Everyman, I will go with thee,
and be thy guide

William Makepeace Thackeray

A
SHABBY GENTEEL
STORY
AND
OTHER WRITINGS

Edited by
D. J. TAYLOR

EVERYMAN
J. M. DENT • LONDON
CHARLES E. TUTTLE
VERMONT

Chronology, introduction, textual editing and endmatter
© J. M. Dent 1993

This edition first published in Everyman by J. M. Dent 1993

Typeset at ROM-Data Corp. Ltd, Falmouth,
Cornwall, England
Printed in Great Britain by
The Guernsey Press
Co. Ltd, Guernsey, C.I.
for
J. M. Dent
Orion Publishing Group
Orion House
5 Upper St Martin's Lane, London WC2H 9EA
and
Charles E. Tuttle Co. Inc.
28 South Main Street, Rutland, Vermont
05701 USA

British Library Cataloguing-in-Publication Data
is available upon request.

ISBN 0 460 87289 3

CONTENTS

LIST OF ILLUSTRATIONS

NOTE ON THE AUTHOR
AND EDITOR

William Makepeace Thackeray (1811–63) was born in Calcutta into a wealthy Anglo-Indian family. He was sent to England in 1816, and educated at Charterhouse and Trinity College, Cambridge, but left without taking a degree. His marriage to Isabella Shawe, which produced two daughters, was effectively ended by her insanity. Thackeray's first full-length work, *Catherine*, appeared in 1839. Throughout the 1840s he wrote journalism, sketches and short fiction for a variety of newspapers and magazines, including *Fraser's* and *Punch*. *Vanity Fair*, his masterpiece, appeared in serial form from January 1847. His later novels included *Pendennis* (1850), *The History of Henry Esmond* (1852), *The Newcomes* (1855) and *The Virginians* (1859). From 1860 to 1862 he edited *The Cornhill* magazine. *Denis Duval*, his final work, was published posthumously.

D. J. Taylor was born in Norwich in 1960 and educated at Norwich School and St John's College, Oxford, where he read modern history. His books include two novels, *Great Eastern Land* (1986) and *Real Life* (1992), two critical studies, *A Vain Conceit: British Fiction in the '80s* (1989) and *After The War: The Novel and England since 1945* (1993), and, with Marcus Berkmann, *Other People: Portraits from the '90s* (1990). He reviews regularly for the *Independent* and the *Sunday Times*. He lives in London with his wife and their small son.

CHRONOLOGY OF THACKERAY'S LIFE

Year	Age	Life
1811		Born, Calcutta, India, 18 July
1815	4	Death of his father, Richmond Thackeray
1817	6	Sent home to England to the care of his great-grandmother and great-aunt. Mother marries Captain Henry Carmichael Smyth
1829	18	Enters (January) Trinity College, Cambridge
1831	20	Admitted to Middle Temple

CHRONOLOGY OF HIS TIMES

Year	Artistic Events	Historical Events
1811	Jane Austen, *Sense and Sensibility*	
1812	Birth of Dickens Byron, Cantos I and II of *Childe Harold*	
1813	Jane Austen, *Pride and Prejudice*	
1814	Walter Scott, *Waverley* Jane Austen, *Mansfield Park*	
1815	Walter Scott, *Guy Mannering*	Defeat of Napoleon at Waterloo
1816	Jane Austen, *Emma* Walter Scott, *Rob Roy*	
1818	Jane Austen, *Northanger Abbey* and *Persuasion* Mary Shelley, *Frankenstein*	
1819	Walter Scott, *Ivanhoe* Birth of George Eliot	Birth of Queen Victoria. 'Peterloo' massacre
1820		Accession of George IV
1821	Walter Scott, *Kenilworth* Baudelaire, Dostoyevsky Flaubert born Death of Keats	
1822	Death of Shelley	
1824	Walter Scott, *Redgauntlet* Death of Byron	
1828	Birth of Tolstoy	Wellington becomes Prime Minister
1830	Tennyson, *Poems, Chiefly Lyrical* Balzac begins to group his novels into *La Comédie Humaine*	Accession of William IV July Revolution in France; accession of Louis-Philippe

Year	Age	Life
1832–6	21–25	Living mostly in Paris, studying art and contributing to various journals
1836		Marries Isabella Shawe
1837	26	Settles in London (July). *The Yellowplush Correspondence* begins to appear in *Fraser's Magazine* (November)
1839	28	*Catherine* serialized in *Fraser's Magazine* (May to February 1840)
1840	29	*A Shabby Genteel Story* serialized in *Fraser's*. *The Paris Sketch Book*. Thackeray's wife becomes mentally ill. He entrusts his children to the care of his mother in Paris
1841	30	*The Second Funeral of Napoleon* *The Great Hoggarty Diamond*
1842	31	First contribution to *Punch*
1843	32	*The Irish Sketch Book*
1844	33	*Barry Lyndon* serialized in *Fraser's*
1845	34	Writing early draft of *Vanity Fair*. Moves his wife, judged incurably insane, from Paris to London
1846	35	*Notes of a Journey from Cornhill to Grand Cairo*. *The Snobs of England* published in *Punch* *Mrs Perkins's Ball*
1847–8	36–7	*Vanity Fair* published in monthly numbers

Year	Artistic Events	Historical Events
1832	Deaths of Goethe, Scott	Passing of first Reform Bill
1833	Carlyle, *Sartor Resartus*	
	Dickens, *Sketches by Boz*	Slavery abolished throughout the British Empire. First steamship crossing of the Atlantic
1834	Balzac, *Le Père Goriot*	
1836	Dickens, *Pickwick Papers*	Newspaper Tax reduced
1837	Carlyle, *The French Revolution*	Accession of Queen Victoria
1838	Dickens, *Oliver Twist* and *Nicholas Nickleby*	Working Men's Association drafts People's Charter
1839	Stendhal, *La Chartreuse de Parme*	Chartist riots
1840		Queen Victoria marries Prince Albert
1841	Dickens, *Barnaby Rudge* and *The Old Curiosity Shop* Carlyle, *On Heroes, Hero-worship and the Heroic in Literature* *Punch* founded	
1843	Dickens, *A Christmas Carol*	
1844	Dickens, *Martin Chuzzlewit*	
1845		Potato famine begins in Ireland
1846	Balzac, *La Cousine Bette*	Louis Napoleon escapes to England

Year   Age   Life

1848–50	37–9	*Pendennis* published in monthly numbers; interrupted, September–November 1849, by a serious illness
1851	40	Resigns from *Punch*
1852	41	*The History of Henry Esmond*
1853–5	42–3	*The Newcomes* published in parts (October 1853–August 1855)
1854	43	*The Rose and the Ring*
1857	46	Stands for Parliament in Oxford; defeated. *The Virginians,* in parts (November 1857–October 1859)
1859	48	Becomes first editor of *The Cornhill Magazine*
1860	49	*Lovel the Widower* published in *Cornhill. The Four Georges* published in *Cornhill. The Roundabout Papers* published in *Cornhill* (to 1863)

Year	Artistic Events	Historical Events
1847	Charlotte Brontë, *Jane Eyre* Emily Brontë, *Wuthering Heights*	
1848	Dickens, *Dombey and Son* Elizabeth Gaskell, *Mary Barton* Macaulay, *History of England* (first two volumes) Dumas *fils*, *La Dame aux Camélias*	Revolutions across Europe Cholera epidemic in England Chartist movement collapses
1849	Charlotte Brontë, *Shirley*	
1850	Deaths of Wordsworth, Balzac Dickens, *David Copperfield* *Household Words* founded	
1851	Melville, *Moby-Dick*	The Great Exhibition opens in Hyde Park
1852	Harriet Beecher Stowe, *Uncle Tom's Cabin*	Louis Napoleon proclaimed Emperor Napoleon III Death of Wellington
1853	Dickens, *Bleak House* Charlotte Brontë, *Villette* Dickens, *Hard Times*	Crimean War begins
1855	Trollope, *The Warden* Death of Charlotte Brontë	
1857	Dickens, *Little Dorrit* Trollope, *Barchester Towers* Flaubert, *Madame Bovary* Baudelaire, *Les Fleurs du mal*	Indian Mutiny
1858	George Eliot, *Scenes of Clerical Life* Carlyle, *Frederick the Great*	
1859	Dickens, *A Tale of Two Cities* George Eliot, *Adam Bede* Wilkie Collins, *The Woman in White* George Eliot, *The Mill on the Floss*	

Year	Age	Life
1861–2	50–1	*Philip* published in *Cornhill*
1862	51	Resigns editorship of *Cornhill*
1863	52	Begins writing *Denis Duval*. Dies.
1864		*Denis Duval* (uncompleted) published in *Cornhill*

Year	Artistic Events	Historical Events
1861	Dickens, *Great Expectations* George Eliot, *Silas Marner* Trollope, *Framley Parsonage* Turgenev, *Fathers and Sons* Dostoyevsky, *The House of the Dead*	Death of Prince Albert Commencement of American Civil War
1862	George Eliot, *Romola* Trollope, *Orley Farm* Hugo, *Les Misérables* Elizabeth Gaskell, *Sylvia's Lovers*	

A SHABBY
GENTEEL STORY
AND
OTHER WRITINGS

INTRODUCTION

INTRODUCTION

Thackeray's collected works extend to twenty-six hardback volumes. It is a bold hand that disturbs them on the second-hand bookseller's shelves, and for everyone who has ever ploughed his way through *Philip* or *The Virginians* – novels which now retain only a faint curiosity value – there must be a dozen readers of *North and South* or *The Mill on the Floss*. It is Thackeray's misfortune that, with two or three exceptions, the books on which he made his reputation should have almost disappeared from sight. *Vanity Fair* remains an early Victorian classic, the *Book of Snobs* has its admirers, and no study of nineteenth-century children's literature can quite ignore *The Rose and the Ring*, but the great works of his maturity, *Esmond* and *The Newcomes*, lie in the Victorian remainder bin along with obscurities like *Mrs Caudle's Curtain Lectures* and *A Gallery of Literary Portraits*. We tend to take Thackeray's position in the mid-nineteenth-century pantheon for granted, but in fact this process of diminishment has been going on for over a century. Carlyle might have thought *The Newcomes* one of the *grandest* novels in the language, yet by the 1880s critics such as Henley and Lang were busying themselves with questions such as 'Is Thackeray a cynic?' (a question which had in any case been asked long before Thackeray's death), and when Henry James wrote his famous attack on the 'loose baggy monsters' of the Victorian novel, the author of *The Virginians* was one of his principal quarries. The response of a bustling proto-modernist like James is understandable, for there is a peculiar woodenness about Thackeray's later work, a sad slackening of interest and design, and it is this rather than the eternal complaints about cynicism that led to the reaction against him. With the exception of a few things written at the very end of his life – *Lovel the Widower,* for instance or certain of the *Roundabout Papers* produced during his time as editor of the *Cornhill* magazine – his post-*Vanity Fair* career is, as John Carey puts it, the history of a capitulation.

That Thackeray's genius should have fallen apart in this depressing way is a measure of his complex relation to his time. There is a rather obvious irony in the process by which the cutting young satirist of *Punch* and *Fraser's Magazine* transformed himself into the sedate and sentimental fogey of *The Newcomes*, and the irony lies in Thackeray's inability to prevent himself falling victim to the attitudes he had burlesqued in his early work. Elevated to the status of a grand literary panjandrum after the success of *Vanity Fair*, he was never quite sure of his stance towards the society which he had once poked fun at but simultaneously wanted to become a part of. Like Evelyn Waugh, perhaps, a century later he was prepared to sneer at those who toadied to aristocrats while complaining that lords no longer asked him to dinner. Throughout the second half of his career Thackeray was writing against the grain of his own nature, and it shows. The result is a series of intermittently dull and unhappy books, in which the sharp opinions of the early days are progressively watered down, youthful hard-headedness is coated over with sentiment, and – as Thackeray was perfectly well aware of this slide into mediocrity – the reader is presented with the spectacle of an author falling asleep over his work and then recovering himself almost from paragraph to paragraph. Nearly any chapter of *The Newcomes* picked at random will give a good idea of its curiously erratic composition. Nothing could be more flat than the prose which discusses female constancy, the virtues of old Colonel Newcome or the value of a public school education, and the flatness is compounded by a feeling that the writer knows that he is being false to himself. But then, almost by accident, Thackeray touches on something that really interests him – the exact shade which an artist would need to use in painting Ethel Newcome's hair, say, or the gaming tables at Baden – and suddenly the style is back to its old racy, colloquial excellence. The value of *The Newcomes* lies almost entirely in these digressions, and the sense of an older voice intermittently reasserting itself amid a great deal of studied gentility. The scene in which the Reverend Honeyman gets imprisoned for debt, for example, is more or less irrelevant from the point of view of plot, but somehow it is worth a hundred encomia of the old Colonel simply because Thackeray is genuinely absorbed in the exposure of human folly. As a result his description of the debtor's prison in Cursitor Street has a kind of conviction that the sham sentiment and the nods to his middle-class readers never manage to bring off.

To turn from the self-conscious 'fine writing' of Thackeray's later novels to his early work as a reporter and a magazine essayist can be a bracing experience. His great period as a journalist and sketch-writer lasted from about 1840 to 1848, an apprenticeship which produced the marvellous pieces of reportage 'Going to see a Man Hanged' and 'The Second Funeral of Napoleon', a mass of burlesques and comic fragments and the longer stories, which we would probably now call novellas, *A Little Dinner at Timmins's, The Fatal Boots* and *A Shabby Genteel Story*. As literary journalism, it has a restless, rackety quality which reflects the circumstances of its composition: written in haste, against deadlines, begun or abandoned to satisfy fleeting private whims. *A Shabby Genteel Story*, for instance, grinds to a halt after a hundred pages, presumably because its author lost interest (*Philip*, written twenty years later, is an unsatisfactory sequel). But the chopped-up, fragmentary form of Thackeray's early work is an important part of its charm. *Vanity Fair*, conceived in the mid-1840s but not published until 1847-8, has the same sprawling air, a jumble of queer impressionist glimpses, scraps of detail, pieces of wayside moralising, any one of which can be detached from the plot without the reader noticing. Orwell thought that one of the great advantages of *Vanity Fair* was that you could pick up the narrative at almost any stage and still have a reasonable idea of what was going on. In saying this he was making an important point about Thackeray's attraction as a writer, his ability to saturate narrative with detail and create a world which, though bristling with intrigue, has a curiously lived-in feeling, simultaneously exotic and familiar. At the same time there is a way in which all that is memorable about *Vanity Fair* grows out of the sketches that precede it. Thackeray's minor characters, the shabby procession of cashiered officers and card-sharpers such as Captain Rook and the Honourable Mr Deuceace, are as much at home in Becky Sharp's entourage as in an early piece like 'Captain Rook and Mr Pigeon'. Even a very early sketch, 'The Artists', which describes the painters' colonies of Soho, is a prefiguration of the scenes descrying Becky's home life with her profligate, portrait-painting father, and from here it is only a short step to Mr Gandish's academy and the detailed account of the 1830s artists' world that occupies the first half of *The Newcomes*.

The rackety, restless sweep of these early pieces also reflects their grounding in Thackeray's own life. For a man born into affluence and the splendour of early nineteenth-century Anglo–Indian society, the 1840s were a series of humiliations. By his early thirties Thackeray had thrown away a fortune – mostly on gambling, but also in ill-advised literary ventures – acquired a wife who went mad, leaving him with the care of two children, and a termagent mother-in-law, and been reduced to hack-work of the dreariest sort – something he found doubly disagreeable as it meant being polite to people he considered his social inferiors. Even the gradual confirmation of his abilities brought its own fatal quota of distress, and the continual reminders of his poverty were guaranteed to take the bloom off relatively exalted commissions. When he went to Ireland in 1842 on the journey that eventually produced the *Irish Sketchbook*, he had to deposit the family plate with his publishers, Chapman and Hall, as 'a kind of genteel pawn'. As it was, success hung in the balance for several years. *Vanity Fair* was very nearly a failure, rescued only after the twelfth number and producing a fraction of the sales of *Dombey and Son*, which ran concurrently. The embarrassments and indignities of these times – nothing very much, perhaps, compared to the trials of a Dickens or a Gissing, but distressing to a man of Thackeray's background and temperament – produced a reservoir of personal experience which filtered through into his published work. The fleecing of impressionable young men by the seedy spongers of 'Captain Rook and Mr Pigeon' mirrors his own experience at the gaming tables, and the succession of rebarbative mothers-in-law – Mrs Gashleigh in *A Little Dinner at Timmins's*, Mrs Captain Budge in 'Hobson's Choice' – harks back to his own dealings with the redoubtable Mrs Shawe. This immersion in his own experience gives Thackeray's early work an oddly personal quality. It is a cliché, of course, to say that a writer resembles a character from his own novels, but Thackeray is present in his writings in a way that many Victorian novelists are not. In the guise of 'Michael Angelo Titmarsh', 'Mr Spec' or 'The Fat Contributor' – only three on an extensive list of authorial personae – he pops up continually, inserting himself into *A Shabby Genteel Story*'s list of wedding guests, attending the Timmins's pretentious dinner party. In much the same way his more straightforward pieces of reportage are rarely detached, for the reader is always conscious of Thackeray at his elbow, so to speak, simultaneously describing and criticising a spectacle which consequently becomes a matter of joint appreciation. The sight of the author at large in his own text performs a double function. Most obviously, it imparts a nice ambiguity to some of the moral judgments – after all, the Thackeray who discourses so wittily on the collective gluttony of 'A Dinner in the City' had presumably worked his way through seven courses himself – but at the same time it gives the subjects on which he touches a tangible authenticity, the feeling that the world of Timmins, Mrs Gashleigh and the Lough Corrib railway dispute is the author's own.

And, curiously enough, it *is* a world. The early nineteenth century comes alive under Thackeray's hand in a way quite unlike that of any other writer. *A Shabby Genteel Story* is barely a chapter old before the reader is plunged into a tremendous sub-universe made up of the melancholy history of the firm of Gann, Blubbery and Gann, small-town snobbery and tip-top fashionable swells. For a social chronicler Thackeray's range is surprisingly narrow. As Orwell points out, he could rarely be got to see the working class as anything other than servants – though he was capable of sympathising with the servant class as a whole – and he tends to notice the effects of social phenomena rather than their causes. However, this narrowness can work to Thackeray's advantage. In particular, his interest in the club-lounging, prize-fighting, rat-catching side of Victorian life, with its faded bucks in padded stays and decadent young men, enabled him to create characters that were beyond the range of a Dickens or a Trollope. Major Pendennis seems a rather subtle creation compared to the pantomime aristocrats of *Nicholas Nickleby*. Lord Cinqbars in *A Shabby Genteel Story* belongs to a distinctive early Victorian genre – the lisping young sprig of nobility with his dandified airs and his passion for 'intrigues' – but the sharpness of the portrait stops him from merely being a type.

This eye for human quiddity is especially important when it comes to determining what it is that Thackeray writes about, and the way he approaches his task. Broadly speaking he wrote at a time when social barriers were markedly more fluid than they had once been or were subsequently to become. To read nearly any novel of the 1840s is to enter a world of clamorous social upheaval, in which new money, founded on industrial and business expertise, is beginning to infiltrate the older *rentier* class. A characteristic symbol of this social battle is the alliance between blood and commercial know-how. Mr Dombey, whose social origins are obscure but whose financial cachet is sufficient to allow him to marry the quasi-aristocratic Edith Granger, is a man of his time. Sir Brian Newcome, the son of a self-made man, who becomes a Tory MP, acquires a baronetcy and marries the niece of the Marquis of Steyne, belongs to the same category of up-wardly mobile entrepreneur. Understandably, the knock-on effects of this process of assimilation were felt further along the social ladder. While in a late period novel like *The Newcomes* Thackeray takes a keen interest in the ability of an older, aristo-cratic society to sustain and reinvent itself through infusions of mercantile money, his early work is pitched rather lower down the social scale, at about the level of the professional middle class, with occasional variations upward (Fitzroy Timmins is a barrister on nodding terms with the local MP) and downward (the Ganns in *A Shabby Genteel Story*). Whatever the precise gradations of status, nearly all of Thackeray's early work is concerned with social advancement: the Timminses, who *would* give their little dinner, Stubbs in *The Fatal Boots* and his 'marriage in high life', Mrs Hobson with her hankering for a manservant. The early sketches are full of this type of vainglory, and the satire is nearly always directed at the type of mind which regards an invitation to dine with a peer as an absolute guarantee of moral excellence. As a writer Thackeray is at his best when observing social distinctions – his high-flown passages are invariably failures – and their corollary, the dreadful sham of 'keeping up appearances'. In fact the exposure of the debt-bilking, fly-by-night side of Victorian life, in which the possession of a house in Mayfair is pretty sure to be balanced by a grocer's bill a yard long is a kind of obsession with him. In the Ganns' attempt to eke out a spurious gentility with the proceeds of a lodging house can perhaps be detected the origins of the famous chapter in *Vanity Fair* describing the lavish lifestyle of Mr and Mrs Rawdon Crawley, 'How to live well on nothing a year'.

Typically Thackeray achieves these effects by way of an intense comic specificity, an attention to detail which can sometimes become rather stifling. Any modern reader of Thackeray's work must be struck by its practicality. He is one of the few Victorian novelists from whom you could find out how to order a dinner or a suit of clothes, and in 'Memorials of Gourmandising' he produced an extended version of the modern restaurant column. One result of this absorption in milieu is a chronic digressiveness, a continual shifting away from the main progress of the story in search of fragments of detail which fascinate Thackeray simply because they are detail. When Fitch the painter falls in love with Caroline Gann we get three stanzas of his sententious poetry. Similarly, Mrs Timmins's social crusade is prefaced with all manner of information about her previous triumphs, how she outdanced Mrs Rowdy in the Scythe Mazurka at the Polish ball, headed by Mrs Hugh Slasher, thereby revenging herself for Mrs Rowdy's victory at the bazaar in aid of the Daughters of Decayed Muffin Men, etc., etc. It is worth pointing out that these digressions are not simply incidental: they are also there to make an artistic point. One can acknowledge Walter Bagehot's complaint that Thackeray had a compulsion to 'amass petty detail to prove that tenth-rate people were ever striving to be ninth-rate people' while wondering if this doesn't miss an important part of Thackeray's acuteness, for nearly every scrap of superfluous material that he intrudes into his character sketches turns out to have some bearing on the finished portrait. The details about Mrs Timmins's marital life, for example, and Mrs Rowdy's allegations that she threw over Captain Higgs on the instructions of her mother, are not just an optional garnish, but the first hint of the underlying tension that exists between Rosa and Mrs Gashleigh. The description of Mrs Topham Sawyer sitting down to breakfast in her Madonna front, a kind of artificial hairpiece fashionable at the time, has a similar effect in harnessing people to their environment by way of specifics. Another writer would have said merely that she wore a wig. By going into detail and hinting at the absurdity of a haughty old woman got up in the style of a biblical painting, Thackeray manages to burlesque Mrs Sawyer out of existence.

Amid all these accretions of detail, the moral point is usually a very simple one. The 'message' of a piece like *A Little Dinner at Timmins's* is straightforward: don't live above your income; don't nurture foolish illusions, balanced by the feeling that such injunctions are largely futile, that the average human being *will* always nurture foolish dreams, and it is of this that the fundamental comedy of human life consists. It is impossible to read the early Thackeray for very long without being pulled up sharply by his matter-of-factness, his casual acceptance of rogues and rascals,

his delight in pointing out that even the most outwardly scrupulous people are still motivated by selfishness and vanity. The
idealism that animates a contemporary like Dickens is to him a
flying in the face of human nature. In the context of Victorian
notions of improvement and self-help, this can make some of his
judgments look highly subversive. One of his favourite themes,
for instance, is that to come down in the world is not necessarily
a bad thing. The Ganns in *A Shabby Genteel Story* are, if they did
but know it, far happier in flyblown lower-middle-class Margate
than they would have been in polite society, the husband a figure
of consuming interest to his fellow-drinkers at the Bag of Nails,
his wife able to brag on endlessly about her noble forebears to a
circle of acquaintances who treat her with unfeigned respect.
Thackeray takes up this theme again in *The Newcomes*, going so
far as to suggest that one of the principal joys of human existence
lies not in living with your equals but with your inferiors. Society
is naturally competitive and only a fool would try to pretend
otherwise. Only a fool, too, would shuffle people unhesitatingly
into categories marked 'good' and 'bad'. For all the contempt
levelled at the Captain Rooks of this world, a sketch like 'Captain
Rook and Mr Pigeon' is surprisingly even-handed. Rook may be
a heartless villain, but Pigeon is almost as bad for allowing himself
to be duped. Measured by any really exacting set of values, most
human lives will be judged a failure: amid general unworthiness,
all we can hope for is to end up a little less unworthy than the
average. These attitudes might make Thackeray a very imperfect
moralist, by the lofty standards of the mid-nineteenth century, but
they give his best work a kind of sharp-eyed common sense, a
refusal to settle for easy sentiment when hard experience suggests
otherwise. The passages in *Vanity Fair* in which the Sedleys,
having lost their money, are accompanied to their new lodgings
in Fulham by an aged retainer who protests undying loyalty are
typical examples of this. Dickens would have painted the scene
up with a rosy glow of faithful servitude. Thackeray, being
Thackeray, treats the ensuing quarrel between Mrs Clapp and her
former employees as the most natural thing in the world.

The Sedleys are a good example of what might be called the
regressive tendency in Thackeray's writing. His characters have a
habit of returning to the point in life where they began, cancelling
out the achievements of their interim careers by over-reach or
foolishness. Colonel Newcome ends up a pensioner in the

almshouses attached to the school of his boyhood. By transferring himself from the grandeur of Russell Square to the faded gentility of the Fulham Road, old Mr Sedley is returning – figuratively if not literally – to the circumstances of his early life. In a sense this is what Thackeray did himself throughout his own career. As a general rule, his gaze is wholly backward-looking, and even the very early pieces of reportage are shot through with an aching nostalgia. In preferring the past to the present Thackeray was doing no more than follow the general tendency of the Victorian novel – *Middlemarch*, after all, is set at the time of the Reform Bill, and Dickens's novels typically lag twenty or thirty years behind the date of their composition – but there is a peculiar intensity about his evocations of bygone experience. George Eliot's abiding interest might lie in the repercussions of 1832, but Thackeray's gaze extends even further back to the Regency world of his boyhood. Ultimately there is a way in which this vanished paradise of Miss Decamp's dance and footmen in floury wigs – a sort of fairy-tale world crammed with light and colour – is more real to him than his adult life. The great inventions and scientific discoveries of the 1840s are at best a noisy inconvenience, and if he mentions the existence of the steam train it is generally as a the prelude to a lament about the decline of the stage coach. Usually Thackeray's nostalgia emerges through his obsession with arte-facts: books, types of food, styles of dress. Bob Stubbs's desire for a pair of top-boots (*The Fatal Boots*) reflects Thackeray's own juvenile yearnings, and it is rare for two or three chapters of his occasional writings to pass without some mention of confection-ery, rout-cakes, the tart woman and so forth. The literature of Thackeray's childhood, too, supplies an enduring theme to his work. It is significant, perhaps, that *Manfrone: or, the One-handed Monk* and Mrs Porter's novels, which Caroline Gann pores over in *A Shabby Genteel Story* should turn up again in 'Tunbridge Toys', a piece written at the very end of his life. There are differences of emphasis, certainly, and the reminiscences of Thackeray's later years can be quite wooden in their sorrowings over irrecoverable time, but the elegiac note is a constant. One of the most attractive features of Thackeray's writing, even at the age of thirty, is his apparent ability to measure experience and sensation by yardsticks which frequently predate his own birth.

'Going to see A Man Hanged', first published in 1840 in *Fraser's*, is perhaps the most striking conflation of these early techniques. An eye-witness account of the public execution of a Swiss valet convicted of murdering his master, it appears at first to be no more than a series of digressions: the recent debates in the House of Commons; notorious executions of the past; the composition of the crowd; Rabelais, Fielding and Dickens. Courvoisier's despatch, when it comes, is done in a few sharp brush strokes – the death bell making 'a dreadful quick, feverish kind of jangling noise', the victim himself, who 'opened his hands in a helpless kind of way, and clasped them once or twice together' – but you are suddenly conscious that it is the centrepiece in a panorama of early Victorian England, and that in assembling all his incidental remarks about Lord John, the crowd shouting 'butter fingers' after the clumsy execution of the Cato Street conspirators, the comments of the onlookers, Thackeray is saying something profoundly important not only about the structure of early Victorian society but human psychology. When he writes about his disgust for murder, 'but it was for *the murder I saw done*', the reader emerges with the queer sense not only of history having come alive, but of something else, something at once awful and universal, walking side by side with him down Snow Hill past the murmering crowd into the silent dawn.

D. J. Taylor

A NOTE ON THE TEXT

———

There is no complete modern edition of Thackeray's works, although a new collected Riverside edition is in preparation. The last such attempt was George Saintsbury's 17-volume Oxford collected edition of 1908. With a few minor enhancements to Thackeray's occasionally erratic punctuation, the present volume reproduces the collected edition begun by Smith, Elder in 1878.

A SHABBY GENTEEL STORY

Chapter I

At that remarkable period when Louis XVIII was restored a second time to the throne of his fathers, and all the English who had money or leisure rushed over to the Continent, there lived in a certain boarding-house at Brussels a genteel young widow, who bore the elegant name of Mrs Wellesley Macarty.

In the same house and room with the widow lived her mamma, a lady who was called Mrs Crabb. Both professed to be rather fashionable people. The Crabbs were of a very old English stock, and the Macartys were, as the world knows, County Cork people; related to the Sheenys, Finnigans, Clancys, and other distinguished families in their part of Ireland. But Ensign Wellesley Mac, not having a shilling, ran off with Miss Crabb, who possessed the same independence; and after having been married about six months to the lady, was carried off suddenly, on the 18 of June, 1815, by a disease very prevalent in those glorious times – the fatal cannon-shot morbus. He, and many hundred young fellows of his regiment, the Clonakilty Fencibles, were attacked by this epidemic on the same day, at a place about ten miles from Brussels, and there perished. The ensign's lady had accompanied her husband to the Continent, and about five months after his death brought into the world two remarkably fine female children.

Mrs Wellesley's mother had been reconciled to her daughter by this time – for, in truth, Mrs Crabb had no other child but her runaway Juliana, to whom she flew when she heard of her destitute condition. And, indeed, it was high time that some one should come to the young widow's aid; for as her husband did not leave money, nor anything that represented money, except a number of tailors' and bootmakers' bills, neatly docketed, in his writing-desk, Mrs Wellesley was in danger of starvation, should no friendly person assist her.

Mrs Crabb, then, came off to her daughter, whom the Sheenys, Finnigans, and Clancys refused, with one scornful voice, to assist. The fact is that Mr Crabb had once been butler to a lord, and his

lady a lady's-maid; and at Crabb's death Mrs Crabb disposed of
the Ram hotel and posting-house, where her husband had made
three thousand pounds, and was living in genteel ease in a country
town, when Ensign Macarty came, saw, and ran away with
Juliana. Of such a connexion it was impossible that the great
Clancys and Finnigans could take notice; and so once more
Widow Crabb was compelled to share with her daughter her small
income of a hundred and twenty a year.

Upon this, at a boarding-house in Brussels, the two managed
to live pretty smartly, and to maintain an honourable reputation.
The twins were put out, after the foreign fashion, to nurse, at a
village in the neighborhood; for Mrs Macarty had been too ill to
nurse them; and Mrs Crabb could not afford to purchase that
most expensive article, a private wet-nurse.

There had been numberless tiffs and quarrels between mother
and daughter when the latter was in her maiden state; and Mrs
Crabb was, to tell the truth, in no wise sorry when her Jooly
disappeared with the Ensign, – for the old lady dearly loved a
gentleman, and was not a little flattered at being the mother to Mrs
Ensign Macarty. Why the Ensign should have run away with this
lady at all, as he might have had her for the asking, is no business
of ours; nor are we going to rake up old stories and village scandals,
which insinuate that Miss Crabb ran away with *him*, for with these
points the writer and the reader have nothing to do.

Well, then, the reconciled mother and daughter lived once more
together, at Brussels. In the course of a year, Mrs Macarty's sorrow
had much abated; and having a great natural love of dress, and a
tolerably handsome face and person, she was induced, without
much reluctance, to throw her weeds aside, and to appear in the
most becoming and varied costumes which her means and ingenu-
ity could furnish. Considering, indeed, the smallness of the former,
it was agreed on all hands that Mrs Crabb and her daughter
deserved wonderful credit – that is, they managed to keep up as
respectable an appearance as if they had five hundred a year; and
at church, at tea-parties, and abroad in the streets, to be what is
called quite the gentlewomen. If they starved at home, nobody saw
it; if they patched and pieced, nobody (it was to be hoped) knew
it: if they bragged about their relations and property, could any
one say them nay? Thus they lived hanging on with desperate
energy to the skirts of genteel society; Mrs Crabb, a sharp woman,
rather respected her daughter's superior rank; and Mrs Macarty

did not quarrel so much as heretofore with her Mamma, on whom herself and her two children were entirely dependent.

While affairs were at this juncture it happened that a young Englishman, James Gann, Esq., of the great oil-house of Gann, Blubbery and Gann (as he took care to tell you before you had been an hour in his company), – it happened, I say, that James Gann, Esq., came to Brussels for a month for the purpose of perfecting himself in the French language; and while in that capital went to lodge at the very boarding-house which contained Mrs Crabb and her daughter. Gann was young, weak, inflammable; he saw and adored Mrs Wellesley Macarty; and she, who was at this period all but engaged to a stout old wooden-legged Scotch regimental surgeon, pitilessly sent Dr M Lint about his business and accepted the addresses of Mr Gann. How the young man arranged matters with his papa the senior partner, I don't know; but it is certain that there was a quarrel, and afterwards a reconciliation; and it is also known that James Gann fought a duel with the surgeon, – receiving the Æsculapian fire, and discharging his own bullet into the azure skies. About nine thousand times in the course of his after-years did Mr Gann narrate the history of the combat; it enabled him to go through life with the reputation of a man of courage, and won for him, as he said with pride, the hand of his Juliana; perhaps this was rather a questionable benefit.

One part of the tale, however, honest James never did dare to tell, except when peculiarly excited by wrath or liquor; it was this: that on the day after the wedding, and in the presence of many friends who had come to offer their congratulations, a stout nurse, bearing a brace of chubby little ones, made her appearance; and these rosy urchins, springing forward at the sight of Mrs James Gann, shouted affectionately, '*Maman! maman!*' at which the lady, blushing rosy red, said, 'James, these two are yours'; and poor James well nigh fainted at this sudden paternity so put upon him. 'Children!' screamed he, aghast; 'whose children?' at which Mrs Crabb, majestically checking him, said, 'These, my dear James, are the daughters of the gallant and good Ensign Macarty, whose widow you yesterday led to the altar. May you be happy with her, and may these blessed children' (tears) 'find in you a father, who shall replace him that fell in the field of glory!'

Mrs Crabb, Mrs James Gann, Mrs Major Lolly, Mrs Piffler, and several ladies present, set up a sob immediately; and James Gann, a good-humoured, soft-hearted man, was taken quite aback. Kissing his lady hurriedly, he vowed that he would take care of the poor little things, and proposed to kiss them likewise; which caress the darlings refused with many roars. Gann's fate was sealed from that minute; and he was properly henpecked by his wife and mother-in-law during the life of the latter. Indeed it was to Mrs Crabb that the stratagem of the infant concealment was due; for when her daughter innocently proposed to have or to see the children, the old lady strongly pointed out the folly of such an arrangement, which might, perhaps, frighten away Mr Gann from the delightful matrimonial trap into which (lucky rogue!) he was about to fall.

Soon after the marriage the happy pair returned to England, occupying the house in Thames Street, City, until the death of Gann senior; when his son, becoming head of the firm of Gann and Blubbery, quitted the dismal precincts of Billingsgate and colonised in the neighbourhood of Putney; where a neat box, a couple of spare bedrooms, a good cellar, and a smart gig to drive into and out from town, made a real gentleman of him. Mrs Gann treated him with much scorn, to be sure, called him a sot, and abused hugely the male companions that he brought down with him to Putney. Honest James would listen meekly, would yield, and would bring down a brace more friends the next day, with whom he would discuss his accustomed number of bottles of port. About this period a daughter was born to him, called Caroline Brandenburg Gann; so named after a large mansion near Hammersmith, and an injured queen who lived there at the time of the little girl's birth, and who was greatly compassioned and patronised by Mrs James Gann, and other ladies of distinction. Mrs James *was* a lady in those days, and gave evening-parties of the very first order.

At this period of time Mrs James Gann sent the twins, Rosalind Clancy and Isabella Finnigan Wellesley Macarty, to a boarding-school for young ladies, and grumbled much at the amount of the half-years' bills which her husband was called upon to pay for them; for though James discharged them with perfect good-humour, his lady began to entertain a mean opinion indeed of her pretty young children. They could expect no fortune, she said, from Mr Gann, and she wondered that he should think of bringing them up expensively, when he had a darling child of his own, for whom he was bound to save all the money that he could lay by.

Grandmamma, too, doted on the little Caroline Brandenburg,

and vowed that she would leave her three thousand pounds to this dear infant; for in this way does the world show its respect for that most respectable thing prosperity. Who in this life get the smiles, and the acts of friendship, and the pleasing legacies? – The rich. And I do, for my part, heartily wish that some one would leave me a trifle – say twenty thousand pounds – being perfectly confident that some one else would leave me more; and that I should sink into my grave worth a plum* at least.

Little Caroline then had her maid, her airy nursery, her little carriage to drive in, the promise of her grandmamma's consols, and that priceless treasure – her Mamma's undivided affection. Gann, too, loved her sincerely, in his careless, good-humoured way; but he determined, notwithstanding, that his step-daughters should have something handsome at his death, but – but for a great BUT.

Gann and Blubbery were in the oil line, – have we not said so? Their profits arose from contracts for lighting a great number of streets in London; and about this period GAS came into use. Gann and Blubbery appeared in the *Gazette*; and, I am sorry to say, so bad had been the management of Blubbery, – so great the extravagance of both partners and their ladies, – that they only paid their creditors fourteenpence halfpenny in the pound.

When Mrs Crabb heard of this dreadful accident – Mrs Crabb, who dined thrice a week with her son-in-law; who never would have been allowed to enter the house at all had not honest James interposed his good-nature between her quarrelsome daughter and herself – Mrs Crabb, I say, proclaimed James Gann to be a swindler, a villain, a disreputable, tipsy, vulgar man, and made over her money to the Misses Rosalind Clancy and Isabella Finnigan Macarty; leaving poor little Caroline without one single maravedi. Half of one thousand five hundred pounds allotted to each was to be paid at marriage, the other half on the death of Mrs James Gann, who was to enjoy the interest thereof. Thus do we rise and fall in this world – thus does Fortune shake her swift wings, and bid us abruptly to resign the gifts (or rather loans) which we have had from her.

How Gann and his family lived after their stroke of misfortune, I know not; but as the failing tradesman is going through the process of bankruptcy, and for some months afterwards, it may be remarked that he has usually some mysterious means of subsistence – stray spars of the wreck of his property, on which he manages to seize, and to float for a while. During his retirement, in an obscure lodging in Lambeth, where the poor fellow was so tormented by his wife as to be compelled to fly to the public-house for refuge, Mrs Crabb died; a hundred a year thus came into the possession of Mrs Gann; and some of James's friends, who thought him a good fellow in his prosperity, came forward and furnished a house, in which they placed him, and came to see and comfort him. Then they came to see him not quite so often; then they found out that Mrs Gann was a sad tyrant, and a silly woman; then the ladies declared *her* to be insupportable, and *Gann* to be a low tipsy fellow: and the gentlemen could but shake their heads, and admit that the charge was true. Then they left off coming to see him altogether; for such is the way of the world, where many of us have good impulses, and are generous on an occasion, but are wearied by perpetual want, and begin to grow angry at its importunities – being very properly vexed at the daily recurrence of hunger, and the impudent unreasonableness of starvation. Gann, then, had a genteel wife and children, a furnished house, and a hundred pounds a year. How should he live? The wife of James Gann, Esq., would never allow him to demean himself by taking a clerk's place; and James himself, being as idle a fellow as ever was known, was fain to acquiesce in this determination of hers, and to wait for some more genteel employment. And a curious list of such genteel employments might be made out, were one inclined to follow this interesting subject far; shabby compromises with the world, into which poor fellows enter, and still fondly talk of their 'position', and strive to imagine that they are really working for their bread.

Numberless lodging-houses are kept by the females of families who have met with reverses: are not 'boarding-houses, with a select musical society, in the neighbourhood of the squares,' maintained by such? Do not the gentlemen of the boarding-houses issue forth every morning to the City, or make believe to go thither, on some mysterious business which they have? After a certain period Mrs James Gann kept a lodging-house (in her own words, received 'two inmates into her family'), and Mr Gann had his mysterious business.

In the year 1835, when this story begins, there stood in a certain back street in the town of Margate a house, on the door of which might be read, in gleaming brass, the name of Mr GANN. It was the work of a single smutty servant-maid to clean this brass-plate every morning, and to attend as far as possible to the wants of Mr

Gann, his family, and lodgers; and his house being not very far from the sea, and as you might, by climbing up to the roof, get a sight between two chimneys of that multitudinous element, Mrs Gann set down her lodgings as fashionable; and declared on her cards that her house commanded 'a fine view of the sea.'

On the wire window-blind of the parlour was written, in large characters, the word OFFICE; and here it was that Gann's services came into play. He was very much changed, poor fellow! and humbled; and from two cards that hung outside the blind I am led to believe that he did not disdain to be agent to the 'London and Jamaica Ginger-Beer Company,' and also for a certain preparation called 'Gaster's Infants' Farinacio, or Mothers' Invigorating Substitute ' – a damp, black, mouldy half-pound packet of which stood in permanence at one end of the 'office' mantelpiece; while a fly-blown ginger-beer bottle occupied the other extremity. Nothing else indicated that this ground-floor chamber was an office, except a huge black inkstand, in which stood a stumpy pen, richly crusted with ink at the nib, and to all appearance for many months enjoying a sinecure.

To this room you saw every day, at two o'clock, the *employé* from the neighbouring hotel bring two quarts of beer; and if you called at that hour, a tremendous smoke, and smell of dinner, would gush out upon you from the 'office', as you stumbled over sundry battered tin dish-covers, which lay gaping at the threshold. Thus had that great bulwark of gentility, the dining at six o'clock, been broken in; and the reader must therefore judge that the house of Gann was in a demoralised state.

Gann certainly was. After the ladies had retired to the back-parlour (which, with yellow gauze round the frames, window-curtains, a red silk cabinet piano, and an album, was still tolerably genteel), Gann remained to transact business in the office. This took place in the presence of friends, and usually consisted in the production of a bottle of gin from the corner cupboard, or, mayhap, a *litre* of brandy, which was given by Gann with a knowing wink, and a fat finger placed on a twinkling red nose: when Mrs G. was out, James would also produce a number of pipes, that gave this room a constant and agreeable odour of shag tobacco.

In fact Mr Gann had nothing to do from morning till night. He was now a fat, bald-headed man of fifty; a dirty dandy on weekdays, with a shawl-waistcoat, a tuft of hair to his great double chin, a snuffy shirt-frill, and enormous breast-pin and seals: he had a pilot-coat, with large mother-of-pearl buttons, and always wore a great rattling telescope, with which he might be seen for hours on the sea-shore or the pier, examining the ships, the bathing-machines, the ladies' schools as they paraded up and down the esplanade, and all other objects which the telescopic view might give him. He knew every person connected with every one of the Deal and Dover coaches, and was sure to be witness to the arrival or departure of several of them in the course of the day; he had a word for the ostler about 'that grey mare', a nod for the 'shooter' or guard, and a bow for the dragsman; he could send parcels for nothing up to town; had twice had Sir Rumble Tumble (the noble driver of the Flash-o'-lightning-light-four-inside-post-coach) 'up at his place', and took care to tell you that some of the party were pretty considerably 'sewn up', too. He did not frequent the large hotels; but in revenge he knew every person who entered or left them; and was a great man at the Bag of Nails and the Magpie and Punchbowl, where he was president of a club; he took the bass in 'Mynheer Van Dunk', 'The Wolf', and many other morsels of concerted song, and used to go backwards and forwards to London in the steamers as often as ever he liked, and have his 'grub', too, on board. Such was James Gann. Many people, when they wrote to him, addressed him James Gann, Esq.*

His reverses and former splendours afforded a never-failing theme of conversation to honest Gann and the whole of his family; and it may be remarked that such pecuniary misfortunes, as they are called, are by no means misfortunes to people of certain dispositions, but actually pieces of good luck. Gann, for instance, used to drink liberally of port and claret when the house of Gann and Blubbery was in existence, and was henceforth compelled to imbibe only brandy and gin. Now he loved these a thousand times more than the wine; and had the advantage of talking about the latter, and of his great merit in giving them up. In those prosperous days, too, being a gentleman, he could not frequent the public house as he did at present; and the sanded tavern-parlour was Gann's supreme enjoyment. He was obliged to spend many hours daily in a dark unsavoury room in an alley off Thames Street; and Gann hated books and business, except of other people's. His tastes were low; he loved public-house jokes and company; and now being fallen, was voted at the Bag of Nails and the Magpie before mentioned a tip-top fellow and real gentleman, whereas he had been considered an ordinary vulgar man by his fashionable associates at Putney. Many men are there who are made to fall, and to profit by the tumble.

As for Mrs G., or Jooly, as she was indifferently called by her husband, she, too, had gained by her losses. She bragged of her former acquaintances in the most extraordinary way, and to hear her you would fancy that she was known to and connected with half the peerage. Her chief occupation was taking medicine, and mending and altering her gowns. She had a huge taste for cheap finery, loved raffles, tea-parties, and walks on the pier, where she flaunted herself and daughters as gay as butterflies. She stood upon her rank, did not fail to tell her lodgers that she was 'a gentlewoman', and was mighty sharp with Becky the maid, and poor Carry, her youngest child.

For the tide of affection had turned now, and the 'Misses Wellesley Macarty' were the darlings of their mother's heart, as Caroline had been in the early days of Putney prosperity. Mrs Gann respected and loved her elder daughters, the stately heiresses of £1,500, and scorned poor Caroline, who was likewise scorned (like Cinderella in the sweetest of all stories) by her brace of haughty, thoughtless sisters. These young women were tall, well-grown, black-browed girls, little scrupulous, fond of fun, and having great health and spirits. Caroline was pale and thin, and had fair hair and meek grey eyes; nobody thought her a beauty in her moping cotton gown: whereas the sisters, in flaunting printed muslins, with pink scarfs, and artificial flowers, and brass *ferronnières*,* and other fallals, were voted very charming and genteel by the Ganns' circle of friends. They had pink cheeks, white shoulders, and many glossy curls stuck about their shining foreheads, as damp and as black as leeches. Such charms, Madam, cannot fail of having their effect; and it was very lucky for Caroline that she did not possess them, for she might have been rendered as vain, frivolous, and vulgar as these young ladies were.

While these enjoyed their pleasures and tea-parties abroad, it was Carry's usual fate to remain at home, and help the servant in the many duties which were required in Mrs Gann's establishment. She dressed that lady and her sisters, brought her papa his tea in bed, kept the lodgers' bills, bore their scoldings if they were ladies, and sometimes gave a hand in the kitchen if any extra piecrust or cookery was required. At two she made a little toilet

for dinner, and was employed on numberless household darnings
and mendings in the long evenings, while her sisters giggled over
the jingling piano, Mamma sprawled on the sofa, and Gann was
over his glass at the club. A weary lot, in sooth, was yours, poor
little Caroline! since the days of your infancy, not one hour of
sunshine, no friendship, no cheery playfellows, no mother's love;
but that being dead, the affection which would have crept round
it, withered and died too. Only James Gann, of all the household,
had a good-natured look for her, and a coarse word of kindness;
nor, indeed, did Caroline complain, nor shed many tears, nor call
for death, as she would if she had been brought up in genteeler
circles. The poor thing did not know her own situation; her misery
was dumb and patient; it is such as thousands and thousands of
women in our society bear, and pine, and die of; made up of sums
of small tyrannies, and long indifference, and bitter wearisome
injustice, more dreadful to bear than any tortures that we of the
stronger sex are pleased to cry *Ai! Ai!* about. In our intercourse
with the world – (which is conducted with that kind of cordiality
that we see in Sir Harry and my lady in a comedy – a couple of
painted grinning fools, talking parts that they have learned out of
a book) – as we sit and look at the smiling actors, we get a glimpse
behind the scenes from time to time; and alas for the wretched
nature that appears there! – among women especially, who deceive even more than men, having more to hide, feeling more,
living more than we who have our business, pleasure, ambition,
which carries us abroad. Ours are the great strokes of misfortune,
as they are called, and theirs the small miseries. While the male
thinks, labours, and battles without, the domestic woes and
wrongs are the lot of the women; and the little ills are so bad, so
infinitely fiercer and bitterer than the great, that I would not
change my condition – no, not to be Helen, Queen Elizabeth, Mrs
Coutts,* or the luckiest she in history.

Well, then, in the manner we have described lived the Gann
family. Mr Gann all the better for his 'misfortunes', Mrs Gann
little the worse; the two young ladies greatly improved by the
circumstance, having been cast thereby into a society where their
expected three thousand pounds made great heiresses of them;
and poor Caroline, as luckless a being as any that the wide sun
shone upon. Better to be alone in the world and utterly friendless,
than to have sham friends and no sympathy; ties of kindred which
bind one as it were to the corpse of relationship, and oblige one

to bear through life the weight and the embraces of this lifeless, cold connexion.

I do not mean to say that Caroline would ever have made use of this metaphor, or suspected that her connexion with her Mamma and sisters was anything so loathsome. She felt that she was ill-treated, and had no companion; but was not on that account envious, only humble and depressed, not desiring so much to resist as to bear injustice, and hardly venturing to think for herself. This tyranny and humility served her in place of education, and formed her manners, which were wonderfully gentle and calm. It was strange to see such a person growing up in such a family; the neighbours spoke of her with much scornful compassion. 'A poor half-witted thing,' they said, 'who could not say bo! to a goose'; and I think it is one good test of gentility to be thus looked down on by vulgar people.

It is not to be supposed that the elder girls had reached their present age without receiving a number of offers of marriage, and been warmly in love a great many times. But many unfortunate occurrences had compelled them to remain in their virgin condition. There was an attorney who had proposed to Rosalind; but finding that she would receive only £750 down, instead of £1,500, the monster had jilted her pitilessly, handsome as she was. An apothecary, too, had been smitten by her charms; but to live in a shop was beneath the dignity of a Wellesley Macarty, and she waited for better things. Lieutenant Swabber, of the coastguard service, had lodged two months at Gann's; and if letters, long walks, and town-talk could settle a match, a match between him and Isabella must have taken place. Well, Isabella was not married; and the lieutenant, a colonel in Spain, seemed to have given up all thoughts of her. She meanwhile consoled herself with a gay young wine-merchant, who had lately established himself at Brighton, kept a gig, rode out with the hounds, and was voted perfectly genteel; and there was a certain French marquess, with the most elegant black moustachios, who had made a vast impression upon the heart of Rosalind, having met her first at the circulating library, and afterwards, by the most extraordinary series of chances, coming upon her and her sister daily in their walks upon the pier.

Meek little Caroline, meanwhile, trampled upon though she was, was springing up to womanhood; and though pale, freckled, thin, meanly-dressed, had a certain charm about her which some people might prefer to the cheap splendours and rude red and white of the Misses Macarty. In fact we have now come to a period of her history when, to the amaze of her mamma and sisters, and not a little to the satisfaction of James Gann, Esquire, she actually inspired a passion in the breast of a very respectable young man.

Chapter II

HOW MRS GANN RECEIVED TWO LODGERS

It was the winter season when the events recorded in this history occurred; and as at that period not one out of a thousand lodging-houses in Margate are let, Mrs Gann, who generally submitted to occupy her own first and second floors during this cheerless season, considered herself more than ordinarily lucky when circumstances occurred which brought no less than two lodgers to her establishment.

She had to thank her daughters for the first inmate; for, as these two young ladies were walking one day down their own street, talking of the joys of the last season, and the delight of the raffles and singing at the libraries, and the intoxicating pleasures of the Vauxhall balls, they were remarked and evidently admired by a young gentleman who was sauntering listlessly up the street.

He stared, and it must be confessed that the fascinating girls stared too, and put each other's head into each other's bonnet, and giggled and said, 'Lor'!' and then looked hard at the young gentleman again. Their eyes were black, their cheeks were very red. Fancy how Miss Bella's and Miss Linda's hearts beat when the gentleman, dropping his glass out of his eye, actually stepped across the street and said, 'Ladies, I am seeking for lodgings, and should be glad to look at those which I see are to let in your house.'

'How did the conjuror know it was our house?' thought Bella and Linda (they always thought in couples). From the very simple fact that Miss Bella had just thrust into the door a latchkey.

Most bitterly did Mrs James Gann regret that she had not on her best gown when a stranger – a stranger in February – actually called to look at the lodgings. She made up, however, for the slovenliness of her dress by the dignity of her demeanour; and asked the gentleman for references, informed him that she was a gentlewoman, and that he would have peculiar advantages in her establishment; and, finally, agreed to receive him at the rate of twenty shillings per week. The bright eyes of the young ladies had done the business; but to this day Mrs James Gann is convinced that her peculiar dignity of manner, and great fluency of brag regarding her family, have been the means of bringing hundreds of lodgers to her house, who but for her would never have visited it.

'Gents,' said Mr James Gann, at the Bag of Nails that very evening, 'we have got a new lodger, and I'll stand glasses round to his jolly good health!'

The new lodger, who was remarkable for nothing except very black eyes, a sallow face, and a habit of smoking cigars in bed until noon, gave his name George Brandon, Esq. As to his temper and habits, when humbly requested by Mrs Gann to pay in advance, he laughed and presented her with a bank-note, never quarrelled with a single item in her bills, walked much, and ate two mutton-chops per diem. The young ladies, who examined all the boxes and letters of the lodgers, as young ladies will, could not find one single document relative to their new inmate, except a tavern-bill of the White Hart, to which the name of George Brandon, Esquire, was prefixed. Any other papers which might elucidate his history were locked up in a Bramah box, likewise marked G. B.; and though these were but unsatisfactory points by which to judge a man's character, there was a something about Mr Brandon which caused all the ladies at Mrs Gann's to vote he was quite a gentleman.

When this was the case, I am happy to say it would not unfrequently happen that Miss Rosalind or Miss Isabella would appear in the lodger's apartments, bearing in the breakfast-cloth, or blushingly appearing with the weekly bill, apologising for Mamma's absence, 'and hoping that everything was to the gentleman's liking.'

Both the Misses Wellesley Macarty took occasion to visit Mr Brandon in this manner, and he received both with such a fascinating ease and gentleman-like freedom of manner, scanning their points from head to foot, and fixing his great black eyes so earnestly on their faces, that the blushing creatures turned away abashed, and yet pleased, and had many conversations about him.

'Law, Bell,' said Miss Rosalind, 'what a chap that Brandon is! I don't half like him,* I do declare!' Than which there can be no greater compliment from a woman to a man.

'No more do I neither,' says Bell. 'The man stares so, and says such things! Just now, when Becky brought his paper and sealing-wax – the silly girl brought black and red too – I took them up to ask which he would have, and what do you think he said?'

'Well, dear, what?' said Mrs Gann.

' "Miss Bell," says he, looking at me, and with such eyes! "I'll keep everything: the red wax, because it's like your lips; the black wax, because it's like your hair; and the satin paper, because it's like your skin!" Wasn't it genteel?'

'Law, now!' exclaimed Mrs Gann.

'Upon my word, I think it's very rude!' said Miss Lindy; 'and if he'd said so to me, I'd have slapped his face for his imperence!' And much to her credit Miss Lindy went to his room ten minutes after to see if he *would* say anything to her. What Mr Brandon said I never knew; but the little pang of envy which had caused Miss Lindy to retort sharply upon her sister, had given place to a pleased good-humour, and she allowed Bella to talk about the new lodger as much as ever she liked.

And now if the reader is anxious to know what was Mr Brandon's character he had better read the following letter from him. It was addressed to no less a person than a viscount; and given, perhaps, with some little ostentation to Becky the maid, to carry to the post. Now Becky before she executed such errands always showed the letters to her mistress or one of the young ladies (it must not be supposed that Miss Caroline was a whit less curious on these matters than her sisters); and when the family beheld the name of Lord Viscount Cinqbars upon the superscription their respect for their lodger was greater than ever it had been:

MARGATE, *February* 1835.

My dear Viscount – For a reason I have, on coming down to Margate, I with much gravity informed the people of the White Hart that my name was Brandon, and intend to bear that honourable appellation during my stay. For the same reason (I am a modest man, and love to do good in secret), I left the public hotel immediately, and am now housed in private lodgings, humble, and at a humble price. I am here, thank Heaven, quite alone. Robinson Crusoe had as much society in his island as I in this of Thanet. In compensation I sleep a great deal, do nothing, and walk much, silent, by the side of the roaring sea, like Calchas, priest of Apollo.

The fact is, that until Papa's wrath is appeased, I must live with the utmost meekness and humility, and have barely enough money in my possession to pay such small current expenses as fall on me here, where strangers are many and credit does not exist. I pray you, therefore, to tell Mr Snipson the tailor, Mr Jackson the bootmaker, honest Solomonson the discounter of bills, and all such friends in London and Oxford as may make inquiries after me, that I am at this very moment at the city of Munich in Bavaria, from which I shall not return until my marriage with Miss Goldmore, the great Indian heiress; who, upon my honour, will have me, I believe, any day for the asking.

Nothing else will satisfy my honoured father, I know, whose purse has already bled pretty freely for me, I must confess, and who has taken the great oath that never is broken, to bleed no more unless this marriage is brought about. Come it must. I can't work, I can't starve, and I can't live under a thousand a year.

Here, to be sure, the charges are not enormous; for your edification read my week's bill:

George Brandon, Esquire,

To Mrs James Gann.

	£.	s.	d.
A week's lodging	1	0	0
Breakfast, cream, eggs	0	9	0
Dinner (fourteen mutton-chops) .	0	10	6
Fire, boot-cleaning, &c	0.	3	6
	£2	3	0

Settled, Juliana Gann.

Juliana Gann! Is it not a sweet name? it sprawls over half the paper. Could you but see the owner of the name, my dear fellow! I love to examine the customs of natives of all countries, and upon my word there are some barbarians in our own less known, and more worthy of being known, than Hottentots, wild Irish, Otaheiteans, or any such savages. If you could see the airs that this woman gives herself; the rouge, ribands, rings, and other female gimcracks that she wears; if you could hear her reminiscences of past times, 'when she and Mr Gann moved in the very genteelest circles of society'; of the peerage, which she knows by heart; and of the fashionable novels, in every word of which she believes, you would be proud of your order, and admire the intense respect which the *canaille* show towards it. There never was such an old woman, not even our tutor at Christchurch.

'There is a he Gann, a vast, bloated old man, in a rough coat, who has met me once, and asked me, with a grin, if my mutton-chops was to my liking? The satirical monster! What *can* I eat in this place but mutton-chops? A great bleeding beef-steak, or a filthy, reeking *gigot à l'eau*, with a turnip poultice? I should die if I did. As for fish in a watering-place, I never touch it; it is sure to be bad. Nor care I for little sinewy, dry, black-legged fowls. Cutlets are my only resource; I have them nicely enough broiled by a little humble companion of the family (a companion, ye gods, in *this* family!), who blushed hugely when she confessed that the cooking was hers, and that her name was Caroline. For drink I indulge in gin, of which I consume two wine-glasses daily, in two tumblers of cold water; it is the only liquor that one can be sure to find genuine in a common house in England.

This Gann, I take it, has similar likings, for I hear him occasionally at midnight floundering up the stairs (his boots dirty in the passage) – floundering, I say, up the stairs, and cursing the candlestick, whence escape now and anon the snuffers and extinguisher, and with brazen rattle disturb the silence of the night. Thrice a week, at least, does Gann breakfast in bed – sure sign of pridian intoxication; and thrice a week, in the morning, I hear a hoarse voice roaring for 'my soda-water'. How long have the rogues drunk soda-water?

At nine, Mrs Gann and daughters are accustomed to breakfast; a handsome pair of girls, truly, and much followed, as I hear, in the quarter. These dear creatures are always paying me visits – visits with the tea-kettle, visits with the newspaper (one brings it, and one comes for it); but the one is always at the other's heels, and so one cannot show oneself to be that dear, gay seducing fellow that one has been, at home and on the Continent. Do you remember *cette chère marquise* at Pau? That cursed conjugal pistol-bullet still plays the deuce with my shoulder. Do you remember Betty Bundy, the butcher's daughter? A pretty race of fools are we to go mad after such women, and risk all – oaths, prayers, promises, long wearisome courtships – for what? – for vanity, truly. When the battle is over, behold your conquest! Betty Bundy is a vulgar country wench; and *cette belle marquise* is old, rouged, and has false hair. *Vanitas vanitatum*! what a moral man I will be some day or other!

I have found an old acquaintance (and be hanged to him!), who has come to lodge in this very house. Do you recollect at Rome a young artist, Fitch by name, the handsome gaby with the large beard, that mad Mrs Carrickfergus was doubly mad about? On the second floor of Mrs Gann's house dwells this youth. His beard brings the *gamins* of the streets trooping and yelling about him; his fine braided coats have grown somewhat shabby now; and the poor fellow is, like your humble servant (by the way, have you a 500 franc billet to spare?) – like your humble servant, I say, very low in pocket. The young Andrea bears up gaily, however; twangles his guitar, paints the worst pictures in the world, and pens sonnets to his imaginary mistress's eyebrow. Luckily the rogue did not know my name, or I should have been compelled to unbosom to him and when I called out to him, dubious as to my name, 'Don't you know me? I met you in Rome. My name is Brandon,' the painter was perfectly satisfied, and majestically bade me welcome.

Fancy the continence of this young Joseph – he has absolutely run away from Mrs Carrickfergus! 'Sir,' said he, with some hesitation and blushes, when I questioned him about the widow, 'I was compelled to leave Rome in consequence of the fatal fondness of that woman. I am an 'andsome man, sir, – I know it – all the chaps in the Academy want me for a model; and that woman, sir, is sixty. Do you think I would ally myself with her; sacrifice my happiness for the sake of a creature that's as hugly as an 'arpy? I'd rather starve, sir. I'd rather give up my heart hart and my 'opes of rising in it than do a haction so dishhhhonourable.'

There is a stock of virtue for you! and the poor fellow half starved. He lived at Rome upon the seven portraits that the Carrickfergus ordered of him, and, as I fancy, now does not make twenty pounds in the year. O rare chastity! O wondrous silly hopes! O *motus animorum, atque O certamina tanta! – pulveris exigui jactu*, in such an insignificant little lump of mud as this! Why the deuce does not the fool marry the widow? His betters would. There was a captain of dragoons, an Italian prince, and four sons of Irish peers, all at her feet; but the Cockney's beard and whiskers have overcome them all. Here my paper has come to an end; and I have the honour to bid your lordship a respectful farewell.

G. B.

Of the young gentleman who goes by the name of Brandon, the reader of the above letter will not be so misguided, we trust, as to have a very exalted opinion. The noble viscount read this document to a supper-party in Christchurch, in Oxford, and left it in a bowl of milk-punch; whence a scout abstracted it, and handed it over to us. My lord was twenty years of age when he received the epistle, and had spent a couple of years abroad before going to the university under the guardianship of the worthy individual who called himself George Brandon.

Mr Brandon was the son of a half-pay* colonel of good family, who, honouring the great himself, thought his son would vastly benefit by an acquaintance with them, and sent him to Eton, at cruel charges upon a slender purse. From Eton the lad went to Oxford, took honours there, frequented the best society, followed with a kind of proud obsequiousness all the tufts of the university, and left it owing exactly two thousand pounds. Then there came storms at home; fury on the part of the stern old 'governor'; and final payment of the debt. But while this settlement was pending, Master George had contracted many more debts among bill-discounters, and was glad to fly to the Continent as tutor to young Lord Cinqbars, in whose company he learned every one of the vices in Europe; and having a good natural genius, and a heart not unkindly, had used these qualities in such an admirable manner as to be at twenty-seven utterly ruined in purse and principle – an idler, a spendthrift, and a glutton. He was free of his money; would spend his last guinea for a sensual gratification; would borrow from his neediest friend; had no kind of conscience or remorse left, but believed himself to be a good-natured devil-may-care fellow; had a good deal of wit, and indisputably good manners, and a pleasing, dashing frankness in conversation with men. I should like to know how many such scoundrels our universities have turned out; and how much ruin has been caused by that accursed system which is called in England 'the education of a gentleman'. Go, my son, for ten years to a public school, that 'world in miniature'; learn 'to fight for yourself' against the time when your real struggles shall begin. Begin to be selfish at ten years of age; study for other ten years; get a competent knowledge of boxing, swimming, rowing, and cricket, with a pretty knack of Latin hexameters and a decent smattering of Greek plays, – do this, and a fond father shall bless you – bless the two thousand pounds which he has spent in acquiring all these benefits for you. And, besides, what else have you not learned? You have been many hundreds of times to chapel, and have learned to consider the religious service performed there as the vainest parade in the world. If your father is a grocer, you have been beaten for his sake, and have learned to be ashamed of him. You have learned to forget (as how should you remember, being separated from them for three-fourths of your time?) the ties and natural affections of home. You have learned, if you have a kindly heart and an open hand, to compete with associates much more wealthy than yourself; and to consider money as not much, but honour – the honour of dining and consorting with your betters – as a great deal. All this does the public-school and college boy learn; and woe be to his knowledge! Alas, what natural tenderness and kindly clinging filial affection is he taught to trample on and despise! My friend Brandon had gone through this process of education, and had been irretrievably ruined by it – his heart and his honesty had been ruined by it, that is to say; and he had received, in return for them a small quantity of classics and mathematics – pretty compensation for all he had lost in gaining them!

But I am wandering most absurdly from the point; right or wrong, so nature and education had formed Mr Brandon, who is one of a considerable class. Well, this young gentleman was established at Mrs Gann's house; and we are obliged to enter into all these explanations concerning him, because they are necessary to the right understanding of our story – Brandon not being altogether a bad man, nor much worse than many a one who goes through a course of regular selfish swindling all his life long and dies religious, resigned, proud of himself, and universally respected by others; for this eminent advantage has the getting-and-keeping scoundrel over the extravagant and careless one.

One day, then, as he was gazing from the window of his lodging-house, a cart, containing a vast number of easels, portfolios, wooden cases of pictures, and a small carpet-bag that might hold a change of clothes, stopped at the door. The vehicle was accompanied by a remarkable young fellow – dressed in a frock-coat covered over with frogs, a dirty turned-down shirt-collar, with a blue satin cravat, and a cap placed wonderfully on one ear – who had evidently hired apartments at Mr Gann's. This new lodger was no other than Mr Andrew Fitch;* or, as he wrote on his cards, without the prefix,

---

ANDREA FITCH

Preparations had been made at Gann's for the reception of Mr Fitch, whose aunt (an auctioneer's lady in the town) had made arrangements that he should board and lodge with the Gann family, and have the apartments on the second floor as his private rooms. In these, then, young Andrea was installed. He was a youth of a poetic temperament, loving solitude; and where is such to be found more easily than on the storm-washed shores of Margate in winter? Then the boarding-house keepers have shut up their houses and gone away in anguish; then the taverns take their carpets up, and you can have your choice of a hundred and twenty beds in any one of them; then but one dismal waiter remains to superintend this vast echoing pile of loneliness, and the landlord pines for summer; then the flys for Ramsgate stand tenantless beside the pier; and about four sailors, in pea-jackets, are to be seen in the three principal streets; in the rest, silence, closed shutters, torpid chimneys enjoying their unnatural winter sinecure – not the clack of a patten* echoing over the cold dry flags!

This solitude had been chosen by Mr Brandon for good reasons of his own; Gann and his family would have fled, but that they had no other house wherein to take refuge; and Mrs Hammerton, the auctioneer's lady, felt so keenly the kindness which she was doing to Mrs Gann, in providing her with a lodger at such a period, that she considered herself fully justified in extracting from the latter a bonus of two guineas, threatening on refusal to send her darling nephew to a rival establishment over the way.

Andrea was here, then, in the loneliness that he loved – a fantastic youth, who lived but for his art; to whom the world was like the Coburg Theatre, and he in a magnificent costume acting a principal part. His art, and his beard and whiskers, were the darlings of his heart. His long pale hair fell over a high polished brow, which looked wonderfully thoughtful; and yet no man was more guiltless of thinking. He was always putting himself into attitudes; he never spoke the truth; and was so entirely affected and absurd, as to be quite honest at last: for it is my belief that the man did not know truth from falsehood any longer, and when he was alone, when he was in company, nay, when he was unconscious and sound asleep snoring in bed, one complete lump of affectation. When his apartments on the second floor were arranged according to his fancy, they made a tremendous show. He had a large Gothic chest, in which he put his wardrobe (namely, two velvet waistcoats, four varied satin under ditto, two pairs braided trousers, two shirts, half-a-dozen false collars, and a couple of pairs of dreadfully dilapidated Blucher boots*. He had some pieces of armour; some China jugs and Venetian glasses; some bits of old damask rags to drape his doors and windows: and a rickety lay figure, in a Spanish hat and cloak, over which slung a long Toledo rapier, and a guitar, with a riband of dirty sky-blue.

Such was our poor fellow's stock in trade. He had some volumes of poems – *Lalla Rookh*, and the sterner compositions of Byron; for, to do him justice, he hated *Don Juan*, and a woman was in his eyes an angel; a hangel, alas! he would call her, for nature and the circumstances of his family had taken sad Cockney advantages over Andrea's pronunciation.

The Misses Wellesley Macarty were not, however, very squeamish with regard to grammar, and, in this dull season, voted Mr

Fitch an elegant young fellow. His immense beard and whiskers gave them the highest opinion of his genius; and before long the intimacy between the young people was considerable, for Mr Fitch insisted upon drawing the portraits of the whole family. He painted Mrs Gann in her rouge and ribands, as described by Mr Brandon; Mr Gann, who said that his picture would be very useful to the artist, as every soul in Margate knew him; and the Misses Macarty (a neat group, representing Miss Bella embracing Miss Linda, who was pointing to a pianoforte).

'I suppose you'll do my Carry next?' said Mr Gann, expressing his approbation of the last picture.

'Law, sir,' said Miss Linda, 'Carry, with her red hair! – it would be *ojus*.'

'Mr Fitch might as well paint Becky, our maid,' said Miss Bella.

'Carry is quite impossible, Gann,' said Mrs Gann; 'she hasn't a gown fit to be seen in. She's not been at church for thirteen Sundays in consequence.'

'And more shame for you, ma'am,' said Mr Gann, who liked his child; 'Carry *shall* have a gown, and the best of gowns.' And jingling three and twenty shillings in his pocket, Mr Gann determined to spend them all in the purchase of a robe for Carry. But alas, the gown never came; half the money was spent that very evening at the Bag of Nails.

'Is that – that young lady, your daughter?' said Mr Fitch, surprised, for he fancied Carry was a humble companion of the family.

'Yes, she is, and a very good daughter too, sir,' answered Mr Gann. '*Fetch* and Carry I call her, or else Carryvan – she's so useful. Ain't you, Carry?'

'I'm very glad if I am, Papa,' said the young lady who was blushing violently, and in whose presence all this conversation had been carried on.

'Hold your tongue, miss,' said her mother; 'you are very expensive to us, that you are, and need not brag about the work you do. You would not live on charity, would you, like some folks?' (here she looked fiercely at Mr Gann); 'and if your sisters and me starve to keep you and some folks, I presume you are bound to make us some return.'

When any allusion was made to Mr Gann's idleness and extravagance, or his lady showed herself in any way inclined to be angry, it was honest James's habit not to answer, but to take his hat and walk abroad to the public-house; or if haply she scolded him at night, he would turn his back and fall a-snoring. These were the only remedies he found for Mrs James's bad temper, and the first of them he adopted on hearing these words of his lady, which we have just now transcribed.

Poor Caroline had not her father's refuge of flight, but was obliged to stay and listen; and a wondrous eloquence, God wot! had Mrs Gann upon the subject of her daughter's ill-conduct. The first lecture Mr Fitch heard, he set down Caroline for a monster. Was she not idle, sulky, scornful, and a sloven? For these and many more of her daughter's vices Mrs Gann vouched, declaring that Caroline's misbehaviour was hastening her own death, and finishing by a fainting fit. In the presence of all these charges, there stood Miss Caroline, dumb, stupid, and careless; nay, when the fainting-fit came on, and Mrs Gann fell back on the sofa, the unfeeling girl took the opportunity to retire, and never offered to smack her Mamma's hands, to give her the smelling-bottle, or to restore her with a glass of water.

One stood close at hand; for Mr Fitch, when this first fit occurred, was sitting in the Gann parlour, painting that lady's portrait; and he was making towards her with his tumbler, when Miss Linda cried out, 'Stop! the water's full of paint;' and straight-away burst out laughing. Mrs Gann jumped up at this, cured suddenly, and left the room, looking somewhat foolish.

'You don't know Ma,' said Miss Linda, still giggling; 'she's always fainting.'

'Poor thing!' cried Fitch; 'very nervous, I suppose?'

Oh, very!' answered the lady, exchanging arch glances with Miss Bella.

'Poor dear lady!' continued the artist; 'I pity her from my hindmost soul. Doesn't the himmortal bard of Havon observe, how sharper than a serpent's tooth it is to have a thankless child? And is it true, Ma'am, that that young woman has been the ruin of her family?'

'Ruin of her fiddlestick!' replied Miss Bella. 'Law, Mr Fitch, you don't know Ma yet; she is in one of her tantrums.'

'What, then, it *isn't* true?' cried simple-minded Fitch. To which neither of the young ladies made any answer in words, nor could the little artist comprehend why they looked at each other, and burst out laughing. But he retired pondering on what he had seen and heard; and being a very soft young fellow, most implicitly believed the accusations of poor dear Mrs Gann, and thought her daughter Caroline was no better than a Regan or Goneril.

A time, however, was to come when he should believe her to be a most pure and gentle Cordelia; and of this change in Fitch's opinions we shall speak in Chapter III.

Chapter III

A SHABBY GENTEEL DINNER,
AND OTHER INCIDENTS OF A LIKE NATURE

Mr Brandon's letter to Lord Cinqbars produced, as we have said, a great impression upon the family of Gann; an impression which was considerably increased by their lodger's subsequent behaviour: for although the persons with whom he now associated were of a very vulgar, ridiculous kind, they were by no means so low or ridiculous that Mr Brandon should not wish to appear before them in the most advantageous light; and, accordingly, he gave himself the greatest airs when in their company, and bragged incessantly of his acquaintance and familiarity with the nobility. Mr Brandon was a tuft-hunter* of the genteel sort; his pride being quite as slavish, and his haughtiness as mean and cringing, in fact, as poor Mrs Gann's stupid wonder and respect for all the persons whose names are written with titles before them. O free and happy Britons, what a miserable, truckling, cringing race ye are!

The reader has no doubt encountered a number of such swaggerers in the course of his conversation with the world – men of a decent middle rank, who affect to despise it, and herd only with persons of the fashion. This is an offence in a man which none of us can forgive; we call him tuft-hunter, lickspittle, sneak, unmanly; we hate, and profess to despise him. I fear it is no such thing. We envy Lickspittle, that is the fact; and therefore hate him. Were he to plague us with the stories of Jones and Brown, our familiars, the man would be a simple bore, his stories heard patiently; but so

soon as he talks of my lord or the duke, we are in arms against
him. I have seen a whole merry party in Russell Square grow
suddenly gloomy and dumb, because a pert barrister, in a loud,
shrill voice, told a story of Lord This or the Marquis of That. We
all hated that man; and I would lay a wager that every one of the
fourteen persons assembled round the boiled turkey and saddle of
mutton (not to mention side-dishes from the pastry-cook's opposite the British Museum) – I would wager, I say, that every one was
muttering inwardly, 'A plague on that fellow! he knows a lord, and
I never spoke to more than three in the whole course of my life.'
To our betters we can reconcile ourselves, if you please, respecting
them very sincerely, laughing at their jokes, making allowance for
their stupidities, meekly suffering their insolence; but we can't
pardon our equals going beyond us. A friend of mine who lived
amicably and happily among his friends and relatives at Hackney,
was on a sudden disowned by the latter, cut by the former, and
doomed in innumerable prophecies to ruin, because he kept a
footboy, – a harmless little blowsy-faced urchin, in light snuff-coloured clothes, glistening over with sugar-loaf buttons. There is
another man, a great man, a literary man, whom the public loves,
and who took a sudden leap from obscurity into fame and wealth.
This was a crime; but he bore his rise with so much modesty, that
even his brethren of the pen did not envy him. One luckless day he
set up a one-horse chaise; from that minute he was doomed.

'Have you seen his new carriage?' says Snarley.

'Yes,' says Yow, 'he's so consumedly proud of it, that he can't
see his old friends while he drives.'

'Ith it a donkey-cart,' lisps Simper, 'thith gwand cawwiage? I
always thaid that the man, from hith thtyle, wath fitted to be a
vewy dethent cothtermonger.'

'Yes, yes,' cries old Candour, 'a sad pity indeed! – dreadfully
extravagant, I'm told – bad health – expensive family – works going
down every day – and now he must set up a carriage forsooth!'

Snarley, Yow, Simper, Candour hate their brother. If he is
ruined, they will be kind to him and just; but he is successful, and
woe be to him!

This trifling digression of half a page or so, although it seems to
have nothing to do with the story in hand, has, nevertheless, the
strongest relation to it; and you shall hear what.

In one word, then, Mr Brandon bragged so much, and assumed

such airs of superiority, that after a while he perfectly disgusted Mrs Gann and the Misses Macarty, who were gentlefolks themselves, and did not at all like his way of telling them that he was their better. Mr Fitch was swallowed up in his hart, as he called it, and cared nothing for Brandon's airs. Gann, being a low-spirited fellow, completely submitted to Mr Brandon, and looked up to him with deepest wonder. And poor little Caroline followed her father's faith, and in six weeks after Mr Brandon's arrival at the lodgings had grown to believe him the most perfect, finished, polished, agreeable of mankind. Indeed, the poor girl had never seen a gentleman before, and towards such her gentle heart turned instinctively. Brandon never offended her by hard words; insulted her by cruel scorn, such as she met with from her mother and her sisters; there was a quiet manner about the man quite different to any that she had before seen amongst the acquaintances of her family; and if he assumed a tone of superiority in his conversation with her and the rest, Caroline felt that he *was* their superior, and as such admired and respected him.

What happens when in the innocent bosom of a girl of sixteen such sensations arise? What has happened ever since the world began?

I have said that Miss Caroline had no friend in the world but her father, and must here take leave to recall that assertion; – a friend she most certainly had, and that was honest Becky, the smutty maid, whose name has been mentioned before. Miss Caroline had learned, in the course of a life spent under the tyranny of her mamma, some of the notions of the latter, and would have been very much offended to call Becky her friend: but friends, in fact, they were; and a great comfort it was for Caroline to descend to the calm kitchen from the stormy back-parlour, and there vent some of her little woes to the compassionate servant of all work.

When Mrs Gann went out with her daughters, Becky would take her work and come and keep Miss Caroline company; and if the truth must be told, the greatest enjoyment the pair used to have was in these afternoons, when they read together out of the precious greasy, marble-covered volumes that Mrs Gann was in the habit of fetching from the library. Many and many a tale had the pair so gone through. I can see them over *Manfrone; or, The One-handed Monk** – the room dark, the street silent, the hour ten – the tall red, lurid candlewick waggling down, the flame flickering pale upon Miss Caroline's pale face as she read out, and lighting up honest Becky's goggling eyes, who sat silent, her work in her lap: she had not done a stitch of it for an hour. As the trapdoor slowly opens, and the scowling Alonzo, bending over the sleeping Imoinda, draws his pistol, cocks it, looks well if the priming be right, places it then to the sleeper's ear, and – *thunder-under-under* – down fall the snuffers! Becky has had them in her hand for ten minutes, afraid to use them. Up starts Caroline, and flings the book back into her mamma's basket. It is that lady returned with her daughters from a tea-party, where two young gents from London have been mighty genteel indeed.

For the sentimental, too, as well as for the terrible, Miss Caroline and the cook had a strong predilection, and had wept their poor eyes out over *Thaddeus of Warsaw** and the *Scottish Chiefs**. Fortified by the examples drawn from those instructive volumes, Becky was firmly convinced that her young mistress would meet with a great lord some day or other, or be carried off, like Cinderella, by a brilliant prince, to the mortification of her elder sisters, whom Becky hated. And when, therefore, the new lodger came, lonely, mysterious, melancholy, elegant, with the romantic name of George Brandon – when he wrote a letter directed to a lord, and Miss Caroline and Becky together examined the superscription, such a look passed between them as the pencil of Leslie* or Maclise* could alone describe for us. Becky's orbs were lighted up with a preternatural look of wondering wisdom; whereas, after an instant, Caroline dropped hers, and blushed, and said, 'Nonsense, Becky!'

'*Is* it nonsense?' said Becky, grinning and snapping her fingers with a triumphant air; 'the cards comes true; I knew they would. Didn't you have king and queen of hearts three deals running? What did you dream about last Tuesday, tell me that?'

But Miss Caroline never did tell, for her sisters came bouncing down the stairs, and examined the lodger's letter. Caroline, however, went away musing much upon these points; and she began to think Mr Brandon more wonderful and beautiful every day.

In the meantime, while Miss Caroline was innocently indulging in her inclination for the brilliant occupier of the first floor, it came to pass that the tenant of the second was inflamed by a most romantic passion for her.

For, after partaking for about a fortnight of the family dinner, and passing some evenings with Mrs Gann and the young ladies,

Mr Fitch, though by no means quick of comprehension, began to perceive that the nightly charges that were brought against poor Caroline could not be founded upon truth. 'Let's see,' mused he to himself. 'Tuesday, the old lady said her daughter was bringing her grey hairs with sorrow to the grave, because the cook had not boiled the potatoes. Wednesday, she said Caroline was an assassin, because she could not find her own thimble. Thursday, she vows Caroline has no religion, because that old pair of silk stockings were not darned. And this can't be,' reasoned Fitch, deeply. 'A gal hain't a murderess because her Ma can't find her thimble. A woman that goes to slap her grown-up daughter on the back, and before company too, for such a paltry thing as a hold pair of stockings, can't be surely a-speaking the truth.' And thus gradually his first impression against Caroline wore away. As this disappeared, pity took possession of his soul – and we know what pity is akin to; and, at the same time, a corresponding hatred for the oppressors of a creature so amiable.

To sum up, in six short weeks after the appearance of the two gentlemen, we find our chief *dramatis personæ* as follows:

> Caroline, an innocent young woman, in love with Brandon
> Fitch, a celebrated painter, almost in love with Caroline.
> Brandon, a young gentleman, in love with himself.

At first he was pretty constant in his attendance upon the Misses Macarty, when they went out to walk, nor were they displeased at his attentions; but he found that there were a great number of Margate beaux – ugly, vulgar fellows as ever were – who always followed in the young ladies' train, and made themselves infinitely more agreeable than he was. These men Mr Brandon treated with a great deal of scorn: and, in return, they hated him cordially. So did the ladies speedily: his haughty manners, though quite as impertinent and free, were not half so pleasant to them as Jones's jokes or Smith's charming romps; and the girls gave Brandon very shortly to understand that they were much happier without him. 'Ladies, your humble,' he heard Bob Smith say, as that little linendraper came skipping to the door from which they were issuing. 'The sun's hup and trade is down; if you're for a walk, I'm your man.' And Miss Linda and Miss Bella each took an arm of Mr Smith, and sailed down the street. 'I'm glad you ain't got that proud gent with the glass hi,' said Mr Smith; 'he's the most hillbred, supercilious beast I ever see.'

'So he is,' says Bella.

'Hush!' says Linda.

The 'proud gent with the glass hi' was at this moment lolling out of the first-floor window, smoking his accustomed cigar; and his eye-glass was fixed upon the ladies, to whom he made a very low bow. It may be imagined how fond he was of them afterwards, and what looks he cast at Mr Bob Smith the next time he met him. Mr Bob's heart beat for a day afterwards; and he found he had business in town.

But the love of society is stronger than even pride; and the great Mr Brandon was sometimes fain to descend from his high station and consort with the vulgar family with whom he lodged. But, as we have said, he always did this with a wonderfully condescending air, giving his associates to understand how great was the honour he did them.

One day, then, he was absolutely so kind as to accept of an invitation from the ground-floor, which was delivered in the passage by Mr James Gann, who said, 'It was hard to see a gent eating mutton-chops from week's end to week's end; and if Mr Brandon had a mind to meet a devilish good fellow as ever was, my friend Swigby, a man who rides his horse, and has his five hundred a year to spend, and to eat a prime cut out of as good a leg of pork (though he said it) as ever a knife was stuck into, they should dine that day at three o'clock sharp, and Mrs G. and the gals would be glad of the honour of his company.'

The person so invited was rather amused at the terms in which Mr Gann conveyed his hospitable message; and at three o'clock made his appearance in the back parlour, whence he had the honour of conducting Mrs Gann (dressed in a sweet yellow *mousseline de laine*, with a large red turban, a *ferronnière*, and a smelling-bottle attached by a ring to a very damp, fat hand) to the 'office', where the repast was set out. The Misses Macarty were in costumes equally tasty: one on the guest's right hand; one near the boarder, Mr Fitch – who, in a large beard, an amethyst, velvet waistcoat, his hair fresh wetted, and parted accurately down the middle to fall in curls over his collar, would have been irresistible if the collar had been a little, little whiter than it was.

Mr Brandon, too, was dressed in his very best suit; for though he affected to despise his hosts very much, he wished to make the most favourable impression upon them, and took care to tell Mrs Gann that he and Lord So-and-so were the only two men in the world who were in possession of that particular waistcoat which she admired: for Mrs Gann was very gracious, and had admired the waistcoat, being desirous to impress with awe Mr Gann's friend and admirer Mr Swigby – who, man of fortune as he was, was a constant frequenter of the club at the Bag of Nails.

About this club and its supporters Mr Gann's guest, Mr Swigby, and Gann himself, talked very gaily before dinner; all the jokes about all the club being roared over by the pair.

Mr Brandon, who felt he was the great man of the party, indulged himself in his great propensities without restraint, and told Mrs Gann stories about half the nobility. Mrs Gann conversed knowingly about the Opera; and declared that she thought Taglion the sweetest singer in the world.

'Mr – a – Swigby, have you ever seen Lablache dance?' asked Mr Brandon of that gentleman, to whom he had been formally introduced.

'At Vauxhall is he?' said Mr Swigby, who was just from town.

'Yes, on the tight-rope; a charming performer.'

On which Mr Gann told how he had been to Vauxhall when the princes were in London; and his lady talked of these knowingly. And then they fell to conversing about fireworks and rack-punch; Mr Brandon assuring the young ladies that Vauxhall was the very pink of the fashion, and longing to have the honour of dancing a quadrille with them there. Indeed Brandon was so very sarcastic, that not a single soul at table understood him.

The table, from Mr Brandon's plan of it, which was afterwards sent to my Lord Cinqbars, was arranged as follows:

	Miss Caroline	Mr Fitch	Miss L Macarty	
	1	Potatoes	3	
Mr James Gann	A roast leg of pork, with sage and onions	Three shreds of celery in a glass	Boiled haddock, removed by hashed mutton	Mrs James Gann
	2	Cabbage	4	
	Mr Swigby	Miss B Macarty	Mr Brandon	

1 and 2 are pots of porter; 3, a quart of ale, Mrs Gann's favourite drink; 4, a bottle of fine old golden sherry, the real

produce of the Uva grape, purchased at the Bag of Nails Hotel for
1s. 9D. by Mr J. Gann.

Mr Gann. 'Taste that sherry, sir. Your 'ealth, and my services
to you, sir. That wine, sir, is given me as a particular favour by
my – ahem! – my wine-merchant, who only will part with a small
quantity of it, and imports it direct, sir, from – ahem! – from – –.'

Mr Brandon. 'From Xeres, of course. It is, I really think, the
finest wine I ever tasted in my life – at a commoner's table, that
is.'

Mrs Gann. 'Oh, in course, a commoner's table! – we have no
titles, sir (Mr Gann, I will trouble you for some more crackling),
though my poor dear girls are related, by their blessed father's
side, to some of the first nobility in the land, I assure you.'

Mr Gann. 'Gammon, Jooly my dear. Them Irish nobility, you
know, what are they? And besides, it's my belief that the gals are
no more related to them than I am.'

Miss Bella (to Mr Brandon, confidentially). 'You must find that
poor Par is sadly vulgar, Mr Brandon.'

Mrs Gann. 'Mr Brandon has never been accustomed to such
language, I am sure; and I entreat you will excuse Mr Gann's
rudeness, sir.'

Miss Linda. 'Indeed, I assure you, Mr Brandon, that we've high
connexions as well as low; as high as some people's connexions,
per'aps, though we are not always talking of the nobility.' This
was a double shot: the first barrel of Miss Linda's sentence hit her
stepfather, the second part was levelled directly at Mr Brandon.
'Don't you think I'm right, Mr Fitch?'

Mr Brandon. 'You are quite right, Miss Linda, in this as in every
other instance; but I am afraid Mr Fitch has not paid proper
attention to your excellent remark: for, if I don't mistake the
meaning of that beautiful design which he has made with his fork
upon the tablecloth, his soul is at this moment wrapped up in his
art.'

This was exactly what Mr Fitch wished that all the world
should suppose. He flung back his hair, and stared wildly for a
moment, and said, 'Pardon me, madam: it is true my thoughts
were at that moment far away in the regions of my hart.' He was
really thinking that his attitude was a very elegant one, and that
a large garnet ring which he wore on his forefinger must be
mistaken by all the company for a ruby.

'Art is very well,' said Mr Brandon; 'but with such pretty

natural objects before you, I wonder you were not content to think of them.'

'Do you mean the mashed potatoes, sir?' said Andrea Fitch, wondering.

'I mean Miss Rosalind Macarty,' answered Brandon, gallantly, and laughing heartily at the painter's simplicity. But this compliment could not soften Miss Linda, who had an uneasy conviction that Mr Brandon was laughing at her, and disliked him accordingly.

At this juncture, Miss Caroline entered and took the place marked as hers, to the left hand of Mr Gann, vacant. An old rickety wooden stool was placed for her, instead of that elegant and commodious Windsor chair which supported every other person at table; and by the side of the plate stood a curious old battered tin mug, on which the antiquarian might possibly discover the inscription of the word 'Caroline'. This, in truth, was poor Caroline's mug and stool, having been appropriated to her from childhood upwards; and here it was her custom meekly to sit, and eat her daily meal.

It was well that the girl was placed near her father, else I do believe she would have been starved; but Gann was much too good-natured to allow that any difference should be made between her and her sisters. There are some meannesses which are too mean even for man – woman, lovely woman alone, can venture to commit them. Well, on the present occasion, and when the dinner was half over, poor Caroline stole gently into the room and took her ordinary place. Caroline's pale face was very red; for the fact must be told that she had been in the kitchen helping Becky, the universal maid; and having heard how the great Mr Brandon was to dine with them upon that day, the simple girl had been showing her respect for him by compiling, in her best manner, a certain dish, for the cooking of which her papa had often praised her. She took her place, blushing violently when she saw him, and if Mr Gann had not been making a violent clattering with his knife and fork, it is possible that he might have heard Miss Caroline's heart thump, which it did violently. Her dress was somehow a little smarter than usual; and Becky the maid, who brought in that remove of hashed mutton which has been set down in the bill of fare, looked at her young lady with a good deal of complacency, as, loaded with plates, she quitted the room. Indeed the poor girl deserved to be looked at: there was an air of gentleness and innocence about her that was apt to please some persons much more than the bold beauties of her sisters. The two young men did not fail to remark this; one of them, the little painter, had long since observed it.

'You are very late, miss,' cried Mrs Gann, who affected not to know what had caused her daughter's delay. 'You're always late!' and the elder girls stared and grinned at each other knowingly, as they always did when Mamma made such attacks upon Caroline, who only kept her eyes down upon the tablecloth, and began to eat her dinner without saying a word.

'Come, my dear,' cried honest Gann, 'if she is late you know why. A girl can't be here and there too, as I say; can they, Swigby?'

'Impossible!' said Swigby.

'Gents,' continued Mr Gann, 'our Carry, you must know, has been down stairs making the pudding for her old pappy; and a good pudding she makes, I can tell you.'

Miss Caroline blushed more vehemently than ever; the artist stared her full in the face; Mrs Gann said, 'Nonsense' and 'stuff,' very majestically; only Mr Brandon interposed in Caroline's favour.

'I would sooner that my wife should know how to make a pudding,' said he, 'than how to play the best piece of music in the world!'

'Law, Mr Brandon! I, for my part, wouldn't demean myself by any such kitchen-work!' cries Miss Linda.

'Make puddens, indeed; it's ojous!' cries Bella.

'For you, my loves, of course!' interposed their mamma. 'Young women of your family and circumstances is not expected to perform any such work. It's different with Miss Caroline, who, if she does make herself useful now and then, don't make herself near so useful as she should, considering that she's not a shilling, and is living on our charity, like some other folks.'

Thus did this amiable woman neglect no opportunity to give her opinions about her husband and daughter. The former, however, cared not a straw; and the latter, in this instance, was perfectly happy. Had not kind Mr Brandon approved of her work; and could she ask for more?

'Mamma may say what she pleases to-day,' thought Caroline. 'I am too happy to be made angry by her.'

Poor little mistaken Caroline, to think you were safe against three women! The dinner had not advanced much further when

Miss Isabella, who had been examining her younger sister curiously for some short time, telegraphed Miss Linda across the table, and nodded, and winked, and pointed to her own neck; a very white one, as I have before had the honour to remark, and quite without any covering, except a smart necklace of twenty-four rows of the lightest blue glass beads, finishing in a neat tassel. Linda had a similar ornament of a vermilion colour; whereas Caroline, on this occasion, wore a handsome new collar up to the throat, and a brooch, which looked all the smarter for the shabby frock over which they were placed. As soon as she saw her sister's signals, the poor little thing, who had only just done fluttering and blushing, fell to this same work over again. Down went her eyes once more, and her face and neck lighted up to the colour of Miss Linda's sham cornelian.

'What's the gals giggling and ogling about?' said Mr Gann, innocently.

'What is it, my darling loves?' said stately Mrs Gann.

'Why, don't you see, Ma?' said Linda. 'Look at Miss Carry! I'm blessed if *she has not got on Becky's collar and brooch* that Sims the pilot gave her!'

The young ladies fell back in uproarious fits of laughter, and laughed all the time that their mamma was thundering out a speech, in which she declared that her daughter's conduct was unworthy a gentlewoman, and bid her leave the room and take off those disgraceful ornaments.

There was no need to tell her; the poor little thing gave one piteous look at her father, who was whistling, and seemed indeed to think the matter a good joke; and after she had managed to open the door and totter into the passage, you might have heard her weeping there, weeping tears more bitter than any of the many she had shed in the course of her life. Down she went to the kitchen, and when she reached that humble place of refuge, first pulled at her neck and made as if she would take off Becky's collar and brooch, and then flung herself into the arms of that honest scullion, where she cried and cried till she brought on the first fit of hysterics that ever she had had.

This crying could not at first be heard in the parlour, where the young ladies, Mrs Gann, Mr Gann, and his friend from the Bag of Nails were roaring at the excellence of the joke. Mr Brandon, sipping sherry, sat by, looking very sarcastically and slyly from one party to the other; Mr Fitch was staring about him too, but with a very different expression, anger and wonder inflaming his bearded countenance. At last, as the laughing died away and a faint voice of weeping came from the kitchen below, Andrew could bear it no longer, but bounced up from his chair and rushed out of the room exclaiming, –

'By Jove, it's too bad!'

'What does the man mean?' said Mrs Gann.

He meant that he was from that moment over head and ears in love with Caroline, and that he longed to beat, buffet, pummel, thump, tear to pieces, those callous ruffians who so pitilessly laughed at her.

'What's that chop wi' the beard in such tantrums about?' said the gentleman from the Bag of Nails.

Mr Gann answered this query by some joke, intimating that 'per'aps Mr Fitch's dinner did not agree with him,' at which these worthies roared again.

The young ladies said, 'Well, now, upon my word!'

'Mighty genteel behaviour, truly!' cried Mamma; 'but what can you expect from the poor thing?'

Brandon only sipped more sherry, but he looked at Fitch as the latter flung out of the room, and his countenance was lighted up by a more unequivocal smile.

These two little adventures were followed by a silence of some few minutes, during which the meats remained on the table, and no signs were shown of that pudding upon which poor Caroline had exhausted her skill. The absence of this delicious part of the repast was first remarked by Mr Gann; and his lady, after jangling at the bell for some time in vain, at last begged one of her daughters to go and hasten matters.

'*Becky!*' shrieked Miss Linda, from the hall, but Becky replied not. 'Becky, are we to be kept waiting all day?' continued the lady in the same shrill voice. 'Mamma wants the pudding!'

'*Tell her to fetch it herself!*' roared Becky, at which remark Gann and his facetious friend once more went off into fits of laughter.

'This is too bad!' said Mrs G., starting up; 'she shall leave the house this instant!' and so no doubt Becky would, but that the lady owed her five quarters' wages; which she, at that period, did not feel inclined to pay.

Well, the dinner at last was at an end; the ladies went away to

tea, leaving the gentlemen to their wine; Brandon, very conde-
scendingly, partaking of a bottle of port, and listening with
admiration to the toasts and sentiments with which it is still the
custom among persons of Mr Gann's rank of life to preface each
glass of wine. As thus:

Glass 1. 'Gents,' says Mr Gann, rising, 'this glass I need say
nothing about. Here's the king, and long life to him and the
family!'

Mr Swigby, with his glass, goes knock, knock, knock on the
table; and saying gravely 'The king!' drinks off his glass, and
smacks his lips afterwards.

Mr Brandon, who had drunk half his, stops in the midst and
says, 'Oh, "the king"'

Mr Swigby. 'A good glass of wine that, Gann my boy!'

Mr Brandon. 'Capital, really; though, upon my faith, I'm no
judge of port.'

Mr Gann (*smacks*). 'A fine fruity wine as ever I tasted. I suppose
you, Mr B., are accustomed only to claret. I've 'ad it too, in my
time, sir, as Swigby there very well knows. I travelled, sir, *sure le
Continong*, I assure you, and drank my glass of claret with the
best man in France, or England either. I wasn't always what I am,
sir.'

Mr Brandon. 'You don't look as if you were.'

Mr Gann. 'No, sir. Before that – – gas came in, I was head, sir,
of one of the fust 'ouses in the hoil-trade, Gann, Blubbery &
Gann, sir – Thames Street, City. I'd my box at Putney, as good a
gig and horse as my friend there drives.'

Mr Swigby. 'Ay, and a better too, Gann, I make no doubt.'

Mr Gann. 'Well, *say* a better. I *had* a better, if money could
fetch it, sir; and I didn't spare that, I warrant you. No, no, James
Gann didn't grudge his purse, sir; and had his friends around him,
as he's 'appy to 'ave now, sir. Mr Brandon, your 'ealth, sir, and
may we hoften meet under this ma'ogany. Swigby, my boy, God
bless you!'

Mr Brandon. 'Your very good health.'

Mr Swigby. 'Thank you, Gann. Here's to you, and long life and
prosperity and happiness to you and yours. Bless you, Jim my boy;
Heaven bless you! I say this, Mr Bandon – Brandon – what's your
name – there ain't a better fellow in all Margate than James Gann
– no, nor in all England. Here's Mrs Gann, gents, and the family.
Mrs Gann!' (*drinks*.)

Mr Brandon. 'Mrs Gann. Hip, hip, hurrah!' (*drinks.*)

Mr Gann. 'Mrs Gann, and thank you, gents. A fine woman Mr B.; ain't she now? Ah, if you'd seen 'er when I married her! Gad, she *was* fine then – an out-and-outer, sir! *Such* a figure!'

Mr Swigby. 'You'd choose none but a good 'un, I war'nt. Ha, ha, ha!'

Mr Gann. 'Did I ever tell you of my duel along with the regimental doctor? No! Then I will. I was a young chap, you see, in those days; and when I saw her at Brussels – (*Brusell,* they call it) – I was right slick up over head and ears in love with her at once. But what was to be done? There was another gent in the case – a regimental doctor, sir – a reg'lar dragon. 'Faint heart,' says I, 'never won a fair lady,' and so I made so bold. She took me, sent the doctor to the right about. I met him one morning in the park at Brussels, and stood to him, sir, like a man. When the affair was over, my second, a leftenant of dragoons, told me, 'Gann,' says he, 'I've seen many a man under fire – I'm a Waterloo man,' says he, – 'and have rode by Wellington many a long day; but I never, for coolness, see such a man as you.' Gents, here's the Duke of Wellington and the British army!' *(The gents drink.)*

Mr Brandon. 'Did you kill the doctor, sir?'

Mr Gann. 'Why, no, sir; I shot in the hair.'

Mr Brandon. 'Shot him in the hair? Egad, that was a severe shot, and a very lucky escape the doctor had of it! Whereabout in the hair? a whisker, sir; or perhaps, a pigtail?'

Mr Swigby. 'Haw, haw, haw! shot'n in the *hair* – capital, capital!'

Mr Gann, who has grown very red. 'No, sir, there may be some mistake in my pronunciation, which I didn't expect to have laughed at, at my hown table.'

Mr Brandon. 'My dear sir! I protest and vow – '

Mr Gann. 'Never mind it, sir. I gave you my best, and did my best to make you welcome. If you like better to make fun of me, do, sir. That may be the *genteel* way, but hang me if it's *hour* way; is it, Jack? *Our* way; I beg your pardon, sir.'

Mr Swigby. 'Jim, Jim! for Heaven's sake! – peace and harmony of the evening – conviviality – social enjoyment – didn't mean it – did you mean anything, Mr What-d'-ye-call-'im?'

Mr Brandon. 'Nothing, upon my honour as a gentleman!'

Mr Gann. 'Well, then, there's my hand!' and good-natured Gann tried to forget the insult, and to talk as if nothing had occurred: but he had been wounded in the most sensitive point in which a man can be touched by his superior, and never forgot Brandon's joke. That night at the club, when dreadfully tipsy, he made several speeches on the subject, and burst into tears many times. The pleasure of the evening was quite spoiled; and, as the conversation became vapid and dull, we shall refrain from reporting it. Mr Brandon speedily took leave, but had not the courage to face the ladies at tea; to whom, it appears, the reconciled Becky had brought that refreshing beverage.

Chapter IV

IN WHICH MR FITCH PROCLAIMS HIS LOVE, AND MR BRANDON PREPARES FOR WAR

From the splendid hall in which Mrs Gann was dispensing her hospitality, the celebrated painter, Andrea Fitch, rushed forth in a state of mind even more delirious than that which he usually enjoyed. He looked abroad into the street: all there was dusk and lonely; the rain falling heavily, the wind playing Pandean pipes and whistling down the chimney-pots. 'I love the storm,' said Fitch, solemnly; and he put his great Spanish cloak round him in the most approved manner (it was of so prodigious a size that the tail of it, as it twirled over his shoulder, whisked away a lodging-card from the door of the house opposite Mr Gann's). 'I love the storm and solitude' said he, lighting a large pipe filled of the fragrant Oronooko*; and thus armed, he passed rapidly down the street, his hat cocked over his ringlets.

Andrea did not like smoking, but he used a pipe as a part of his profession as an artist, and as one of the picturesque parts of his costume; in like manner, though he did not fence, he always travelled about with a pair of foils; and quite unconscious of music, nevertheless had a guitar constantly near at hand. Without such properties a painter's spectacle is not complete; and now he determined to add to them another indispensable requisite – a mistress. 'What great artist was ever without one?' thought he. Long, long had he sighed for some one whom he might love, some one to whom he might address the poems which he was in the habit of making. Hundreds of such fragments had he composed, addressed to Leila, Ximena, Ada – imaginary beauties, whom he courted in dreamy verse. With what joy would he replace all those by a real charmer of flesh and blood! Away he went, then, on this evening – the tyranny of Mrs Gann towards poor Caroline having awakened all his sympathies in the gentle girl's favour – determined now and for ever to make her the mistress of his heart. Monna-Lisa, the Fornarina, Leonardo, Raphael – he thought of all these, and vowed that his Caroline should be made famous and live for ever on his canvas. While Mrs Gann was preparing for her friends, and entertaining them at tea and whist; while Caroline, all unconscious of the love she inspired, was weeping up stairs in her little garret; while Mr Brandon was enjoying the refined conversation of Gann and Swigby, over their glass and pipe in the office, Andrea walked abroad by the side of the ocean; and, before he was wet through, walked himself into the most fervid affection for poor persecuted Caroline. The reader might have observed him (had not the night been very dark, and a great deal too wet to allow a sensible reader to go abroad on such an errand) at the sea-shore standing on a rock, and drawing from his bosom a locket which contained a curl of hair tied up in riband. He looked at it for a moment, and then flung it away from him into the black boiling waters below him.

'No other 'air but thine, Caroline, shall ever rest near this 'art!' he said, and kissed the locket and restored it to its place. Light -minded youth, whose hair was it that he thus flung away? How many times had Andrea shown that very ringlet in strictest confidence to several brethren of the brush, and declared that it was the hair of a dear girl in Spain whom he loved to madness? Alas! 'twas but a fiction of his fevered brain; every one of his friends had a locket of hair, and Andrea, who had no love until now, had clipped this precious token from the wig of a lovely lay-figure, with cast-iron joints and a cardboard head, that had stood for some time in his atelier. I don't know that he felt any shame about the proceeding, for he was of such a warm imagination that he had grown to believe that the hair did actually come from a girl in Spain, and only parted with it on yielding to a superior attachment.

This attachment being fixed on, the young painter came home wet through; passed the night in reading Byron; making sketches, and burning them; writing poems to Caroline, and expunging them with pitiless india-rubber. A romantic man makes a point of sitting up all night, and pacing his chamber; and you may see many a composition of Andrea's dated 'Midnight, 10th of March, A. F.,' with his peculiar flourish over the initials. He was not sorry to be told in the morning, by the ladies at breakfast, that he looked dreadfully pale; and answered, laying his hand on his forehead and shaking his head gloomily, that he could get no sleep: and then he would heave a huge sigh; and Miss Bella and Miss Linda would look at each other and grin according to their wont. He was glad, I say, to have his woe remarked, and continued his sleeplessness for two or three nights; but he was certainly still more glad when he heard Mr Brandon, on the fourth morning, cry out, in a shrill, angry voice to Becky the maid, to give the gentleman up stairs his compliments – Mr Brandon's compliments – and tell him that he could not get a wink of sleep for the horrid trampling he kept up. 'I am hanged if I stay in the house a night longer,' added the first floor sharply, 'if that Mr Fitch kicks up such a confounded noise!' Mr Fitch's point was gained, and henceforth he was as quiet as a mouse; for his wish was not only to be in love, but to let everybody know that he was in love, or where is the use of a *belle passion*?

So, whenever he saw Caroline, at meals, or in the passage, he used to stare at her with the utmost power of his big eyes, and fall to groaning most pathetically. He used to leave his meals untasted, groan, heave sighs, and stare incessantly. Mrs Gann and her eldest daughters were astonished at these manœuvres; for they never suspected that any man could possibly be such a fool as to fall in love with Caroline. At length the suspicion came upon them, created immense laughter and delight; and the ladies did not fail to rally Caroline in their usual elegant way. Gann, too, loved a joke (much polite waggery had this worthy man practised in select inn-parlours for twenty years past), and would call poor Caroline 'Mrs F.'; and say that, instead of *Fetch* and Carry, as he used to name her, he should style her *Fitch* and Carry for the future; and laugh at this great pun, and make many others of a similar sort that set Caroline blushing.

Indeed, the girl suffered a great deal more from this raillery than at first may be imagined; for after the first awe inspired by Fitch's whiskers had passed away, and he had drawn the young ladies' pictures, and made designs in their albums, and in the midst of their jokes and conversation had remained perfectly silent, the Gann family had determined that the man was an idiot: and, indeed, were not very wide of the mark. In everything except his own peculiar art honest Fitch *was* an idiot; and as upon the subject of painting the Ganns, like most people of their class in England, were profoundly ignorant, it came to pass that he would breakfast and dine for many days in their company, and not utter one single syllable. So they looked upon him with extreme pity and contempt, as a harmless, good-natured, crack-brained creature, quite below them in the scale of intellect, and only to be endured because he paid a certain number of shillings weekly to the Gann exchequer. Mrs Gann in all companies was accustomed to talk about her idiot. Neighbours and children used to peer at him as he strutted down the street: and though every young lady, including my dear Caroline, is flattered by having a lover, at least they don't like such a lover as this. The Misses Macarty (after having set their caps at him very fiercely, and quarrelled concerning him on his first coming to lodge at their house) vowed and protested now that he was no better than a chimpanzee; and Caroline and Becky agreed that this insult was as great as any that could be paid to the painter. 'He's a good creature too,' said Becky, 'crack-brained as he is. Do you know, miss, he gave me half a sovereign to buy a new collar, after that business t'other day?'

'And did – Mr – , – , did the first floor say anything?' asked Caroline.

'Didn't he! he's a funny gentleman, that Brandon, sure enough; and when I took him up breakfast next morning, asked about Sims the pilot, and what I gi'ed Sims for the collar and brooch – he, he!'

And this was indeed a correct report of Mr Brandon's conversation with Becky; he had been infinitely amused with the whole transaction, and wrote his friend the viscount a capital facetious account of the manners and customs of the native inhabitants of the Isle of Thanet.

And now, when Mr Fitch's passion was fully developed – as far, that is, as sighs and ogles could give it utterance – a curious instance of that spirit of contradiction for which our race is remarkable was seen in the behaviour of Mr Brandon. Although Caroline, in the depths of her little silly heart, had set him down for her divinity, her wondrous fairy prince, who was to deliver her from her present miserable durance, she had never by word or deed acquainted Brandon with her inclination for him, but had, with instinctive modesty, avoided him more sedulously than before. He, too, had never bestowed a thought upon her. How should such a Jove as Mr Brandon, from the cloudy summit of his fashionable Olympus, look down and perceive such an humble, retiring being as poor little Caroline Gann? Thinking her at first not disagreeable, he had never, until the day of the dinner, bestowed one single further thought upon her; and only when exasperated by the Miss Macartys' behaviour towards him, did he begin to think how sweet it would be to make them jealous and unhappy.

'The uncouth grinning monsters,' said he, 'with their horrible court of Bob Smiths and Jack Joneses, daring to look down upon me, a gentleman, – me, the celebrated *mangeur des cœurs* – a man of genius, fashion, and noble family! If I could but revenge myself on them! What injury can I invent to wound them?'

It is curious to what points a man in his passion will go. Mr Brandon had long since, in fact, tried to do the greatest possible injury to the young ladies; for it had been, at the first dawn of his acquaintance, as we are bound with much sorrow to confess, his fixed intention to ruin one or the other of them. And when the young ladies had, by their coldness and indifference to him, frustrated this benevolent intention, he straightway fancied that they had injured him severely, and cast about for means to revenge himself upon them.

This point is, to be sure, a very delicate one to treat, – for in words, at least, the age has grown to be wonderfully moral, and refuses to hear discourses upon such subjects. But human nature, as far as I am able to learn, has not much changed since the time when Richardson wrote and Hogarth painted, a century ago. There are wicked Lovelaces abroad, ladies, now as then, when it was considered no shame to expose the rogues; and pardon us, therefore, for hinting that such there be. Elegant acts of *rouerie*, such as that meditated by Mr Brandon, are often performed still by dashing young men of the world, who think no sin of an *amourette*, but glory in it, especially if the victim be a person of mean condition. Had Brandon succeeded (such is the high moral state of our British youth), all his friends would have pronounced him, and he would have considered himself, to be a very lucky, captivating dog; nor, as I believe, would he have had a single pang of conscience for the rascally action which he had committed. This supreme act of scoundrelism has man permitted to himself – to deceive women. When we consider how he has availed himself of the privilege so created by him, indeed one may sympathise with the advocates of woman's rights who point out this monstrous wrong. We have read of that wretched woman of old whom the pious Pharisees were for stoning incontinently; but we don't hear that they made any outcry against *the man* who was concerned in the crime. Where was he? Happy, no doubt, and easy in mind, and regaling some choice friends over a bottle with the history of his success.

Being thus injured, then, Mr Brandon longed for revenge. How should he repay these impertinent young women for slighting his addresses? '*Pardi*,' said he; 'just to punish their pride and insolence, I have a great mind to make love to their sister.'

He did not, however, for some time condescend to perform this threat. Eagles such as Brandon do not sail down from the clouds in order to pounce upon small flies, and soar airwards again, contented with such an ignoble booty. In a word, he never gave a minute's thought to Miss Caroline, until further circumstances occurred which caused this great man to consider her as an object somewhat worthy of his remark.

The violent affection suddenly exhibited by Mr Fitch, the painter, towards poor little Caroline was the point which determined Brandon to begin to act.

My dear Viscount [wrote he to the same Lord Cinqbars whom he formerly addressed] – Give me joy; for in a week's time it is my intention to be violently in love – and love is no small amusement in a wateringplace in winter.

I told you about the fair Juliana Gann and her family. I forgot whether I mentioned how the Juliana had two fair daughters, the Rosalind and the Isabella; and another, Caroline by name, not so good-looking as her half-sisters, but, nevertheless, a pleasing young person.

Well, when I came hither I had nothing to do but to fall in love with the two handsomest; and did so, taking many walks with them, talking much nonsense; passing long dismal evenings over horrid tea with them and their mamma: laying regular siege, in fact, to these Margate beauties, who, according to the common rule in such cases, could not, I thought, last long.

Miserable deception! disgusting aristocratic blindness! [Mr Brandon always assumed that his own high birth and eminent position were granted.]

Would you believe it, that I, who have seen, fought, and conquered in so many places, should have been ignominiously defeated here? Just as American Jackson defeated our Peninsular veterans, I, an old Continental conqueror too, have been overcome by this ignoble enemy. These women have entrenched themselves so firmly in their vulgarity, that I have been beaten back several times with disgrace, being quite unable to make an impression. The monsters, too, keep up a dreadful fire from behind their entrenchments; and besides have raised the whole country against me: in a word, all the snobs of their acquaintance are in arms. There is Bob Smith, the linendraper; Harry Jones, who keeps the fancy tea-shop; young Glauber, the apothecary; and sundry other persons, who are ready to eat me when they see me in the streets; and are all at the beck of the victorious Amazons.

How is a gentleman to make head against such a *canaille* as this? – a regular *jacquerie*. Once or twice I have thought of retreating; but a retreat, for sundry reasons I have, is inconvenient. I can't go to London; I am known at Dover; I believe there is a bill against me at Canterbury; at Chatham there are sundry quartered regiments whose recognition I should be unwilling to risk. I must stay here – and be hanged to the place – until my better star shall rise.

But I am determined that my stay shall be to some purpose; and so to show how persevering I am, I shall make one more trial upon the third daughter, – yes, upon the third daughter, a family Cinderella, who shall, I am determined, make her sisters *crever* with envy. I merely mean fun, you know – not mischief, – for Cinderella is but a little child: and, besides, I am the most harmless fellow breathing, but must have my joke. Now Cinderella has a lover, the bearded painter of whom I spoke to you in a former letter. He has lately plunged into the most extraordinary fits of passion for her, and is more mad than even he was before. Woe betide you, O painter! I have nothing to do: a month to do that nothing in; in that time, mark my words, I will laugh at that painter's beard. Should you like a lock of it, or a sofa stuffed with it? there is beard enough: or should you like to see a specimen of poor little Cinderella's golden ringlets? Command your slave. I wish I had paper enough to write you an account of a grand Gann dinner at which I assisted, and of a scene which there took place; and how Cinderella was dressed out, not by a fairy, but by a charitable kitchen-maid, and was turned out of the room by her indignant mamma for appearing in the scullion's finery. But my *forte* does not lie in such descriptions of polite life. We drank port, and toasts after dinner: here is the *menu*, and the names and order of the eaters.

The bill of fare has been given already, and need not, therefore, be again laid before the public.

'What a fellow that is!' said young Lord Cinqbars, reading the letter to his friends, and in a profound admiration of his tutor's genius.

'And to think that he was a reading man too, and took a double first,' cried another; 'why, the man's an *Admirable Crichton*.'*

'Upon my life, though, he's a little too bad,' said a third, who was a moralist. And with this a fresh bowl of milk-punch came reeking from the college butteries, and the jovial party discussed that.

Chapter V

CONTAINS A GREAT DEAL OF COMPLICATED LOVE-MAKING

The Misses Macarty were excessively indignant that Mr Fitch should have had the audacity to fall in love with their sister; and poor Caroline's life was not, as may be imagined, made much the happier by the envy and passion thus excited. Mr Fitch's amour was the source of a great deal of pain to her. Her mother would tauntingly say, that as both were beggars, they could not do better than marry; and declared, in the same satirical way, that she should like nothing better than to see a large family of grandchildren about her, to be plagues and burdens upon her, as her daughter was. The short way would have been, when the young painter's intentions were manifest, which they pretty speedily were, to have requested him immediately to quit the house; or, as Mr Gann said, 'to give him the sack at once'; to which measure the worthy man indignantly avowed that he would have resort. But his lady would not allow of any such rudeness; although, for her part, she professed the strongest scorn and contempt for the painter. For the painful fact must be stated: Fitch had a short time previously paid no less a sum than a whole quarter's board and lodging in advance, at Mrs Gann's humble request, and he possessed his landlady's receipt for that sum; the mention of which circumstance silenced Gann's objections at once. And indeed it is pretty certain that, with all her taunts to her daughter and just abuse of Fitch's poverty, Mrs Gann in her heart was not altogether averse to the match. In the first place, she loved match-making; next, she would be glad to be rid of her daughter at any rate; and, besides, Fitch's aunt, the auctioneer's wife, was rich, and had no children; painters, as she had heard, make often a great deal of money, and Fitch might be a clever one, for aught she knew. So he was allowed to remain in the house, an undeclared but very assiduous lover; and to sigh, and to moan, and make verses and portraits of his beloved, and build castles in the air as best he might, Indeed our humble Cinderella was in a very curious position. She felt a tender passion for the first floor, and was adored by the second floor, and had to wait upon both at the summons of the bell of either; and as the poor little thing was compelled not to notice any of the sighs and glances which the painter bestowed upon her, she also had schooled herself to maintain a quiet demeanour towards, Mr Brandon, and not allow him to discover the secret which was labouring in her little breast.

I think it may be laid down as a pretty general rule, that most romantic little girls of Caroline's age have such a budding sentiment as this young person entertained; quite innocent, of course; nourished and talked of in delicious secrecy to the *confidante* of the hour. Or else what are novels made for? Had Caroline read of Valancourt and Emily for nothing, or gathered no good example from those five tear-fraught volumes which describe the loves of Miss Helen Mar and Sir William Wallace? Many a time had she depicted Brandon in a fancy costume such as the fascinating Valancourt wore; or painted herself as Helen, tying a sash round her knight's cuirass, and watching him forth to battle. Silly fancies, no doubt; but consider, madam, the poor girl's age and education; the only instruction she had ever received was from these tender, kind-hearted, silly books: the only happiness which Fate had allowed her was in this little silent world of fancy. It would be hard to grudge the poor thing her dreams; and many such did she have, and impart blushingly to honest Becky, as they sate by the humble kitchen-fire.

Although it cost her heart a great pang, she had once ventured to implore her mother not to send her up stairs to the lodgers' rooms, for she shrank at the notion of the occurrence that

Brandon should discover her regard for him; but this point had never entered Mrs Gann's sagacious head. She thought her daughter wished to avoid Fitch, and sternly bade her do her duty, and not give herself such impertinent airs; and, indeed, it can't be said that poor Caroline was very sorry at being compelled to continue to see Brandon. To do both gentlemen justice, neither ever said a word unfit for Caroline to hear. Fitch would have been torn to pieces by a thousand wild horses rather than have breathed a single syllable to hurt her feelings; and Brandon, though by no means so squeamish on ordinary occasions, was innately a gentleman, and, from taste rather than from virtue, was carefully respectful in his behaviour to her.

As for the Misses Macarty themselves, it has been stated that they had already given away their hearts several times; Miss Isabella being at this moment attached to a certain young wine-merchant, and to Lieutenant or Colonel Swabber of the Spanish service; and Miss Rosalind having a decided fondness for a foreign nobleman, with black moustachios, who had paid a visit to Margate. Of Miss Bella's lovers, Swabber had disappeared; but she still met the wine-merchant pretty often, and it is believed had gone very nigh to accept him. As for Miss Rosalind, I am sorry to say that the course of her true love ran by no means smoothly: the Frenchman had turned out to be not a marquess, but a billiard-marker; and a sad, sore subject the disappointment was with the neglected lady.

We should have spoken of it long since, had the subject been one that was much canvassed in the Gann family; but once when Gann had endeavoured to rally his stepdaughter on this unfortunate attachment (using for the purpose those delicate turns of wit for which the honest gentleman was always famous), Miss Linda had flown into such a violent fury, and comported herself in a way so dreadful, that James Gann, Esquire, was fairly frightened out of his wits by the threats, screams, and imprecations which she uttered. Miss Bella, who was disposed to be jocose likewise, was likewise awed into silence; for her dear sister talked of tearing her eyes out that minute, and uttered some hints, too, regarding love-matters personally affecting Miss Bella herself, which caused that young lady to turn pale-red, to mutter something about 'wicked lies,' and to leave the room immediately. Nor was the subject ever again broached by the Ganns. Even when Mrs Gann once talked about that odious French impostor, she was stopped immediately, not by the lady concerned, but by Miss Bella, who cried, sharply, 'Mamma, hold your tongue, and don't vex our dear Linda by alluding to any such stuff.' It is most probable that the young ladies had had a private conference, which, beginning a little fiercely at first, had ended amicably: and so the marquess was mentioned no more.

Miss Linda, then, was comparatively free (for Bob Smith, the linendraper, and young Glauber, the apothecary, went for nothing); and, very luckily for her, a successor was found for the faithless Frenchman, almost immediately.

This gentleman was a commoner, to be sure; but had a good estate of five hundred a year, kept his horse and gig, and was, as Mr Gann remarked, as good a fellow as ever lived. Let us say at once that the new lover was no other than Mr Swigby. From the day when he had been introduced to the family he appeared to be very much attracted by the two sisters; sent a turkey off his own farm, and six bottles of prime Hollands,* to Mr and Mrs Gann, in presents; and, in ten short days after his first visit, had informed his friend Gann that he was violently in love with two women whose names he would never – never breathe. The worthy Gann knew right well how the matter was; for he had not failed to remark Swigby's melancholy, and to attribute it to its right cause.

Swigby was forty-eight years of age, stout, hearty, gay, much given to drink, and had never been a lady's man, or, indeed, passed half-a-dozen evenings in ladies' society. He thought Gann the noblest and finest fellow in the world. He never heard any singing like James's, nor any jokes like his; nor had met with such an accomplished gentleman or man of the world. 'Gann has his faults,' Swigby would say at the Bag of Nails; 'which of us has not? – but I tell you what, he's the greatest trump I ever see.' Many scores of scores had he paid for Gann, many guineas and crown-pieces had he lent him, since he came into his property some three years before. What were Swigby's former pursuits I can't tell. What need we care? Hadn't he five hundred a year now, and a horse and gig? Ay, that he had.

Since his accession to fortune, this gay young bachelor had taken his share (what he called 'his whack') of pleasure; had been at one – nay, perhaps, at two – public-houses every night; and had been tipsy, I make no doubt, nearly a thousand times in the course of the three years. Many people had tried to cheat him; but no, no! he knew what was what, and in all matters of money was simple and shrewd. Gann's gentility won him; his bragging, his *ton*, and the stylish tuft on his chin. To be invited to his house was a proud moment; and when he went away, after the banquet described in the last chapter, he was in a perfect ferment of love and liquor.

'What a stylish woman is that Mrs Gann!' thought he, as he tumbled into bed at his inn; 'fine she must have been as a gal! fourteen stone now, without saddle or bridle, and no mistake. And them Miss Macartys. Jupiter! what spanking, handsome, elegant creatures! – real elegance in both on 'em! Such hair! – black's the word – as black as my mare; such cheeks, such necks and shoulders!' At noon he repeated these observations to Gann himself, as he walked up and down the pier with that gentleman, smoking Manilla cheroots. He was in raptures with his evening. Gann received his praises with much majestic good-humour.

'Blood, sir!' said he, 'blood's everything! Them gals have been brought up as few ever have. I don't speak of myself; but their mother – their mother's a lady, sir. Show me a woman in England as is better bred or knows the world more than my Juliana!'

'It's impawssible,' said Swigby.

'Think of the company we've kep', sir, before our misfortunes – the fust in the land. Brandenburg House, sir – England's injured queen.* Law bless you! Juliana was always there.'

'I make no doubt, sir; you can see it in her,' said Swigby solemnly.

'And as for those gals, why, ain't they related to the fust families in Ireland, sir? – In course they are. As I said before, blood's everything; and those young women have the best of it: they are connected with the reg'lar old noblesse.'

'They have the best of everything, I'm sure,' said Swigby, 'and deserve it too,' and relapsed into his morning remarks. 'What creatures! what elegance! what hair and eyes, sir! – black, and all's black, as I say. What complexion, sir! – ay, and what *makes*, too! Such a neck and shoulders I never see!'

Gann, who had his hands in his pockets (his friend's arm being hooked into one of his), here suddenly withdrew his hand from its hiding-place, clenched his fist, assumed a horrible knowing grin, and gave Mr Swigby such a blow in the ribs as well nigh sent him into the water. 'You sly dog!' said Mr Gann, with inexpressible emphasis; 'you've found *that* out, too, have you? Have a care, Joe my boy, – have a care.'

And herewith Gann and Joe burst into tremendous roars of laughter, fresh explosions taking place at intervals of five minutes during the rest of the walk. The two friends parted exceedingly happy; and when they met that evening at The Nails Gann drew Swigby mysteriously into the bar, and thrust into his hand a triangular piece of pink paper, which the latter read:

Mrs Gann and the Misses Macarty request the honour and pleasure of Mr Swigby's company (if you have no better engagement) to tea to-morrow evening at half-past five.

> *Margaretta Cottage, Salamanca Road North,*
> *Thursday evening.*

The faces of the two gentlemen were wonderfully expressive of satisfaction as this communication passed between them. And I am led to believe that Mrs Gann had been unusually pleased with her husband's conduct on that day, for honest James had no less than thirteen and sixpence in his pocket, and insisted, as usual, upon standing glasses all round. Joe Swigby, left alone in the little parlour behind the bar, called for a sheet of paper, a new pen and a wafer, and in the space of half-an-hour concocted a very spirited and satisfactory answer to this note; which was carried off by Gann, and duly delivered. Punctually at half-past five Mr Joseph Swigby knocked at Margaretta Cottage door, in his new coat with glistering brass buttons, his face clean-shaved, and his great ears shining over his great shirt-collar delightfully bright and red.

What happened at this tea-party it is needless here to say; but Swigby came away from it quite as much enchanted as before, and declared that the duets sung by the ladies in hideous discord were the sweetest music he had ever heard. He sent the gin and the turkey the next day; and, of course, was invited to dine.

The dinner was followed up on his part by an offer to drive all the young ladies and their mamma into the country; and he hired a very smart barouche to conduct them. The invitation was not declined; and Fitch, too, was asked by Mr Swigby, in the height of his good-humour, and accepted with the utmost delight. 'Me and Joe will go on the box,' said Gann. 'You four ladies and Mr Fitch shall go inside. Carry must go bodkin;* but she ain't very big.'

'Carry, indeed, will stop at home,' said her mamma; 'she's not fit to go out.'

At which poor Fitch's jaw fell; it was in order to ride with her that he had agreed to accompany the party; nor could he escape now, having just promised so eagerly.

'Oh, don't let's have that proud Brandon,' said the young ladies, when the good-natured Mr Swigby proposed to ask that gentleman; and therefore he was not invited to join them in their excursion: but he stayed at home very unconcernedly, and saw the barouche and its load drive off. Somebody else looked at it from the parlour-window with rather a heavy heart, and that some one was poor Caroline. The day was bright and sunshiny; the spring was beginning early; it would have been pleasant to have been a lady for once, and to have driven along in a carriage with prancing horses. Mr Fitch looked after her in a very sheepish, melancholy way; and was so dismal and silly during the first part of the journey, that Miss Linda, who was next to him, said to her papa that she would change places with him; and actually mounted the box by the side of the happy, trembling Mr Swigby. How proud he was, to be sure! How knowingly did he spank the horses along, and fling out the shillings at the turnpikes!

'Bless you, *he* don't care for change!' said Gann, as one of the toll-takers offered to render some coppers; and Joe felt infinitely obliged to his friend for setting off his amiable qualities in such a way.

O mighty Fate, that over us miserable mortals rulest supreme, with what small means are thy ends effected! – with what scornful ease and mean instruments does it please thee to govern mankind! Let each man think of the circumstances of his life, and how its lot has been determined. The getting up a little earlier or later, the turning down this street or that, the eating of this dish or the other, may influence all the years and actions of a future life. Mankind walks down the left-hand side of Regent Street instead of the right, and meets a friend who asks him to dinner, and goes, and finds the turtle remarkably good, and the iced punch very cool and pleasant; and, being in a merry, jovial, idle mood, has no objection to a social rubber of whist – nay, to a few more glasses of that cool punch. In the most careless, good-humoured way, he loses a few points; and still feels thirsty, and loses a few more points; and, like a man of spirit, increases his stakes, to be sure, and just by that walk down Regent Street is ruined for life. Or he walks down the right-hand side of Regent Street instead of the left, and, good heavens! who is that charming young creature who has just stepped into her carriage from

Mr Fraser's shop, and to whom and her mamma Mr Fraser has made the most elegant bow in the world? It is the lovely Miss Moidore, with a hundred thousand pounds, who has remarked your elegant figure, and regularly drives to town on the first of the month, to purchase her darling Magazine. You drive after her as fast as the hack-cab will carry you. She reads the Magazine the whole way. She stops at her papa's elegant villa at Hampstead, with a conservatory, a double coach-house, and a parklike paddock. As the lodge-gate separates you from that dear girl, she looks back just once, and blushes. *Erubuit, salva est res.* She has blushed, and you are all right. In a week you are introduced to the family, and pronounced a charming young fellow of high principles. In three weeks you have danced twenty-nine quadrilles with her, and whisked her through several miles of waltzes. In a month Mrs O'Flaherty has flung herself into the arms of her mother, just having come from a visit to the village of Gretna, near Carlisle; and you have an account at your banker's ever after. What is the cause of all this good fortune? – a walk on a particular side of Regent Street. And so true and indisputable is this fact, that there's a young north-country gentleman with whom I am acquainted that daily paces up and down the above-named street for many hours, fully expecting that such an adventure will happen to him; for which end he keeps a cab in readiness at the corner of Vigo Lane.

Now, after a dissertation in this history, the reader is pretty sure to know that a moral is coming; and the facts connected with our tale, which are to be drawn from the above little essay on fate, are simply these:–1. If Mr Fitch had not heard Mr Swigby invite *all* the ladies, he would have refused Swigby's invitation, and stayed at home. 2. If he had not been in the carriage, it is quite certain that Miss Rosalind Macarty would not have been seated by him on the back seat. 3. If he had not been sulky, she never would have asked her papa to let her take his place on the box. 4. If she had not taken her papa's place on the box, not one of the circumstances would have happened which did happen; and which were as follows:

1. Miss Bella remained inside.

2. Mr Swigby, who was wavering between the two, like a certain animal between two bundles of hay, was determined by this circumstance, and made proposals to Miss Linda, whispering to Miss Linda: 'Miss, I ain't equal to the like of you; but I'm

hearty, healthy, and have five hundred a year. Will you marry me?' In fact, this very speech had been taught him by cunning Gann, who saw well enough that Swigby would speak to one or other of his daughters. And to it the young lady replied, also in a whispering, agitated tone, 'Law, Mr S! What an odd man! How can you?' And, after a little pause, added, '*Speak to Mamma.*'

3. (And this is the main point of my story.) If little Caroline had been allowed to go out, she never would have been left alone with Brandon at Margate. When Fate wills that something should come to pass, she sends forth a million of little circumstances to clear and prepare the way.

In the month of April (as indeed in half-a-score of other months of the year) the reader may have remarked that the cold north-east wind is prevalent; and that when, tempted by a glimpse of sunshine, he issues forth to take the air, he receives not only it, but such a quantity of it as is enough to keep him shivering through the rest of the miserable month. On one of these happy days of English weather (it was the very day before the pleasure-party described in the last chapter) Mr Brandon, cursing heartily his country, and thinking how infinitely more congenial to him were the winds and habits prevalent in other nations, was marching over the cliffs near Margate, in the midst of a storm of shrill east wind which no ordinary mortal could bear, when he found perched on the cliff, his fingers blue with cold, the celebrated Andrea Fitch, employed in sketching a land or a sea scape on a sheet of grey paper.

'You have chosen a fine day for sketching,' said Mr Brandon bitterly, his thin aquiline nose peering out livid from the fur collar of his coat.

Mr Fitch smiled, understanding the allusion.

'An hartist, sir,' said he, 'doesn't mind the coldness of the weather. There was a chap in the Academy who took sketches twenty degrees below zero in Hiceland – Mount 'Ecla, sir! *E* was the man that gave the first hidea of Mount 'Ecla for the Surrey Zoological Gardens.'

'He must have been a wonderful enthusiast!' said Mr Brandon; 'I fancy that most would prefer to sit at home, and not numb their fingers in such a freezing storm as this!'

'Storm, sir!' replied Fitch, majestically; 'I live in a storm, sir! A true hartist is never so 'appy as when he can have the advantage to gaze upon yonder tempestuous hocean in one of its hangry moods.'

'Ay, there comes the steamer,' answered Mr Brandon; 'I can fancy that there are a score of unhappy people on board who are not artists, and would wish to behold your ocean quiet.'

'They are not poets, sir: the glorious hever-changing expression of the great countenance of Nature is not seen by them. I should consider myself unworthy of my hart, if I could not bear a little privation of cold or 'eat for its sake. And besides, sir, whatever their hardships may be, such a sight hamply repays me; for, although my private sorrows may be (has they are) tremendous, I never can look abroad upon the green hearth and hawful sea, without in a measure forgetting my personal woes and wrongs; for what right has a poor creature like me to think of his affairs in the presence of such a spectacle as this? I can't, sir; I feel ashamed of myself; I bow my 'ead and am quiet. When I set myself to examining hart, sir (by which I mean nature), I don't dare to think of anything else.'

'You worship a very charming and consoling mistress,' answered Mr Brandon, with a supercilious air, lighting and beginning to smoke a cigar; 'your enthusiasm does you credit.'

'If you have another,' said Andrea Fitch, 'I should like to smoke one, for you seem to have a real feeling about hart, and I was a-getting so deucedly cold here, that really there was scarcely any bearing of it.'

'The cold is very severe,' replied Mr Brandon.

'No, no, it's not the weather, sir!' said Mr Fitch; 'it's here, sir, here' (pointing to the left side of his waistcoat).

'What! you, too, have had sorrows?'

'Sorrows, sir! hagonies – hagonies, which I have never unfolded to any mortal! I have hendured halmost hevery thing. Poverty, sir, 'unger, hobloquy, 'opeless love! but for my hart, sir, I should be the most miserable wretch in the world!'

And herewith Mr Fitch began to pour forth into Mr Brandon's ears the history of some of those sorrows under which he laboured, and which he communicated to every single person who would listen to him.

Mr Brandon was greatly amused by Fitch's prattle, and the latter told him under what privations he had studied his art: how he had starved for three years in Paris and Rome, while labouring at his profession; how meanly jealous the Royal Academy was which would never exhibit a single one of his pictures; how he had been driven from the Heternal City by the attentions of an immense fat Mrs Carrickfergus, who absolutely proposed marriage to him; and how he was at this moment (a fact of which Mr Brandon was already quite aware) madly and desperately in love with one of the most beautiful maidens in this world. For Fitch, having a mistress to his heart's desire, was boiling with impatience to have a confidant; what, indeed, would be the joy of love, if one were not allowed to speak of one's feelings to a friend who could know how to sympathise with them? Fitch was sure Brandon did, because Brandon was the very first person with whom the painter had talked since he had come to the resolution recorded in the last chapter.

'I hope she is as rich as that unlucky Mrs Carrickfergus, whom you treated so cruelly?' said the confidant, affecting entire ignorance.

'Rich, sir? no, I thank Heaven, she has not a penny!' said Fitch.

'I presume, then, you are yourself independent,' said Brandon, smiling; 'for in the marriage state, one or the other of the parties concerned should bring a portion of the filthy lucre.'

'Haven't I my profession, sir?' said Fitch majestically, having declared five minutes before that he starved in his profession. 'Do you suppose a painter gets nothing? Haven't I horders from the first people in Europe? – commissions, sir, to hexecute 'istory-pieces, battle-pieces, haltar-pieces?'

'Master-pieces, I am sure,' said Brandon, bowing politely; 'for a gentleman of your astonishing genius can do no other.'

The delighted artist received this compliment with many blushes, and vowed and protested that his performances were not really worthy of such high praise; but he fancied Mr Brandon a great connoisseur, nevertheless, and unburdened his mind to him in a manner still more open. Fitch's sketch was by this time finished; and, putting his drawing implements together, he rose, and the gentlemen walked away. The sketch was hugely admired by Mr Brandon, and when they came home, Fitch, culling it dexterously out of his book, presented it in a neat speech to his friend, 'the gifted hamateur'.

'The gifted hamateur' received the drawing with a profusion of thanks, and so much did he value it, that he had actually torn off a piece to light a cigar with, when he saw that words were written on the other side of the paper, and deciphered the following:

SONG OF THE VIOLET

A humble flower long time I pined,
  Upon the solitary plain,
And trembled at the angry wind,
  And shrunk before the bitter rain.
And, oh! 'twas in a blessed hour,
  A passing wanderer chanced to see
And, pitying the lonely flower,
  To stoop and gather me.

I fear no more the tempest rude,
  On dreary heath no more I pine,
But left my cheerless solitude,
  To deck the breast of Caroline.
Alas! our days are brief at best,
  Nor long I fear will mine endure,
Though shelter'd here upon a breast
  So gentle and so pure.

It draws the fragrance from my leaves,
  It robs me of my sweetest breath;
And every time it falls and heaves,
  It warns me of my coming death.
But one I know would glad forego
  All joys of life to be as I;
An hour to rest on that sweet breast,
  And then, contented, die.

                                  Andrea

When Mr Brandon had finished the perusal of these verses, he
laid them down with an air of considerable vexation. 'Egad!' said
he, 'this fellow, fool as he is, is not so great a fool as he seems;
and if he goes on this way, may finish by turning the girl's head.
They can't resist a man if he but presses hard enough – I know
they can't!' And here Mr Brandon mused over his various experience, which confirmed his observation, that be a man ever so
silly, a gentlewoman will yield to him out of sheer weariness. And
he thought of several cases in which, by the persevering application of copies of verses, young ladies had been brought from
dislike to sufferance of a man, from sufferance to partiality, and
from partiality to St George's, Hanover Square.* 'A ruffian who
murders his *h*'s to carry off such a delicate little creature as that!'
cried he in a transport: 'it shall never be if I can prevent it!' He

thought Caroline more and more beautiful every instant, and was himself by this time almost as much in love with her as Fitch himself.

Mr Brandon, then, saw Fitch depart in Swigby's carriage with no ordinary feelings of pleasure. Miss Caroline was not with them. 'Now is my time!' thought Brandon; and, ringing the bell, he inquired with some anxiety, from Becky, where Miss Caroline was? It must be confessed that mistress and maid were at their usual occupation, working and reading novels in the back parlour. Poor Carry! what other pleasure had she?

She had not gone through many pages, or Becky advanced many stitches in the darning of that tablecloth which the good housewife, Mrs Gann, had confided to her charge, when an humble knock was heard at the door of the sitting-room, that caused the blushing Caroline to tremble and drop her book, as Miss Lydia Languish* does in the play.

Mr George Brandon entered with a very demure air. He held in his hand a black satin neck-scarf, of which a part had come to be broken. He could not wear it in its present condition, that was evident; but Miss Caroline was blushing and trembling a great deal too much to suspect that this wicked Brandon had himself torn his own scarf with his own hands one moment before he entered the room. I don't know whether Becky had any suspicions of this fact, or whether it was only the ordinary roguish look which she had when anything pleased her, that now lighted up her eyes and caused her mouth to expand smilingly, and her fat red cheeks to gather up into wrinkles.

'I have had a sad misfortune,' said he, 'and should be very much obliged indeed to Miss Caroline to repair it.' (Caroline was said with a kind of tender hesitation that caused the young woman, so named, to blush more than ever.) 'It is the only stock I have in the world, and I can't go barenecked into the streets; can I, Mrs Becky?'

'No, sure,' said Becky.

'Not unless I was a celebrated painter, like Mr Fitch,' added Mr Brandon, with a smile, which was reflected speedily upon the face of the lady whom he wished to interest. 'Those great geniuses,' he added, 'may do anything.'

'For,' says Becky, 'hee's got enough beard on hees faze to keep hees neck warm!' At which remark, though Miss Caroline very properly said, 'For shame, Becky!' Mr Brandon was so convulsed with laughter, that he fairly fell down upon the sofa on which Miss Caroline was seated. How she startled and trembled, as he flung his arm upon the back of the couch! Mr Brandon did not attempt to apologise for what was an act of considerable impertinence, but continued mercilessly to make many more jokes concerning poor Fitch, which were so cleverly suited to the comprehension of the maid and the young mistress, as to elicit a great number of roars of laughter from the one, and to cause the other to smile in spite of herself. Indeed, Brandon had gained a vast reputation with Becky in his morning colloquies with her, and she was ready to laugh at any single word which it pleased him to utter. How many of his good things had this honest scullion carried down stairs to Caroline? and how pitilessly had she contrived to *estropier* them in their passage from the drawing-room to the kitchen!

Well then, while Mr Brandon 'was a-going on,' as Becky said, Caroline had taken his stock, and her little fingers were occupied in repairing the damage he had done to it. Was it clumsiness on her part? Certain it is that the rent took several minutes to repair: of them the *mangeur de cœurs* did not fail to profit, conversing in an easy, kindly, confidential way, which set our fluttering heroine speedily at rest, and enabled her to reply to his continual queries, addressed with much adroitness and an air of fraternal interest, by a number of those pretty little timid whispering yeses and noes, and those gentle, quick looks of the eyes, wherewith young and modest maidens are wont to reply to the questions of seducing young bachelors. Dear yeses and noes, how beautiful you are when gently whispered by pretty lips! – glances of quick innocent eyes, how charming are you! – and how charming the soft blush that steals over the cheek, towards which the dark lashes are drawing the blue-veined eyelids down. And here let the writer of this solemnly declare, upon his veracity, that he means nothing but what is right and moral. But look, I pray you, at an innocent bashful girl of sixteen: if she be but good, she must be pretty. She is a woman now, but a girl still. How delightful all her ways are! How exquisite her instinctive grace! All the arts of all the Cleopatras are not so captivating as her nature. Who can resist her confiding simplicity, or fail to be touched and conquered by her gentle appeal to protection?

All this Mr Brandon saw and felt, as many a gentleman educated in this school will. It is not because a man is a rascal himself that he cannot appreciate virtue and purity very keenly; and our hero did feel for this simple, gentle, tender, artless creature a real respect and sympathy – a sympathy so fresh and delicious, that he was but too glad to yield to it and indulge in it, and which he mistook, probably, for a real love of virtue, and a return to the days of his innocence.

Indeed, Mr Brandon, it was no such thing. It was only because vice and debauch were stale for the moment, and this pretty virtue new. It was only because your cloyed appetite was long unused to this simple meat that you felt so keen a relish for it; and I thought of you only the last blessed Saturday, at Mr Lovegrove's, West India Tavern, Blackwall, where a company of fifteen epicures, who had scorned the turtle, pooh-poohed the punch, and sent away the whitebait, did suddenly and simultaneously make a rush upon – a dish of *beans and bacon*. And if the assiduous reader of novels will think upon some of the most celebrated works of that species, which have lately appeared in this and other countries, he will find, amidst much debauch of sentiment and enervating dissipation of intellect, that the writers have from time to time a returning appetite for innocence and freshness, and indulge us with occasional repasts of beans and bacon. How long Mr Brandon remained by Miss Caroline's side I have no means of judging; it is probable, however, that he stayed a much longer time than was necessary for the mending of his black-satin stock. I believe, indeed, that he read to the ladies a great part of the *Mysteries of Udolpho*,* over which they were engaged; and interspersed his reading with many remarks of his own, both tender and satirical. Whether he was in her company half an hour or four hours, this is certain, that the time slipped away very swiftly with poor Caroline; and when a carriage drove up to the door, and shrill voices were heard crying, 'Becky!' 'Carry!' and Rebecca the maid starting up, cried, 'Lor', here's missus!' and Brandon jumped rather suddenly off the sofa, and fled up the stairs – when all these events took place, I know Caroline felt very sad indeed, and opened the door for her parents with a very heavy heart.

Swigby helped Miss Linda off the box with excessive tenderness. Papa was bustling and roaring in high good-humour, and called for 'hot water and tumblers immediately'. Mrs Gann was gracious; and Miss Bell sulky, as she had good reason to be, for she insisted upon taking the front seat in the carriage before her sister, and had lost a husband by that very piece of obstinacy.

Mr Fitch, as he entered, bestowed upon Caroline a heavy sigh and a deep stare, and silently ascended to his own apartment. He was lost in thought. The fact is, he was trying to remember some verses regarding a violet, which he had made five years before, and which he had somehow lost from among his papers. So he went up stairs, muttering.

> A humble flower long since I pined
> Upon a solitary plain –

Chapter VI

DESCRIBES A SHABBY GENTEEL MARRIAGE, AND MORE LOVE-MAKING

It will not be necessary to describe the particulars of the festivities which took place on the occasion of Mr Swigby's marriage to Miss Macarty. The happy pair went off in a postchaise and four to the bridegroom's country-seat, accompanied by the bride's blushing sister; and when the first week of their matrimonial bliss was ended, that worthy woman, Mrs Gann, with her excellent husband, went to visit the young couple. Miss Caroline was left, therefore, sole mistress of the house, and received especial cautions from her mamma as to prudence, economy, the proper management of the lodgers' bills, and the necessity of staying at home.

Considering that one of the gentlemen remaining in the house was a declared lover of Miss Caroline, I think it is a little surprising that her mother should leave her unprotected; but in this matter the poor are not so particular as the rich; and so this young lady was consigned to the guardianship of her own innocence and the lodgers' loyalty: nor was there any reason why Mrs Gann should doubt the latter. As for Mr Fitch, he would have far preferred to be torn to pieces by ten thousand wild horses, rather than to offer to the young woman any unkindness or insult; and how was Mrs Gann to suppose that her other lodger was a whit less loyal? that he had any partiality for a person of whom he always spoke as a mean, insignificant little baby? So, without any misgivings, and in a one-horse fly with Mr Gann by her side, with a bran new green coat and gilt buttons, Juliana Gann went forth to visit her beloved child, and console her in her married state.

And here, were I allowed to occupy the reader with extraneous matters, I could give a very curious and touching picture of the Swigby *ménage*. Mrs S, I am very sorry to say, quarrelled with her husband on the third day after their marriage, – and for what, pr'thee? Why, because he would smoke, and no gentleman ought to smoke. Swigby, therefore, patiently resigned his pipe, and with it one of the quietest, happiest, kindest companions of his solitude. He was a different man after this; his pipe was as a limb of his body. Having on Tuesday conquered the pipe, Mrs Swigby on Thursday did battle with her husband's rum-and-water, a drink of an odious smell, as she very properly observed; and the smell was doubly odious, now that the tobacco-smoke no longer perfumed the parlour-breeze, and counteracted the odours of the juice of West India sugar-canes. On Thursday, then, Mr Swigby and rum held out pretty bravely. Mrs S. attacked the punch with some sharp-shooting, and fierce charges of vulgarity; to which S replied, by opening the battery of oaths (chiefly directed to his own eyes, however), and loud protestations that he would never surrender. In three days more, however, the rum-and-water was gone. Mr Swigby, defeated and prostrate, had given up that stronghold; his young wife and sister were triumphant; and his poor mother, who occupied her son's house, and had till now taken her place at the head of his table, saw that her empire was for ever lost, and was preparing suddenly to succumb to the imperious claims of the mistress of the mansion.

All this, I say, I wish I had the liberty to describe at large, as also to narrate the arrival of majestic Mrs Gann; and a battle-royal which speedily took place between the two worthy mothers-in-law. Noble is the hatred of ladies who stand in this relation to each other; each sees what injury the other is inflicting upon her darling child; each mistrusts, detests, and to her offspring privily abuses the arts and crimes of the other. A house with a wife is often warm enough; a house with a wife and her mother is rather warmer than any spot on the known globe; a house with two mothers-in-law is so excessively hot, that it can be likened to no place on earth at all, but one must go lower for a simile. Think of a wife who despises her husband, and teaches him manners; of an elegant sister, who joins in rallying him (this was almost the only point of union between Bella and Linda now, – for since the marriage, Linda hated her sister consumedly). Think, I say, of two mothers-in-law – one, large, pompous, and atrociously genteel – another coarse and shrill, determined not to have her son put upon, – and you may see what a happy fellow Joe Swigby was, and into what a piece of good luck he had fallen.

What would have become of him without his father-in-law? Indeed one shudders to think; but the consequence of that gentleman's arrival and intervention was speedily this: about four o'clock, when the dinner was removed, and the quarrelling used commonly to set in, the two gents took their hats, and sallied out; and as one has found when the body is inflamed that the application of a stringent medicine may cause the ill to disappear for a while, only to return elsewhere with greater force; in like manner, Mrs Swigby's sudden victory over the pipe and rum-and-water, although it had caused a temporary cessation of the evil of which she complained, was quite unable to stop it altogether; it disappeared from one spot only to rage with more violence elsewhere. In Swigby's parlour, rum and tobacco odours rose no more (except, indeed, when Mrs Gann would partake of the former as a restorative); but if you could have seen the Half-Moon and Snuffers down the village; if you could have seen the good dry skittle-ground which stretched at the back of that inn, and the window of the back-parlour which superintended that skittle-ground; if the hour at which you beheld these objects was evening, what time the rustics, from their toils released, trolled the stout ball amidst the rattling pins (the oaken pins that standing in the sun did cast long shadows on the golden sward); if you had remarked all this, I say, you would have also seen in the back parlour a tallow candle twinkling in the shade, and standing on a little greasy table. Upon the greasy table was a pewter porter-pot, and to the left a teaspoon glittering in a glass of gin; close to each of these two delicacies was a pipe of tobacco; and behind the pipes sat Mr Gann and Mr Swigby, who now made the Half-Moon and Snuffers their usual place of resort, and forgot their married cares.

In spite of all our promises of brevity, these things have taken some space to describe; and the reader must also know that some short interval elapsed ere they occurred. A month at least passed away before Mr Swigby had decidedly taken up his position at the little inn: all this time, Gann was staying with his son-in-law, at the latter's most earnest request; and Mrs Gann remained under the same roof at her own desire. Not the hints of her daughter, nor the broad questions of the dowager Mrs Swigby, could induce honest Mrs Gann to stir from her quarters. She had had her lodgers' money in advance, as was the worthy woman's custom; she knew Margate in April was dreadfully dull, and she determined to enjoy the country until the jovial town season arrived. The Canterbury coachman, whom Gann knew, and who passed through the village, used to take her cargo of novels to and fro; and the old lady made herself as happy as circumstances would allow. Should anything of importance occur during her mamma's absence, Caroline was to make use of the same conveyance, and inform Mrs Gann in a letter.

Miss Caroline looked at her papa and mamma, as the vehicle which was to bear them to the newly-married couple moved up the street; but, strange to say, she did not feel that heaviness of heart which she before had experienced when forbidden to share the festivities of her family, but was on this occasion more happy than any one of them – so happy, that the young woman felt quite ashamed of herself; and Becky was fain to remark how her mistress's cheek flushed, and her eyes sparkled (and turned perpetually to the door), and her whole little frame was in a flutter.

'I wonder if he will come,' said the little heart; and the eyes turned and looked at that well-known sofa-corner, where *he* had been placed a fortnight before. He looked exactly like Lord Byron, that he did, with his pale brow, and his slim bare neck; only not half so wicked – no, no. She was sure that her – her Mr B –, her Bran –, her *George*, was as good as he was beautiful. Don't let us be angry with her for calling him George; the girl was bred in an humble sentimental school; she did not know enough of society to be squeamish; she never thought that she could be his really, and gave way in the silence of her fancy to the full extent of her affection for him. She had not looked at the door above twenty-five times – that is to say, her parents had not quitted the house ten minutes – when, sure enough, the latch did rattle, the door opened, and, with a faint blush on his cheek, divine George entered. He was going to make some excuse, as on the former occasion; but he looked first into Caroline's face, which was beaming with joy and smiles; and the little thing, in return, regarded him, and – made room for him on the sofa. O sweet instinct of love! Brandon had no need of excuses, but sate down, and talked away as easily, happily, and confidentially, and neither took any note of time. Andrea Fitch (the sly dog!) witnessed the Gann departure with feelings of exultation, and had laid some deep plans of his own with regard to Miss Caroline. So strong was his confidence in his friend on the first floor, that Andrea actually descended to those apartments, on his way to Mrs Gann's parlour, in order to consult Mr Brandon, and make known to him his plan of operations.

It would have made your heart break, or, at the very least, your sides ache, to behold the countenance of poor Mr Fitch, as he thrust his bearded head in at the door of the parlour. There was Brandon lolling on the sofa, at his ease; Becky in full good-humour; and Caroline, always absurdly inclined to blush, blushing at Fitch's appearance more than ever! She could not help looking from him slyly and gently into the face of Mr Brandon. That gentleman saw the look, and did not fail to interpret it. It was a confession of love – an appeal for protection. A thrill of delightful vanity shot through Brandon's frame, and made his heart throb, as he noticed this look of poor Caroline. He answered it with one of his own that was cruelly wrong, cruelly triumphant, and sarcastic; and he shouted out to Mr Fitch, with a loud, disconcerted tone, which only made that young painter feel more awkward than ever he had been. Fitch made some clumsy speech regarding his dinner, – whether that meal was to be held, in the absence of the parents, at the usual hour, and then took his leave.

The poor fellow had been pleasing himself with the notion of taking this daily meal *tête-à-tête* with Caroline. What progress would he make in her heart during the absence of her parents! Did it not seem as if the first marriage had been arranged on purpose to facilitate his own? He determined thus his plan of campaign. He would make, in the first place, the most beautiful drawing of Caroline that ever was seen. 'The conversations I'll 'ave with her during the sittings,' says he, 'will carry me a pretty long way; the drawing itself will be so beautiful, that she can't resist that. I'll write her verses in her halbum, and make designs hallusive of my passion for her.' And so our pictorial *Alnaschar** dreamed and dreamed. He had, ere long, established himself in a house in Newman Street,* with a footman to open the door. Caroline was up stairs, his wife, and her picture the crack portrait of the Exhibition. With her by his side, Andrea Fitch felt he could do anything. Half-a-dozen carriages at his door – a hundred guineas for a Kit-Cat portrait. Lady Fitch, Sir Andrew Fitch, the President's chain, – all sorts of bright visions floated before his imagination; and as Caroline was the first precious condition of his preferment, he determined forthwith to begin, and realise that.

But O disappointment! on coming down to dinner at three o'clock to that charming *tête-à-tête*, he found no less than four covers laid on the table, Miss Caroline blushing (according to custom) at the head of it; Becky, the maid, grinning at the foot; and Mr Brandon sitting quietly on one side, as much at home, forsooth, as if he had held that position for a year.

The fact is that the moment after Fitch retired, Brandon, inspired by jealousy, had made the same request which had been brought forward by the painter; nor must the ladies be too angry with Caroline, if, after some scruples and struggles, she yielded to the proposal. Remember that the girl was the daughter of a boarding-house, accustomed to continual dealings with her mamma's lodgers, and up to the present moment thinking herself as safe among them as the young person who walked through Ireland with a bright gold wand, in the song of *Mr Thomas Moore*.* On the point, however, of Brandon's admission, it must be confessed, for Caroline's honour, that she did hesitate. She felt that she entertained very different feelings towards him to those with which any other lodger or man had inspired her, and made a little movement of resistance at first. But the poor girl's modesty overcame this, as well as her wish. Ought she to avoid him? Ought she not to stifle any preference which she might feel towards him, and act towards him with the same indifference which she would show to any other person in a like situation? Was not Mr Fitch to dine at table as usual, and had she refused him? So reasoned she in her heart. Silly little cunning heart! it knew that all these reasons were lies, and that she *should* avoid the man; but she was willing to accept of any pretext for meeting, and so made a kind of compromise with her conscience. Dine he should; but Becky should dine too, and be a protector to her. Becky laughed loudly at the idea of this, and took her place with huge delight.

It is needless to say a word about this dinner, as we have already described a former meal; suffice it to say, that the presence of Brandon caused the painter to be excessively sulky and uncomfortable; and so gave his rival, who was gay, triumphant, and at his ease, a decided advantage over him. Nor did Brandon neglect to use this to the utmost. When Fitch retired to his own apartments – not jealous as yet, for the simple fellow believed every word of Brandon's morning conversation with him – but vaguely annoyed and disappointed, Brandon assailed him with all the force of ridicule; at all his manners, words, looks, he joked mercilessly; laughed at his low birth (Miss Gann, be it remembered, had been taught to pique herself upon her own family), and invented a series of stories concerning his past life which made the ladies – for Becky, being in the parlour, must be considered as such – conceive the greatest contempt and pity for the poor painter.

After this, Mr Brandon would expatiate with much eloquence upon his own superior attractions and qualities. He talked of his cousin, Lord So-and-so, with the easiest air imaginable; told Caroline what princesses he had danced with at foreign courts; frightened her with accounts of dreadful duels he had fought; in a word, 'posed' before her as a hero of the most sublime kind. How the poor little thing drank in all his tales; and how she and Becky (for they now occupied the same bedroom) talked over them at night!

Miss Caroline, as Mr Fitch has already stated, had in her possession, like almost every young lady in England, a little square book called an album, containing prints from annuals; hideous designs of flowers; old pictures of faded fashions, cut out and pasted into the leaves; and small scraps of verses selected from Bryon, Landon* or Mrs Hemans*: and written out in the girlish hand of the owner of the book. Brandon looked over this work with a good deal of curiosity – for he contended, always, that a girl's disposition might be learned from the character of this museum of hers – and found here several sketches by Mr Fitch for which, before that gentleman had declared his passion for her, Caroline had begged. These sketches the sentimental painter had illustrated with poetry, which, I must confess, Caroline thought charming, until now, when Mr Brandon took occasion to point out how wretchedly poor the verses were (as indeed was the fact) and to parody them all. He was not unskilful at this kind of exercise, and at the drawing of caricatures, and had soon made a dozen of both parodies and drawings, which reflected cruelly upon the person and the talents of the painter.

What now did this wicked Mr Brandon do? He, in the first place, drew a caricature of Fitch; and, secondly, having gone to a gardener's near the town, and purchased there a bunch of violets, he presented them to Miss Caroline, and wrote Mr Fitch's own verses before given into her album. He signed them with his own initials, and thus declared open war with the painter.

Chapter VII

WHICH BRINGS A GREAT NUMBER OF PEOPLE
TO MARGATE BY THE STEAMBOAT

The events which this history records began in the month of February. Time had now passed, and April had arrived, and with it that festive season so loved by schoolboys, and called the Easter holidays. Not only schoolboys, but men, profit by this period of leisure – such men, especially, as have just come into enjoyment of their own cups and saucers, and are in daily expectation of their whiskers – college men, I mean, – who are persons more anxious than any others to designate themselves and each other by the manly title.

Among other men, then, my Lord Viscount Cinqbars, of Christ Church, Oxon, received a sum of money to pay his quarter's bill, and having written to his papa that he was busily engaged in reading for the 'little-go', and must, therefore, decline the delight he had promised himself of passing the vacation at Cinqbars Hall – and having, the day after his letter was despatched, driven to town tandem with young Tom Tufthunt, of the same university – and having exhausted the pleasures of the metropolis – the theatres, the Cider-cellars, the Finish, the station-houses, and other places which need by no means be here particularised –

Lord Cinqbars, I say, growing tired of London at the end of ten days, quitted the metropolis somewhat suddenly: nor did he pay his hotel bill at Long's before his departure; but he left that document in possession of the landlord, as a token of his (my Lord Cinqbars') confidence in his host.

Tom Tufthunt went with my lord, of course (although of an aristocratic turn in politics, Tom loved and respected a lord as much as any democrat in England). And whither do you think this worthy pair of young gentlemen were bound? To no less a place than Margate: for Cinqbars was filled with a longing to go and see his old friend Brandon, and determined, to use his own elegant words, 'to knock the old buck up.'

There was no adventure of consequence on board the steamer which brought Lord Cinqbars and his friend from London to Margate, and very few passengers besides. A wandering Jew or two were set down at Gravesend; the Rev Mr Wackerbart, and six unhappy little pupils whom the reverend gentleman had pounced upon in London, and was carrying back to his academy near Herne Bay; some of those inevitable persons of dubious rank who seem to have free tickets, and always eat and drink hugely with the captain; and a lady and her party, formed the whole list of passengers.

The lady – a very fat lady – had evidently just returned from abroad. Her great green travelling chariot was on the deck, and on all her imperials were pasted fresh large bills, with the words INCE'S BRITISH HOTEL, BOULOGNE-SUR-MER; for it is the custom of that worthy gentleman to seize upon and plaster all the luggage of his guests with tickets, on which his name and residence are inscribed – by which simple means he keeps himself perpetually in their recollection, and brings himself to the notice of all other persons who are in the habit of peering at their fellow-passengers' trunks, to find out their names. I need not say what a large class this is.

Well; this fat lady had a courier, a tall, whiskered man, who spoke all languages, looked like a field-marshal, went by the name of Donnerwetter, and rode on the box; a French maid, Mademoiselle Augustine; and a little black page, called Saladin, who rode in the rumble. Saladin's whole business was to attend a wheezy fat white poodle, who usually travelled inside with his mistress and her fair *compagnon de voyage*, whose name was Miss Runt. This fat lady was evidently a person of distinction. During the first

part of the voyage, on a windy, sunshiny April day, she paced the
deck stoutly, leaning on the arm of poor little Miss Runt; and after
they had passed Gravesend, when the vessel began to pitch a good
deal, retired to her citadel, the travelling-chariot, to and from
which the steward, the stewardess, and the whiskered courier
were continually running with supplies – of sandwiches first, and
afterwards of very hot brandy-and-water: for the truth must be
told, it was rather a rough afternoon, and the poodle was sick;
Saladin was as bad; the French maid, like all French maids, was
outrageously ill; the lady herself was very unwell indeed; and poor
dear sympathising Runt was qualmish.

'Ah, Runt!' would the fat lady say in the intervals, 'what a thing
this malady de mare is! Oh, mong jew! Oh – oh!'

'It is indeed, dear madam,' said Runt, and went 'Oh – Oh!' in
chorus.

'Ask the steward if we are near Margate, Runt.' And Runt did,
and asked this question every five minutes as people do on these
occasions.

'Issy Monsieur Donnerwetter: ally dimandy ung pew d'o sho
poor mwaw.'

'Et de l'eau de fie afec, n'est-ce-bas, Matame?' said Mr
Donnerwetter.

'Wee, wee, comme vous vouly.'

And Donnerwetter knew very well what 'comme vous vouly'
meant, and brought the liquor exactly in the wished-for state.

'Ah, Runt, Runt! there's something even worse than sea-sick-
ness. Heigh-ho!'

'Dear, dear Marianne, don't flutter yourself,' cries Runt,
squeezing a fat paw of her friend and patroness between her
own bony fingers. 'Don't agitate your nerves, dear. I know you're
miserable; but haven't you got a friend in your faithful Runty?'

'You're a good creater, that you are,' said the fat lady, who
seemed herself to be a good-humoured old soul; 'and I don't know
what I should have done without you. Heigh-ho!'

'Cheer up, dear! you'll be happier when you get to Margate:
you know you will,' cried Runt, very knowingly.

'What do you mean, Elizabeth?'

'You know very well, dear Marianne. I mean that there's some
one there will make you happy; though he's a nasty wretch, that
he is, to have treated my darling, beautiful Marianne so.'

'Runt, Runt, don't abuse that best of men. Don't call me

beautiful – I'm not, Runt; I have been, but I ain't now; and oh! no woman in the world is assy bong poor lui.'

'But an angel is; and you are, as you always was, an angel – as good as an angel, as kind as an angel, as beautiful as one.'

'Ally dong,' said her companion, giving her a push; 'you flatter me, Runt, you know you do.'

'May I be struck down dead if I don't say the truth; and if he refuses you, as he did at Rome – that is, after all his attentions and vows, he's faithless to you, – I say he's a wretch, that he is; and I will say he's a wretch, and he is a wretch – a nasty, wicked wretch!'

'Elizabeth, if you say that, you'll break my heart, you will! Vous casserez mong pover cure.' But Elizabeth swore, on the contrary, that she would die for her Marianne, which consoled the fat lady a little.

A great deal more of this kind of conversation took place during the voyage; but as it occurred inside a carriage, so that to hear it was very difficult, and as possibly it was not of that edifying nature which would induce the reader to relish many chapters of it, we shall give no further account of the ladies' talk: suffice it to say, that about half-past four o'clock the journey ended, by the vessel bringing up at Margate Pier. The passengers poured forth, and hied to their respective homes or inns. My Lord Cinqbars and his companion (of whom we have said nothing, as they on their sides had scarcely spoken a word the whole way, except 'deuce-ace,' 'quarter-tray,' 'sizes,' and so on – being occupied ceaselessly in drinking bottled stout and playing backgammon) ordered their luggage to be conveyed to Wright's Hotel, whither the fat lady and suite followed them. The house was vacant, and the best rooms in it were placed, of course, at the service of the new comers. The fat lady sailed out of her bedroom towards her saloon, just as Lord Cinqbars, cigar in mouth, was swaggering out of his parlour. They met in the passage; when, to the young lord's surprise, the fat lady dropped him a low curtsey, and said –

'Munseer le Vecomte de Cinqbars, sharmy de vous voir. Vous vous rappelez de mwaw, n'est-ce-pas? Je vous ai vew à Rome – shay l'ambassadure, vous savy.'

Lord Cinqbars stared her in the face, and pushed by her without a word, leaving the fat lady rather disconcerted.

'Well, Runt, I'm sure,' said she, 'he need not be so proud; I've met him twenty times at Rome, when he was a young chap with his tutor.'

'Who the devil can that fat foreigner be?' mused Lord Cinqbars. 'Hang her, I've seen her somewhere; but I'm cursed if I understand a word of her jabber.' And so, dismissing the subject, he walked on to Brandon's.

'Dang it, it's a strange thing!' said the landlord of the hotel; 'but both my lord and the fat woman in number nine have asked their way to Mother Gann's lodging' – for so did he dare to call that respectable woman!

It was true: as soon as number nine had eaten her dinner, she asked the question mentioned by the landlord; and, as this meal occupied a considerable time, the shades of evening had by this time fallen upon the quiet city; the silver moon lighted up the bay, and, supported by a numerous and well-appointed train of gas-lamps, illuminated the streets of a town – of autumn eves so crowded and so gay; of gusty April nights, so desolate. At this still hour (it might be half-past seven) two ladies passed the gates of Wright's Hotel, 'in shrouding mantle wrapped, and velvet cap.' Up the deserted High Street toiled they, by gaping rows of empty bathing-houses, by melancholy Jolly's French bazaar, by mouldy pastry-cooks, blank reading-rooms, by fishmongers who never sold a fish, mercers who vended not a yard of riband – because, as yet, the season was not come – and Jews and Cockneys still remained in town. At High Street's corner, near to Hawley Square, they passed the house of Mr Fincham, chemist, who doth not only healthful drugs supply, but likewise sells cigars – the worst cigars that ever mortal man gave threepence for.

Up to this point, I say, I have had a right to accompany the fat lady and Miss Runt; but whether, on arriving at Mr Fincham's, they turned to the left, in the direction of the Royal Hotel, or to the right, by the beach, the bathing-machines, and queer rickety old row of houses, called Buenos Ayres, no power on earth shall induce me to say; suffice it, they went to Mrs Gann's. Why should we set all the world gadding to a particular street, to know where that lady lives? They arrived before that lady's house at about eight o'clock. Every house in the street had bills on it except hers (bitter mockery, as if anybody came down at Easter!), and at Mrs Gann's house there was a light in the garret, and another in the two-pair front. I believe I have not mentioned before, that all the front windows were bow or bay-windows; but so much the reader may know.

The two ladies, who had walked so far, examined wistfully the plate on the door, stood on the steps for a short time, retreated, and conversed with one another.

'Oh, Runty!' said the stouter of the two, 'he's here – I know he's here, mong cure le dee – my heart tells me so.' And she put a large hand upon a place on her left side, where there once had been a waist.

'Do you think he looks front or back, dear?' asked Runt. 'P'raps he's not at home.'

'That – that's his croisy,' said the stout person; 'I know it is;' and she pointed with instinctive justice to the two-pair. 'Ecouty!' she added, 'he's coming; there's some one at that window. Oh, mong jew, mong jew! c'est André, c'est lui!'

The moon was shining full on the face of the bow-windows of Mrs Gann's house; and the two fair spies, who were watching on the other side, were, in consequence, completely in shadow. As the lady said, a dark form was seen in the two-pair front; it paced the room for a while, for no blinds were drawn. It then flung itself on a chair; its head on its hands; it then began to beat its brows wildly, and paced the room again. Ah! how the fat lady's heart throbbed as she looked at all this!

She gave a piercing shriek – almost fainted! and little Runt's knees trembled under her, as with all her might she supported, or rather pushed up, the falling figure of her stout patroness – who saw at that instant Fitch come to the candle with an immense pistol in his hand, and give a most horrible grin as he looked at it, and clasped it to his breast.

'Unhand me, Runt; he's going to kill himself! It's for me! I know it is – I will go to him! Andrea, my Andrea!' And the fat lady was pushing for the opposite side of the way, when suddenly the second-floor window went clattering up, and Fitch's pale head was thrust out.

He had heard a scream and had possibly been induced to open the window in consequence; but by the time he had opened it he had forgotten everything, and put his head vacantly out of the window, and gazed, the moon shining cold on his pale features.

'Pallid horb!' said Fitch, 'shall I ever see thy light again? Will another night see me on this hearth, or view me, stark and cold, a lifeless corpse?' He took his pistol up, and slowly aimed it at a chimney-pot opposite. Fancy the fat lady's sensations, as she beheld her lover standing in the moonlight, and exercising this deadly weapon.

'Make ready – present – fire!' shouted Fitch, and did instanta-neously, not fire off, but lower his weapon. 'The bolt of death is sped!' continued he, clapping his hand on his side, 'The poor painter's life is over! Caroline, Caroline, I die for thee!'

'Runt, Runt, I told you so!' shrieked the fat lady. 'He is dying for me, and Caroline's my second name.'

What the fat lady would have done more, I can't say; for Fitch, disturbed out of his reverie by her talking below, looked out, frowning vacantly, and saying, 'Ulloh! we've hinterlopers 'ere!' suddenly banged down the window, and pulled down the blinds.

This gave a check to the fat lady's projected rush, and discon-certed her a little. But she was consoled by Miss Runt, promised to return on the morrow, and went home happy in the idea that her Andrea was faithful to her.

Alas, poor fat lady! little did you know the truth. It was Caroline Gann, Fitch was raving about; and it was a part of his last letter to her, to be delivered after his death, that he was spouting out of the window.

Was the crazy painter going to fight a duel, or was he going to kill himself? This will be explained in the next chapter.

Chapter VIII

WHICH TREATS OF WAR AND LOVE, AND MANY THINGS THAT ARE NOT TO BE UNDERSTOOD IN CHAP. VII

Fitch's verses, inserted in a previous chapter of this story (and of which lines, by the way, the printer managed to make still greater nonsense than the ingenious bard ever designed), had been com-posed many years before; and it was with no small trouble and thought that the young painter called the greater part of them to memory again, and furbished up a copy for Caroline's album. Unlike the love of most men. Andrea's passion was not characterised by jealousy and watchfulness, otherwise he would not have failed to perceive certain tokens of intelligence passing from time to time between Caroline and Brandon, and the lady's evident coldness to himself. The fact is, the painter was in love with being in love – entirely absorbed in the consideration of the fact that he, Andrea Fitch, was at last enamoured; and he did not mind his mistress much more than Don Quixote did Dulcinea del Toboso.

Having rubbed up his verses, then, and designed a pretty emblematical outline which was to surround them, representing an arabesque of violets, dewdrops, fairies, and other objects, he came down one morning, drawing in hand; and having informed Caroline, who was sitting very melancholy in the parlour, pre-occupied, with a pale face and red eyes, and not caring twopence for the finest drawing in the world – having informed her that he was going to make in her halbum a humble hoffering of his hart, poor Fitch was just on the point of sticking in the drawing with gum, as painters know very well how to do, when his eye lighted upon a page of the album, in which nestled a few dried violets and – his own verses, signed with the name of George Brandon.

'Miss Caroline – Miss Gann, mam!' shrieked Fitch, in a tone of voice which made the young lady start out of a profound reverie, and cry, nervously, 'What in heaven is the matter?'

'These verses, madam – a faded violet – word for word, gracious 'eavens! every word!' roared Fitch, advancing with the book.

She looked at him rather vacantly, and as the violets caught her eye, put out her hand, and took them. 'Do you know the hawthor, Miss Gann, of "The faded Violets"?'

'Author? O yes; they are – they are George's!' She burst into tears as she said that word; and, pulling the little faded flowers to pieces, went sobbing out of the room.

Dear, dear little Caroline! she has only been in love two months, and is already beginning to feel the woes of it!

It cannot be from want of experience – for I have felt the noble passion of love many times these forty years, since I was a boy of twelve (by which the reader may form a pretty good guess of my age!) it cannot be, I say, from want of experience that I am unable to describe, step by step, the progress of a love-affair; nay, I am perfectly certain that I could, if I chose, make a most astonishing and heart-rending *liber amoris*; but, nevertheless, I always feel a vast repugnance to the following out of a subject of this kind, which I attribute to a natural diffidence and sense of shame that prevent me from enlarging on a theme that has in it something sacred – certain arcana which an honest man, although initiated into them, should not divulge.

If such coy scruples and blushing delicacy prevent one from passing the threshold even of an honourable love, and setting down, at so many guineas or shillings per page, the pious emotions and tendernesses of two persons chastely and legally engaged in sighing, ogling, hand-squeezing, kissing, and so forth (for with such outward signs I believe that the passion of love is expressed), – if a man feel, I say, squeamish about describing an innocent love, he is doubly disinclined to describe a guilty one; and I have always felt a kind of loathing for the skill of such geniuses as Rousseau or Richardson, who could paint with such painful accuracy all the struggles and woes of Eloise and Clarissa – all the wicked arts and triumphs of such scoundrels as Lovelace.

We have in this history a scoundrelly Lovelace in the person going by the name of George Brandon, and a dear, tender, innocent, yielding creature on whom he is practising his infernal skill; and whether the public feel any sympathy for her or not, the writer can only say, for his part, that he heartily loves and respects poor little Caroline, and is quite unwilling to enter into any of the slow, painful, wicked details of the courtship which passed between her and her lover.

Not that there was any wickedness on her side, poor girl! or that she did anything but follow the natural and beautiful impulses of an honest little female heart, that leads it to truth and love, and worship a being of the other sex, whom the eager fancy invests with all sorts of attributes of superiority. There was no wild, conceited tale that Brandon told Caroline which she did not believe, – no virtue which she could conceive or had read of in novels with which she did not endow him. Many long talks had they, and many sweet, stolen interviews, during the periods in which Caroline's father and mother were away making merry at the house of their son-in-law; and while she was left under the care of her virtue and of Becky the maid. Indeed, it was a blessing that the latter was left in the joint guardianship. For Becky, who had such an absurd opinion of her young lady's merits as to fancy that she was a fit wife for any gentleman of the land, and that any gentleman might be charmed and fall in love with her, had some instinct, or possibly some experience, as to the passions and errors of youth, and warned Caroline accordingly. 'If he's really in love,

Miss, and I think he be, he'll marry you; if he won't marry you, he's a rascal, and you're too good for him, and must have nothing to do with him.' To which Caroline replied, that she was sure Mr Brandon was the most angelic, high-principled of human beings, and that she was sure his intentions were of the most honourable description.

We have before described what Mr Brandon's character was. He was not a man of honourable intentions at all. But he was a gentleman of so excessively eager a temperament, that if properly resisted by a practised coquette, or by a woman of strong principles, he would sacrifice anything to obtain his ends – nay, marry to obtain them; and, considering his disposition, it is only a wonder that he had not been married a great number of times already; for he had been in love perpetually since his seventeenth year. By which the reader may pretty well appreciate the virtue or the prudence of the ladies with whom hitherto our inflammable young gentleman had had to do.

The fruit, then, of all his stolen interviews, of all his prayers, vows, and protestations to Caroline, had been only this, – that she loved him; but loved him as an honest girl should, and was ready to go to the altar with him when he chose. He talked about his family, his peculiar circumstances, his proud father's curse. Little Caroline only sighed, and said her dearest George must wait until he could obtain his parent's consent. When pressed harder, she would burst into tears, and wonder how one so good and affectionate as he could propose to her anything unworthy of them both. It is clear to see that the young lady had read a vast number of novels, and knew something of the nature of love; and that she had a good principle and honesty of her own, which set her lover's schemes at naught: indeed, she had both these advantages, – her education, such as it was, having given her the one, and her honest nature having endowed her with the other.

On the day when Fitch came down to Caroline with his verses, Brandon had pressed these unworthy propositions upon her. She had torn herself violently away from him, and rushed to the door; but the poor little thing fell back before she could reach it, screaming in a fit of hysterics which brought Becky to her aid, and caused Brandon to leave her, abashed. He went out; she watched him go, and stole up into his room, and laid on his table the first letter she had ever written to him. It was written in pencil, in a trembling, school-girl hand, and contained simply the following words:

George, you have almost broken my heart. Leave me if you will, and if you dare not act like an honest man. If ever you speak to me so again as you did this morning, I declare solemnly before Heaven, I will take poison.

C.

Indeed, the poor thing had read romances to some purpose; without them, it is probable, she never would have thought of such a means of escape from a lover's persecutions; and there was something in the girl's character that made Brandon feel sure that she would keep her promise. How the words agitated him! He felt a violent mixture of raging disappointment and admiration, and loved the girl ten thousand times more than ever.

Mr Brandon had scarcely finished the reading of this document, and was yet agitated by the various passions which the perusal of it created, when the door of his apartment was violently flung open, and some one came in. Brandon started and turned round, with a kind of dread that Caroline had already executed her threat, and that a messenger was come to inform him of her death. Mr Andrea Fitch was the intruder. His hat was on – his eyes were glaring; and if the beards of men did stand on end anywhere but in poems and romances, his, no doubt, would have formed round his countenance a bristling auburn halo. As it was, Fitch only looked astonishingly fierce, as he stalked up to the table, his hands behind his back. When he had arrived at this barrier between himself and Mr Brandon, he stopped, and, speechless, stared that gentleman in the face.

'May I beg, Mr Fitch, to know what has procured me the honour of this visit?' exclaimed Mr Brandon, after a brief pause of wonder.

'Honour! – ha, ha, ha!' growled Mr Fitch, in a most sardonic, discordant way – 'honour!'

'Well, sir, honour or no honour, I can tell you, my good man, it certainly is no pleasure!' said Brandon, testily. 'In plain English, then, what the devil has brought you here?'

Fitch plumped the album down on the table close to Mr Brandon's nose, and said, 'That has brought me, sir – that halbum, sir; or, I ask your pardon, that a – album – ha, ha, ha!'

'Oh, I see!' said Mr Brandon, who could not refrain from a smile. 'It was a cruel trick of mine, Fitch, to rob you of your verses; but all's fair in love.'

'Fitch, sir! don't Fitch me, sir! I wish to be hintimate honly with men of h-honour, not with forgers, sir; not with 'artless miscreants! Miscreants, sir, I repeat; vipers, sir; b – b – b – blackguards, sir!'

'Blackguards, sir!' roared Mr Brandon, bouncing up; 'blackguards, you dirty cockney mountebank! Quit the room, sir, or I'll fling you out of the window!'

'Will you, sir? try, sir; I wish you may get it, sir. I'm a hartist, sir, and as good a man as you. Miscreant, forger, traitor, come on!'

And Mr Brandon *would* have come on, but for a circumstance that deterred him; and this was, that Mr Fitch drew from his bosom a long, sharp, shining, waving poniard of the middle ages, that formed a part of his artistical properties, and with which he had armed himself for this encounter.

'Come on, sir!' shrieked Fitch, brandishing this fearful weapon. 'Lay a finger on me, and I bury this blade in your treacherous 'art. Ha! do you tremble?'

Indeed, the aristocratic Mr Brandon turned somewhat pale.

'Well, well,' said he, 'what do you want? Do you suppose I am to be bullied by your absurd melodramatic airs! It was, after all, but a joke, sir, and I am sorry that it has offended you. Can I say more? – what shall I do?'

'You shall hapologise; not only to me, sir, but you shall tell Miss Caroline, in my presence, that you stole those verses from me, and used them quite unauthorised by me.'

'Look you, Mr Fitch, I will make you another set of verses quite as good, if you like; but what you ask is impossible.'

'I will 'asten myself, then, to Miss Caroline, and acquaint her with your dastardly forgery, sir. I will hopen her heyes, sir!'

'You may hopen her heyes, as you call them, if you please: but I tell you *fairly*, that the young lady will credit me rather than you; and if you swear ever so much that the verses are yours, I must say that – '

'Say what, sir?'

'Say that you *lie*, sir!' said Mr Brandon, stamping on the ground. 'I'll make you other verses, I repeat; but this is all I can do, and now go about your business!'

'Curse your verses, sir! liar and forger yourself! Hare you a coward as well, sir? A coward! yes, I believe you are; or will you meet me to-morrow morning like a man, and give me satisfaction for this hinfamous hinsult?'

'Sir,' said Mr Brandon, with the utmost stateliness and scorn,

'If you wish to murder me as you do the king's English, I won't balk you. Although a man of my rank is not called upon to meet a blackguard of your condition, I will, nevertheless, grant you your will. But have a care; by heavens, I won't spare you, and I can hit an ace of hearts at twenty paces!'

'Two can play at that,' said Mr Fitch, calmly; 'and if I can't hit a hace of 'arts at twenty paces, I can hit a man at twelve, and to-morrow I'll try.' With which, giving Mr Brandon a look of the highest contempt, the young painter left the room.

What were Mr Brandon's thoughts as his antagonist left him? Strange to say, rather agreeable. He had much too great a contempt for Fitch to suppose that so low a fellow would ever think seriously of fighting him, and reasoned with himself thus:

'This Fitch, I know, will go off to Caroline, tell her the whole transaction, frighten her with the tale of a duel, and then she and I shall have a scene. I will tell her the truth about those infernal verses, menace death, blood, and danger, and then –'

Here he fell back into a charming reverie; the wily fellow knew what power such a circumstance would give him over a poor weak girl, who would do anything rather than that her beloved should risk his life. And with this dastardly speculation as to the price he should ask for refraining from meeting Fitch, he was entertaining himself when, much to his annoyance, that gentleman again came into the room.

'Mr Brandon,' said he, 'you have insulted me in the grossest and cruellest way.'

'Well, sir, are you come to apologise?' said Brandon sneeringly.

'No, I'm not come to apologise, Mr Aristocrat: it's past that. I'm come to say this, sir, that I take you for a coward; and that, unless you will give me your solemn word of honour not to mention a word of this quarrel to Miss Gann, which might prevent our meeting, I will never leave you till we *do* fight!'

'This is outrageous, sir! Leave the room, or by heavens I'll not meet you at all!'

'Heasy sir; easy, I beg your pardon, I can force you to that!'

'And how, pray, sir?'

'Why, in the first place, here's a stick, and I'll 'orsewhip you; and here are a pair of pistols, and we can fight now!'

'Well, sir, I give you my honour,' said Mr Brandon, in a diabolical rage; and added, 'I'll meet you to-morrow, not now; and you need not be afraid that I'll miss you!'

'Hadew, sir,' said the chivalrous little Fitch; 'bon giorno, sir, as we used to say at Rome.' And so, for the second time, he left Mr Brandon, who did not like very well the extraordinary courage he had displayed.

'What the deuce has exasperated the fellow so?' thought Brandon.

Why, in the first place, he had crossed Fitch in love; and, in the second, he had sneered at his pronunciation and his gentility, and Fitch's little soul was in a fury which nothing but blood would allay: he was determined, for the sake of his hart and his lady, to bring this proud champion down.

So Brandon was at last left to his cogitations; when, confusion! about five o'clock came another knock at his door.

'Come in!' growled the owner of the lodgings.

A sallow, blear-eyed, rickety, undersized creature, tottering upon a pair of high-heeled lacquered boots, and supporting himself upon an immense gold-knobbed cane, entered the room with his hat on one side and a jaunty air. It was a white hat with a broad brim, and under it fell a great deal of greasy lank hair, that shrouded the cheek-bones of the wearer. The little man had no beard to his chin, appeared about twenty years of age, and might weigh, stick and all, some seven stone. If you wish to know how this exquisite was dressed, I have the pleasure to inform you that he wore a great sky-blue embroidered satin stock, in the which figured a carbuncle that looked like a lambent gooseberry. He had a shawl-waistcoat of many colours; a pair of loose blue trousers, neatly strapped to show his little feet: a brown cut-away coat with brass buttons, that fitted tight round a spider waist; and over all a white or drab surtout, with a sable collar and cuffs, from which latter on each hand peeped five little fingers covered with lemon-coloured kid gloves. One of these hands he held constantly to his little chest; and, with a hoarse thin voice, he piped out.

'George, my buck! how goes it?'

We have been thus particular in our description of the costume of this individual (whose inward man strongly corresponded with his manly and agreeable exterior), because he was the person whom Mr Brandon most respected in the world.

'Cinqbars!' exclaimed our hero: 'why, what the deuce has brought you to Margate?'

'Fwendship, my old cock!' said the Honourable Augustus

Frederick Ringwood, commonly called Viscount Cinqbars, for indeed it was he. 'Fwendship and the *City of Canterbuwy* steamer!' and herewith his lordship held out his right-hand forefinger to Brandon, who inclosed it most cordially in all his. 'Wathn't it good of me, now George, to come down and conthole you in thith curthed, thtupid place – hay now?' said my lord, after these salutations.

Brandon swore he was very glad to see him, which was very true, for he had no sooner set his eyes upon his lordship, than he had determined to borrow as much money from him as ever he could induce the young nobleman to part with.

'I'll tell you how it wath, my boy: you thee I wath thtopping at Long'th, when I found, by Jove, that the governor wath come to town! Cuth me if I didn't meet the infarnal old family dwag, with my mother, thithterth, and all, ath I wath dwiving a hack-cab with Polly Tomkinth in the Pawk! Tho when I got home, "Hang it!" thayth I to Tufthunt, "Tom my boy," thaith I, "I've just theen the governor, and must be off!" "What, back to Ockthford?" thaith Tom. "No," thaith I, "that *won't* do. Abroad – to Jewicho – anywhere. Egad, I have it! I'll go down to Margate and thee old George, that I will." And tho off I came the very next day; and here I am, and thereth dinner waiting for uth at the hotel, and thixth bottleth of champagne in ithe, and thum thalmon: tho you mutht come.'

To this proposition Mr Brandon readily agreed, being glad enough of the prospect of a good dinner and some jovial society, for he was low and disturbed in spirits, and so promised to dine with his friend at the Sun.

The two gentlemen conversed for some time longer. Mr Brandon was a shrewd fellow, and knew perfectly well a fact of which, no doubt, the reader has a notion – namely, that Lord Cinqbars was a ninny; but nevertheless, Brandon esteemed him highly as a lord. We pardon stupidity in lords; nature or instinct, however sarcastic a man may be among ordinary persons, renders him towards men of quality benevolently blind: a divinity hedges not only the king, but the whole peerage.

'That's the girl, I suppose,' said my lord, knowingly winking at Brandon: 'that little pale girl, who let me in, I mean. A nice little filly upon my honour, Georgy my buck!'

'Oh – that – yes – I wrote, I think, something about her,' said Brandon, blushing slightly; for, indeed, he now began to wish that his friend should make no comments upon a young lady with whom he was so much in love.

'I suppose it's all up now?' continued my lord, looking still more knowing. 'All over with her, hay? I saw it was by her looks, in a minute.'

'Indeed you do me a great deal too much honour. Miss – ah – Miss Gann is a very respectable young person, and I would not for the world have you to suppose that I would do anything that should the least injure her character.'

At this speech Lord Cinqbars was at first much puzzled; but, in considering it, was fully convinced that Brandon was a deeper dog than ever. Boiling with impatience to know the particulars of this delicate intrigue, this cunning diplomatist determined he would pump the whole story out of Brandon by degrees; and so, in the course of half an hour's conversation that the young men had together, Cinqbars did not make less than forty allusions to the subject that interested him. At last Brandon cut him short rather haughtily, by begging that he would make no further allusions to the subject, as it was one that was excessively disagreeable to him.

In fact, there was no mistake about it now. George Brandon was in love with Caroline. He felt that he was while he blushed at his friend's alluding to her, while he grew indignant at the young lord's coarse banter about her.

Turning the conversation to another point, he asked Cinqbars about his voyage, and whether he had brought any companion with him to Margate; whereupon my lord related all his feats in London, how he had been to the watchhouse, how many bottles of champagne he had drunk, how he had 'milled'* a policeman, &c. &c.; and he concluded by saying that he had come down with Tom Tufthunt, who was at the inn at that very moment smoking a cigar.

This did not increase Brandon's good-humour; and when Cinqbars mentioned his friend's name, Brandon saluted it mentally with a hearty curse. These two gentlemen hated each other of old. Tufthunt was a small college man of no family, with a foundation fellowship; and it used to be considered that a sporting fellow of a small college was a sad, raffish, disreputable character. Tufthunt, then, was a vulgar fellow, and Brandon a gentleman, so they hated each other. They were both toadies of the same nobleman, so they hated each other. They had had some quarrel at college about a disputed bet, which Brandon knew he owed, and so they hated each other; and in their words about it Brandon had threatened to horsewhip Tufthunt, and called him a 'sneaking, swindling, small college snob'; and so little Tufthunt, who had not resented the words, hated Brandon far more than Brandon hated him. The latter only had a contempt for his rival, and voted him a profound bore and vulgarian.

So, although Mr Tufthunt did not choose to frequent Mr Brandon's rooms, he was very anxious that his friend, the young lord, should not fall into his old bear-leader's hands again, and came down to Margate to counteract any influence which the arts of Brandon might acquire.

'Curse the fellow!' thought Tufthunt in his heart (there was a fine reciprocity of curses between the two men); 'he has drawn Cinqbars already for fifty pounds this year, and will have some half of his last remittance, if I don't keep a look-out, the swindling thief!'

And so frightened was Tufthunt at the notion of Brandon's return to power and dishonest use of it, that he was at the time on the point of writing to Lord Ringwood to tell him of his son's doings, only he wanted some money deucedly himself. Of Mr Tufthunt's physique and history it is necessary merely to say that he was the son of a country attorney, who was agent to a lord; he had been sent to a foundation-school, where he distinguished himself for ten years, by fighting and being flogged more than any boy of the five hundred. From the foundation-school he went to college with an exhibition, which was succeeded by a fellowship, which was to end in a living. In his person Mr Tufthunt was short and bow-legged; he wore a sort of clerico-sporting costume, consisting of a black straight-cut coat and light drab breeches, with a vast number of buttons at the ankles; a sort of dress much affectioned by sporting gentlemen of the university in the author's time.

Well, Brandon said he had some letters to write, and promised to follow his friend, which he did; but, if the truth must be told, so infatuated was the young man become with his passion, with the resistance he had met with, and so nervous from the various occurrences of the morning, that he passed the half hour during which he was free from Cinqbars' society in kneeling, imploring, weeping at Caroline's little garret-door, which had remained pitilessly closed to him. He was wild with disappointment, mortification – mad longing to see her. The cleverest coquette in

Europe could not have so inflamed him. His first act on entering
the dinner-room was to drink off a large tumbler of champagne;
and when Cinqbars, in his elegant way, began to rally him upon
his wildness, Mr Brandon only growled and cursed with frightful
vehemency, and applied again to the bottle. His face, which had
been quite white, grew a bright red; his tongue, which had been
tied, began to chatter vehemently; before the fish was off the table
Mr Brandon showed strong symptoms of intoxication; before the
dessert appeared, Mr Tufthunt, winking knowingly to Lord
Cinqbars, had begun to draw him out; and Brandon, with a
number of shrieks and oaths, was narrating the history of his
attachment.

'Look you, Tufthunt,' said he, wildly; 'hang you, I hate you,
but I *must* talk! I've been, for two months now, in this cursed hole;
in a rickety lodging, with a vulgar family; as vulgar, by Jove, as
you are yourself!'

Mr Tufthunt did not like this style of address half so much as
Lord Cinqbars, who was laughing immoderately, and to whom
Tufthunt whispered rather sheepishly, 'Pooh, pooh, he's drunk!'

'*Drunk!* no sir,' yelled out Brandon; 'I'm mad, though, with the
prudery of a little devil of fifteen, who has cost me more trouble
than it would take me to seduce every one of your sisters – ha, ha!
every one of the Miss Tufthunts, by Jove! Miss Suky Tufthunt,
Miss Dolly Tufthunt, Miss Anna-Marie Tufthunt, and the whole
bunch. Come, sir, don't sit scowling at *me*, or I'll brain you with
the decanter.' (Tufthunt was down again on the sofa.) 'I've borne
with the girl's mother, and her father, and her sisters, and a cook
in the house, and a scoundrel of a painter, that I'm going to fight
about her; and for what? – why, for a letter, which says, "George,
I'll kill myself! George, I'll kill myself!" – ha, ha! a little devil like
that *killing* herself – ha, ha! and I – I who – who adore her, who
am mad for – '

'Mad, I believe he is,' said Tufthunt; and at this moment Mr
Brandon was giving the most unequivocal signs of madness; he
plunged his head into the corner of the sofa, and was kicking his
feet violently into the cushions.

'You don't understand him, Tufty, my boy,' said Lord
Cinqbars, with a very superior air. 'You ain't up to these things,
I tell you; and I suspect, by Jove, that you never were in love in
your life. I know what it is, sir. And as for Brandon, Heaven bless
you! I've often seen him in that way when we were abroad. When

he has an intrigue, he's mad about it. Let me see, there was the Countess Fritzch, at Baden-Baden; there was the woman at Pau; and that girl – at Paris, was it? – no, at Vienna. He went on just so about them all; but I'll tell you what, when *we* do the thing, we do it easier, my boy, hay?'

And so saying, my lord cocked up his little sallow, beardless face into a grin, and then fell to eying a glass of execrable claret across a candle. *An intrigue,* as he called it, was the little creature's delight; and until the time should arrive when he could have one himself, he loved to talk of those of his friends.

As for Tufthunt, we may fancy how that gentleman's previous affection for Brandon was increased by the latter's brutal addresses to him. Brandon continued to drink and to talk, though not always in the sentimental way in which he had spoken about his loves and injuries. Growing presently madly jocose as he had before been madly melancholy, he narrated to the two gentlemen the particulars of his quarrel with Fitch, mimicking the little painter's manner in an excessively comic way, and giving the most ludicrous account of his person, kept his companions in a roar of laughter. Cinqbars swore that he would see the fun in the morning, and agreed that if the painter wanted a second, either he or Tufthunt would act for him.

Now my Lord Cinqbars had an excessively clever servant, a merry rogue whom he had discovered in the humble capacity of scout's assistant at Christchurch, and raised to be his valet. The chief duties of the valet were to black his lord's beautiful boots, that we have admired so much, and put his lordship to bed when overtaken with liquor. He heard every word of the young men's talk (it being his habit, much encouraged by his master, to join occasionally in the conversation); and in the course of the night, when at supper with Monsieur Donnerwetter and Mdlle Augustine, he related every word of the talk above stairs, mimicking Brandon quite as cleverly as the latter had mimicked Fitch. When then, after making his company laugh by describing Brandon's love-agonies, Mr Tom informed them how that gentleman had a rival, with whom he was going to fight a duel the next morning – an artist-fellow with an immense beard, whose name was Fitch, to his surprise Mdlle Augustine burst into a scream of laughter, and exclaimed, '*Feesh, Feesh! c'est notre homme;* – it is our man, sare! Saladin, remember you Mr Fish?'

Saladin said gravely, 'Missa Fis, Missa Fis! know 'um quite

well, Missa Fis! Painter-man, big beard, gib Saladin bit injyrubby, Missis lub Missa Fis!'

It was too true, the fat lady was the famous *Mrs Carrick Fergus*, and she had come all the way from Rome in pursuit of her adored painter.

Chapter IX

WHICH THREATENS DEATH,
BUT CONTAINS A GREAT DEAL OF MARRYING

As the morrow was to be an eventful day in the lives of all the heroes and heroines of this history, it will be as well to state how they passed the night previous. Brandon, like the English before the battle of Hastings, spent the evening in feasting and carousing; and Lord Cinqbars, at twelve o'clock, his usual time after his usual quantity of drink, was carried up to bed by the servant kept by his lordship for that purpose. Mr Tufthunt took this as a hint to wish Brandon good-night, at the same time promising that he and Cinqbars would not fail him in the morning about the duel.

Shall we confess that Mr Brandon, whose excitement now began to wear off, and who had a dreadful headache, did not at all relish the idea of the morrow's combat?

'If,' said he, 'I shoot this crack-brained painter, all the world will cry out, 'Murder!' If he shoot me, all the world will laugh at me! And yet, confound him! he seems so bent upon blood, that there is no escaping a meeting.'

'At any rate,' Brandon thought, 'there will be no harm in a letter to Caroline.' So, on arriving at home, he sat down and wrote a very pathetic one; saying that he fought in her cause, and if he died, his last breath should be for her. So having written, he jumped into bed, and did not sleep one single wink all night.

As Brandon passed his night like the English, Fitch went through his like the Normans, in fasting, and mortification, and meditation. The poor fellow likewise indited a letter to Caroline: a very long and strong one, interspersed with pieces of poetry, and containing the words we have just heard him utter out of the window. Then he thought about making his will: but he recollected, and, indeed, it was a bitter thought to the young man, that there was not one single soul in the wide world who cared for him – except, indeed, thought he, after a pause, that poor Mrs Carrickfergus at Rome, who *did* like me, and was the only person who ever bought my drawings. So he made over all his sketches to her, regulated his little property, found that he had money enough to pay his washerwoman; and so, having disposed of his worldly concerns, Mr Fitch also jumped into bed, and speedily fell into a deep sleep. Brandon could hear him snoring all night, and did not feel a bit the more comfortable because his antagonist took matters so unconcernedly.

Indeed, our poor painter had no guilty thoughts in his breast, nor any particular revenge against Brandon, now that the first pangs of mortified vanity were over. But, with all his vagaries, he was a man of spirit; and after what had passed in the morning, the treason that had been done him, and the insults heaped upon him, he felt that the duel was irrevocable. He had a misty notion, imbibed somewhere, that it was the part of a gentleman's duty to fight duels, and had long been seeking for an opportunity. 'Suppose I do die,' said he, 'what's the odds? Caroline doesn't care for me. Dr Wackerbart's boys won't have their drawing-lesson next Wednesday; and no more will be said of poor Andrea.'

And now for the garret. Caroline was wrapped up in her own woes, poor little soul! and in the arms of the faithful Becky cried herself to sleep. But the slow hours passed on; and the tide, which had been out, now came in; and the lamps waxed fainter and fainter; and the watchman cried six o'clock; and the sun arose and gilded the minarets of Margate; and Becky got up and scoured the steps, and the kitchen, and made ready the lodgers' breakfasts; and at half past eight there came a thundering rap at the door, and two gentlemen, one with a mahogany case under his arm, asked for Mr Brandon, and were shown up to his room by the astonished Becky, who was bidden by Mr Brandon to get breakfast for three.

The thundering rap awakened Mr Fitch, who rose and dressed himself in his best clothes, gave a twist of the curling-tongs to his beard, and conducted himself throughout with perfect coolness. Nine o'clock struck, and he wrapped his cloak round him, and put under his cloak that pair of foils which we have said he possessed, and did not know in the least how to use. However, he had heard his *camarades d'atelier*, at Paris and Rome, say that they were the best weapons for duelling; and so forth he issued.

Becky was in the passage as he passed down; she was always scrubbing there. 'Becky,' said Fitch, in a hollow voice, 'here is a letter; if I should not return in half an hour, give it to Miss Gann, and promise on your honour that she shall not have it sooner.' Becky promised. She thought the painter was at some of his mad tricks. He went out of the door saluting her gravely.

But he went only a few steps and came back again. 'Becky,' said he, 'you – you've always been a good girl to me, and here's something for you; per'aps we sha'n't – we sha'n't see each other for some time.' The tears were in his eyes as he spoke, and he handed her over seven shillings and fourpence halfpenny, being every farthing he possessed in the world.

'Well, I'm sure!' said Becky; and that was all she said, for she pocketed the money and fell to scrubbing again.

Presently the three gentlemen up stairs came clattering down. 'Lock bless you, don't be in such a 'urry!' exclaimed Becky; 'it's full herly yet, and the water's not biling.'

'We'll come back to breakfast, my dear,' said one, a little gentleman in high-heeled boots; 'and, I thay, mind and have thum thoda-water.' And he walked out, twirling his cane. His friend with the case followed him. Mr Brandon came last.

He too turned back after he had gone a few paces. 'Becky,' said he, in a grave voice, 'if I am not back in half-an-hour, give that to Miss Gann.'

Becky was fairly flustered by this; and after turning the letters round and round, and peeping into the sides, and looking at the seals very hard, she like a fool determined that she would not wait half-an-hour, but carry them up to Miss Caroline; and so up she mounted, finding pretty Caroline in the act of lacing her stays.

And the consequences of Becky's conduct was that little Carry left off lacing her stays (a sweet little figure the poor thing looked in them; but that is neither here nor there), took the letters, looked at one which she threw down directly; at the other, which she eagerly opened, and having read a line or two, gave a loud scream, and fell down dead in a fainting fit.

Waft us, O Muse! to Mr Wright's hotel, and quick narrate what chances there befell. Very early in the morning Mdlle Augustine made her appearance in the apartment of Miss Runt, and with great glee informed that lady of the event which was about to take place. 'Figurez-vous, mademoiselle, que notre homme va se battre – oh, but it will be droll to see him sword in hand!'

'Don't plague me with your ojous servants' quarrels, Augustine; that horrid courier is always quarrelling and tipsy.'

'Mon Dieu, qu'elle est bête!' exclaimed Augustine: 'but I tell you it is not the courier; it is he, l'objet, le peintre dont madame s'est amourachée, Monsieur Feesh.'

'Mr Fitch!' cried Runt, jumping up in the bed. 'Mr Fitch going to fight! Augustine, my stockings – quick, my *robe-de-chambre* – tell me when, how, where?'

And so Augustine told her that the combat was to take place at nine that morning, behind the Windmill, and that the gentleman with whom Mr Fitch was to go out had been dining at the hotel the night previous, in company with the little milor, who was to be his second.

Quick as lightning flew Runt to the chamber of her patroness. That lady was in a profound sleep; and I leave you to imagine what were her sensations on awaking and hearing this dreadful tale.

Such is the force of love, that although, for many years, Mrs Carrickfergus had never left her bed before noon, although in all her wild wanderings after the painter she, nevertheless, would have her tea and cutlet in bed, and her doze likewise, before she set forth on a journey – she now started up in an instant, forgetting her nap, mutton-chops, everything, and began dressing with a promptitude which can only be equalled by Harlequin when disguising himself in a pantomime. She would have had an attack of nerves, only she knew there was no time for it; and I do believe that twenty minutes were scarcely over her head, as the saying is, when her bonnet and cloak were on, and with her whole suit, and an inn-waiter or two whom she pressed into her service, she was on full trot to the field of action. For twenty years before, and from that day to this, Marianne Carrickfergus never had or has walked so quickly.

'Hullo, here'th a go!' exclaimed Lord Viscount Cinqbars, as they arrived on the ground behind the Windmill; 'cuth me, there'th only one man!'

This was indeed the case; Mr Fitch, in his great cloak, was pacing slowly up and down the grass, his shadow stretching far in the sunshine. Mr Fitch was alone too; for the fact is, he had never thought about a second. This is admitted frankly, bowing with much majesty to the company as they came up. 'But that, gents,' said he, 'will make no difference, I hope, nor prevent fair play from being done.' And, flinging off his cloak, he produced the foils, from which the buttons had been taken off. He went up to Brandon, and was for offering him one of the weapons, just as they do at the theatre. Brandon stepped back rather abashed: Cinqbars looked posed; Tufthunt delighted. 'Ecod,' said he, 'I hope the bearded fellow will give it him.'

'Excuse me, sir,' said Mr Brandon; 'as the challenged party, I demand pistols.'

Mr Fitch, with great presence of mind and gracefulness, stuck the swords into the grass.

'Oh, pithtolth of courth,' lisped my lord; and presently called aside Tufthunt, to whom he whispered something in great glee; to which Tufthunt objected at first, saying, 'No, d – him, let him fight.' 'And your fellowship and living, Tufty, my boy?' interposed my lord; and then they walked on. After a couple of minutes, during which Mr Fitch was employed in examining Mr Brandon from the toe upwards to the crown of his head, or hat, just as Mr Widdicombe does Mr Cartlich before those two gentlemen proceed to join in combat on the boards of *Astley's Amphitheatre* (indeed poor Fitch had no other standard of chivalry) – when Fitch had concluded this examination, of which Brandon did not know what the deuce to make, Lord Cinqbars came back to the painter, and gave him a nod.

'Sir,' said he, 'as you have come unprovided with a second, I, with your leave, will act as one. My name is Cinqbars – Lord Cinqbars; and though I had come to the ground to act as the friend of my friend here, Mr Tufthunt will take that duty upon him; and as it appears to me there can be no other end to this unhappy affair, we will proceed at once.'

It is a marvel how Lord Cinqbars ever made such a gentlemanly speech. When Fitch heard that he was to have a lord for a second, he laid his hand on his chest, and vowed it was the greatest h-honour of his life; and was turning round to walk towards his ground, when my lord, gracefully thrusting his tongue into his cheeks, and bringing his thumb up to his nose, twiddled about his fingers for a moment, and said to Brandon, 'Gammon!'

Mr Brandon smiled, and heaved a great, deep refreshing sigh.

The truth was, a load was taken off his mind, of which he was very glad to be rid; for there was something in the coolness of that crazy painter that our fashionable gentleman did not at all approve of.

'I think, Mr Tufthunt,' said Lord Cinqbars, very loud, 'that considering the gravity of the case – threatening horsewhipping, you know, lie on both sides, and lady in the case – I think we must have the barrier-duel!'

'What's that?' asked Fitch.

'The simplest thing in the world; and,' in a whisper, 'let me add, the best for you. Look here. We shall put you at twenty paces, and a hat between you. You walk forward and fire when you like. When you fire, you stop; and you both have the liberty of walking up to the hat. Nothing can be more fair than that.'

'Very well,' said Fitch; and, with a great deal of preparation, the pistols were loaded.

'I tell you what,' whispered Cinqbars to Fitch, 'if I hadn't chosen this way you were a dead man. If he fires he hits you dead. You must not let him fire, but have him down first.'

'I'll try,' said Fitch, who was a little pale, and thanked his noble friend for his counsel. The hat was placed and the men took their places.

'Are you all ready?'

'Ready,' said Brandon.

'Advance when I drop my handkerchief.' And presently down it fell, Lord Cinqbars crying, 'Now!'

The combatants both advanced, each covering his man. When he had gone about six paces, Fitch stopped, fired, and – missed. He grasped his pistol tightly, for he was very near dropping it; and then stood biting his lips, and looking at Brandon, who grinned savagely, and walked up to the hat.

'Will you retract what you said of me yesterday, you villain?' said Brandon.

'I can't.'

'Will you beg for life?'

'No.'

'Then take a minute, and make your peace with God, for you are a dead man.'

Fitch dropped his pistol to the ground, shut his eyes for a moment, and flinging up his chest and clenching his fists, said, '*Now I'm ready*.'

Brandon *fired* – and strange to say, Andrea Fitch, as he gasped and staggered backwards, saw, or thought he saw, Mr Brandon's pistol flying up in the air, where it went off, and heard that gentleman yell out an immense oath in a very audible voice. When he came to himself, a thick stick was lying at Brandon's feet; Mr Brandon was capering about the ground, and cursing and shaking a maimed elbow, and a whole posse of people were rushing upon them. The first was the great German courier, who rushed upon Brandon, and shook that gentleman, and shouting, 'Schelm! spitzbube! blagárd! goward!' in his ear. 'If I had not drown my stick and brogen his damt arm, he wod have murdered dat boor young man.'

The German's speech contained two unfounded assertions; in the first place Brandon would not have murdered Fitch; and, secondly, his arm was not broken – he had merely received a blow on that part which anatomists call the funny bone: a severe blow, which sent the pistol spinning into the air, and caused the gentleman to scream with pain. Two waiters seized upon the murderer too; a baker, who had been brought from his rounds, a bellman, several boys, – were yelling around him, and shouting out, 'Pole-e-eace!'

Next to these came, panting and blowing, some women. Could Fitch believe his eyes? – that fat woman in red satin! – yes – no – yes – he was, he was in the arms of Mrs Carrickfergus!

The particulars of this meeting are too delicate to relate. Suffice it that somehow matters were explained, Mr Brandon was let loose, and a fly was presently seen to drive up, into which Mr Fitch consented to enter with his new-found friend.

Brandon had some good movements in him. As Fitch was getting into the carriage he walked up to him and held out his left hand: 'I can't offer you my right hand, Mr Fitch, for that cursed courier's stick has maimed it; but I hope you will allow me to apologise for my shameful conduct to you, and to say that I never in my life met a more gallant fellow than yourself.'

'That he is, by Jove!' said my Lord Cinqbars.

Fitch blushed as red as a peony, and trembled very much. 'And yet,' said he, 'you would have murdered me just now, Mr Brandon. I can't take your 'and, sir.'

'Why, you great flat,' said my lord, wisely, 'he couldn't have hurt you, nor you him. There wath no ballth in the pithtolth.'

'What,' said Fitch, starting back, 'do you gents call that *a joke?* Oh, my lord, my lord!' And here poor Fitch actually burst into tears on the red satin bosom of Mrs Carrickfergus: she and Miss Runt were crying as hard as they could. And so, amidst much shouting and huzzaing, the fly drove away.

'What a blubbering, abthurd donkey!' said Cinqbars, with his usual judgement; 'ain't he, Tufthunt?'

Tufthunt of course said yes; but Brandon was in a virtuous mood. 'By heavens! I think his tears do the man honour. When I came out with him this morning, I intended to act fairly by him. And as for Mr Tufthunt, who calls a man a coward because he cries – Mr Tufthunt knows well what a pistol is, and that some men don't care to face it, brave as they are.'

Mr Tufthunt understood the hint, and bit his lips and walked on. And as for that worthy moralist, Mr Brandon, I am happy to say that there was some good fortune in store for him, which, though similar in kind to that bestowed lately upon Mr Fitch, was superior in degree.

It was no other than this, that forgetting all maidenly decency and decorum, before Lord Viscount Cinqbars and his friend, that silly little creature, Caroline Gann, rushed out from the parlour into the passage – she had been at the window ever since she was rid of her fainting fit! and ah! what agonies of fear had that little panting heart endured during the half-hour of her lover's absence! – Caroline Gann, I say, rushed into the passage, and leaped upon the neck of Brandon, and kissed him, and called him her dear, dear, dear darling George, and sobbed, and laughed, until George, taking her round the waist gently, carried her into the little dingy parlour, and closed the door behind him.

'Egad,' cried Cinqbars, 'this is quite a *thene!* Hullo, Becky, Polly, what's your name? – bring uth up the breakfatht; and I hope you've remembered the thoda-water. Come along up thtairth, Tufty my boy.'

When Brandon came up stairs and joined them, which he did in a minute or two, consigning Caroline to Becky's care, his eyes were full of tears; and when Cinqbars began to rally him in his usual delicate way, Brandon said gravely, 'No laughing, sir, if you please; for I swear that that lady before long shall be my wife.'

'Your wife! – and what will your father say, and what will your duns say, and what will Miss Goldmore say, with her hundred thousand pounds?' cried Cinqbars.

'Miss Goldmore be hanged,' said Brandon, 'and the duns too; and my father may reconcile it to himself as he can.' And here Brandon fell into a reverie.

'It's no use thinking,' he cried, after a pause. 'You see what a girl it is, Cinqbars. I love her – by heavens, I'm mad with love for her! She shall be mine, let what will come of it. And besides,' he added, in a lower tone of voice, 'why need, why need my father know anything about it?'

'O flames and furies, what a lover it is!' exclaimed his friend. 'But, by Jove, I like your spirit; and hang all governors, say I. Stop – a bright thought! If you must marry, why here's Tom Tufthunt, the very man to do your business.' Little Lord Cinqbars was delighted with the excitement of the affair, and thought to himself, 'By Jove, this *is* an intrigue!'

'What, is Tufthunt in orders?' said Brandon.

'Yes,' replied that reverend gentleman: 'don't you see my coat? I took orders six weeks ago, on my fellowship. Cinqbars' governor has promised me a living.'

'And you shall marry George here, so you shall.'

'What, without a licence?'

'Hang the licence! – we won't peach, will we, George?'

'Her family must know nothing of it,' said George, 'or *they* would.'

'Why should they? Why shouldn't Tom marry you in this very room without any church or stuff at all?'

Tom said: 'You'll hold me out, my lord, if anything comes of it; and, if Brandon likes, why, I *will*. He's done for if he does,' muttered Tufthunt, 'and I have had my revenge on him, the bullying, supercilious blackleg.'

And so on that very day, in Brandon's room, without a licence, and by that worthy clergyman the Rev Thomas Tufthunt, with my Lord Cinqbars for the sole witness, poor Caroline Gann, who knew no better, who never heard of licences, and did not know what banns meant, was married in a manner to the person calling himself George Brandon; George Brandon not being his real name.

No writings at all were made, and the ceremony merely read through. Becky, Caroline's sole guardian, when the poor girl kissed her, and, blushing, showed her gold ring, thought all was in order: and the happy couple set off for Dover that day, with fifty pounds which Cinqbars lent the bridegroom.

Becky received a little letter from Caroline, which she promised to carry to her mamma at Swigby's: and it was agreed that she was to give warning, and come and live with her young lady. Next morning Lord Cinqbars and Tufthunt took the boat for London; the latter uneasy in mind, the former vowing that 'he'd never spent such an exciting day in his life, and loved an intrigue of all things.'

Next morning, too, the great travelling-chariot of Mrs Carrickfergus rolled away with a bearded gentleman inside. Poor Fitch had been back to his lodgings to try one more chance with Caroline, and he arrived in time – to see her get into a postchaise alone with Brandon.

Six weeks afterwards *Galignani's Messenger** contained the following announcement:

Married, at the British embassy, by Bishop Luscombe, Andrew Fitch, Esq., to Marianne Caroline Matilda, widow of the late Antony Carrickfergus, of Lombard Street and Gloucester Place, Esquire. The happy pair, after a magnificent *déjeuner*, set off for the south in their splendid carriage-and-four. Miss Runt officiated as bride's-maid; and we remarked among the company Earl and Countess Crabs, General Sir Rice Curry, K.C.B., Colonel Wapshot, Sir Charles Swang, the Hon Algernon Percy Deuceace and his lady, Count Punter, and others of the *élite* of the fashionable now in Paris. The bridegroom was attended by his friend Michael Angelo Titmarsh, Esquire; and the lady was given away by the Right Hon the Earl of Crabs. On the departure of the bride and bridegroom the festivities were resumed, and many a sparkling bumper of Meurice's champagne was quaffed to the health of the hospitable and interesting couple.

And with one more marriage this chapter shall conclude. About this time the British Auxiliary Legion came home from Spain; and Lieut-General Swabber, a knight of San Fernando, of the order of Isabella the Catholic, of the Tower and Sword, who, as plain Lieutenant Swabber, had loved Miss Isabella Macarty, as a general now actually married her. I leave you to suppose how glorious Mrs Gann was, and how Gann got tipsy at the Bag of Nails; but as her daughters each insisted upon their £30 a year income, and Mrs Gann had so only £60 left, she was obliged still to continue the lodging-house at Margate, in which have occurred the most interesting passages of this *Shabby Genteel Story*.

Becky never went to her young mistress, who was not heard of after she wrote the letter to her parent saying that she was married to Mr Brandon; but, for *particular reasons*, her dear husband wished to keep his marriage secret, and for the present her beloved parents must be content to know she was happy. Gann missed his little Carry at first a good deal, but spent more and more of his time at the alehouse, as his house with only Mrs Gann in it was too hot for him. Mrs Gann talked unceasingly of her daughter the Squire's lady, and her daughter the general's wife; but never once mentioned Caroline after the first burst of wonder and wrath at her departure.

God bless thee, poor Caroline! Thou art happy now, for some short space at least; and here, therefore, let us leave thee.

GOING TO SEE A MAN HANGED

July 1840

X, who had voted with Mr Ewart for the abolition of the punishment of death, was anxious to see the effect on the public mind of an execution, and asked me to accompany him to see Courvoisier killed.* We had not the advantage of a sheriff's order, like the 'six hundred noblemen and gentlemen' who were admitted within the walls of the prison; but determined to mingle with the crowd at the foot of the scaffold, and take up our positions at a very early hour.

As I was to rise at three in the morning, I went to bed at ten, thinking that five hours' sleep would be amply sufficient to brace me against the fatigues of the coming day. But, as might have been expected, the event of the morrow was perpetually before my eyes through the night, and kept them wide open. I heard all the clocks in the neighbourhood chime the hours in succession; a dog from some court hard by kept up a pitiful howling; at one o'clock, a cock set up a feeble, melancholy crowing; shortly after two the daylight came peeping grey through the window-shutters; and by the time that X arrived, in fulfilment of his promise, I had been asleep about half-an-hour. He, more wise, had not gone to rest at all, but had remained up all night at the Club, along with Dash and two or three more. Dash is one of the most eminent wits in London, and had kept the company merry all night with appropriate jokes about the coming event. It is curious that a murder is a great inspirer of jokes. We all like to laugh and have our fling about it; there is a certain grim pleasure in the circumstance – a perpetual jingling antithesis between life and death, that is sure of its effect.

In mansion or garret, on down or straw, surrounded by weeping friends and solemn oily doctors, or tossing unheeded upon scanty hospital beds, there were many people in this great city to whom that Sunday night was to be the last of any that they should pass on earth here. In the course of half-a-dozen dark, wakeful hours, one had leisure to think of these (and a little, too, of that certain supreme night, that shall come at one time or other, when he who writes shall be stretched upon the last bed, prostrate in the last struggle, taking the last look of dear faces that have cheered us here, and lingering – one moment more – ere we part for the tremendous journey); but, chiefly, I could not help thinking, as each clock sounded, what is *he* doing now? has *he* heard it in his little room in Newgate yonder? Eleven o'clock. He has been writing until now. The gaoler says he is a pleasant man enough to be with; but he can hold out no longer, and is very weary. 'Wake me at four,' says he, 'for I have still much to put down.' From eleven to twelve the gaoler hears how he is grinding his teeth in his sleep. At twelve he is up in his bed, and asks, 'Is it the time?' He has plenty more time yet for sleep; and he sleeps, and the bell goes on tolling. Seven hours more – five hours more. Many a carriage is clattering through the streets, bringing ladies away from evening parties; many bachelors are reeling home after a jolly night; Covent Garden is alive and the light coming through the cell-window turns the gaoler's candle pale. Four hours more! 'Courvoisier,' says the gaoler, shaking him, 'it's four o'clock now, and I've woke you as you told me; but there's no call for you *to get up yet*.' The poor wretch leaves his bed, however, and makes his last toilet; and then falls to writing, to tell the world how he did the crime for which he has suffered. This time he will tell the truth, and the whole truth. They bring him his breakfast 'from the coffee-shop opposite – tea, coffee, and thin bread and butter.' He will take nothing, however, but goes on writing. He has to write to his mother – the pious mother far away in his own country – who reared him and loved him; and even now has sent him her forgiveness and her blessing. He finishes his memorials and letters, and makes his will, disposing of his little miserable property of books and tracts that pious people have furnished him with. '*Ce 6 Juillet, 1840. François Benjamin Courvoisier vous donne ceci, mon ami, pour souvenir.*' He has a token for his dear friend the gaoler; another for his dear friend the under-sheriff. As the day of the convict's death draws nigh, it is painful to see how he fastens upon everybody who approaches him, how pitifully he clings to them and loves them.

While these things are going on within the prison (with which we are made accurately acquainted by the copious chronicles of such events which are published subsequently), X's carriage has driven up to the door of my lodgings, and we have partaken of

an elegant *déjeuner* that has been prepared for the occasion. A
cup of coffee at half-past three in the morning is uncommonly
pleasant; and X – enlivens us with the repetition of the jokes that
Dash has just been making. Admirable, certainly – they must have
had a merry night of it, that's clear; and we stoutly debate
whether, when one has to get up so early in the morning, it is best
to have an hour or two of sleep, or wait and go to bed afterwards
at the end of the day's work. That fowl is extraordinarily tough
– the wing, even, is as hard as a board; a slight disappointment,
for there is nothing else for breakfast. 'Will any gentleman have
some sherry and soda-water before he sets out? It clears the brains
famously.' Thus primed, the party sets out. The coachman has
dropped asleep on the box, and wakes up wildly as the hall-door
opens. It is just four o'clock. About this very time they are waking
up poor – pshaw! who is for a cigar? X does not smoke himself;
but vows and protests, in the kindest way in the world, that he
does not care in the least for the new drab-silk linings in his
carriage. Z, who smokes, mounts, however, the box. 'Drive to
Snow Hill,' says the owner of the chariot. The policemen, who
are the only people in the street, and are standing by, look
knowing – they know what it means well enough.

How cool and clean the streets look, as the carriage startles the
echoes that have been asleep in the corners all night. Somebody
has been sweeping the pavements clean in the night-time surely;
they would not soil a lady's white satin shoes, they are so dry and
neat. There is not a cloud or a breath in the air, except Z's cigar,
which whiffs off, and soars straight upwards in volumes of white,
pure smoke. The trees in the squares look bright and green – as
bright as leaves in the country in June. We who keep late hours
don't know the beauty of London air and verdure; in the early
morning they are delightful – the most fresh and lively companions possible. But they cannot bear the crowd and the bustle of
mid-day. You don't know them then – they are no longer the same
things. We have come to Gray's Inn; there is actually dew upon
the grass in the gardens; and the windows of the stout old red
houses are all in a flame.

As we enter Holborn the town grows more animated; and there
are already twice as many people in the streets as you see at
mid-day in a German *Residenz* or an English provincial town. The
gin-shop keepers have many of them taken their shutters down,
and many persons are issuing from them pipe in hand. Down they

go along the broad bright street, their blue shadows marching *after* them; for they are all bound the same way, and are bent like us upon seeing the hanging.

It is twenty minutes past four as we pass St Sepulchre's: by this time many hundred people are in the street, and many more are coming up Snow Hill. Before us lies Newgate Prison; but something a great deal more awful to look at, which seizes the eye at once, and makes the heart beat, is

There it stands black and ready, jutting out from a little door in the prison. As you see it, you feel a kind of dumb electric shock, which causes one to start a little, and give a sort of gasp for breath. The shock is over in a second; and presently you examine the object before you with a certain feeling of complacent curiosity. At least, such was the effect that the gallows produced upon the writer, who is trying to set down all his feelings as they occurred, and not to exaggerate them at all.

After the gallows-shock had subsided, we went down into the crowd, which was very numerous, but not dense as yet. It was evident that the day's *business* had not begun. People sauntered up, and formed groups, and talked; the new comers asking those who seemed *habitués* of the place about former executions; and did the victim hang with his face towards the clock or towards Ludgate Hill? and had he the rope round his neck when he came on the scaffold, or was it put on by Jack Ketch* afterwards? and had Lord W taken a window, and which was he? I may mention the noble Marquis's name, as he was not at the exhibition. A pseudo W was pointed out in an opposite window, towards whom all the people in our neighbourhood looked eagerly, and with great respect too. The mob seemed to have no sort of ill-will against him, but sympathy and admiration. This noble lord's personal courage and strength have won the plebs over to him. Perhaps his exploits against policemen have occasioned some of this popularity; for the mob hate them, as children the schoolmaster.

Throughout the whole four hours, however, the mob was extraordinarily gentle and good-humoured. At first we had leisure to talk to the people about us; and I recommend X's brother senators of both sides of the House to see more of this same people and to appreciate them better. Honourable Members are battling and struggling in the House; shouting, yelling, crowing, hear-hearing, pooh-poohing, making speeches of three columns, and gaining 'great Conservative triumphs,' or 'signal successes of the Reform cause', as the case may be. Three hundred and ten gentlemen of good fortune, and able for the most part to quote Horace, declare solemnly that unless Sir Robert comes in, the nation is ruined. Three hundred and fifteen on the other side swear by their great gods that the safety of the empire depends upon Lord John; and to this end they quote Horace too. I declare that I have never been in a great London crowd without thinking of what they call the two 'great' parties in England with wonder. For which of the two great leaders do these people care, I pray you? When Lord Stanley withdrew his Irish bill the other night,* were they in transports of joy, like worthy persons who read the *Globe* and the *Chronicle*? or when he beat the Ministers, were they wild with delight, like honest gentlemen who read the *Post* and the *Times*? Ask yonder ragged fellow, who has evidently frequented debating-clubs, and speaks with good sense and shrewd good- nature. He cares no more for Lord John than he does for Sir Robert; and, with due respect be it said, would mind very little if both of them were ushered out by Mr Ketch, and took their places under yonder black beam. What are the two great parties to him, and those like him? Sheer wind, hollow humbug, absurd claptraps; a silly mummery of dividing and debating, which does not in the least, however it may turn, affect his condition. It has been so ever since the happy days when Whigs and Tories began; and a pretty pastime no doubt it is for both. August parties, great balances of British freedom: are not the two sides quite as active, and eager, and loud, as at their very birth, and ready to fight for place as stoutly as ever they fought before? But lo! in the meantime, whilst you are jangling and brawling over the accounts, *Populus*, whose estate you have administered while he was an infant, and could not take care of himself – Populus has been growing and growing, till he is every bit as wise as his guardians. Talk to our ragged friend. He is not so polished, perhaps, as a member of the 'Oxford and Cambridge Club'; he has not been to Eton; and never read Horace in his life:

but he can think just as soundly as the best of you; he can speak quite as strongly in his own rough way; he has been reading all sorts of books of late years, and gathered together no little information. He is as good a man as the common run of us; and there are ten million more men in the country as good as he, – ten million, for whom we, in our infinite superiority, are acting as guardians, and to whom, in our bounty, we give – exactly nothing. Put yourself in their position, worthy sir. You and a hundred others find yourselves in some lone place, where you set up a government. You take a chief, as is natural; he is the cheapest order-keeper in the world. You establish half-a-dozen worthies, whose families you say have the privilege to legislate for you for ever; half-a-dozen more, who shall be appointed by a choice of thirty of the rest: and the other sixty, who shall have no choice, vote, place, or privilege, at all. Honourable sir, suppose that you are one of the last sixty: how will you feel, you who have intelligence, passions, honest pride, as well as your neighbour; how will you feel towards your equals, in whose hands lie all the power and all the property of the community? Would you love and honour them, tamely acquiesce in their superiority, see their privileges, and go yourself disregarded without a pang? you are not a man if you would. I am not talking of right or wrong, or debating questions of government. But ask my friend there, with the ragged elbows and no shirt, what he thinks? You have your party, Conservative or Whig, as it may be. You believe that an aristocracy is an institution necessary, beautiful, and virtuous. You are a gentleman, in other words, and stick by your party.

And our friend with the elbows (the crowd is thickening hugely all this time) sticks by *his*. Talk to him of Whig or Tory, he grins at them: of virtual representation, pish! He is a *democrat*, and will stand by his friends, as you by yours; and they are twenty millions, his friends, of whom a vast minority now, a majority a few years hence, will be as good as you. In the meantime we shall continue electing, and debating, and dividing, and having every day new triumphs for the glorious cause of Conservatism, or the glorious cause of Reform, until –

What is the meaning of this unconscionable republican tirade – *àpropos* of a hanging? Such feelings, I think, must come across any man in a vast multitude like this. What good sense and intelligence have most of the people by whom you are surrounded;

how much sound humour does one hear bandied about from one
to another! A great number of coarse phrases are used, that would
make ladies in drawing-rooms blush; but the morals of the men
are good and hearty. A ragamuffin in the crowd (a powdery baker
in a white sheep's-wool cap) uses some indecent expression to a
woman near: there is an instant cry of shame, which silences the
man, and a dozen people are ready to give the woman protection.
The crowd has grown very dense by this time, it is about six
o'clock, and there is great heaving, and pushing, and swaying to
and fro; but round the women the men have formed a circle, and
keep them as much as possible out of the rush and trample. In one
of the houses near us, a gallery has been formed on the roof. Seats
were here let, and a number of persons of various degrees were
occupying them. Several tipsy, dissolute-looking young men, of
the Dick Swiveller cast, were in this gallery. One was lolling over
the sunshiny tiles, with a fierce sodden face, out of which came a
pipe, and which was shaded by long matted hair, and a hat cocked
very much on one side. This gentleman was one of a party which
had evidently not been to bed on Sunday night, but had passed it
in some of those delectable night-houses in the neighbourhood of
Covent Garden. The debauch was not over yet, and the women
of the party were giggling, drinking, and romping, as is the wont
of these delicate creatures; sprawling here and there, and falling
upon the knees of one or other of the males. Their scarfs were off
their shoulders, and you saw the sun shining down upon the bare
white flesh, and the shoulder-points glittering like burning-
glasses. The people about us were very indignant at some of the
proceedings of this debauched crew, and at last raised up such a
yell as frightened them into shame, and they were more orderly
for the remainder of the day. The windows of the shops opposite
began to fill apace, and our before-mentioned friend with ragged
elbows pointed out a celebrated fashionable character who occupied one of them; and, to our surprise, knew as much about him
as the *Court Journal* or the *Morning Post*. Presently he entertained
us with a long and pretty accurate account of the history of
Lady –, and indulged in a judicious criticism upon her last work.
I have met with many a country gentleman who had not read half
as many books as this honest fellow, this shrewd *prolétaire* in a
black shirt. The people about him took up and carried on the
conversation very knowingly, and were very little behind him in
point of information. It was just as good a company as one meets

on common occasions. I was in a genteel crowd in one of the galleries at the Queen's coronation; indeed, in point of intelligence, the democrats were quite equal to the aristocrats. How many more such groups were there in this immense multitude of nearly forty thousand, as some say? How many more such throughout the country? I never yet, as I said before, have been in an English mob, without the same feeling for the persons who composed it, and without wonder at the vigorous, orderly good sense and intelligence of the people.

The character of the crowd was as yet, however, quite festive. Jokes bandying about here and there, and jolly laughs breaking out. Some men were endeavouring to climb up a leaden pipe on one of the houses. The landlord came out, and endeavoured with might and main to pull them down. Many thousand eyes turned upon this contest immediately. All sorts of voices issued from the crowd, and uttered choice expressions of slang. When one of the men was pulled down by the leg, the waves of this black mob-ocean laughed innumerably; when one fellow slipped away, scrambled up the pipe, and made good his lodgment on the shelf, we were all made happy, and encouraged him by loud shouts of admiration. What is there so particularly delightful in the spectacle of a man clambering up a gas-pipe? Why were we kept for a quarter of an hour in deep interest gazing upon this remarkable scene? Indeed it is hard to say: a man does not know what a fool he is until he tries; or, at least, what mean follies will amuse him. The other day I went to Astley's, and saw a clown come in with a foolscap and pinafore, and six small boys who represented his school-fellows. To them enters schoolmaster; horses clown, and flogs him hugely on the back part of his pinafore. I never read anything in Swift, Boz, Rabelais, Fielding, Paul de Kock, which delighted me so much as this sight, and caused me to laugh so profoundly. And why? What is there so ridiculous in the sight of one miserably rouged man beating another on the breech? Tell us where the fun lies in this and the before-mentioned episode of the gas-pipe? Vast, indeed, are the capacities and ingenuities of the human soul that can find, in incidents so wonderfully small, means of contemplation and amusement.

Really the time passed away with extraordinary quickness. A thousand things of the sort related here came to amuse us. First the workmen knocking and hammering at the scaffold, mysterious clattering of blows was heard within it, and a ladder painted black was carried round, and into the interior of the edifice by a small side-door. We all looked at this little ladder and at each other – things began to be very interesting. Soon came a squad of policemen; stalwart, rosy-looking men, saying much for City feeding; well-dressed, well-limbed, and of admirable good-humour. They paced about the open space between the prison and the barriers which kept in the crowd from the scaffold. The front line, as far as I could see, was chiefly occupied by blackguards and boys – professional persons, no doubt, who saluted the policemen on their appearance with a volley of jokes and ribaldry. As far as I could judge from faces, there were more blackguards of sixteen and seventeen than of any maturer age; stunted, sallow, ill-grown lads, in rugged fustian, scowling about. There were a considerable number of girls, too, of the same age; one that Cruikshank and Boz might have taken as a study for Nancy. The girl was a young thief's mistress evidently; if attacked, ready to reply without a particle of modesty; could give as good ribaldry as she got; made no secret (and there were several inquiries) as to her profession and means of livelihood. But with all this, there was something good about the girl; a sort of devil-may-care candour and simplicity that one could not fail to see. Her answers to some of the coarse questions put to her, were very ready and good-humoured. She had a friend with her of the same age and class, of whom she seemed to be very fond, and who looked up to her for protection. Both of these women had beautiful eyes. Devil-may-care's were extraordinarily bright and blue, and admirably fair complexion, and a large red mouth full of white teeth. *Au reste*, ugly, stunted, thick-limbed, and by no means a beauty. Her friend could not be more than fifteen. They were not in rags, but had greasy cotton shawls, and old, faded, rag-shop bonnets. I was curious to look at them, having, in late fashionable novels, read many accounts of such personages. Bah! what figments these novelists tell us! Boz, who knows life well, knows that his Miss Nancy is the most unreal fantastical personage possible; no more like a thief's mistress than one of Gesner's shepherdesses resembles a real country wench. He dare not tell the truth concerning such young ladies. They have, no doubt, virtues like other human creatures; nay, their position engenders virtues that are not called into exercise among other women. But on these an honest painter of human nature has no right to dwell; not being able to paint the whole portrait, he has no right to present one or two favourable points as characterising the whole; and therefore, in fact, had better leave the picture alone altogether. The new French literature is essentially false and worthless from this very error – the writers giving us favourable pictures of monsters, and (to say nothing of decency or morality) pictures quite untrue to nature.

But yonder, glittering through the crowd in Newgate Street – see, the Sheriffs' carriages are slowly making their way. We have been here three hours! Is it possible that they can have passed so soon? Close to the barriers where we are, the mob has become so dense that it is with difficulty a man can keep his feet. Each man, however, is very careful in protecting the women, and all are full of jokes and good-humour. The windows of the shops opposite are now pretty nearly filled by the persons who hired them. Many young dandies are there with moustaches and cigars; some quiet, fat, family-parties, of simple, honest tradesmen and their wives, as we fancy, who are looking on with the greatest imaginable calmness, and sipping their tea. Yonder is the sham Lord W, who is flinging various articles among the crowd; one of his companions, a tall, burly man, with large moustaches, has provided himself with a squirt, and is aspersing the mob with brandy-and-water. Honest gentleman! high-bred aristocrat! genuine lover of humour and wit! I would walk some miles to see thee on the tread-mill, thee and thy Mohawk crew!

We tried to get up a hiss against these ruffians, but only had a trifling success; the crowd did not seem to think their offence very heinous; and our friend, the philosopher in the ragged elbows, who had remained near us all the time, was not inspired with any such savage disgust at the proceedings of certain notorious young gentlemen, as I must confess fills my own particular bosom. He only said, 'So-and-so is a lord, and they'll let him off,' and then discoursed about Lord Ferrers being hanged. The philosopher knew the history pretty well, and so did most of the little knot of persons about him, and it must be a gratifying thing for young gentlemen to find that their actions are made the subject of this kind of conversation.

Scarcely a word had been said about Courvoisier all this time. We were all, as far as I could judge, in just such a frame of mind as men are in when they are squeezing at the pit-door of a play, or pushing for a review or a Lord Mayor's show. We asked most of the men who were near us, whether they had seen many executions? most of them had, the philosopher especially;

whether the sight of them did any good? 'For the matter of that, no; people did not care about them at all; nobody ever thought of it after a bit.' A countryman, who had left his drove in Smithfield, said the same thing; he had seen a man hanged at York, and spoke of the ceremony with perfect good sense, and in a quiet, sagacious way.

J. S., the famous wit, now dead, had, I recollect, a good story upon the subject of executing, and of the terror which the punishment inspires. After Thistlewood* and his companions were hanged, their heads were taken off, according to the sentence, and the executioner, as he severed each, held it up to the crowd, in the proper orthodox way, saying, 'Here is the head of a traitor!' At the sight of the first ghastly head the people were struck with terror, and a general expression of disgust and fear broke from them. The second head was looked at also with much interest, but the excitement regarding the third head diminished. When the executioner had come to the last of the heads, he lifted it up, but, by some clumsiness, allowed it to drop. At this the crowd yelled out, '*Ah, Butter-fingers!*' – the excitement had passed entirely away. The punishment had grown to be a joke – Butter-fingers was the word – a pretty commentary, indeed, upon the august nature of public executions, and the awful majesty of the law.

It was past seven now; the quarters rang and passed away; the crowd began to grow very eager and more quiet, and we turned back every now and then and looked at St Sepulchre's clock. Half an hour, twenty-five minutes. What is he doing now? He has his irons off by this time. A quarter: he's in the press-room now, no doubt. Now at last we had come to think about the man we were going to see hanged. How slowly the clock crept over the last quarter! Those who were able to turn round and see (for the crowd was now extraordinarily dense) chronicled the time, eight minutes, five minutes; at last – ding, dong, dong, dong! – the bell is tolling the chimes of eight.

Between the writing of this line and the last, the pen has been put down, as the reader may suppose, and the person who is addressing him has gone through a pause of no very pleasant thoughts and recollections. The whole of the sickening, ghastly, wicked scene passes before the eyes again; and, indeed, it is an awful one to see, and very hard and painful to describe.

As the clock began to strike, an immense sway and movement swept over the whole of that vast dense crowd. They were all uncovered directly, and a great murmur arose, more awful, bizarre, and indescribable than any sound I had ever before heard. Women and children began to shriek horribly. I don't know whether it was the bell I heard; but a dreadful quick, feverish kind of jangling noise mingled with the noise of the people, and lasted for about two minutes. The scaffold stood before us, tenantless and black; the black chain was hanging down ready from the beam. Nobody came. 'He has been respited,' some one said; another said, 'He has killed himself in prison.'

Just then, from under the black prison-door, a pale, quiet head peered out. It was shockingly bright and distinct; it rose up directly, and a man in black appeared on the scaffold, and was silently followed by about four more dark figures. The first was a tall grave man: we all knew who the second man was. *'That's he – that's he!'* you heard the people say, as the devoted man came up.

I have seen a cast of the head since, but, indeed, should never have known it. Courvoisier bore his punishment like a man, and walked very firmly. He was dressed in a new black suit, as it seemed: his shirt was open. His arms were tied in front of him. He opened his hands in a helpless kind of way, and clasped them once or twice together. He turned his head here and there, and looked about him for an instant with a wild, imploring look. His mouth was contracted into a sort of pitiful smile. He went and placed himself at once under the beam, with his face towards St Sepulchre's. The tall, grave man in black twisted him round swiftly in the other direction, and, drawing from his pocket a night-cap, pulled it tight over the patient's head and face. I am not ashamed to say that I could look no more, but shut my eyes as the last dreadful act was going on, which sent this wretched, guilty soul into the presence of God.

If a public execution is beneficial – and beneficial it is, no doubt, or else the wise laws would not encourage forty thousand people to witness it – the next useful thing must be a full description of such a ceremony, and all its *entourages*, and to this end the above pages are offered to the reader. How does an individual man feel under it? In what way does he observe it – how does he view all the phenomena connected with it – what induces him, in the first instance, to go and see it – and how is he moved by it afterwards? The writer has discarded the magazine 'We' altogether, and spoken face to face with the reader, recording every one of the impressions felt by him as honestly as he could.

I must confess, then (for 'I' is the shortest word, and the best in this case), that the sight has left on my mind an extraordinary feeling of terror and shame. It seems to me that I have been abetting an act of frightful wickedness and violence, performed by a set of men against one of their fellows; and I pray God that it may soon be out of the power of any man in England to witness such a hideous and degrading sight. Forty thousand persons (say the Sheriffs), of all ranks and degrees – mechanics, gentlemen, pickpockets, members of both Houses of Parliament, street-walkers, newspaper-writers, gather together before Newgate at a very early hour; the most part of them give up their natural quiet night's rest, in order to partake of this hideous debauchery, which is more exciting than sleep, or than wine, or the last new ballet, or any other amusement they can have. Pickpocket and Peer each is tickled by the sight alike, and has that hidden lust after blood which influences our race. Government, a Christian government, gives us a feast every now and then: it agrees – that is to say – a majority in the two Houses agrees, that for certain crimes it is necessary that a man should be hanged by the neck. Government commits the criminal's soul to the mercy of God, stating that here on earth he is to look for no mercy; keeps him for a fortnight to prepare, provides him with a clergyman to settle his religious matters (if there be time enough, but Government can't wait); and on a Monday morning, the bell tolling, the clergyman reading out the word of God, 'I am the resurrection and the life,' 'The Lord giveth and the Lord taketh away' – on a Monday morning, at eight o'clock, this man is placed under a beam, with a rope connecting it and him; a plank disappears from under him, and those who have paid for good places may see the hands of the Government agent, Jack Ketch, coming up from his black hole, and seizing the prisoner's legs, and pulling them, until he is quite dead – strangled.

Many persons, and well-informed newspapers, say that it is mawkish sentiment to talk in this way, morbid humanity, cheap philanthropy, that any man can get up and preach about. There is the *Observer*, for instance, a paper conspicuous for the tremendous sarcasm which distinguishes its articles, and which falls cruelly foul of the *Morning Herald*. 'Courvoisier is dead,' says the *Observer*; 'he died as he had lived – a villain; a lie was in his mouth. Peace be to his ashes. We war not with the dead.' What a magnanimous *Observer*! From this, *Observer* turns to the *Herald*, and says, '*Fiat justitia ruat cœlum.*' So much for the *Herald*.

We quote from memory, and the quotation from the *Observer* possibly is – *De mortuis nil nisi bonum*; or, *Omne ignotum pro magnifico*; or, *Sero nunquam est ad bonos mores via*; or, *Ingenuas didicisse fideliter artes emollit mores nec sinit esse feros*: all of which pithy Roman apophthegms would apply just as well.

'Peace be to his ashes. He died a villain.' This is both benevolence and reason. Did he die a villain? The *Observer* does not want to destroy him body and soul, evidently, from that pious wish that his ashes should be at peace. Is the next Monday but one after the sentence the time necessary for a villain to repent in? May a man not require more leisure – a week more – six months more – before he has been able to make his repentance sure before Him who died for us all? – for all, be it remembered – not alone for the judge and jury, or for the sheriffs, or for the executioner who is pulling down the legs of the prisoner – but for him too, murderer and criminal as he is, whom we are killing for his crime. Do we want to kill him body and soul? Heaven forbid! My lord in the black cap specially prays that heaven may have mercy on him; but he must be ready by Monday morning.

Look at the documents which came from the prison of this unhappy Courvoisier during the few days which passed between his trial and execution. Were ever letters more painful to read? At first, his statements are false, contradictory, lying. He has not repented then. His last declaration seems to be honest, as far as the relation of the crime goes. But read the rest of his statement, the account of his personal history, and the crimes which he committed in his young days – then 'how the evil thought came to him to put his hand to the work' – it is evidently the writing of a mad, distracted man. The horrid gallows is perpetually before him; he is wild with dread and remorse. Clergymen are with him ceaselessly; religious tracts are forced into his hands; night and day they ply him with the heinousness of his crime, and exhortations to repentance. Read through that last paper of his; by heaven, it is pitiful to read it. See the Scripture phrases brought in now and anon; the peculiar terms of tract-phraseology (I do not wish to speak of these often meritorious publications with disrespect); one knows too well how such language is learned – imitated from the priest at the bed-side, eagerly seized and appropriated, and confounded by the poor prisoner.

But murder is such a monstrous crime (this is the great argument) – when a man has killed another it is natural that he should be killed. Away with your foolish sentimentalists who say no – it is *natural*. That is the word, and a fine philosophical opinion it is – philosophical and Christian. Kill a man, and you must be killed in turn; that is the unavoidable *sequitur*. You may talk to a man for a year upon the subject, and he will always reply to you, 'It is natural, and therefore it must be done. Blood demands blood.'

Does it? The system of compensations might be carried on *ad infinitum* – an eye for an eye, a tooth for a tooth, as by the old Mosaic law. But (putting the fact out of the question, that we have had this statute repealed by the Highest Authority), why, because you lose your eye, is that of your opponent to be extracted likewise? Where is the reason for the practice? And yet it is just as natural as the death dictum, founded precisely upon the same show of sense. Knowing, however, that revenge is not only evil, but useless, we have given it up on all minor points. Only to the last we stick firm, contrary though it be to reason and to Christian law.

There is some talk, too, of the terror which the sight of this spectacle inspires, and of this we have endeavoured to give as good a notion as we can in the above pages. I fully confess that I came away down Snow Hill that morning with a disgust for murder, but it was for *the murder I saw done*. As we made our way through the immense crowd, we came upon two little girls of eleven and twelve years: one of them was crying bitterly, and begged, for heaven's sake, that some one would lead her from that horrid place. This was done, and the children were carried into a place of safety. We asked the elder girl – and a very pretty one – what brought her into such a neighbourhood? The child grinned knowingly, and said, 'We've koom to see the mon hanged!' Tender law, that brings out babes upon such errands, and provides them with such gratifying moral spectacles!

This is the 20th of July, and I may be permitted for my part to declare that, for the last fourteen days, so salutary has the impression of the butchery been upon me, I have had the man's face continually before my eyes; that I can see Mr Ketch at this moment, with an easy air, taking the rope from his pocket; that I feel myself ashamed and degraded at the brutal curiosity which took me to that brutal sight; and that I pray to Almighty God to cause this disgraceful sin to pass from among us, and to cleanse our land of blood.

THE ARTISTS

It is confidently stated that there was once a time when the quarter of Soho* was thronged by the fashion of London. Many wide streets are there in the neighbourhood, stretching cheerfully towards Middlesex Hospital in the north, bounded by Dean Street in the west, where the lords and ladies of William's time used to dwell – till in Queen Anne's time, Bloomsbury put Soho out of fashion, and Great Russell Street became the pink of the mode.

Both these quarters of the town have submitted to the awful rule of nature, and are now to be seen undergoing the dire process of decay. Fashion has deserted Soho, and left her in her gaunt, lonely old age. The houses have a vast, dingy, mouldy, dowager look. No more beaux, in mighty periwigs, ride by in gilded clattering coaches; no more lackeys accompany them, bearing torches, and shouting for precedence. A solitary policeman paces these solitary streets, – the only dandy in the neighbourhood. You hear the milkman yelling his milk with a startling distinctness, and the clack of a servant-girl's pattens* sets people a-staring from the windows.

With Bloomsbury we have here nothing to do; but as genteel stock-brokers inhabit the neighbourhood of Regent's Park – as lawyers have taken possession of Russell Square – so Artists have seized upon the desolate quarter of Soho. They are to be found in great numbers in Berners Street. Up to the present time, naturalists have never been able to account for this mystery of their residence. What has a painter to do with Middlesex Hospital? He is to be found in Charlotte Street, Fitzroy Square. And why? Philosophy cannot tell, any more than why milk is found in a cocoa-nut.

Look at Newman Street. Has earth, in any dismal corner of her great round face, a spot more desperately gloomy? The windows are spotted with wafers, holding up ghastly bills, that tell you the house is 'To Let'. Nobody walks there – not even an old-clothes-man: the first inhabited house has bars to the windows, and bears the name of 'Ahasuerus, officer to the Sheriff of Middlesex'; and here, above all places, must painters take up their quarters – day by day must these reckless people pass Ahasuerus's treble gate. There was my poor friend Tom Tickner (who did those sweet things for 'The Book of Beauty'). Tom, who could not pay his washerwoman, lived opposite the bailiff's; and could see every miserable debtor, or greasy Jew writ-bearer that went in or out of his door. The street begins with a bailiff's, and ends with a hospital. I wonder how men live in it, and are decently cheerful, with this gloomy, double-barrelled moral pushed perpetually into their faces. Here, however, they persist in living, no one knows why; owls may still be found roosting in Netley Abbey, and a few Arabs are to be seen at the present minute in Palmyra.

The ground-floors of the houses where painters live are mostly make-believe shops, black empty warehouses, containing fabulous goods. There is a sedan-chair opposite a house in Rathbone Place, that I have myself seen every day for forty-three years. The house has commonly a huge india-rubber-coloured door, with a couple of glistening brass-plates and bells. A portrait painter lives on the first-floor; a great historical genius inhabits the second. Remark the first-floor's middle drawing-room window; it is four feet higher than its two companions, and has taken a fancy to peep into the second-floor front. So much for the outward appearance of their habitations, and for the quarters in which they commonly dwell. They seem to love solitude, and their mighty spirits rejoice in vastness and gloomy ruin.

I don't say a word here about those geniuses who frequent the thoroughfares of the town, and have picture-frames containing a little gallery of miniature peers, beauties, and general officers, in the Quadrant, the passages about St. Martin's Lane, the Strand, and Cheapside. Lord Lyndhurst is to be seen in many of these gratis exhibitions – Lord Lyndhurst cribbed from Chalon; Lady Peel from Sir Thomas; Miss Croker from the same; the Duke*; from ditto; an original officer in the Spanish Legion; a colonel or so, of the Bunhill-Row Fencibles; a lady on a yellow sofa, with four children in little caps and blue ribands. We have all of us seen these pretty pictures, and are aware that our own features may be 'done in this style'. Then there is the man on the chain-pier at Brighton, who pares out your likeness in sticking-plaster; there is Miss Croke, or Miss Runt, who gives lessons in Poonah-painting, japanning, or mezzotinting; Miss Stump, who attends ladies' schools with large chalk heads from Le Brun or the Cartoons;

Rubbery, who instructs young gentlemen's establishments in pencil; and Sepio, of the Water-Colour Society, who paints before eight pupils daily, at a guinea an hour, keeping his own drawings for himself.

All these persons, as the most indifferent reader must see, equally belong to the tribe of Artists (the last not more than the first), and in an article like this should be mentioned properly. But though this paper has been extended from eight pages to sixteen, not a volume would suffice to do justice to the biographies of the persons above mentioned. Think of the superb Sepio, in a light-blue satin cravat, and a light-brown coat, and yellow kids, tripping daintily from Grosvenor Square to Gloucester Place, a small sugar-loaf boy following, who carries his morocco portfolio. Sepio scents his handkerchief, curls his hair, and wears, on a great coarse fist a large emerald ring that one of his pupils gave him. He would not smoke a cigar for the world; he is always to be found at the opera; and gods! how he grins, and waggles his head about, as Lady Flummery nods to him from her box.

He goes to at least six great parties in the season. At the houses where he teaches, he has a faint hope that he is received as an equal, and propitiates scornful footmen by absurd donations of sovereigns. The rogue has plenty of them. He has a stock-broker, and a power of guinea-lessons stowed away in the Consols. There are a number of young ladies of genius in the aristocracy, who admire him hugely; he begs you to contradict the report about him and Lady Smigsmag; every now and then he gets a present of game from a marquis; the City ladies die to have lessons of him; he prances about the Park on a high-bred cock-tail, with lacquered boots and enormous high heels; and he has a mother and sisters somewhere – washerwomen, it is said, in Pimlico.

How different is his fate to that of poor Rubbery, the school drawing-master! Highgate, Homerton, Putney, Hackney, Hornsey, Turnham Green, are his resorts; he has a select seminary to attend at every one of these places; and if, from all these nurseries of youth, he obtains a sufficient number of half-crowns to pay his week's bills, what a happy man is he!

He lives most likely in a third floor in Howland Street, and has commonly five children, who have all a marvellous talent for drawing – all save one, perhaps, that is an idiot, which a poor, sick mother is ever carefully tending. Sepio's great aim and battle in life is to be considered one of the aristocracy; honest Rubbery would fain be thought a gentleman, too; but, indeed, he does not know whether he is so or not. Why be a gentleman? – a gentleman Artist does not obtain the wages of a tailor; Rubbery's butcher looks down upon him with a royal scorn; and his wife, poor gentle soul (a clergyman's daughter, who married him in the firm belief that her John would be knighted, and make an immense fortune) – his wife, I say, has many fierce looks to suffer from Mrs Butcher, and many meek excuses or prayers to proffer, when she cannot pay her bill, – or when worst of all, she has humbly to beg for a little scrap of meat upon credit, against John's coming home. He has five-and-twenty miles to walk that day, and must have something nourishing when he comes in – he is killing himself, poor fellow, she knows he is: and Miss Crick has promised to pay him his quarter's charge on the very next Saturday. 'Gentlefolks, indeed,' says Mrs Butcher; 'pretty gentlefolks these, as can't pay for half-a-pound of steak!' Let us thank heaven that the Artist's wife has her meat, however – there is good in that shrill, fat, mottle-faced Mrs Brisket, after all.

Think of the labours of that poor Rubbery. He was up at four in the morning, and toiled till nine upon a huge damp icy lithographic stone; on which he has drawn the 'Star of the Wave', or the 'Queen of the Tourney', or, 'She met at Almack's', for Lady Flummery's last new song. This done, at half-past nine, he is to be seen striding across Kensington Gardens, to wait upon the before-named Miss Crick, at Lamont House. Transport yourself in imagination to the Misses Kittle's seminary, Potzdam Villa, Upper Homerton, four miles from Shoreditch; and at half-past two, Professor Rubbery is to be seen swinging along towards the gate. Somebody is on the look-out for him; indeed it is his eldest daughter, Marianne, who has been pacing the shrubbery, and peering over the green railings this half-hour past. She is with the Misses Kittle on the 'mutual system', a thousand times more despised than the butchers' and the grocers' daughters, who are educated on the same terms, and whose papas are warm men in Aldgate. Wednesday is the happiest day of Marianne's week: and this the happiest hour of Wednesday. Behold! Professor Rubbery wipes his hot brows and kisses the poor thing, and they go in together out of the rain, and he tells her that the twins are well out of the measles, thank God! and that Tom has just done the Antinous, in a way that must make him sure of the Academy prize, and that mother is better of her rheumatism now. He has brought her a letter, in large round-hand, from Polly; a famous soldier, drawn by little Frank; and when, after his two hours' lesson, Rubbery is off again, our dear Marianne cons over the letter and picture a hundred times with soft tearful smiles, and stows them away in an old writing-desk, amidst a heap more of precious home relics, wretched trumpery scraps and baubles, that you and I, Madam, would sneer at; but that in the poor child's eyes (and, I think, in the eyes of One who knows how to value widows' mites and humble sinners' offerings) are better than banknotes and Pitt diamonds. O kind heaven, that has given these treasures to the poor! Many and many an hour does Marianne lie awake with full eyes, and yearn for that wretched old lodging in Howland Street, where mother and brothers lie sleeping; and, gods! what a fête it is, when twice or thrice in the year she comes home!

I forget how many hundred millions of miles, for how many billions of centuries, how many thousands of decillions of angels, peris, houris, demons, afreets, and the like, Mahomet travelled, lived, and counted, during the time that some water was falling from a bucket to the ground; but have we not been wandering most egregiously away from Rubbery, during the minute in which his daughter is changing his shoes, and taking off his reeking mackintosh in the hall of Potzdam Villa? She thinks him the finest artist that ever cut an HB; that's positive: and as a drawing-master, his merits are wonderful; for at the Misses Kittle's annual vacation festival, when the young ladies' drawings are exhibited to their mammas and relatives (Rubbery attending in a clean shirt, with his wife's large brooch stuck in it, and drinking negus along with the very best); – at the annual festival, I say, it will be found that the sixty-four drawings exhibited – 'Tintern Abbey', 'Kenilworth Castle', 'Horse – from Carl Vernet', 'Head – from West', or what not (say sixteen of each sort) – are the one exactly as good as the other; so that, although Miss Slamcoe gets the prize, there is really no reason why Miss Timson, who is only four years old, should not have it; her design being accurately stroke for stroke, tree for tree, curl for curl, the same as Miss Slamcoe's, who is eighteen. The fact is, that of these drawings, Rubbery, in the course of the year, has done every single stroke, although the girls and their parents are ready to take their affidavits (or, as I heard once a great female grammarian say, their *affies davit*) that the drawing-master has never been near the sketches. This is the way with them; but mark! – when young ladies come home, are settled in life, and mammas of families, – can they design so much as a horse, or a dog, or a 'moo-cow', for little Jack who bawls out for them? Not they! Rubbery's pupils have no more notion of drawing, any more than Sepio's of painting, when that eminent artist is away.

Between these two gentlemen, lie a whole class of teachers of drawing, who resemble them more or less. I am ashamed to say that Rubbery takes his pipe in the parlour of an hotel, of which the largest room is devoted to the convenience of poor people, amateurs of British gin: whilst Sepio trips down to the Club, and has a pint of the smallest claret: but of course the tastes of men vary; and you find them simple or presuming, careless or prudent, natural and vulgar, or false and atrociously genteel, in all ranks and stations of life.

As for the other persons mentioned at the beginning of this discourse, viz. the cheap portrait-painter, the portrait-cutter in sticking-plaster, and Miss Croke, the teacher of mezzotint and Poonah-painting – nothing need be said of them in this place, as we have to speak of matters more important. Only about Miss Croke, or about other professors of cheap art, let the reader most sedulously avoid them. Mezzotinto is a take-in, Poonah-painting a rank, villanous deception. So is 'Grecian art without brush or pencils.' These are only small mechanical contrivances, over which young ladies are made to lose time. And now, having disposed of these small skirmishers who hover round the great body of Artists, we are arrived in presence of the main force, that we must begin to attack in form. In the 'partition of the earth', as it has been described by Schiller, the reader will remember that the poet, finding himself at the end of the general scramble without a single morsel of plunder, applied passionately to Jove, who pitied the poor fellow's condition, and complimented him with a seat in the Empyrean. 'The strong and the cunning,' says Jupiter, 'have seized upon the inheritance of the world, whilst thou wert star-gazing and rhyming: not one single acre remains wherewith I can endow thee; but, in revenge, if thou art disposed to visit me in my own heaven, come when thou wilt, it is always open to thee.'

The cunning and strong have scrambled and struggled more on our own little native spot of earth than in any other place on the world's surface; and the English poet (whether he handles a pen or a pencil) has little other refuge than that windy, unsubstantial one which Jove has vouchsafed to him. Such airy board and lodging is, however, distasteful to many; who prefer, therefore, to give up their poetical calling, and, in a vulgar beef-eating world, to feed upon and fight for vulgar beef.

For such persons (among the class of painters), it may be asserted that portrait-painting was invented. It is the Artist's compromise with heaven; 'the light of common day', in which, after a certain quantity of 'travel from the East', the genius fades at last. Abbé Barthélemy (who sent Le Jeune Anacharsis travelling through Greece in the time of Plato – travelling through ancient Greece in lace ruffles, red heels, and a pig-tail), – Abbé Barthélemy, I say, declares that somebody was once standing against a wall in the sun, and that somebody else traced the outline of somebody's shadow; and so painting was 'invented'. Angelica Kauffmann has made a neat picture of this neat subject; and very well worthy she was of handling it. Her painting *might* grow out of a wall and a piece of charcoal; and honest Barthélemy might be satisfied that he had here traced the true origin of the art. What a base pedigree have these abominable Greek, French, and High-Dutch heathens invented for that which is divine! – a wall, ye gods, to be represented as the father of that which came down radiant from you! The man who invented such a blasphemy, ought to be impaled upon broken bottles, or shot off pitilessly by spring-guns, nailed to the bricks like a dead owl or a weasel, or tied up – a kind of vulgar Prometheus – and baited for ever by the house-dog.

But let not our indignation carry us too far. Lack of genius in some, of bread in others, of patronage in a shop-keeping world, that thinks only of the useful, and is little inclined to study the sublime, has turned thousands of persons calling themselves, and wishing to be, Artists, into so many common face-painters, who must look out for the 'kalon' in the fat features of a red-gilled Alderman, or, at best, in a pretty, simpering, white-necked beauty from 'Almack's'. The dangerous charms of these latter, especially, have seduced away many painters; and we often think that this very physical superiority which English ladies possess, this tempting brilliancy of health and complexion, which belongs to them more than to any others, has operated upon our Artists as a serious disadvantage, and kept them from better things. The French call such beauty '*La beauté du Diable*'; and a devilish power it has truly; before our Armidas and Helens how many Rinaldos and Parises have fallen, who are content to forget their glorious calling, and slumber away their energies in the laps of these soft tempters. O ye British enchantresses! I never see a gilded annual-book, without likening it to a small island near Cape Pelorus, in Sicily, whither, by twanging of harps, singing of ravishing melodies, glancing of voluptuous eyes, and the most beautiful fashionable undress in the world, the naughty sirens lured the passing sea-man.* Steer clear of them, ye Artists! pull, pull for your lives, ye crews of Suffolk Street and the Water-Colour gallery! stop your ears, bury your eyes, tie yourselves to the mast, and away with you from the gaudy, smiling 'Books of Beauty'. Land, and you are ruined! Look well among the flowers on yonder beach – it is whitened with the bones of painters.

For my part, I never have a model under seventy, and her with several shawls and a cloak on. By these means the imagination gets fair play, and the morals remain unendangered.

Personalities are odious; but let the British public look at the pictures of the celebrated Mr Shalloon – the moral British public – and say whether our grandchildren (or the grandchildren of the exalted personages whom Mr Shalloon paints) will not have a queer idea of the manners of their grandmammas, as they are represented in the most beautiful, dexterous, captivating water-colour drawings that ever were? Heavenly powers, how they simper and ogle! with what gimcracks of lace, ribbons, ferronnières, smelling-bottles, and what not, is every one of them overloaded! What shoulders, what ringlets, what funny little pug-dogs do they most of them exhibit to us! The days of Lancret and Watteau are lived over again, and the court ladies of the time of Queen Victoria look as moral as the immaculate countesses of the days of Louis Quinze. The last President of the Royal Academy* is answerable for many sins, and many imitators; especially for that gay, sim-pering, meretricious look which he managed to give to every lady who sat to him for her portrait; and I do not know a more curious contrast than that which may be perceived by any one who will examine a collection of his portraits by the side of some by Sir Joshua Reynolds. They seem to have painted different races of people; and when one hears very old gentlemen talking of the superior beauty that existed in their early days (as very old gentlemen, from Nestor downwards, have and will), one is in-clined to believe that there is some truth in what they say; at least, that the men and women under George the Third were far superior to their descendants in the time of George the Fourth.

*Sir Thomas Lawrence.

Whither has it fled – that calm matronly grace, or beautiful virgin innocence, which belonged to the happy women who sat to Sir Joshua? Sir Thomas's ladies are ogling out of their gilt frames, and asking us for admiration; Sir Joshua's sit quiet, in maiden meditation fancy free, not anxious for applause, but sure to command it; a thousand times more lovely in their sedate serenity than Sir Thomas's ladies in their smiles, and their satin ball-dresses.

But this is not the general notion, and the ladies prefer the manner of the modern Artist. Of course, such being the case, the painters must follow the fashion. One could point out half-a-dozen Artists who, at Sir Thomas's death, have seized upon a shred of his somewhat tawdry mantle. There is Carmine, for instance, a man of no small repute, who will stand as the representative of his class.

Carmine has had the usual education of a painter in this country; he can read and write – that is, has spent years drawing the figure – and has made his foreign tour. It may be that he had original talent once, but he has learned to forget this, as the great bar to his success; and must imitate, in order to live. He is among Artists what a dentist is among surgeons – a man who is employed to decorate the human head, and who is paid enormously for so doing. You know one of Carmine's beauties at any exhibition, and see the process by which they are manufactured. He lengthens the noses, widens the foreheads, opens the eyes, and gives them the proper languishing leer; diminishes the mouth, and infallibly tips the ends of it with a pretty smile of his favourite colour. He is a personable, white-handed, bald-headed, middle-aged man now, with that grave blandness of look which one sees in so many prosperous empty-headed people. He has a collection of little stories and court gossip about Lady This, and 'my particular friend, Lord So-and-so', which he lets off in succession to every sitter: indeed, a most bland, irreproachable, gentleman-like man. He gives most patronising advice to young Artists, and makes a point of praising all – not certainly too much, but in a gentleman-like, indifferent, simpering way. This should be the maxim with prosperous persons, who have had to make their way, and wish to keep what they have made. They praise everybody, and are called good-natured, benevolent men. Surely no benevolence is so easy; it simply consists in lying, and smiling, and wishing everybody well. You will get to do so quite naturally at last, and at no expense of truth. At first, when a man has feelings of his own – feelings of love or of anger – this perpetual grin and good-humour is hard to maintain. I used to imagine, when I first knew Carmine, that there were some particular springs in his wig (that glossy, oily, curl crop of chestnut hair) that pulled up his features into a smile, and kept the muscles so fixed for the day. I don't think so now, and should say he grinned, even when he was asleep and his teeth were out; the smile does not lie in the manufacture of the wig, but in the construction of the brain. Claude Carmine has the organ of *don't-care-a-damn-ativeness* wonderfully developed; not that reckless don't-care-a-damn-ativeness which leads a man to disregard all the world, and himself into the bargain. Claude stops before he comes to himself; but beyond that individual member of the Royal Academy, has not a single sympathy for a single human creature. The account of his friends' deaths, woes, misfortunes, or good luck, he receives with equal good-nature; he gives three splendid dinners per annum, Gunter, Dukes, Fortnum and Mason, everything; he dines out the other three hundred and sixty-two days in the year, and was never known to give away a shilling, or to advance, for one half-hour, the forty pounds per quarter wages that he gives to Mr Scumble, who works the backgrounds, limbs, and draperies of his portraits.

He is not a good painter: how should he be; whose painting as it were never goes beyond a whisper, and who would make a general simpering as he looked at an advancing cannon-ball? – but he is not a bad painter, being a keen, respectable man of the world, who has a cool head, and knows what is what. In France, where tigerism used to be the fashion among the painters, I make no doubt Carmine would have let his beard and wig grow, and looked the fiercest of the fierce; but with us a man must be genteel; the perfection of style (in writing and in drawing-rooms) being '*de ne pas en avoir*,' Carmine of course is agreeably vapid. His conversation has accordingly the flavour and briskness of a clear, brilliant, stale bottle of soda-water, – once in five minutes or so, you see rising up to the surface a little bubble – a little tiny shining point of wit, – it rises and explodes feebly, and then dies. With regard to wit, people of fashion (as we are given to understand) are satisfied with a mere *soupçon* of it. Anything more were indecorous; a genteel stomach could not bear it: Carmine knows the exact proportions of the dose, and would not venture to administer to his sitters anything beyond the requisite quantity.

There is a great deal more said here about Carmine – the man, than Carmine – the Artist; but what can be written about the

latter? New ladies in white satin, new Generals in red, new Peers
in scarlet and ermine, and stout Members of Parliament pointing
to inkstands and sheets of letter-paper, with a Turkey-carpet
beneath them, a red curtain above them, a Doric pillar supporting
them, and a tremendous storm of thunder and lightning lowering
and flashing in the background, spring up every year, and take
their due positions 'upon the line' in the Academy, and send their
compliments of hundreds to swell Carmine's heap of Consols. If
he paints Lady Flummery for the tenth time, in the character of
the tenth Muse, what need have we to say anything about it? The
man is a good workman, and will manufacture a decent article at
the best price; but we should no more think of noticing each, than
of writing fresh critiques upon every new coat that Nugee or Stultz
turned out. The papers say, in reference to his picture 'No. 591.
"Full-length portrait of her Grace the Duchess of Doldrum.
Carmine, R.A." Mr Carmine never fails; this work, like all others
by the same artist, is excellent' – or, 'No. 591, &c. The lovely
Duchess of Doldrum has received from Mr Carmine's pencil
ample justice; the *chiar' oscuro* of the picture is perfect; the
likeness admirable; the keeping and colouring have the true
Titianesque gusto; if we might hint a fault, it has the left ear of
the lap-dog a 'little' out of drawing.'

Then, perhaps, comes a criticism which says:–'The Duchess of
Doldrum's picture by Mr Carmine is neither better nor worse than
five hundred other performances of the same artist. It would be
very unjust to say that these portraits are bad, for they have really
a considerable cleverness; but to say that they were good, would
be quite as false; nothing in our eyes was ever further from being
so. Every ten years Mr Carmine exhibits what is called an original
picture of three inches square, but beyond this, nothing original
is to be found in him: as a lad, he copied Reynolds, then Opie,
then Lawrence; then having made a sort of style of his own, he
has copied himself ever since,' &c.

And then the critic goes on to consider the various parts of
Carmine's pictures. In speaking of critics, their peculiar relationship with painters ought not to be forgotten; and as in a former
paper we have seen how a fashionable authoress has her critical
toadies, in like manner has the painter his enemies and friends in
the press; with this difference, probably, that the writer can bear
a fair quantity of abuse without wincing, while the artist not
uncommonly grows mad at such strictures, considers them as

personal matters, inspired by a private feeling of hostility, and hates the critic for life who has ventured to question his judgment in any way. We have said before, poor Academicians, for how many conspiracies are you made to answer! We may add now, poor critics, what black personal animosities are discovered for you, when you happen (right or wrong, but according to your best ideas) to speak the truth! Say that Snooks's picture is badly coloured, –'O heavens!' shrieks Snooks, 'what can I have done to offend this fellow?' Hint that such a figure is badly drawn – and Snooks instantly declares you to be his personal enemy, actuated only by envy and vile pique. My friend Pebbler, himself a famous Artist, is of opinion that the critic should *never* abuse the painter's performances, because, says he, the painter knows much better than any one else what his own faults are, and because you never do him any good. Are men of the brush so obstinate? – very likely: but the public – the public? are we not to do our duty by it too; and, aided by our superior knowledge and genius for the fine arts, point out to it the way it should go? Yes, surely; and as by the efforts of dull or interested critics many bad painters have been palmed off upon the nation as geniuses of the first degree; in like manner, the sagacious and disinterested (like some we could name) have endeavoured to provide this British nation with pure principles of taste – or at least, to prevent them from adopting such as are impure.

Carmine, to be sure, comes in for very little abuse; and, indeed, he deserves but little. He is a fashionable painter, and preserves the golden mediocrity which is necessary for the fashion. Let us bid him good-bye. He lives in a house all to himself, most likely – has a footman, sometimes a carriage; is apt to belong to the 'Athenæum'; and dies universally respected; that is, not one single soul cares for him dead, as he, living, did not care for one single soul.

Then, perhaps, we should mention M'Gilp, or Blather, rising young men, who will fill Carmine's place one of these days, and occupy his house in —, when the fulness of time shall come, and (he borne to a narrow grave in the Harrow Road by the whole mourning Royal Academy) they shall leave their present first floor in Newman Street, and step into his very house and shoes.

There is little difference between the juniors and the seniors; they grin when they are talking of him together, and express a perfect confidence that they can paint a head against Carmine any day – as very likely they can. But until his demise, they are occupied with painting people about the Regent's Park and Russell Square; are very glad to have the chance of a popular clergyman, or a college tutor, or a mayor of Stoke Poges after the Reform Bill. Such characters are commonly mezzotinted afterwards; and the portrait of our esteemed townsman So-and-so, by that talented artist Mr M'Gilp, of London, is favourably noticed by the provincial press, and is to be found over the sideboards of many country gentlemen. If they come up to town, to whom do they go? To M'Gilp, to be sure; and thus, slowly, his practice and his prices increase.

The Academy student is a personage that should not be omitted here; he resembles very much, outwardly, the medical student, and has many of the latter's habits and pleasures. He very often wears a broad-brimmed hat and a fine dirty crimson velvet waistcoat, his hair commonly grows long, and he has braiding to his pantaloons. He works leisurely at the Academy, he loves theatres, billiards, and novels, and has his house-of-call somewhere in the neighbourhood of St. Martin's Lane, where he and his brethren meet and sneer at Royal Academicians. If you ask him what line of art he pursues, he answers with a smile exceedingly supercilious, 'Sir, I am an historical painter'; meaning that he will only condescend to take subjects from Hume, or Robertson, or from the classics – which he knows nothing about. This stage of an historical painter is only preparatory, lasting perhaps from eighteen to five-and-twenty, when the gentleman's madness begins to disappear, and he comes to look at life sternly in the face, and to learn that man shall not live by historical painting alone. Then our friend falls to portrait-painting, or annual-painting, or makes some other such sad compromise with necessity.

He has probably a small patrimony, which defrays the charge of his studies and cheap pleasures during his period of apprenticeship. He makes the *obligé* tour to France and Italy, and returns from those countries with a multitude of spoiled canvases, and a large pair of moustaches, with which he establishes himself in one of the dingy streets of Soho before mentioned. There is poor Pipson, a man of indomitable patience, and undying enthusiasm for his profession. He could paper Exeter Hall with his studies from the life, and with portraits in chalk and oil of French *sapeurs* and Italian brigands, that kindly descend from their mountain-caverns, and quit their murderous occupations, in order to sit to young gentlemen at Rome, at the rate of tenpence an hour. Pipson returns from abroad, establishes himself, has his cards printed, and waits and waits for commissions for great historical pictures. Meanwhile, night after night, he is to be found at his old place in the Academy, copying the old life-guardsman – working, working away – and never advancing one jot. At eighteen, Pipson copied statues and life-guardsmen to admiration; at five-and-thirty he can make admirable drawings of life-guardsmen and statues. Beyond this he never goes; year after year his historical picture is returned to him by the envious Academicians, and he grows old, and his little patrimony is long since spent; and he earns nothing himself. How does he support hope and life? – that is the wonder. No one knows until he tries (which God forbid he should!) upon what a small matter hope and life can be supported. Our poor fellow lives on from year to year in a miraculous way; tolerably cheerful in the midst of his semi-starvation, and wonderfully confident about next year, in spite of the failures of the last twenty-five. Let us thank God for imparting to us, poor weak mortals, the inestimable blessing of *vanity*. How many half-witted votaries of the arts – poets, painters, actors, musicians – live upon this food, and scarcely any other! If the delusion were to drop from Pipson's eyes, and he should see himself as he is – if some malevolent genius were to mingle with his feeble brains one fatal particle of common sense, – he would just walk off Waterloo Bridge, and abjure poverty, incapacity, cold lodgings, unpaid baker's bills, ragged elbows, and deferred hopes, at once and for ever.

We do not mean to depreciate the profession of historical painting, but simply to warn youth against it as dangerous and unprofitable. It is as if a young fellow should say, 'I will be a Raffaelle or a Titian – a Milton or a Shakespeare,' and if he will count up how many people have lived since the world began, and how many there have been of the Raffaelle or Shakespeare sort, he can calculate to a nicety what are the chances in his favour. Even successful historical painters, what are they? – in a worldly point of view, they mostly inhabit the second floor, or have great desolate studios in back premises, whither life-guardsmen, old-clothesmen, blackamoors, and other 'properties' are conducted, to figure at full length as Roman conquerors, Jewish high-priests, or Othellos on canvas. Then there are gay, smart, water-colour painters, – a flourishing and pleasant trade. Then there are shabby, fierce-looking geniuses, in ringlets, and all but rags, who paint, and whose pictures are never sold, and who vow they are the objects of some general and scoundrelly conspiracy. There are landscape-painters, who travel to the uttermost ends of the earth and brave heat and cold, to bring to the greedy British public views of Cairo, Calcutta, St Petersburg, Timbuctoo. You see English artists under the shadow of the Pyramids, making sketches of the Copts, perched on the backs of dromedaries, accompanying a caravan across the desert, or getting materials for an annual in Iceland or Siberia. What genius and what energy do not they all exhibit – these men, whose profession, in this wise country of ours, is scarcely considered as liberal!

If we read the works of the Reverend Dr Lempriere, Monsieur Winckelmann, Professor Plato, and others who have written concerning the musty old Grecians, we shall find that the Artists of those barbarous times meddled with all sorts of trades besides their own, and dabbled in fighting, philosophy, metaphysics, both Scotch and German, politics, music, and the deuce knows what. A rambling sculptor, who used to go about giving lectures in those days, Socrates by name, declared that the wisest of men in his time were artists. This Plato, before mentioned, went through a regular course of drawing, figure and landscape, black-lead, chalk, with or without stump, sepia, water-colour, and oils. Was there ever such absurdity known? Among these benighted heathens, painters were the most accomplished gentlemen, – and the most accomplished gentlemen were painters; the former would make you a speech, or read you a dissertation on Kant, or lead you a regiment – with the very best statesman, philosopher, or soldier in Athens. And they had the folly to say, that by thus busying and accomplishing themselves in all manly studies, they were advancing eminently in their own peculiar one. What was the consequence? Why, that fellow Socrates not only made a miserable fifth-rate sculptor, but was actually hanged for treason.

And serve him right. Do *our* young artists study anything beyond the proper way of cutting a pencil, or drawing a model? Do you hear of *them* hard at work over books, and bothering their brains with musty learning? Not they, forsooth: we understand the doctrine of division of labour, and each man sticks to his trade. Artists do not meddle with the pursuits of the rest of the world; and, in revenge, the rest of the world does not meddle with Artists. Fancy an Artist being a senior wrangler or a politician; and on the other hand, fancy a real gentleman turned painter! No, no; ranks are defined. A real gentleman may get money by the law, or by wearing a red coat and fighting, or a black one and preaching; but that he should sell himself to *Art* – forbid it, heaven! And do not let your ladyship on reading this cry, 'Stuff! – stupid envy, rank republicanism, – an artist *is* a gentleman.' Madam, would you like to see your son, the Honourable Fitzroy Plantagenet, a painter? You would die sooner; the escutcheon of the Smigsmags would be blotted for ever, if Plantagenet ever ventured to make a mercantile use of a bladder of paint.

Time was – some hundred years back – when writers lived in Grub Street, and poor ragged Johnson shrunk behind a screen in Cave's parlour – that the author's trade was considered a very mean one; which a gentleman of family could not take up but as an amateur. This absurdity is pretty nearly worn out now, and I do humbly hope and pray for the day when the other shall likewise disappear. If there be any nobleman with a talent that way, why – why don't we see him among the R.A.'s?

501	The Schoolmaster. Sketch taken abroad	Brum, Henry, Lord, *R.A. F.R.S. S.A. of the National Institute of France.*
502	View of the Artist's residence at Windsor	Maconkey, Right Honourable T.B.
503	Murder of the Babes in the Tower	Rustle, Lord J. Pill, Right Honourable Sir Robert.
504	A little Agitation	O Carrol, Daniel, M.R.I.A.

Fancy, I say, such names as these figuring in the catalogue of the Academy: and why should they not? The real glorious days of the art (which wants equality and not patronage) will revive then. Patronage – a plague on the word! – it implies inferiority; and in the name of all that is sensible, why is a respectable country gentleman, or a city attorney's lady, or any person of any rank, however exalted, to 'patronise' an Artist!

There are some who sigh for the past times, when magnificent, swaggering Peter Paul Rubens (who himself patronised a queen) rode abroad with a score of gentlemen in his train, and a purse-bearer to scatter ducats; and who love to think how he was made an English knight and a Spanish grandee, and went of embassies as if he had been a born marquis. Sweet it is to remember, too, that Sir Antony Vandyck, K.B., actually married out of the peerage: and that when Titian dropped his mahlstick, the Emperor Charles V picked it up (O gods! what heroic self-devotion)

– picked it up, saying, 'I can make fifty dukes, but not one Titian'.
Nay, was not the Pope of Rome going to make Raffaelle a
Cardinal – and were not these golden days?

Let us say at once, 'No.' The very fuss made about cert in
painters in the sixteenth and seventeenth centuries shows that the
body of artists had no rank or position in the world. They hung
upon single patrons: and every man who holds his place by such
a tenure, must feel himself an inferior, more or less. The times are
changing now, and as authors are no longer compelled to send
their works abroad under the guardianship of a great man and a
slavish dedication, painters, too, are beginning to deal directly
with the public. Who are the great picture-buyers now? – the
engravers and their employers, the people – 'the only source of
legitimate power,' as they say after dinner. A fig then for
Cardinal's hats! were Mr O'Connell in power to-morrow, let us
hope he would not give one, not even a paltry bishopric *in
partibus*, to the best painter in the Academy. What need have they
of honours out of the profession? Why are they to be be-knighted
like a parcel of aldermen? – for my part, I solemnly declare, that
I will take nothing under a peerage, after the exhibition of my
great picture, and don't see, if painters *must* have titles conferred
upon them for eminent services, why the Marquis of Mulready or
the Earl of Landseer should not sit in the House as well as any
law or soldier lord.

The truth to be elicited from this little digressive dissertation is
this painful one – that young Artists are not generally as well
instructed as they should be; and let the Royal Academy look to
it, and give some sound courses of lectures to their pupils on
literature and history, as well as on anatomy, or light and shade.

MEMORIALS OF
GOURMANDISING

In a letter to Oliver Yorke, Esquire, by M. A. Titmarsh

PARIS, *May* 1841

Sir – The man who makes the best salads in London, and whom, therefore, we have facetiously called Sultan Saladin – a man who is conspicuous for his love and practice of all the polite arts – music, to wit, architecture, painting, and cookery – once took the humble personage who writes this into his library, and laid before me two or three volumes of manuscript year-books, such as, since he began to travel and to observe, he has been in the habit of keeping.

Every night, in the course of his rambles, his highness the sultan (indeed, his port is sublime, as, for the matter of that, are all the wines in his cellar) sets down with an iron pen, and in the neatest handwriting in the world, the events and observations of the day; with the same iron pen he illuminates the leaf of his journal by the most faithful and delightful sketches of the scenery which he has witnessed in the course of the four-and-twenty hours; and if he has dined at an inn or restaurant, gasthaus, posada, albergo, or what not, invariably inserts into his logbook the bill of fare. The sultan leads a jolly life – a tall stalwart man, who every day about six o'clock in London and Paris, at two in Italy, in Germany and Belgium at an hour after noon, feels the noble calls of hunger agitating his lordly bosom (or its neighbourhood, that is), and replies to the call by a good dinner. Ah! it is wonderful to think how the healthy and philosophic mind can accommodate itself in all cases to the varying circumstances of the time – how, in its travels through the world, the liberal and cosmopolite stomach recognises the national dinner-hour! Depend upon it that, in all countries, nature has wisely ordained and suited to their exigencies *the dishes of a people*. I mean to say that olla podrida* is good in Spain (though a plateful of it, eaten in Paris, once made me so dreadfully ill that it is a mercy I was spared ever to eat another dinner); I mean to say, and have proved it, that sauerkraut is good in Germany; and I make no doubt that whale's blubber is a very tolerable dish in Kamtschatka, though I have never visited the country. Cannibalism in the South Seas, and sheepsheadism in Scotland, are the only practices that one cannot, perhaps, reconcile with this rule – at least, whatever a man's private opinions may be, the decencies of society oblige him to eschew the expression of them upon subjects which the national prejudice has precluded from free discussion.

Well, after looking through three or four of Saladin's volumes, I grew so charmed with them, that I used to come back every day and study them. I declare there are bills of fare in those books over which I have cried; and the reading of them, especially about an hour before dinner, has made me so ferociously hungry, that, in the first place, the sultan (a kind-hearted generous man, as every man is who loves his meals) could not help inviting me to take potluck with him; and, secondly, I could eat twice as much as upon common occasions, though my appetite is always good.

Lying awake, then, of nights, or wandering solitary abroad on wide commons, or by the side of silent rivers, or at church when Doctor Snufflem was preaching his favourite sermon, or stretched on the flat of my back smoking a cigar at the club when X was talking of the corn-laws, or Y was describing that famous run they had with the Z hounds – at all periods, I say, favourable to self-examination, those bills of fare have come into my mind, and often and often I have thought them over. 'Titmarsh,' I have said to myself, 'if ever you travel again, do as the sultan has done, and *keep your dinner-bills*. They are always pleasant to look over; they always will recall happy hours and actions, be you ever so hard pushed for a dinner, and fain to put up with an onion and a crust: of the past fate cannot deprive you. Yesterday is the philosopher's property; and by thinking of it, and using it to advantage, he may gaily go through to-morrow, doubtful and dismal though it be. Try this lamb stuffed with pistachio-nuts; another handful of this pillau. Ho, you rascals! bring round the sherbet there, and never spare the jars of wine – 'tis true Persian, on the honour of a Barmecide!* Is not that dinner in the 'Arabian Nights' a right good dinner? Would you have had Bedreddin to refuse and turn sulky at the windy repast, or to sit down grinning in the face of his grave entertainer, and gaily take what came? Remember what came of the honest fellow's philosophy. He slapped the grim old prince in the face; and the grim old prince, who had invited him but to laugh at him, did presently order a real and substantial repast to be set before him – great pyramids of smoking rice and pillau (a good pillau is one of the best dishes in the world), savoury kids, snow-cooled sherbets, luscious wine of Schiraz; with an accompaniment of moon-faced beauties from the harem, no doubt, dancing, singing, and smiling in the most ravishing manner. Thus should we, my dear friends, laugh at Fate's beard, as we confront him – thus should we, if the old monster be insolent, fall to and box his ears. He has a spice of humour in his composition; and be sure he will be tickled by such conduct.

Some months ago, when the expectation of war between England and France grew to be so strong, and there was such a talk of mobilising national guards, and arming three or four hundred thousand more French soldiers – when such ferocious yells of hatred against perfidious Albion were uttered by the liberal French press, that I did really believe the rupture between the two countries was about immediately to take place; being seriously alarmed, I set off for Paris at once. My good sir, what could we do without our Paris? I came here first in 1815 (when the Duke and I were a good deal remarked by the inhabitants); I proposed but to stay a week; stopped three months, and have returned every year since. There is something fatal in the place – a charm about it – a wicked one very likely – but it acts on us all; and perpetually the old Paris man comes hieing back to his quarters again, and is to be found, as usual, sunning himself in the Rue de la Paix. Painters, princes, gourmands, officers on half-pay – serious old ladies even acknowledge the attraction of the place – are more at ease here than in any other place in Europe; and back they come, and are to be found sooner or later occupying their old haunts.

My darling city improves, too, with each visit, and has some new palace, or church, or statue, or other gimcrack, to greet your eyes withal. A few years since, and lo! on the column of the Place Vendôme, instead of the shabby tri-coloured rag, shone the bronze statue of Napoleon. Then came the famous triumphal arch; a noble building indeed! – how stately and white, and beautiful and strong, it seems to dominate over the whole city! Next was the obelisk; a huge bustle and festival being made to welcome it to the city. Then came the fair asphaltum terraces round about the obelisk; then the fountains to decorate the terraces. I have scarcely been twelve months absent, and behold they have gilded all the Naiads and Tritons; they have clapped a huge fountain in the very midst of the Champs Elysées – a great, glittering, frothing fountain, that to the poetic eye looks like an enormous shaving-brush; and all down the avenue they have placed hundreds of gilded flaring gas-lamps, that make this gayest walk in the world look gayer still than ever. But a truce to such descriptions, which might carry one far, very far, from the object proposed in this paper.

I simply wish to introduce to public notice a brief dinner-journal. It has been written with the utmost honesty and simplicity of purpose; and exhibits a picture or table of the development of the human mind under a series of gastronomic experiments, diversified in their nature, and diversified, consequently, in their effects. A man in London has not, for the most part, the opportunity to make these experiments. You are a family man, let us presume, and you live in that metropolis for half a century. You have on Sunday, say, a leg of mutton and potatoes for dinner. On Monday you have cold mutton and potatoes. On Tuesday, hashed mutton and potatoes; the hashed mutton being flavoured with little damp triangular pieces of toast, which always surrounded that charming dish. Well, on Wednesday, the mutton ended, you have beef: the beef undergoes the same alternations of cookery, and disappears. Your life presents a succession of joints, varied every now and then by a bit of fish and some poultry. You drink three glasses of a brandyfied liquor called sherry at dinner; your excellent lady imbibes one. When she has had her glass of port after dinner, she goes up-stairs with the children, and you fall asleep in your arm-chair. Some of the most pure and precious enjoyments of life are unknown to you. You eat and drink, but you do not know the *art* of eating and drinking; nay, most probably you despise those who do. 'Give me a slice of meat,' say you, very likely, 'and a fig for your gourmands.' You fancy it is very virtuous and manly all this. Nonsense, my good sir; you are indifferent because you are ignorant, because your life is passed in a narrow circle of ideas, and because you are bigotedly blind and pompously callous to the beauties and excellences beyond you.

Sir, *respect your dinner;* idolise it, enjoy it properly. You will be by many hours in the week, many weeks in the year, and many years in your life the happier if you do.

Don't tell us that it is not worthy of a man. All a man's senses are worthy of employment, and should be cultivated as a duty. The senses are the arts. What glorious feasts does Nature prepare for your eye in animal form, in landscape, and painting! Are you to put out your eyes and not see? What royal dishes of melody does her bounty provide for you in the shape of poetry, music, whether windy or wiry, notes of the human voice, or ravishing song of birds! Are you to stuff your ears with cotton, and vow that the sense of hearing is unmanly? – you obstinate dolt you! No, surely; nor must you be so absurd as to fancy that the art of eating is in any way less worthy than the other two. You like your dinner, man; never be ashamed to say so. If you don't like your victuals, pass on to the next article; but remember that every man who has been worth a fig in this world, as poet, painter, or musician, has had a good appetite and a good taste. Ah, what a poet Byron would have been had he taken his meals properly, and allowed himself to grow fat – if nature intended him to grow fat – and not have physicked his intellect with wretched opium pills and acrid vinegar, that sent his principles to sleep, and turned his feelings sour! If that man had respected his dinner, he never would have written 'Don Juan'.

Allons donc! enough sermonising; let us sit down and fall to at once.

I dined soon after my arrival at a very pleasant Paris club, where daily is provided a dinner for ten persons, that is universally reported to be excellent. Five men in England would have consumed the same amount of victuals, as you will see by the bill of fare:

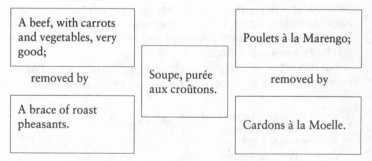

A beef, with carrots and vegetables, very good;	Soupe, purée aux croûtons.	Poulets à la Marengo;
removed by		removed by
A brace of roast pheasants.		Cardons à la Moelle.

Dessert of cheese, pears and Fontainebleau grapes.
Bordeaux red, and excellent Chablis at discretion.

This dinner was very nicely served. A venerable *maître d'hôtel* in black cutting up neatly the dishes on a trencher at the side-table, and several waiters attending in green coats, red plush tights, and their hair curled. There was a great quantity of light in the room; some handsome pieces of plated ware; the pheasants came in with their tails to their backs; and the smart waiters, with their hair dressed and parted down the middle, gave a pleasant, lively, stylish appearance to the whole affair.

Now I certainly dined (by the way, I must not forget to mention that we had with the beef some boiled kidney potatoes, very neatly dished up in a napkin) – I certainly dined, I say; and half an hour afterwards felt, perhaps, more at my ease than I should have done had I consulted my own inclinations, and devoured twice the quantity that on this occasion came to my share. But I would rather, as a man not caring for appearances, dine, as a general rule, off a beef-steak for two at the Café Foy, than sit down to take a tenth part of such a meal every day. There was only one man at the table besides your humble servant who did not put water into his wine; and he – I mean the other – was observed by his friends, who exclaimed, 'Comment! vous buvez sec,' as if to do so was a wonder. The consequence was, that half-a-dozen bottles of wine served for the whole ten of us; and the guests, having dispatched their dinner in an hour, skipped lightly away from it, did not stay to ruminate, and to feel uneasy, and to fiddle about the last and penultimate waistcoat button, as we do after a house-dinner at an English club. What was it that made the charm of this dinner? – for pleasant it was. It was the neat and comfortable manner in which it was served; the pheasant-tails had a considerable effect; that snowy napkin coquettishly arranged round the kidneys gave them a *distingué* air; the light and glittering service gave an appearance of plenty and hospitality that sent everybody away contented.

I put down this dinner just to show English and Scotch housekeepers what may be done, and for what price. Say,

		s.	d.
Soup and fresh bread, } Beef and carrots	prime cost	2	6
Fowls and sauce		3	6
Pheasants (hens)		5	0
Grapes, pears, cheese, vegetables		3	0
		14	0

For fifteen pence *par tête* a company of ten persons may have a dinner set before them – nay, and be made to fancy that they dine well, provided the service is handsomely arranged, that you have a good stock of side-dishes, &c., in your plate-chest, and don't spare the spermaceti.*

As for the wine, that depends on yourself. Always be crying out to your friends, 'Mr So-and-so, I don't drink myself, but pray pass the bottle. Tomkins, my boy, help your neighbour, and never mind me. What! Hopkins, are there two of us on the doctor's list? Pass the wine; *Smith* I'm sure won't refuse it;' and so on. A very good plan is to have the butler (or the fellow in the white waistcoat who 'behaves as sich') pour out the wine when wanted (in half-glasses, of course), and to make a deuced great noise and shouting, 'John, John, why the devil, sir, don't you help Mr Simkins to another glass of wine?' If you point out Simkins once or twice in this way, depend upon it, *he* won't drink a great quantity of your liquor. You may thus keep your friends from being dangerous, by a thousand innocent manœuvres; and, as I have said before, you may very probably make them believe that they have had a famous dinner. There was only one man in our company of ten the other day who ever thought he had not dined; and what was he? a foreigner, – a man of a discontented inquiring spirit, always carping at things, and never satisfied.

Well, next day I dined *au cinquième* with a family (of Irish extraction, by the way), and what do you think was our dinner for six persons? Why, simply,

> Nine dozen Ostend oysters;
> Soup à la mulligatawny;
> Boiled turkey, with celery sauce;
> Saddle of mutton rôti.
> Removes: Plompouding; croûte de macaroni.
> Vin: Beaune ordinaire, volnay, bordeaux, champagne,
>   eau chaude, cognac.

I forget the dessert. Alas! in moments of prosperity and plenty, one is often forgetful: I remember the dessert at the Cercle well enough.

A person whom they call in this country an *illustration littéraire* – the editor of a newspaper, in fact – with a very pretty wife, were of the party, and looked at the dinner with a great deal of good-humoured superiority. I declare, upon my honour, that I helped both the illustration and his lady twice to saddle of mutton; and as for the turkey and celery sauce, you should have seen how our host dispensed it to them! They ate the oysters, they ate the soup ('Diable! mais il est poivré!' said the illustration, with tears in his eyes), they ate the turkey, they ate the mutton, they ate the pudding; and what did our hostess say? Why, casting down her eyes gently, and with the modestest air in the world, she said, –'There is such a beautiful piece of cold beef in the larder; do somebody ask for a little slice of it.'

Heaven bless her for that speech! I loved and respected her for it; it brought the tears to my eyes. A man who could sneer at such a sentiment could have neither heart nor good breeding. Don't you see that it shows

> Simplicity,
> Modesty,
> Hospitality?

Put these against

> Waiters with their hair curled,
> Pheasants roasted with their tails on,
> A dozen spermaceti candles.

Add them up, I say, oh candid reader, and answer in the sum of human happiness, which of the two accounts makes the better figure?

I declare, I know few things more affecting than that little question about the cold beef; and considering calmly our national characteristics, balancing in the scale of quiet thought our defects and our merits, and daily more inclined to believe that there is something in the race of Britons which renders them usually superior to the French family. This is but one of the traits of English character that has been occasioned by the use of roast beef.

It is an immense question, that of diet. Look at the two bills of fare just set down; the relative consumption of ten animals and six. What a profound physical and moral difference may we trace here! How distinct, from the cradle upwards, must have been the thoughts, feelings, education of the parties who ordered those two dinners! It is a fact which does not admit of a question, that the French are beginning, since so many English have come among them, to use beef much more profusely. Everybody at the restaurateur's orders beefsteak and pommes. Will the national character slowly undergo a change under the influence of this dish? Will the French be more simple? broader in the shoulders? less inclined to brag about military glory and such humbug? All this in the dark vista of futurity the spectator may fancy is visible to him, and the philanthropist cannot but applaud the change. This brings me naturally to the consideration of the manner of dressing beefsteaks in this country, and of the merit of that manner.

I dined on a Saturday at the Café Foy, on the Boulevard, in a private room, with a friend. We had

> Potage julienne, with a little purée in it;
> Two entrecôtes aux épinards;
> One perdreau truffé;
> One fromage roquefort;
> A bottle of nuits with the beef;
> A bottle of sauterne with the partridge.

And perhaps a glass of punch, with a cigar, afterwards: but that is neither here nor there. The insertion of the purée into the julienne was not of my recommending; and if this junction is effected at all, the operation should be performed with the greatest care. If you put too much purée, both soups are infallibly spoiled. A much better plan it is to have your julienne by itself, though I will not enlarge on this point, as the excellent friend with whom I dined may chance to see this notice, and may be hurt at the renewal in print of a dispute which caused a good deal of pain to both of us. By the way, we had half-a-dozen sardines while the dinner was getting ready, eating them with delicious bread and butter, for which this place is famous. Then followed the soup. Why the deuce *would* he have the pu – but never mind. After the soup, we had what I do not hesitate to call the very best beefsteak I ever ate in my life. By the shade of Heliogabalus!* as I write about it now, a week after I have eaten it, the old, rich, sweet, piquant, juicy taste comes smacking on my lips again; and I feel something of that exquisite sensation I then had. I am ashamed of the delight which the eating of that piece of meat caused me. G and I had quarrelled about the soup (I said so, and don't wish to return to the subject); but when we began on the steak, we looked at each other, and loved each other. We did not speak – our hearts were too full for that; but we took a bit, and laid down our forks, and looked at one another, and understood each other. There were no two individuals on this wide earth – no two lovers billing in the shade – no mother clasping baby to her heart, more supremely happy than we. Every now and then, we had a glass of honest, firm, generous Burgundy, that nobly supported the meat. As you may fancy, we did not leave a single morsel of the steak; but when it was done, we put bits of bread into the silver dish, and wistfully sopped up the gravy. I suppose I shall never in this world taste anything so good again. But what then? What if I *did* like it excessively? Was my liking unjust or unmanly? Is my regret now puling or unworthy? No. 'Laudo manentem!' as Titmouse says. When it is eaten, I resign myself, and can eat a two-franc dinner at Richard's without ill-humour and without a pang.

Any dispute about the relative excellence of the beefsteak cut from the filet, as is usual in France, and of the *entrecôte*, must henceforth be idle and absurd. Whenever, my dear young friend, you go to Paris, call at once for the *entrecôte*; the filet in comparison to it is a poor *fade* lady's meat. What folly, by the way, is that in England which induces us to attach an estimation to the part of the sirloin that is called the Sunday side, – poor, tender, stringy stuff, not comparable to the manly meat on the other side, handsomely garnished with crisp fat, and with a layer of horn! Give the Sunday side to misses and ladies' maids, for men be the Monday's side, or, better still, a thousand times more succulent and full of flavour – the *ribs of beef*. This is the meat I would eat were I going to do battle with any mortal foe. Fancy a hundred thousand Englishmen, after a meal of stalwart beef ribs, encountering a hundred thousand Frenchmen who had partaken of a trifling collation of soup, turnips, carrots, onions, and Gruyère cheese. Would it be manly to engage at such odds? I say, no.

Passing by Véry's one day, I saw a cadaverous cook with a spatula, thumping a poor beefsteak with all his might. This is not only a horrible cruelty, but an error. They not only beat the beef, moreover, but they soak it in oil. Absurd, disgusting barbarity! Beef so beaten loses its natural spirit; it is too noble for corporal punishment. You may by these tortures and artifices make it soft and greasy, but tender and juicy never.

The landlord of the Café Foy (I have received no sort of consideration from him) knows this truth full well, and follows the simple honest plan; first, to have good meat, and next to hang it a long time. I have instructed him how to do the steaks to a turn; not raw, horribly livid and blue in the midst, as I have seen great flaps of meat (what a shame to think of our fine meat being so treated!), but *cooked* all the way through. Go to the Café Foy then, ask for a *Beefsteak à la Titmarsh*, and you will see what a dish will be set before you. I have dwelt upon this point at too much length, perhaps, for some of my readers; but it can't be helped. The truth is, beef is my weakness; and I do declare, that I derive more positive enjoyment from the simple viand than from any concoction whatever in the whole cook's cyclopædia.

Always drink red wine with beefsteaks; port, if possible; if not, Burgundy, of not too high a flavour – good Beaune, say. This fact, which is very likely not known to many persons who, forsooth, are too magnificent to care about their meat and drink – this simple fact I take to be worth the whole price I shall get for this article.

But to return to dinner. We were left, I think, G and I, sopping up the gravy with bits of bread, and declaring that no power on earth could induce us to eat a morsel more that day. At one time, we thought of countermanding the perdreau aux truffes, that to my certain knowledge had been betruffed five days before.

Poor blind mortals that we were; ungrateful to our appetites, needlessly mistrustful and cowardly. A man may do what he dares; nor does he know, until he tries, what the honest appetite will bear. We were kept waiting between the steak and the partridge some ten minutes or so. For the first two or three minutes we lay back in our chairs quite exhausted indeed. Then we began to fiddle with a dish of toothpicks, for want of anything more savoury; then we looked out of the window; then G got in a rage, rang the bell violently, and asked, 'Pourquoi diable nous fait-on attendre si longtemps?' The waiter grinned. He is a nice good-humoured fellow, Auguste; and I heartily trust that some reader of this may give him a five-franc piece for my sake. Auguste grinned and disappeared.

Presently, we were aware of an odour gradually coming towards us, something musky, fiery, savoury, mysterious – a hot drowsy smell, that lulls the senses, and yet inflames them – the truffes were coming! Yonder they lie, caverned under the full bosom of the red-legged bird. My hand trembled as, after a little pause, I cut the animal in two. G said I did not give him his share of the truffes; I don't believe I did. I spilled some salt into my plate, and a little cayenne pepper – very little: we began, as far as I can remember, the following conversation:

Gustavus. Chop, chop, chop.

Michael Angelo. Globloblob.

G. Gobble.

M.A. Obble.

G. Here's a big one.

M.A. Hobgob. What wine shall we have? I should like some champagne.

G. It's bad here. Have some Sauterne.

M.A. Very well. Hobgobglobglob, &c.

Auguste (opening the Sauterne). Cloo-oo-oo-oop! The cork is out; he pours it into the glass, glock, glock, glock.

Nothing more took place in the way of talk. The poor little partridge was soon a heap of bones – a very little heap. A trufflesque odour was left in the room, but only an odour. Presently, the cheese was brought: the amber Sauterne flask had turned of a sickly green hue; nothing, save half a glass of sediment at the bottom, remained to tell of the light and social spirit that had but one half-hour before inhabited the flask. Darkness fell upon our little chamber; the men in the street began crying, '*Messager! Journal du Soir!*' The bright moon rose glittering over the tiles of the Rue Louis le Grand, opposite, illuminating two glasses of punch that two gentlemen in a small room of the Café Foy did ever and anon raise to their lips. Both were silent; both happy; both were smoking cigars – for both knew that the soothing plant of Cuba is sweeter to the philosopher after dinner than the prattle of all the women in the world. Women – pshaw! The man who, after dinner – after a good dinner – can think about driving home, and shaving himself by candlelight, and enduring a damp shirt, and a pair of tight glazed pumps to show his cobweb stockings and set his feet in a flame; and, having undergone all this, can get into a cold cab, and drive off to No. 222 Harley Street, where Mrs Mortimer Smith is at home; where you take off your cloak in a damp dark back parlour, called Mr Smith's study, and containing, when you arrive, twenty-four ladies' cloaks and tippets, fourteen hats, two pairs of clogs (belonging to two gentlemen of the Middle Temple, who walk for economy, and think dancing at Mrs Mortimer Smith's the height of enjoyment); – the man who can do all this, and walk, gracefully smiling, into Mrs Smith's drawing rooms, where the brown holland bags have been re-

moved from the chandeliers; a man from Kirkman's is thumping
on the piano, and Mrs Smith is standing simpering in the middle
of the room, dressed in red, with a bird of paradise in her turban,
a tremulous fan in one hand, and the other clutching hold of her
little fat gold watch and seals; – the man who, after making his
bow to Mrs Smith, can advance to Miss Jones, in blue crape, and
lead her to a place among six other pairs of solemn-looking
persons, and whisper *fadaises* to her (at which she cries, 'Oh fie,
you naughty man! how can you?') and look at Miss Smith's red
shoulders struggling out of her gown, and her mottled elbows that
a pair of crumpled kid gloves leave in a state of delicious nature;
and, after having gone through certain mysterious quadrille figures with her, lead her back to her mamma, who has just seized
a third glass of muddy negus* from the black footman; – the man
who can do all this may do it, and go hang, for me! And many
such men there be, my Gustavus, in yonder dusky London city.
Be it ours, my dear friend, when the day's labour and repast are
done, to lie and ruminate calmly; to watch the bland cigar smoke
as it rises gently ceiling-wards; to be idle in body as well as mind;
not to kick our heels madly in quadrilles, and puff and pant in
senseless gallopades: let us appreciate the joys of idleness; let us
give a loose to silence; and having enjoyed this, the best dessert
after a goodly dinner, at close of eve, saunter slowly home.

As the dinner above described drew no less than three five-franc
pieces out of my purse, I determined to economise for the next
few days, and either to be invited out to dinner, or else to partake
of some repast at a small charge, such as one may have here. I had
on the day succeeding the truffled partridge a dinner for a shilling,
viz.:

> Bifsteck aux pommes (heu quantum mutatus ab illo!)
> Galantine de volaille
> Fromage de Gruyère.
> Demi-bouteille de vin très-vieux de Mâcon ou Chablis,
> Pain à discrétion.

This dinner, my young friend, was taken about half-past two
o'clock in the day, and was, in fact, a breakfast – a breakfast taken
at a two-franc house, in the Rue Haute Vivienne; it was certainly
a sufficient dinner: I certainly was not hungry for all the rest of
the day. Nay, the wine was decently good, as almost all wine is

in the morning, if one had the courage or the power to drink it.
You see many honest English families marching into these two-
franc eating-houses, at five o'clock, and fancy they dine in great
luxury. Returning to England, however, they inform their friends
that the meat in France is not good; that the fowls are very small,
and black; the kidneys very tough; the partridges and fruit have
no taste in them, and the soup is execrably thin. A dinner at
Williams's, in the Old Bailey, is better than the best of these; and
therefore had the English Cockney better remain at Williams's
than judge the great nation so falsely.

The worst of these two-franc establishments is a horrid air of
shabby elegance which distinguishes them. At some of them, they
will go the length of changing your knife and fork with every dish;
they have grand chimney-glasses, and a fine lady at the counter,
and fine arabesque paintings on the walls; they give you your soup
in a battered dish of plated ware, which has served its best time,
most likely, in a first-rate establishment, and comes here to *étaler*
its second-hand splendour amongst amateurs of a lower grade. I
fancy the very meat that is served to you has undergone the same
degradation, and that some of the mouldy cutlets that are offered
to the two-franc epicures lay once plump and juicy in Véry's
larder. Much better is the sanded floor and the iron fork! Homely
neatness is the charm of poverty: elegance should belong to wealth
alone. There is a very decent place where you dine for thirty-two
sous in the Passage Choiseul. You get your soup in china bowls;
they don't change your knife and fork, but they give you very fit
portions of meat and potatoes, and mayhap a herring with
mustard sauce, a dish of apple fritters, a dessert of stewed prunes,
and a pint of drinkable wine, as I have proved only yesterday.

After two such banyan days*, I allowed myself a little feasting;
and as nobody persisted in asking me to dinner, I went off to the
'Trois Frères' by myself, and dined in that excellent company.

I would recommend a man who is going to dine by himself here,
to reflect well before he orders soup for dinner.

My notion is, that you eat as much after soup as without it, but
you *don't eat with the same appetite*.

Especially if you are a healthy man, as I am – deuced hungry at
five o'clock. My appetite runs away with me; and if I order soup
(which is always enough for two), I invariably swallow the whole
of it; and the greater portion of my *petit pain*, too, before my
second dish arrives.

The best part of a pint of julienne, or purée à la Condé, is very well for a man who has only one dish besides to devour; but not for you and me, who like our fish and our *rôti* of game or meat as well.

Oysters you may eat. They do, for a fact, prepare one to go through the rest of a dinner properly. Lemon and cayenne pepper is the word, depend on it, and a glass of white wine braces you up for what is to follow.

French restaurateur dinners are intended, however, for two people, at least; still better for three; and require a good deal of thought before you can arrange them for one.

Here, for instance, is a recent *menu*:

Trois Fréres Provençaux

	f.	c.
Pain	0	25
Beaune première	3	0
Purée à la Créci	0	75
Turbot aux capres	1	75
Quart poule aux truffes	2	25
Champignons à la Provençale	1	25
Gelée aux pommes	1	25
Cognac	0	30
	10	80

A heavy bill for a single man; and a heavy dinner, too; for I have said before I have a great appetite, and when a thing is put before me I eat it. At Brussels I once ate fourteen dishes; and have seen a lady, with whom I was in love, at the table of a German grand duke, eat seventeen dishes. This is a positive, though disgusting fact. Up to the first twelve dishes she had a very good chance of becoming Mrs Titmarsh, but I have lost sight of her since.

Well, then, I say to you, if you have self-command enough to send away half your soup, order some; but you are a poor creature if you do, after all. If you are a man, and have *not* that self-command, don't have any. The Frenchman cannot live without it, but I say to you that you are better than a Frenchman. I would lay even money that you who are reading this are more than five feet seven in height, and weigh eleven stone; while a Frenchman is five feet four, and does not weight nine. The Frenchman has after his soup a dish of vegetables, where you have one of meat. You are a different and superior animal – a French-beating animal (the history of hundreds of years has shown you to be so); you must have, to keep up that superior weight and sinew, which is the secret of your superiority – as for public institutions, bah! – you must have, I say, simpler, stronger, more succulent food.

Eschew the soup, then, and have the fish up at once. It is the best to begin with fish, if you like it, as every epicure and honest man should, simply boiled or fried in the English fashion, and not tortured and bullied with oil, onions, wine, and herbs, as in Paris it is frequently done.

Turbot with lobster-sauce is too much; turbot à la Hollandaise vulgar; sliced potatoes swimming in melted butter are a mean concomitant for a noble, simple, liberal fish; turbot with capers is the thing. The brisk little capers relieve the dulness of the turbot; the melted butter is rich, bland, and calm – it *should be*, that is to say; not that vapid watery mixture that I see in London; not oiled butter, as the Hollanders have it, but melted, with plenty of thickening matter: I don't know how to do it, but I know it when it is good.

They melt butter well at the 'Rocher de Cancale,' and at the 'Frères'.

Well, this turbot was very good; not so well, of course, as one gets it in London, and dried rather in the boiling; which can't be helped, unless you are a Lucullus or a Cambacérès of a man, and can afford to order one for yourself. This *grandeur d'âme* is very rare; my friend Tom Willows is almost the only man I know who possessed it. Yes, —, one of the wittiest men in London, I once knew to take the whole *intérieur* of a diligence (six places), because he was a little unwell. Ever since I have admired that man. He understands true economy; a mean extravagant man would have contented himself with a single place, and been unwell in consequence. How I am rambling from my subject, however. The fish was good, and I ate up every single scrap of it, sucking the bones and fins curiously. That is the deuce of an appetite, it *must* be satisfied; and if you were to put a roast donkey before me, with the promise of a haunch of venison afterwards, I believe I should eat the greater part of the long-eared animal.

A pint of purée à la Créci, a pain de gruau, a slice of turbot – a man should think about ordering his bill, for he has had enough dinner; but no, we are creatures of superstition and habit, and must have one regular course of meat. Here comes the *poulet à la Marengo*: I hope they've given me the wing.

No such thing. The poulet à la Marengo aux truffes is bad – too oily by far; the truffles are not of this year, as they should be, for there are cartloads in town: they are poor in flavour, and have only been cast into the dish a minute before it was brought to table, and what is the consequence? They do not flavour the meat in the least; some faint trufflesque savour you may get as you are crunching each individual root, but that is all, and that all not worth the having; for as nothing is finer than a good truffle, in like manner nothing is meaner than a bad one. It is merely pompous, windy, and pretentious, like those scraps of philosophy with which a certain eminent novelist decks out his meat.

A mushroom, thought I, is better a thousand times than these tough flavourless roots. I finished every one of them, however, and the fine fat capon's thigh which they surrounded. It was a disappointment not to get a wing, to be sure. They *always* give me legs; but, after all, with a little good-humour and philosophy, a leg of a fine Mans capon may be found very acceptable. How plump and tender the rogue's thigh is! his very drumstick is as fat as the calf of a London footman; and the sinews, which puzzle one so over the lean black hen-legs in London, are miraculously whisked away from the limb before me. Look at it now! Half-a-dozen cuts with the knife, and yonder lies the bone – white, large, stark naked, without a morsel of flesh left upon it, solitary in the midst of a pool of melted butter.

How good the Burgundy smacks after it! I always drink Burgundy at this house, and that not of the best. It is my firm, opinion that a third-rate Burgundy, and a third-rate claret – Beaune and Larose, for instance, are *better* than the best. The Bordeaux enlivens, the Burgundy invigorates; stronger drink only inflames; and where a bottle of good Beaune only causes a man to feel a certain manly warmth of benevolence – a glow something like that produced by sunshine and gentle exercise – a bottle of Chambertin will set all your frame in a fever, swell the extremities, and cause the pulses to throb. Chambertin should *never* be handed round more than twice; and I recollect to this moment the headache I had after drinking a bottle and a half of Romanée-Gélée, for which this house is famous. Somebody else *paid* for the – (no other than you, O Gustavus! with whom I hope to have many a tall dinner on the same charges) – but 'twas in our hot youth, ere experience had taught us that moderation was happiness, and had shown us that it is absurd to be guzzling wine at fifteen francs a bottle.

By the way, I may here mention a story relating to some of Blackwood's men, who dined at this very house. Fancy the fellows trying claret, which they voted sour; then Burgundy, at which they made wry faces, and finished the evening with brandy and *lunel*! This is what men call eating a French dinner. Willows and I dined at the 'Rocher,' and an English family there feeding ordered – mutton chops and potatoes. Why not, in these cases, stay at home? Chops are better chops in England (the best chops in the world are to be had at the Reform Club) than in France. What could literary men mean by ordering lunel? I always rather liked the descriptions of eating in the *Noctes*.* They were gross in all cases, absurdly erroneous in many; but there was manliness about them, and strong evidence of a great, though misdirected and uneducated, genius for victuals.

Mushrooms, thought I, are better than those tasteless truffles, and so ordered a dish to try. You know what a *Provençale* sauce is, I have no doubt? – a rich, savoury mixture of garlic and oil; which, with a little cayenne pepper and salt, impart a pleasant taste to the plump little mushrooms, that can't be described but may be thought of with pleasure.

The only point was, how will they agree with me to-morrow morning? for the fact is, I had eaten an immense quantity of them, and began to be afraid! Suppose we go and have a glass of punch and a cigar! Oh, glorious garden of the Palais Royal! your trees are leafless now, but what matters? Your alleys are damp, but what of that? All the windows are blazing with light and merriment; at least two thousand happy people are pacing up and down the colonnades; cheerful sounds of money chinking are heard as you pass the changers' shops; bustling shouts of 'Garçon!' and 'V'là, monsieur!' come from the swinging doors of the restaurateurs. Look at that group of soldiers gaping at Véfour's window, where lie lobsters, pine-apples, fat truffle-stuffed partridges, which make me almost hungry again. I wonder whether those three fellows with mustachios and a toothpick a piece have had a dinner, or only a toothpick. When the 'Trois Frères' used to be on the first floor, and had a door leading into the Rue de Valois, as well as one into the garden, I recollect seeing three men with toothpicks mount the stair from the street, descend the stair into the garden, and give themselves as great airs as if they had dined for a napoleon a-head. The rogues are lucky if they have had a sixteen-sous dinner; and the next time I dine abroad, I am resolved to have one myself. I never understood why Gil Blas* grew so mighty squeamish in the affair of the cat and the hare. Hare is best, but why should not cat be good?

Being on the subject of bad dinners, I may as well ease my mind of one that occurred to me some few days back. When walking in the Boulevard, I met my friend, Captain Hopkinson, of the half-pay, looking very hungry, and indeed going to dine. In most cases one respects the dictum of a half-pay officer regarding a dining-house. He knows as a general rule where the fat of the land lies, and how to take his share of that fat in the most economical manner.

'I tell you what I do,' says Hopkinson; 'I allow myself fifteen francs a week for dinner (I count upon being asked out twice a week), and so have a three-franc dinner at Richard's, where, for the extra francs, they give me an excellent bottle of wine, and make me comfortable.'

'Why shouldn't they?' I thought. 'Here is a man who has served his country, and no doubt knows a thing when he sees it.' We made a party of four, therefore, and went to the Captain's place to dine.

We had a private room *au second*; a very damp and dirty private room, with a faint odour of stale punch, and dingy glasses round the walls.

We had a soup of purée aux croûtons; a very dingy dubious soup, indeed, thickened, I fancy, with brown paper, and flavoured with the same.

At the end of the soup, Monsieur Landlord came upstairs very kindly, and gave us each a pinch of snuff out of a gold snuff-box.

We had four portions of anguille à la Tartare, very good and fresh (it is best in these places to eat freshwater fish). Each portion was half the length of a man's finger. Dish one was dispatched in no time, and we began drinking the famous wine that our guide recommended. I have cut him ever since. It was four-sous wine – weak, vapid, watery stuff, of the most unsatisfactory nature.

We had four portions of gigot aux haricots – four flaps of bleeding tough meat, cut unnaturally (that is, with the grain: the French gash the meat in parallel lines with the bone). We ate these up as we might, and the landlord was so good as to come up again and favour us with a pinch from his gold box.

With wonderful unanimity, as we were told the place was famous for civet de lièvre, we ordered civet de lièvre for four.

It came up, but we couldn't – really we couldn't. We were obliged to have extra dishes, and pay extra. Gustavus had a mayonnaise of crayfish, and half a fowl; I fell to work upon my cheese, as usual, and availed myself of the discretionary bread. We went away disgusted, wretched, unhappy. We had had for our three francs bad bread, bad meat, bad wine. And there stood the landlord at the door (and be hanged to him!) grinning and offering his box.

We don't speak to Hopkinson any more now when we meet him. How can you trust or be friendly with a man who deceives you in this miserable way?

What is the moral to be drawn from this dinner? It is evident. Avoid pretence; mistrust shabby elegance; cut your coat according to your cloth; if you have but a few shillings in your pocket, aim only at those humble and honest meats which your small store will purchase. At the Café Foy, for the same money, I might have had

	f.	s.
A delicious entrecôte and potatoes	1	5
A pint of excellent wine	0	10
A little bread (meaning a great deal)	0	5
A dish of stewed kidneys	1	0
	3	0

Or at Paolo's:

A bread (as before)	0	5
A heap of macaroni, or raviuoli	0	15
A Milanese cutlet	1	0
A pint of wine	0	10

And ten sous for any other luxury your imagination could suggest. The raviuoli and the cutlets are admirably dressed at Paolo's. Does any healthy man need more?

These dinners, I am perfectly aware, are by no means splendid; and I might, with the most perfect ease, write you out a dozen bills of fare, each more splendid and piquant than the other, in which all the luxuries of the season should figure. But the remarks here set down are the result of experience, not fancy, and intended only for persons in the middling classes of life. Very few men can afford to pay more than five francs daily for dinner. Let us calmly, then, consider what enjoyment may be had for those five francs; how, by economy on one day, we may venture upon luxury the next; how, by a little forethought and care, we may be happy on all days. Who knew and studied this cheap philosophy of life better than old Horace before quoted? Sometimes (when in luck) he chirupped over cups that were fit for an archbishop's supper; sometimes he philosophised over his own *ordinaire* at his own farm. How affecting is the last ode of the first book:

To his serving-boy	*Ad ministram*
Persicos odi,	Dear Lucy, you know what my wish is –
Puer, apparatus;	I hate all your Frenchified fuss:
Displicent nexæ	Your silly entrées and made dishes
Philyrâ coronæ:	Were never intended for us.
Mitte sectari	No footman in lace and in ruffles
Rosa quo locorum	Need dangle behind my arm-chair;
Sera moretur.	And never mind seeking for truffles,
	Although they be ever so rare.
Simplici myrto	But a plain leg of mutton, my Lucy,
Nihil allabores	I pr'ythee get ready at three:
Sedulus curæ:	Have it smoking, and tender, and juicy,
Neque te ministrum	And what better meat can there be?
Dedecet myrtus,	And when it has feasted the master,
Neque me sub arctâ	'Twill amply suffice for the maid;
Vite bibentem.	Meanwhile I will smoke my canaster,
	And tipple my ale in the shade.

Not that this is the truth entirely and for ever. Horatius Flaccus was too wise to dislike a good thing; but it is possible that the Persian apparatus was on that day beyond his means, and so he contended himself with humble fare.

A gentleman, by-the-bye, has just come to Paris to whom I am very kind; and who will, in all human probability, between this and next month, ask me to a dinner at the 'Rocher de Cancale'. If so, something may occur worth writing about; or if you are anxious to hear more on the subject, send me over a sum to my address, to be laid out for you exclusively in eating. I give you my honour I will do you justice, and account for every farthing of it.

One of the most absurd customs at present in use is that of giving your friend – when some piece of good-luck happens to him, such as an appointment as Chief Judge of Owhyhee, or King's advocate to Timbuctoo – of giving your friend, because, forsooth, he may have been suddenly elevated from £200 a year to £2,000, an enormous dinner of congratulation.

Last year, for instance, when our friend, Fred Jowling, got his place of Commissioner at Quashumaboo, it was considered absolutely necessary to give the man a dinner, and some score of us had to pay about fifty shillings a piece for the purpose. I had, so help me Moses! but three guineas in the world at that period; and out of this sum the *bienséances* compelled me to sacrifice five-sixths, to feast myself in company of a man gorged with wealth, rattling sovereigns in his pocket as if they had been so much dross, and capable of treating us all without missing the sum he might expend on us.

Jow himself allowed, as I represented the case to him, that the arrangement *was* very hard; but represented, fairly enough, that this was one of the sacrifices that a man of the world, from time to time, is called to make. 'You, my dear Titmarsh,' said he, 'know very well that I don't care for these grand entertainments' (the rogue, he is a five-bottle man, and just the most finished *gourmet* of my acquaintance!); 'you know that I am perfectly convinced of your friendship for me, though you join in the dinner or not, but – it would look rather queer if you backed out – *it would look rather queer*.' Jow said this in such an emphatic way, that I saw I must lay down my money; and accordingly Mr Lovegrove of Blackwall, for a certain quantity of iced punch, champagne, cider cup, fish, flesh, and fowl, received the last of my sovereigns.

At the beginning of the year Bolter got a place too – Judge-Advocate in the Topinambo Islands, of £3,000 a year, which, he said, was a poor remuneration in consideration of *the practice* which he gave up in town. He may have practised on his laundress, but for anything else I believe the man never had a client in his life.

However, on his way to Topinambo – by Marseilles, Egypt, the Desert, the Persian Gulf, and so on – Bolter arrived in Paris; and I saw from his appearance, and his manner of shaking hands with me, and the peculiar way in which he talked about the 'Rocher de Cancale', that he expected we were to give him a dinner, as we had to Jowling.

There were four friends of Bolter's in the capital besides myself, and among us the dinner question was mooted: we agreed that it should be a simple dinner of ten francs a head, and this was the bill of fare:

1 Oysters (common), nice.
2 Oysters, green of Marennes (very good).
3 Potage, purée de gibier (very fair).

As we were English, they instantly then served us –

4 Sole en matelotte Normande (comme ça).
5 Turbot à la crème au gratin (excellent).
6 Jardinière cutlets (particularly seedy).
7 Poulet à la Marengo (very fair, but why the deuce is one always to be pestered by it?)
8 }
9 } (Entrées of some kind, but a blank in my memory.)
10 A rôt of chevreuil.
11 Ditto of ortolans (very hot, crisp, and nice).
12 Ditto of partridges (quite good and plump).
13 Pointes d'asperges.
14 Champignons à la Provençale (the most delicious mushrooms I ever tasted).
15 Pineapple jelly.
16 Blanc, or red mange.
17 Pencacks. Let everybody who goes to the 'Rocher' order these pancakes; they are arranged with jelly inside, rolled up between various *couches* of vermicelli, flavoured with a *leetle* wine; and, by everything sacred, the most delightful meat possible.
18 Timbale of macaroni.

The jellies and sucreries should have been mentioned in the dessert, and there were numberless plates of trifles, which made the table look very pretty, but need not be mentioned here.

The dinner was not a fine one, as you see. No rarities, no truffles even, no mets de primeur, though there were peas and asparagus in the market at a pretty fair price. But with rarities no man has any business except he have a colossal fortune. Hothouse strawberries, asparagus, &c., are, as far as my experience goes, most *fade*, mean, and tasteless meats. Much better to have a simple dinner of twenty dishes, and content therewith, than to look for impossible splendours and Apician morsels.

In respect of wine. Let those who go to the 'Rocher' take my advice and order Madeira. They have here some pale old East India very good. How they got it is a secret, for the Parisians do not know good Madeira when they see it. Some very fair strong young wine may be had at the Hôtel des Américains, in the Rue Saint Honoré; as, indeed, all West India produce – pineapple rum, for instance. I may say, with confidence, that I never knew what rum was until I tasted this at Paris.

But to the 'Rocher'. The Madeira was the best wine served; though some Burgundy, handed round in the course of dinner, and a bottle of Montrachet, similarly poured out to us, were very fair. The champagne was decidedly not good – poor, inflated, thin stuff. They say the drink we swallow in England is not genuine wine, but brandy-loaded and otherwise doctored for the English market; but, ah, what superior wine! *Au reste*, the French will not generally pay the money for the wine; and it therefore is carried from an ungrateful country to more generous climes, where it is better appreciated. We had claret and speeches after dinner; and very possibly some of the persons present made free with a jug of hot water, a few lumps of sugar, and the horrid addition of a glass of cognac. There can be no worse practice than this. After a dinner of eighteen dishes, in which you have drunk at least thirty-six glasses of wine – when the stomach is full, the brain heavy, the hands and feet inflamed – when the claret begins to pall – you, forsooth, must gorge yourself with brandy-and-water, and puff filthy cigars. For shame! Who ever does it? Does a gentleman drink brandy-and-water? Does a man who mixes in the society of the lovelier half of humanity befoul himself by tobacco smoke? Fie, fie! avoid the practice. I indulge in it always myself; but that is no reason why you, a young man entering into the world, should degrade yourself in any such way. No, no, my dear lad, never refuse an evening party, and avoid tobacco as you would the upas plant.*

By the way, not having my purse about me when the above dinner was given, I was constrained to borrow from Bolter, whom I knew more intimately than the rest; and nothing grieved me more than to find, on calling at his hotel four days afterwards, that he had set off by the mail post for Marseilles. Friend of my youth, dear dear Bolter! if haply this trifling page should come before thine eyes, weary of perusing the sacred rolls of Themis* in thy far-off island in the Indian Sea, thou wilt recall our little dinner in the little room of the Cancalian Coffee-house, and think for a while of thy friend!

Let us now mention one or two places that the Briton, on his arrival here, should frequent or avoid. As a quiet dear house, where there are some of the best rooms in Paris – always the best meat, fowls, vegetables, &c. – we may specially recommend

Monsieur Voisin's café, opposite the Church of the Assumption. A very decent and lively house of restauration is that at the corner of the Rue du Faubourg Montmartre, on the Boulevard. I never yet had a good dinner at Véfour's; *something* is always *manqué* at the place. The grand Vatel is worthy of note, as cheap, pretty, and quiet. All the English houses gentlemen may frequent who are so inclined; but, though the writer of this has many times dined for sixteen sous at Catcomb's, cheek by jowl with a French chasseur or a labourer, he has, he confesses, an antipathy to enter into the confidence of a footman or groom of his own country.

A gentleman who purchases pictures in this town was lately waited upon by a lady, who said she had in her possession one of the greatest rarities in the world – a picture admirable, too, as a work of art – no less than an original portrait of Shakespeare, by his comrade, the famous John Davis. The gentleman rushed off immediately to behold the wonder, and saw a head, rudely but vigorously painted on panel, about twice the size of life, with a couple of hooks drawn through the top part of the board, under which was written:

THE WILLIAM SHAKESPEARE,
BY JOHN DAVIS.

'Voyez-vous, Monsieur,' said the lady; 'il n'y a plus de doute. Le portrait de Shakspeare, du célèbre Davis, et signé même de lui!'

I remember it used to hang up in a silent little street in the Latin quarter, near an old convent, before a quaint old quiet tavern that I loved. It was pleasant to see the old name written up in a strange land, and the well-known friendly face greeting one. There was a quiet little garden at the back of the tavern, and famous good roast beef, clean rooms, and English beer. Where are you now, John Davis? Could not the image of thy august patron preserve thy house from ruin, or rally the faithful around it? Are you unfortunate, Davis? Are you a bankrupt? Let us hope not. I swear to thee, that when, one sunny afternoon, I saw the ensign of thy tavern, I loved thee for thy choice, and doused my cap on entering the porch, and looked around, and thought all friends were here.

In the queer old pleasant novel of the 'Spiritual Quixote' honest Tugwell, the Sancho of the story, relates a Warwickshire legend, which at the time Graves wrote was not much more than a hundred years old; and by which it appears that the owner of New

Place was a famous jesting gentleman, and used to sit at his gate of summer evenings, cutting the queerest merriest jokes with all the passers-by. I have heard from a Warwickshire clergyman that the legend still exists in the country; and Ward's 'Diary' says that Master Shakspeare died of a surfeit, brought on by carousing with a literary friend who had come to visit him from London. And wherefore not? Better to die of good wine and good company than of slow disease and doctors' doses. Some geniuses live on sour misanthropy, and some on meek milk and water. Let us not deal too hardly with those that are of a jovial sort, and indulge in the decent practice of the cup and the platter.

A word or two, by way of conclusion, may be said about the numerous pleasant villages in the neighbourhood of Paris, or rather of the eating and drinking to be found in the taverns of those suburban spots. At Versailles, Monsieur Duboux, at the Hôtel des Reservoirs, has a good cook and cellars, and will gratify you with a heavier bill than is paid at Véry's and the 'Rocher'. On the beautiful terrace of Saint Germain, looking over miles of river and vineyard, of fair villages basking in the meadows, and great tall trees stretching wide round about, you may sit in the open air of summer evenings, and see the white spires of Saint Denis rising in the distance, and the grey arches of Marly to the right, and before you the city of Paris with innumerable domes and towers.

Watching these objects, and the setting sun gorgeously illumining the heavens and them, you may have an excellent dinner served to you by the *chef* of Messire Gallois, who at present owns the pavilion where Louis XIV was born. The *maître d hôtel* is from the 'Rocher', and told us that he came out to Saint Germain for the sake of the air. The only drawback to the entertainment is, that the charges are as atrociously high in price as the dishes provided are small in quantity; and dining at this pavilion on the 15th of April, at a period when a *botte* of asparagus at Paris cost only three francs, the writer of this and a chosen associate had to pay seven francs for about the third part of a *botte* of asparagus, served up to them by Messire Gallois.

Facts like these ought not to go unnoticed. Therefore let the readers of *Fraser's Magazine* who propose a visit to Paris, take warning by the unhappy fate of the person now addressing them, and avoid the place or not, as they think fit. A bad dinner does no harm to any human soul, and the philosopher partakes of such with easy resignation; but a bad and dear dinner is enough to raise the anger of any man, however naturally sweet-tempered, and he is bound to warn his acquaintance of it.

With one parting syllable in praise of the 'Marronniers' at Bercy, where you get capital eels, fried gudgeons fresh from the Seine, and excellent wine of the ordinary kind, this discourse is here closed. 'En telle ou meilleure pensée, Beuueurs très illustres (car à vous non à aultres sont dédiés ces escriptz) reconfortez vostre malheur, et beuuez fraiz si faire se peult.'

CAPTAIN ROOK AND
MR PIGEON

The statistic-mongers and dealers in geography have calculated to a nicety how many quartern loaves, bars of iron, pigs of lead, sacks of wool, Turks, Quakers, Methodists, Jews, Catholics, and Church-of-England men are consumed or produced in the different countries of this wicked world: I should like to see an accurate table showing the rogues and dupes of each nation; the calculation would form a pretty matter for a philosopher to speculate upon. The mind loves to repose and broods benevolently over this expanded theme. What thieves are there in Paris, O heavens! and what a power of rogues with pigtails and mandarin buttons at Pekin! What crowds of swindlers are there at this very moment pursuing their trade at St Petersburg! how many scoundrels are saying their prayers alongside of Don Carlos! how many scores are jobbing under the pretty nose of Queen Christina!* What an inordinate number of rascals is there, to be sure, puffing tobacco and drinking flat small-beer in all the capitals of Germany; or else, without a rag to their ebony backs, swigging quass out of calabashes, and smeared over with palm-oil, lolling at the doors of clay huts in the sunny city of Timbuctoo! It is not necessary to make any more topographical allusions, or, for illustrating the above position, to go through the whole Gazetteer; but he is a bad philosopher who has not all these things in mind, and does not in his speculations or his estimate of mankind duly consider and weigh them. And it is fine and consolatory to think that thoughtful Nature, which has provided sweet flowers for the humming bee; fair running streams for glittering fish; store of kids, deer, goats, and other fresh meat for roaring lions; for active cats, mice; for mice, cheese, and so on; establishing throughout the whole of her realm the great doctrine that where a demand is, there will be a supply (see the romances of Adam Smith, Malthus, and Ricardo, and the philosophical works of Miss Martineau)*. I say it is consolatory to think that, as Nature has provided flies for the food of fishes, and flowers for bees, so she has created fools for rogues;

and thus the scheme is consistent throughout. Yes, observation, with extensive view, will discover Captain Rooks all over the world, and Mr Pigeons made for their benefit. Wherever shines the sun, you are sure to find Folly basking in it; and knavery is the shadow at Folly's heels.

It is not, however, necessary to go to St Petersburg or Pekin for rogues (and in truth I don't know whether the Timbuctoo Captain Rooks prefer cribbage or billiards). 'We are not birds,' as the Irishman says, 'to be in half-a-dozen places at once'; so let us pretermit all considerations of rogues in other countries, examining only those who flourish under our very noses. I have travelled much, and seen many men and cities; and, in truth, I think that our country of England produces the best soldiers, sailors, razors, tailors, brewers, hatters, and rogues, of all. Especially there is no cheat like an English cheat. Our society produces them in the greatest numbers as well as of the greatest excellence. We supply all Europe with them. I defy you to point out a great city of the Continent where half-a-dozen of them are not to be found: proofs of our enterprise and samples of our home manufacture. Try Rome, Cheltenham, Baden, Toeplitz, Madrid, or Tzarskoselo: I have been in every one of them, and give you my honour that the Englishman is the best rascal to be found in all; better than your eager Frenchman; your swaggering Irishman, with a red velvet waistcoat and red whiskers; your grave Spaniard, with horrid goggle eyes and profuse diamond shirt-pins; your tallow-faced German baron, with white moustache and double chin, fat, pudgy, dirty fingers, and great gold thumb-ring; better even than your nondescript Russian – swindler and spy as he is by loyalty and education – the most dangerous antagonist we have. Who has the best coat even at Vienna? who has the neatest britzska at Baden? who drinks the best champagne at Paris? Captain Rook, to be sure, of her Britannic Majesty's service: he *has* been of the service, that is to say, but often finds it convenient to sell out.

The life of a blackleg, which is the name contemptuously applied to Captain Rook in his own country, is such an easy, comfortable, careless, merry one, that I can't conceive why all the world do not turn Captain Rooks; unless, may be, there are some mysteries and difficulties in it which the vulgar know nothing of, and which only men of real genius can overcome. Call on Captain Rook in the day (in London, he lives about St. James's, abroad, he has the very best rooms in the very best hotels), and you will find him at one o'clock dressed in the very finest *robe-de-chambre*, before a breakfast-table covered with the prettiest patties and delicacies possible; smoking, perhaps, one of the biggest Meerschaum pipes you ever saw; reading, possibly, *The Morning Post*, or a novel (he has only one volume in his whole room, and that from a circulating library); or having his hair dressed; or talking to a tailor about waistcoat patterns; or drinking sodawater with a glass of sherry; all this he does every morning, and it does not seem very difficult, and lasts until three. At three, he goes to a horse-dealer's, and lounges there for half an hour; at four he is to be seen at the window of his Club; at five, he is cantering and curvetting in Hyde Park with one or two more (he does not know any ladies, but has many male acquaintances: some, stout old gentlemen riding cobs, who knew his family, and give him a surly grunt of recognition; some, very young lads with pale dissolute faces, little moustaches perhaps, or at least little tufts on their chin, who hail him eagerly as a man of fashion): at seven, he has a dinner at 'Long's' or at the 'Clarendon'; and so to bed very likely at five in the morning, after a quiet game of whist, broiled bones, and punch.

Perhaps he dines early at a tavern in Covent Garden; after which, you will see him at the theatre in a private box (Captain Rook affects the Olympic a good deal). In the box, besides himself, you will remark a young man – very young – one of the lads who spoke to him in the Park this morning, and a couple of ladies: one shabby, melancholy, raw-boned, with numberless small white ringlets, large hands and feet, and a faded light blue silk gown; she has a large cap, trimmed with yellow, and all sorts of crumpled flowers and greasy blonde lace; she wears large gilt ear-rings, and sits back and nobody speaks to her, and she to nobody, except to say, 'Law, Maria, how well you *do* look to-night; there's a man opposite has been staring at you this three hours: I'm blest if it isn't him as we saw in the Park, dear!'

'I wish, Hanna, you'd 'old your tongue, and not bother me about the men. You don't believe Miss 'Ickman, Freddy, do you?' says Maria, smiling fondly on Freddy. Maria is sitting in front: she says she is twenty-three, though Miss Hickman knows very well she is thirty-one, (Freddy is just of age). She wears a purple-velvet gown, three different gold bracelets on each arm, as many rings on each finger of each hand; to one is hooked a gold smelling-bottle: she has an enormous fan, a laced pocket-handkerchief, a Cashmere shawl, which is continually falling off, and exposing, very unnecessarily, a pair of very white shoulders: she talks loud, always lets her playbill drop into the pit, and smells pungently of Mr Delcroix's shop. After this description it is not at all necessary to say who Maria is: Miss Hickman is her companion, and they live together in a very snug little house in Mayfair, which has just been new-furnished *à la Louis Quatorze* by Freddy, as we are positively informed. It is even said that the little carriage, with two little white ponies, which Maria drives herself in such a fascinating way through the Park, was purchased for her by Freddy too; ay, and that Captain Rook got it for him – a great bargain of course.

Such is Captain Rook's life. Can anything be more easy? Suppose Maria says, 'Come home, Rook, and heat a cold chicken with us, and a glass of hiced champagne'; and suppose he goes, and after chicken – just for fun – Maria proposes a little chicken-hazard; – she only plays for shillings, while Freddy, a little bolder, won't mind half-pound stakes himself. Is there any great harm in all this? Well, after half-an-hour, Maria grows tired, and Miss Hickman has been nodding asleep in the corner long ago; so off the two ladies set, candle in hand.

'D – n it, Fred,' says Captain Rook, pouring out for that young gentleman his fifteenth glass of champagne, 'what luck you are in, if you did but know how to back it!'

What more natural, and even kind, of Rook than to say this? Fred is evidently an inexperienced player; and every inexperienced player, and every experienced player knows that there is nothing like backing your luck. Freddy does. Well; fortune is proverbially variable; and it is not at all surprising that Freddy, after having had so much luck at the commencement of the evening, should have the tables turned on him at some time or another – Freddy loses.

It is deuced unlucky, to be sure, that he should have won all the little *coups* and lost all the great ones; but there is a plan which the commonest play-man knows, an infallible means of retrieving yourself at play: it is simply doubling your stake. Say, you lose a guinea: you bet two guineas, which if you win, you win a guinea and your original stake: if you lose, you have but to bet four guineas on the third stake, eight on the fourth, sixteen on the fifth, thirty-two on the sixth, and so on. It stands to reason that you cannot lose *always*; and the very first time you win, all your losings are made up to you. There is but one drawback to this infallible process; if you begin at a guinea, double every time you lose, and lose fifteen times, you will have lost exactly sixteen thousand three hundred and eighty-four guineas; a sum which probably exceeds the amount of your yearly income: mine is considerably under that figure.

Freddy does not play this game then, yet; but being a poor-spirited creature, as we have seen he must be by being afraid to win, he is equally poor-spirited when he begins to lose: he is frightened; that is, increases his stakes, and backs his ill-luck: when a man does this, it is all over with him.

When Captain Rook goes home (the sun is peering through the shutters of the little drawing-room in Curzon Street, and the ghastly footboy – oh, how bleared his eyes look as he opens the door!) – when Captain Rook goes home, he has Freddy's I O U's in his pocket to the amount, say, of three hundred pounds. Some people say that Maria has half of the money when it is paid; but this I don't believe: is Captain Rook the kind of fellow to give up a purse when his hand has once clawed hold of it?

Be this, however, true or not, it concerns us very little. The Captain goes home to King Street, plunges into bed much too tired to say his prayers, and wakes the next morning at twelve to go over such another day as we have just chalked out for him. As for Freddy, not poppy, nor mandragora, nor all the soda-water at the chemist's, can ever medicine him to that sweet sleep which he might have had but for his loss. '*If* I had but played my king of hearts,' sighed Fred, 'and kept back my trump; but there's no standing against a fellow who turns up a king seven times running: if I *had* even but pulled up when Thomas (curse him!) brought up that infernal Curaçoa punch, I should have saved a couple of hundred,' and so on go Freddy's lamentations. O luckless Freddy! dismal Freddy! silly gaby of a Freddy! you are hit now, and there is no cure for you but bleeding you almost to death's door. The homoeopathic maxim of *similia similibus* – which means, I believe, that you are to be cured 'by a hair of the dog that bit you' – must be put in practice with regard to Freddy – only not in homœopathic infinitesimal doses; no hair of the dog that bit him; but, *vice versa*, the dog of the hair that tickled him. Freddy has begun to play; – a mere trifle at first, but he must play it out; he must go the whole dog now, or there is no chance for him. He must play until he can play no more; he *will* play until he has not a shilling left to play with, when, perhaps, he may turn out an honest man, though the odds are against him: the betting is in favour of his being a swindler always; a rich or a poor one, as the case may be. I need not tell Freddy's name, I think* now; it stands on his card:

MR FREDERICK PIGEON

LONG'S HOTEL

I have said the chances are that Frederick Pigeon, Esq, will become a rich or a poor swindler, though the first chance, it must be confessed, is very remote. I once heard an actor, who could not write, speak, or even read English; who was not fit for any trade in the world, and had not the 'nous' to keep an applestall, and scarcely even enough sense to make a Member of Parliament: I once, I say, heard an actor, – whose only qualifications were a large pair of legs, a large voice, and a very large neck, – curse his fate and his profession, by which, do what he would, he could only make eight guineas a week. 'No men,' said he, with a great deal of justice, 'were so ill paid as 'dramatic artists'; they laboured for nothing all their youth, and had no provision for old age.' With this, he sighed, and called for (it was on a Saturday night) the forty-ninth glass of brandy-and-water which he had drunk in the course of the week.

The excitement of his profession, I make no doubt, caused my friend Claptrap to consume this quantity of spirit-and-water, besides beer in the morning, after rehearsal; and I could not help musing over his fate. It is a hard one. To eat, drink, work a little, and be jolly; to be paid twice as much as you are worth, and then to go to ruin; to drop off the tree when you are swelled out, seedy, and over-ripe; and to lie rotting in the mud underneath, until at last you mingle with it.

Now, badly as the actor is paid, (and the reader will the more readily pardon the above episode, because, in reality, it has nothing to do with the subject in hand,) and luckless as his fate is, the lot of the poor blackleg is cast lower still. You never hear of a rich gambler; or of one who wins in the end. Where does all the money go to which is lost among them? Did you ever play a game at loo for sixpences? At the end of the night a great many of those small coins have been lost, and in consequence, won: but ask the table all around; one man has won three shillings; two have neither lost nor won; one rather thinks he has lost; and the three others have lost two pounds each. Is not this the fact, known to everybody who indulges in round games, and especially the noble game of loo? I often think that the devil's books, as cards are called, are let out to us from Old Nick's circulating library, and that he lays his paw upon a certain part of the winnings, and carries it off privily: else, what becomes of all the money?

For instance, there is the gentleman whom the newspapers call 'a noble earl of sporting celebrity'; – if he has lost a shilling, according to the newspaper accounts, he has lost fifty millions: he drops fifty thousand pounds at the Derby, just as you and I would lay down twopence-halfpenny for half an ounce of Macabaw. Who has won these millions? Is it Mr Crockford, or Mr Bond, or Mr Salon-des-Etrangers? (I do not call these latter gentlemen gamblers, for their speculation is a certainty); but who wins his money, and everybody else's money who plays and loses? Much money is staked in the absence of Mr Crockford; many notes are given without the interference of the Bonds; there are hundreds of thousands of gamblers who are *étrangers* even to the *Salon-des-Etrangers*.

No, my dear sir, it is not in the public gambling-houses that the money is lost; it is not in them that your virtue is chiefly in danger. Better by half lose your income, your fortune, or your master's money, in a decent public hell, than in the private society of such men as my friend Captain Rook; but we are again and again digressing; the point is, is the Captain's trade a good one, and does it yield tolerably good interest for outlay and capital?

To the latter question first: – at this very season of May, when the Rooks are very young, have you not, my dear friend, often tasted them in pies? – they are then so tender that you cannot tell the difference between them and pigeons. So, in like manner, our Rook has been in his youth undistinguishable from a pigeon. He does as he has been done by: yea, he has been plucked as even now he plucks his friend Mr Frederick Pigeon. Say that he began the world with ten thousand pounds: every maravedi of this is gone; and may be considered as the capital which he has sacrificed to learn his trade. Having spent £10,000, then, on an annuity of £650, he must look to a larger interest for his money – say fifteen hundred, two thousand, or three thousand pounds, decently to repay his risk and labour. Besides the money sunk in the first place, his profession requires continual annual outlays, as thus –

Horses, carriages (including Epsom, Goodwood, Ascot, &c.)	£500	0	0
Lodgings, servants, and board	350	0	0
Watering-places, and touring	300	0	0
Dinners to give	150	0	0
Pocket-money	150	0	0
Gloves, handkerchiefs, perfumery, and tobacco (very moderate)	150	0	0
Tailor's bills (£100 say, never paid)	0	0	0
Total	£1,600	0	0

I defy any man to carry on the profession in a decent way under the above sum: ten thousand sunk, and sixteen hundred annual expenses; no, it is *not* a good profession: it is *not* good interest for one's money; it is *not* a fair remuneration for a gentleman of birth, industry, and genius: and my friend Claptrap, who growls about *his* pay, may bless his eyes that he was not born a gentleman and bred up to such an unprofitable calling as this. Considering his trouble, his outlay, his birth, and breeding, the Captain is most wickedly and basely rewarded. And when he is obliged to retreat, when his hand trembles, his credit is fallen, his bills laughed at by every money-lender in Europe, his tailors rampant and inexorable – in fact, when the *coup* of life will *sauter* for him no more – who will help the play-worn veteran? As Mitchel sings after Aristophanes –

> In glory he was seen, when his years as yet *were green*;
> But now when his dotage is on him,
> God help him; – for no eye of those who pass him by,
> Throws a look of compassion upon him.

Who indeed will help him? – not his family, for he has bled his father, his uncle, his old grandmother; he has had slices out of his sisters' portions, and quarrelled with his brothers-in-law; the old people are deád; the young ones hate him, and will give him nothing. Who will help him? – not his friends; in the first place, my dear sir, a man's friends very seldom do: in the second place, it is Captain Rook's business not to keep, but to give up his friends. His acquaintances do not last more than a year; the time, namely, during which he is employed in plucking them; then they part. Pigeon has not a single feather left to his tail, and how should he help Rook, whom, *au reste*, he has learned to detest most cordially, and has found out to be a rascal? When Rook's ill day comes, it is simply because he has no more friends; he has exhausted them all, plucked every one as clean as the palm of your hand. And to arrive at this conclusion, Rook has been spending sixteen hundred a year, and the prime of his life, and has moreover sunk ten thousand pounds! *Is* this a proper reward for a gentleman? I say it is a sin and a shame that an English gentleman should be allowed thus to drop down the stream without a single hand to help him.

The moral of the above remarks I take to be this; that black-legging is as bad a trade as can be: and so let parents and guardians look to it, and not apprentice their children to such a villanous, scurvy way of living.

It must be confessed, however, that there are some individuals who have for the profession such a natural genius, that no entreaties or example of parents will keep them from it, and no restraint or occupation occasioned by another calling. They do what Christians do not do; they leave all to follow their master the Devil; they cut friends, families, and good, thriving, profitable trades, to put up with this one, that is both unthrifty and unprofitable. They are in regiments: ugly whispers about certain midnight games at blind-hookey, and a few odd bargains in horseflesh, are borne abroad, and Cornet Rook receives the gentlest hint in the world that he had better sell out.* They are in counting-houses, with a promise of partnership, for which papa is to lay down a handsome premium; but the firm of Hobbs, Bobbs and Higgory can never admit a young gentleman who is a notorious gambler, is much oftener at the races than his desk, and has bills daily falling due at his private banker's. The father, that excellent old man, Sam Rook, so well known on 'Change in the war-time, discovers, at the end of five years, that his son has spent rather more than the four thousand pounds intended for his partnership, and cannot, in common justice to his other thirteen children, give him a shilling more. A pretty pass for flash young Tom Rook, with four horses in stable, a protemporaneous Mrs Rook, very likely, in an establishment near the Regent's Park, and a bill for three hundred and seventy-five pounds coming due on the fifth of next month.

Sometimes young Rook is destined to the bar: and I am glad to introduce one of these gentlemen and his history to the notice of the reader. He was the son of an amiable gentleman, the Reverend Athanasius Rook, who took high honours at Cambridge in the year 1: was a fellow of Trinity in the year 2: and so continued a fellow and tutor of the College until a living fell vacant, on which he seized. It was only two hundred and fifty pounds a year; but the fact is, Athanasius was in love. Miss Gregory, a pretty, demure, simple governess at Miss Mickle's establishment for young ladies in Cambridge (where the reverend gentleman used often of late to take his tea), had caught the eye of the honest college tutor: and in Trinity walks, and up and down the Trumpington Road, he walked with her (and another young lady of course), talked with her, and told his love.

Miss Gregory had not a rap, as might be imagined; but she loved Athanasius with her whole soul and strength, and was the most orderly, cheerful, tender, smiling, bustling little wife that ever a country parson was blest withal. Athanasius took a couple of pupils at a couple of hundred guineas each, and so made out a snug income; ay, and laid by for a rainy day – a little portion for Harriet, when she should grow up and marry, and a help for Tom at college and at the bar. For you must know there were two little Rooks now growing in the rookery; and very happy were father and mother, I can tell you, to put meat down their tender little throats. Oh, if ever a man was good and happy, it was Athanasius; if ever a woman was happy and good, it was his wife: not the whole parish, not the whole county, not the whole kingdom, could produce such a snug rectory, or such a pleasant *ménage*.

Athanasius's fame as a scholar, too, was great; and as his charges were very high, and as he received but two pupils, there was, of course, much anxiety among wealthy parents to place their children under his care. Future squires, bankers, yea, lords and dukes, came to profit by his instructions, and were led by him gracefully over the 'Asses' bridge' into the sublime regions of mathematics, or through the syntax into the pleasant paths of classic lore.

In the midst of these companions, Tom Rook grew up; more fondled and petted, of course, than they; cleverer than they; as handsome, dashing, well-instructed a lad for his years as ever went to college to be a senior wrangler, and went down without any such honour.

Fancy, then, our young gentleman installed at college, whither his father has taken him, and with fond veteran recollections has surveyed hall and grass-plots, and the old porter, and the old fountain, and the old rooms in which he used to live. Fancy the sobs of good little Mrs Rook, as she parted with her boy; and the tears of sweet pale Harriet, as she clung round his neck, and brought him (in a silver paper, slobbered with many tears) a little crimson silk purse (with two guineas of her own in it, poor thing!) Fancy all this, and fancy young Tom, sorry too, but yet restless and glad, panting for the new life opening upon him, the freedom, the joy of the manly struggle for fame, which he vows he will win. Tom Rook, in other words, is installed at Trinity College, attends, lectures, reads at home, goes to chapel, uses wine-parties moderately, and bids fair to be one of the topmost men of his year.

Tom goes down for the Christmas vacation. (What a man he is grown, and how his sister and mother quarrel which shall walk with him down the village; and what stories the old gentleman lugs out with his old port, and how he quotes Æschylus, to be sure!) The pupils are away too, and the three have Tom in quiet. Alas! I fear the place has grown a little too quiet for Tom: however he reads very stoutly of mornings; and sister Harriet peeps with a great deal of wonder into huge books of scribbling-paper, containing many strange diagrams, and complicated arrangements of x's and y's.

May comes, and the college examinations; the delighted parent receives at breakfast, on the 10th of that month, two letters, as follows:

From the Rev. Solomon Snorter to the Rev. Athanasius Rook.

Trinity, May 10.

Dear Credo* – I wish you joy. Your lad is the best man of his year, and I hope in four more to see him at our table. In classics he is, my dear friend, facile princeps; in mathematics he was run hard (entre nous) by a lad of the name of Snick, a Westmoreland man and a sizer. We must keep up Thomas to his mathematics, and I have no doubt we shall make a fellow and a wrangler of him.

I send you his college bill, £105 10s.; rather heavy, but this is the first term, and that you know is expensive: I shall be glad to give you a receipt for it. By the way, the young man is *rather* too fond of amusement, and lives with a very expensive set. Give him a lecture on this score. – Yours,

*This is most probably a joke on the Christian name of Mr Rook.

Sol. Snorter.

Next comes Mr Tom Rook's own letter: it is long, modest; we only give the postscript:

P.S. – Dear Father, I forgot to say that, as I live in the very best set in the University (Lord Bagwig, the Duke's eldest son you know, vows he will give me a living), I have been led into one or two expenses which will frighten you: I lost £30 to the honourable Mr Deuceace (a son of Lord Crabs) at Bagwig's, the other day at dinner; and owe £54 more for desserts and hiring horses, which I can't send into Snorter's bill.* Hiring horses is so deuced expensive; next term I must have a nag of my own, that's positive.

The Rev. Athanasius read the postscript with much less gusto than the letter: however, Tom has done his duty and the old gentleman won't baulk his pleasure; so he sends him £100, with a 'God bless you!' and mamma adds, in a postscript, that 'he must always keep well with his aristocratic friends, for he was made only for the best society.'

A year or two passes on: Tom comes home for the vacations; but Tom has sadly changed; he has grown haggard and pale. At the second year's examination (owing to an unlucky illness) Tom was not classed at all; and Snick, the Westmoreland man, has carried everything before him. Tom drinks more after dinner than his father likes; he is always riding about and dining in the neighbourhood, and coming home, quite odd, his mother says – ill-humoured, unsteady on his feet, and husky in his talk. The Reverend Athanasius begins to grow very, very grave: they have high words, even the father and son; and oh! how Harriet and her mother tremble and listen at the study-door when these disputes are going on!

The last term of Tom's undergraduateship arrives; he is in ill health, but he will make a mighty effort to retrieve himself for his degree; and early in the cold winter's morning – late, late at night – he toils over his books: and the end is that, a month before the examination, Thomas Rook, Esquire, has a brain fever, and Mrs Rook, and Miss Rook, and the Reverend Athanasius Rook, are all lodging at the 'Hoop', an inn in Cambridge town, and day and night round the couch of poor Tom.

O sin, woe, repentance! O touching reconciliation and burst of

---

*It is, or was, the custom for young gentlemen at Cambridge to have unlimited credit with tradesmen, whom the college tutors paid, and then sent the bills to the parents of the young men.

tears on the part of son and father, when one morning at the parsonage, after Tom's recovery, the old gentleman produces a bundle of receipts, and says, with a broken voice, 'There, boy, don't be vexed about your debts. Boys will be boys, I know, and I have paid all demands.' Everybody cries in the house at this news; the mother and daughter most profusely, even Mrs Stokes the old housekeeper, who shakes master's hand, and actually kisses Mr Tom.

Well, Tom begins to read a little for his fellowship, but in vain; he is beaten by Mr Snick, the Westmoreland man. He has no hopes of a living, Lord Bagwig's promises were all moonshine. Tom must go to the bar; and his father, who has long left off taking pupils, must take them again, to support his son in London.

Why tell you what happens when there? Tom lives at the west end of the town, and never goes near the Temple: Tom goes to Ascot and Epsom along with his great friends; Tom has a long bill with Mr Rymell, another long bill with Mr Nugee, he gets into the hands of the Jews – and his father rushes up to London on the outside of the coach to find Tom in a spunging-house in Cursitor Street – the nearest approach he has made to the Temple during his three years' residence in London.

I don't like to tell you the rest of the history. The Reverend Athanasius was not immortal, and he died a year after his visit to the spunging-house, leaving his son exactly one farthing, and his wife one hundred pounds a year, with the remainder to his daughter. But, heaven bless you! the poor things would never allow Tom to want while they had plenty, and they sold out and sold out the three thousand pounds, until, at the end of the three years, there did not remain one single stiver of them; and now Miss Harriet is a governess, with sixty pounds a year, supporting her mother, who lives upon fifty.

As for Tom, he is a regular *leg* now – leading the life already described. When I met him last it was at Baden, where he was on a professional tour, with a carriage, a courier, a valet, a confederate, and a case of pistols. He has been in five duels, he has killed a man who spoke lightly about his honour; and at French or English hazard, at billiards, at whist, at loo, écarté, blind hookey, drawing straws, or beggar-my-neighbour, he will cheat you – cheat you for a hundred pounds or for a guinea, and murder you afterwards if you like.

Abroad, our friend takes military rank, and calls himself Captain

Rook; when asked of what service, he says he was with Don Carlos or Queen Christina; and certain it is that he was absent for a couple of years nobody knows where; he may have been with General Evans, or he may have been at the Sainte Pélagie in Paris, as some people vow he was.

We must wind up this paper with some remarks concerning poor little Pigeon. Vanity has been little Pigeon's failing through life. He is a linendraper's son, and has been left with money: and the silly fashionable works that he has read, and the silly female relatives that he has – (NB All young men with money have silly, flattering she-relatives) – and the silly trips that he has made to watering-places, where he has scraped acquaintance with the Honourable Tom Mountcoffeehouse, Lord Ballyhooly, the celebrated German Prince, Sweller Mobskau, and their like (all Captain Rooks in their way), have been the ruin of him.

I have not the slightest pity in the world for little Pigeon. Look at him! See in what absurd finery the little prig is dressed. Wine makes his poor little head ache, but he will drink because it is manly. In mortal fear he puts himself behind a curvetting camelopard of a cabhorse; or perched on the top of a prancing dromedary, is borne through Rotten Row, when he would give the world to be on his own sofa, or with his own mamma and sisters, over a quiet pool of commerce and a cup of tea. How riding does scarify his poor little legs, and shake his poor little sides! Smoking, how it does turn his little stomach inside out; and yet smoke he will: Sweller Mobskau smokes; Mountcoffeehouse don't mind a cigar; and as for Ballyhooly, he will puff you a dozen in a day, and says very truly that Pontet won't supply *him* with near such good ones as he sells Pigeon. The fact is, that Pontet vowed seven years ago not to give his lordship a sixpence more credit; and so the good-natured nobleman always helps himself out of Pigeon's box.

On the shoulders of these aristocratic individuals, Mr Pigeon is carried into certain clubs, or perhaps we should say he walks into them by the aid of these 'legs'. But they keep him always to themselves. Captain Rooks must rob in companies; but of course, the greater the profits, the fewer the partners must be. Three are positively requisite, however, as every reader must know who has played a game at whist: number one to be Pigeon's partner, and curse his stars at losing, and propose higher play, and 'settle' with number two; number three to transact business with Pigeon, and drive him down to the City to sell out. We have known an instance or two where, after a very good night's work, number three has bolted with the winnings altogether, but the practice is dangerous; not only disgraceful to the profession, but it cuts up your own chance afterwards, as no one will act with you. There is only one occasion on which such a manoeuvre is allowable. Many are sick of the profession, and desirous to turn honest men: in this case, when you can get a good *coup*, five thousand say, bolt without scruple. One thing is clear, the other men *must* be mum, and you can live at Vienna comfortably on the interest of five thousand pounds.

Well, then, in the society of these amiable confederates little Pigeon goes through that period of time which is necessary for the purpose of plucking him. To do this, you must not, in most cases, tug at the feathers so as to hurt him, else he may be frightened, and hop away to somebody else: nor, generally speaking, will the feathers come out so easily at first as they will when he is used to it, and then they drop in handfuls. Nor need you have the least scruple in so causing the little creature to moult artificially: if you don't, somebody else will: a Pigeon goes into the world fated, as Chateaubriand says –

'Pigeon, il va subir le sort de tout pigeon.'

He must be plucked, it is the purpose for which nature has formed him: if you, Captain Rook, do not perform the operation on a green table lighted by two wax-candles, and with two packs of cards to operate with, some other Rook will: are there not railroads, and Spanish bonds, and bituminous companies, and Cornish tin mines, and old dowagers with daughters to marry? If you leave him, Rook of Birchin Lane will have him as sure as fate: if Rook of Birchin Lane don't hit him, Rook of the Stock Exchange will blaze away both barrels at him, which, if the poor trembling flutterer escape, he will fly over and drop into the rookery, where dear old swindling Lady Rook and her daughters will find him and nestle him in their bosoms, and in that soft place pluck him until he turns out as naked as a cannon-ball.

Be not thou scrupulous, O Captain! Seize on Pigeon; pluck him gently but boldly; but, above all, never let him go. If he is a stout cautious bird, of course *you* must be more cautious; if he is excessively silly and scared, perhaps the best way is just to take him around the neck at once, and strip the whole stock of plumage from his back.

The feathers of the human pigeon being thus violently abstracted from him, no others supply their place: and yet I do not pity him. He is now only undergoing the destiny of pigeons, and is, I do believe, as happy in his plucked as in his feathered state. He cannot purse out his breast, and bury his head, and fan his tail, and strut in the sun as if he were a turkey-cock. Under all those fine airs and feathers, he was but what he is now, a poor little meek, silly, cowardly bird, and his state of pride is not a whit more natural to him than his fallen condition. He soon grows used to it. He is too great a coward to despair; much too mean to be frightened because he must live by doing meanness. He is sure, if he cannot fly, to fall somehow or other on his little miserable legs: on these he hops about, and manages to live somewhere in his own mean way. He has but a small stomach, and doesn't mind what food he puts into it. He spunges on his relatives; or else just before his utter ruin he marries and has nine children (and such a family *always* lives); he turns bully most likely, takes to drinking, and beats his wife, who supports him, or takes to drinking too; or he gets a little place, a very little place: you hear he has some tide-waitership, or is clerk to some new milk company, or is lurking about a newspaper. He dies, and a subscription is raised for the Widow Pigeon, and we look no more to find a likeness of him in his children, who are as a new race. Blessed are ye little ones, for ye are born in poverty, and may bear it, or surmount it and die rich. But woe to the pigeons of this earth, for they are born rich that they may die poor.

The end of Captain Rook – for we must bring both him and the paper to an end – is not more agreeable, but somewhat more manly and majestic than the conclusion of Mr Pigeon. If you walk over to the Queen's Bench Prison, I would lay a wager that a dozen such are to be found there in a moment. They have a kind of Lucifer look with them, and stare at you with fierce, twinkling, crow-footed eyes; or grin from under huge grizzly moustaches, as they walk up and down in their tattered brocades. What a dreadful activity is that of a madhouse, or a prison! – a dreary flagged court-yard, a long dark room, and the inmates of it, like the inmates of the ménagerie cages, ceaselessly walking up and down! Mary Queen of Scots says very touchingly:

> Pour mon mal estranger
> Je ne m'arreste en place;
> Mais, J'en ay beau changer

Si ma douleur n'efface!

Up and down, up and down – the inward woe seems to spur the body onwards; and I think in both madhouse and prison you will find plenty of specimens of our Captain Rook. It is fine to mark him under the pressure of this woe, and see how fierce he looks when stirred up by the long pole of memory. In these asylums the Rooks end their lives; or, more happy, they die miserably in a miserable provincial town abroad, and for the benefit of coming Rooks they commonly die early; you as seldom hear of an old Rook (practising his trade) as of a rich one. It is a short-lived trade; not merry, for the gains are most precarious, and perpetual doubt and dread are not pleasant accompaniments of a profession: – not agreeable either, for though Captain Rook does not mind *being* a scoundrel, no man likes to be considered as such, and as such, he knows very well, does the world consider Captain Rook: not profitable, for the expenses of the trade swallow up all the profits of it, and in addition leave the bankrupt with certain habits that have become as nature to him, and which, to live, he must gratify. I know no more miserable wretch than our Rook in his autumn days, at dismal Calais or Boulogne, or at the Bench yonder, with a whole load of diseases and wants, that have come to him in the course of his profession; the diseases and wants of sensuality, always pampered, and now agonising for lack of its unnatural food; the mind, which *must* think now, and has only bitter recollections, mortified ambitions, and unavailing scoundrelisms to con over! Oh, Captain Rook! what nice 'chums' do you take with you into prison; what pleasant companions of exile follow you over the *fines patriæ*, or attend, the only watchers, round your miserable death-bed!

My son, be not a Pigeon in thy dealings with the world – but it is better to be a Pigeon than a Rook.

A DINNER IN THE CITY

I

Out of a mere love of variety and contrast, I think we cannot do better, after leaving the wretched Whitestock among his starving parishioners, than transport ourselves to the City, where we are invited to dine with the Worshipful Company of Bellows-Menders, at their splendid Hall in Marrow-pudding Lane. Next to eating good dinners, a healthy man with a benevolent turn of mind must like, I think, to read about them. When I was a boy, I had by heart the Barmecide's feast in the 'Arabian Nights'; and the culinary passages in Scott's novels (in which works there is a deal of good eating) always were my favourites. The Homeric poems are full, as everybody knows, of roast and boiled: and every year I look forward with pleasure to the newspapers of the 10th of November for the *menu* of the Lord Mayor's feast, which is sure to appear in those journals. What student of history is there who does not remember the City dinner given to the Allied Sovereigns in 1814? It is good even now, and to read it ought to make a man hungry, had he had five meals that day. In a word, I had long, long yearned in my secret heart to be present at a City festival. The last year's papers had a bill of fare commencing with 'four hundred tureens of turtle, each containing five pints'; and concluding with the pine-apples and ices of the dessert. 'Fancy two thousand pints of turtle, my love,' I have often said to Mrs Spec, 'in a vast silver tank, smoking fragrantly, with lovely green islands of calipash and calipee* floating about – why, my dear, if it had been invented in the time of Vitellius* he would have bathed in it!'

'He would have been a nasty wretch,' Mrs Spec said, who thinks that cold mutton is the most wholesome food of man. However, when she heard what great company was to be present at the dinner, the Ministers of State, the Foreign Ambassadors, some of the bench of Bishops, no doubt the Judges, and a great portion of the Nobility, she was pleased at the card which was sent to her husband, and made a neat tie to my white neckcloth before I set off on the festive journey. She warned me to be very cautious, and obstinately refused to allow me the Chubb door-key.

The very card of invitation is a curiosity. It is almost as big as a tea-tray. It gives one ideas of a vast, enormous hospitality. Gog and Magog* in livery might leave it at your door. If a man is to eat up that card, heaven help us, I thought; the Doctor must be called in. Indeed, it was a Doctor who procured me the placard of invitation. Like all medical men who have published a book upon diet, Pillkington is a great gourmand, and he made a great favour of procuring the ticket for me from his brother of the Stock Exchange, who is a Citizen and a Bellows-Mender in his corporate capacity.

We drove in Pillkington's brougham to the place of *mangez vous*, through the streets of the town, in the broad daylight, dressed out in our white waistcoats and ties; making a sensation upon all beholders by the premature splendour of our appearance. There is something grand in that hospitality of the citizens, who not only give you more to eat than other people, but who begin earlier than anybody else. Major Bangles, Captain Canterbury, and a host of the fashionables of my acquaintance, were taking their morning's ride in the Park as we drove through. You should have seen how they stared at us! It gave me a pleasure to be able to remark mentally, 'Look on, gents, we too are sometimes invited to the tables of the great.'

We fell in with numbers of carriages as we were approaching Citywards, in which reclined gentlemen with white neckcloths – grand equipages of foreign ambassadors, whose uniforms, and stars, and gold lace glistened within the carriages, while their servants with coloured cockades looked splendid without: these careered by the Doctor's brougham-horse, which was a little fatigued with his professional journeys in the morning. General Sir Roger Bluff, K. C. B., and Colonel Tucker, were stepping into a cab at the United Service Club as we passed it. The veterans blazed in scarlet and gold lace. It seemed strange that men so famous, if they did not mount their chargers to go to dinner, should ride in any vehicle under a coach-and-six: and instead of having a triumphal car to conduct them to the City, should go thither in a rickety cab, driven by a ragged charioteer smoking a dhoodeen.* In Cornhill we fell into a line, and formed a complete regiment of the aristocracy. Crowds were gathered round the steps of the old hall in Marrow-pudding Lane, and welcomed us nobility and gentry as we stepped out of our equipages at the door. The policemen could hardly restrain the ardour of these low fellows, and their sarcastic cheers were sometimes very unpleasant. There was one rascal who made an observation about the size of my white waistcoat, for which I should have liked to sacrifice him on the spot; but Pillkington hurried me, as the policemen did our little brougham, to give place to a prodigious fine equipage which followed, with immense grey horses, immense footmen in powder, and driven by a grave coachman in an episcopal wig.

A veteran officer in scarlet, with silver epaulets, and a profuse quantity of bullion and silver lace, descended from this carriage between the two footmen, and was nearly upset by his curling sabre, which had twisted itself between his legs, which were cased in duck trousers very tight, except about the knees (where they bagged quite freely), and with rich long white straps. I thought he must be a great man by the oddness of his uniform.

'Who is the General?' says I, as the old warrior, disentangling himself from his scimetar, entered the outer hall. 'Is it the Marquis of Anglesea, or the Rajah of Sarawak?'

I spoke in utter ignorance, as it appeared. 'That! Pooh,' says Pillkington 'that is Mr Champignon, M.P., of Whitehall Gardens and Fungus Abbey, Citizen and Bellows-Mender. His uniform is that of a Colonel of the Diddlesex Militia.' There was no end to similar mistakes on that day. A venerable man with a blue and gold uniform, and a large crimson sword-belt and brass-scabbarded sabre, passed presently, whom I mistook for a foreign ambassador at the least; whereas I found out that he was only a Billingsgate Commissioner – and a little fellow in a blue livery, which fitted him so badly that I thought he must be one of the hired waiters of the company, who had been put into a coat that didn't belong to him, turned out to be a real right honourable gent, who had been a Minister once.

I was conducted upstairs by my friend to the gorgeous drawing-room, where the company assembled, and where there was a picture of George IV. I cannot make out what public companies can want with a picture of George IV. A fellow with a gold chain, and in a black suit, such as the lamented Mr Cooper wore preparatory to execution in the last act of *George Barnwell** bawled out our names as we entered the apartment. 'If my Eliza could hear that gentleman,' thought I, 'roaring out the name of

"Mr Spec!" in the presence of at least two hundred Earls, Prelates, Judges, and distinguished characters!' It made little impression upon them, however; and I slunk into the embrasure of a window, and watched the company.

Every man who came into the room was, of course, ushered in with a roar. 'His Excellency the minister of Topinambo!' the usher yelled; and the Minister appeared, bowing, and in tights. 'Mr Hoggin! The Right Honourable the Earl of Bareacres! Mr Snog! Mr Braddle! Mr Alderman Moodle! Mr Justice Bunker! Lieut-Gen. Sir Roger Bluff! Colonel Tucker! Mr Tims!' with the same emphasis and mark of admiration for us all as it were. The Warden of the Bellows-Menders came forward and made a profusion of bows to the various distinguished guests as they arrived. He, too, was in a court dress, with a sword and bag. His lady must like so to behold him turning out in arms and ruffles, shaking hands with Ministers, and bowing over his wine-glass to their Excellencies the Foreign Ambassadors.

To be in a room with these great people gave me a thousand sensations of joy. Once, I am positive, the Secretary of the Tape and Sealing-Wax Office looked at me, and turning round to a noble lord in a red ribbon, evidently asked, 'Who is that?' Oh, Eliza, Eliza! How I wish you had been there! – or if not there, in the ladies' gallery in the dining-hall, when the music began, and Mr Shadrach, Mr Meshech, and little Jack Oldboy (whom I recollect in the part of *Count Almaviva* any time these forty years), sang *Non nobis, Domine*.

But I am advancing matters prematurely. We are not in the grand dining-hall as yet. The crowd grows thicker and thicker, so that you can't see people bow as they enter any more. The usher in the gold chain roars out name after name: more ambassadors, more generals, more citizens, capitalists, bankers – among them Mr Rowdy, my banker, from whom I shrank guiltily from private financial reasons – and, last and greatest of all, 'The Right Honourable the Lord Mayor!'

That was a shock, such as I felt on landing at Calais for the first time; on first seeing an Eastern bazaar: on first catching a sight of Mrs Spec; a new sensation, in a word. Till death I shall remember that surprise. I saw over the heads of the crowd, first a great sword borne up in the air: then a man in a fur cap of the shape of a flowerpot; then I heard the voice shouting the august name – the crowd separated. A handsome man with a chain and gown stood before me. It was he. He? What do I say? It was his Lordship. I cared for nothing till dinner-time after that.

II

The glorious company of banqueteers were now pretty well all assembled; and I, for my part, attracted by an irresistible fascination, pushed nearer and nearer my Lord Mayor, and surveyed him, as the Generals, Lords, Ambassadors, Judges, and other big-wigs rallied round him as their centre, and, being introduced to his Lordship and each other, made themselves the most solemn and graceful bows; as if it had been the object of that General's life to meet that Judge; and as if that Secretary of the Tape and Sealing-Wax Office, having achieved at length a presentation to the Lord Mayor, had gained the end of his existence, and might go home, singing a *Nunc dimittis*. Don Geronimo de Mulligan y Guayaba, Minister of the Republic of Topinambo (and originally descended from an illustrious Irish ancestor, who hewed out with his pickaxe in the Topinambo mines the steps by which his family have ascended to their present eminence), holding his cocked hat with the yellow cockade close over his embroidered coat-tails, conversed with Alderman Codshead, that celebrated Statesman, who was also in tights, with a sword and bag.

Of all the articles of the splendid court-dress of our aristocracy, I think it is those little bags which I admire most. The dear crisp curly little black darlings! They give a gentleman's back an indescribable grace and air of chivalry. They are at once manly, elegant, and useful (being made of sticking-plaster, which can be applied afterwards to heal many a wound of domestic life). They are something extra appended to men, to enable them to appear in the presence of royalty. How vastly the idea of a Court increases in solemnity and grandeur when you think that a man cannot enter it without a tail!

These thoughts passed through my mind, and pleasingly diverted it from all sensations of hunger, while many friends around me were pulling out their watches, looking towards the great dining-room doors, rattling at the lock, (the door gasped open once or twice, and the nose of a functionary on the other side peeped in among us and entreated peace,) and vowing it was scandalous, monstrous, shameful. If you ask an assembly of Englishmen to a

feast, and accident or the cook delays it, they show their gratitude
in this way. Before the supper-rooms were thrown open at my
friend Mrs Perkins's ball, I recollect Liversage at the door, swearing
and growling as if he had met with an injury. So I thought the
Bellows-Menders' guests seemed heaving into mutiny, when the
great doors burst open in a flood of light, and we rushed, a black
streaming crowd, into the gorgeous hall of banquet.

Every man sprang for his place with breathless rapidity. We
knew where those places were beforehand; for a cunning map had
been put into the hands of each of us by an officer of the Company,
where every plate of this grand festival was numbered, and each
gentleman's place was ticketed off. My wife keeps my card still in
her album; and my dear eldest boy (who has a fine genius and
appetite) will gaze on it for half an hour at a time, whereas he
passes by the copies of verses and the flower-pieces with an entire
indifference.

The vast hall flames with gas, and is emblazoned all over with
the arms of bygone Bellows-Menders. August portraits decorate
the walls. The Duke of Kent in scarlet, with a crooked sabre,
stared me firmly in the face during the whole entertainment. The
Duke of Cumberland, in a huzzar uniform, was at my back, and
I knew was looking down into my plate. The eyes of those gaunt
portraits follow you everywhere. The Prince Regent has been
mentioned before. He has his place of honour over the Great
Bellows-Mender's chair, and surveys the high table glittering with
plate, épergnes, candles, hock-glasses, moulds of blancmange
stuck over with flowers, gold statues holding up baskets of
barley-sugar, and a thousand objects of art. Piles of immense gold
cans and salvers rose up in buffets behind this high table; towards
which presently, and in a grand procession – the band in the
gallery overhead blowing out the Bellows-Menders' march – a
score of City tradesmen and their famous guests walked solemnly
between our rows of tables.

Grace was said, not by the professional devotees who sang 'Non
Nobis' at the end of the meal, but by a chaplain somewhere in the
room, and the turtle began. Armies of waiters came rushing in
with tureens of this broth of the City.

There was a gentleman near us – a very lean old Bellows-
Mender indeed, who had three platefuls. His old hands trembled,
and his plate quivered with excitement, as he asked again and
again. That old man is not destined to eat much more of the green

fat of this life. As he took it, he shook all over like the jelly in the dish opposite to him. He gasped out a quick laugh once or twice to his neighbour, when his two or three old tusks showed, still standing up in those jaws which had swallowed such a deal of calipash. He winked at the waiters, knowing them from former banquets.

This banquet, which I am describing at Christmas, took place at the end of May. At that time the vegetables called pease were exceedingly scarce, and cost six-and-twenty shillings a quart.

'There are two hundred quarts of pease,' said the old fellow, winking with blood-shot eyes, and a laugh that was perfectly frightful. They were consumed with the fragrant ducks, by those who were inclined: or with the venison, which now came in.

That was a great sight. On a centre table in the hall, on which already stood a cold Baron of Beef – a grotesque piece of meat – a dish as big as a dish in a pantomime, with a little Standard of England stuck into the top of it, as if it were round this we were to rally – on this centre table, six men placed as many huge dishes under cover; and at a given signal the master cook and five assistants in white caps and jackets marched rapidly up to the dish-covers, which being withdrawn, discovered to our sight six haunches, on which the six carvers, taking out six sharp knives from their girdles, began operating.

It was, I say, like something out of a Gothic romance, or a grotesque fairy pantomime. Feudal barons must have dined so five hundred years ago. One of those knives may have been the identical blade which Walworth plunged into Wat Tyler's ribs, and which was afterwards caught up into the City Arms, where it blazes. (Not that any man can seriously believe that Wat Tyler was hurt by the dig of the jolly old Mayor in the red gown and chain, any more than that pantaloon is singed by the great poker, which is always forthcoming at the present season). Here we were practising the noble custom of the good old times, imitating our glorious forefathers, rallying round our old institutions, like true Britons. These very flagons and platters were in the room before us, ten times as big as any we use or want now-a-days. They served us a grace-cup as large as a plate-basket, and at the end they passed us a rosewater dish, into which Pepys might have dipped his napkin. Pepys? – what do I say? Richard III, Cœur-de-Lion, Guy of Warwick, Gog and Magog. I don't know how antique the articles are.

Conversation, rapid and befitting the place and occasion, went on all round. 'Waiter, where's the turtle-fins?' – Gobble, gobble. 'Hice Punch or My deary, sir?' 'Smelts or salmon, Jowler my boy?' 'Always take cold beef after turtle.' – Hobble-gobble. 'These year pease have no taste.' Hobble-gobbleobble. 'Jones, a glass of 'Ock with you? Smith, jine us? Waiter, three 'Ocks. S., mind your manners! There's Mrs S. a-looking at you from the gallery.' – Hobble-obbl-gobble-gob-gob-gob. A steam of meats, a flare of candles, a rushing to and fro of waiters, a ceaseless clinking of glass and steel, a dizzy mist of gluttony, out of which I see my old friend of the turtle-soup making terrific play among the pease, his knife darting down his throat.

It is all over. We can eat no more. We are full of Bacchus and fat venison. We lay down our weapons and rest. 'Why, in the name of goodness,' says I, turning round to Pillkington, who had behaved at dinner like a doctor; 'why – ?'

But a great rap, tap, tap proclaimed grace, after which the professional gentlemen sang out, '*Non Nobis*,' and then the dessert and the speeches began; about which we shall speak in the third course of our entertainment.

III

On the hammer having ceased its tapping, Mr Chisel, the immortal toast-master, who presided over the President, roared out to my three professional friends, '*Non Nobis*', and what is called 'the business of the evening' commenced.

First, the Warden of the Worshipful Society of the Bellows-Menders proposed 'Her Majesty' in a reverential voice. We all stood up respectfully, Chisel yelling out to us to 'Charge our glasses.' The royal health having been imbibed, the professional gentlemen ejaculated a part of the National Anthem; and I do not mean any disrespect to them personally, in mentioning that this eminently religious hymn was performed by Messrs, Shadrach and Meshech, two well-known melodists of the Hebrew persuasion. We clinked our glasses at the conclusion of the anthem, making more dents upon the time-worn town old board, where many a man present had clinked for George III, clapped for George IV, rapped for William IV, and was rejoiced to bump the bottom of his glass as a token of reverence for our present Sovereign.

Here, as in the case of the Hebrew melophonists, I would insinuate no wrong thought. Gentlemen, no doubt, have the loyal emotions which exhibit themselves by clapping glasses on the tables. We do it at home. Let us make no doubt that the bellows-menders, tailors, authors, public characters, judges, aldermen, sheriffs, and what not, shout out a health for the Sovereign every night at their banquets, and that their families fill round and drink the same toast from the bottles of half-guinea Burgundy.

'His Royal Highness Prince Albert, and Albert Prince of Wales, and the rest of the Royal Family,' followed, Chisel yelling out the august titles, and all of us banging away with our glasses, as if we were seriously interested in drinking healths to this royal race: as if drinking healths could do anybody any good; as if the imprecations of a company of bellows-menders, aldermen, magistrates, tailors, authors, tradesmen, ambassadors, who did not care a twopenny-piece for all the royal families in Europe, could somehow affect heaven kindly towards their Royal Highnesses by their tipsy vows, under the presidence of Mr Chisel.

The Queen Dowager's health was next prayed for by us Bacchanalians, I need not say with what fervency and efficacy. This prayer was no sooner put up by the Chairman, with Chisel as his Boanerges* of a Clerk, than the elderly Hebrew gentlemen before mentioned began striking up a wild patriotic ditty about the 'Queen of the Isles, on whose sea-girt shores the bright sun smiles, and the ocean roars; whose cliffs never knew, since the bright sun rose, but a people true, who scorned all foes. Oh, a people true, who scorn all wiles, inhabit you, bright Queen of the Isles. Bright Quee – Bright Quee – ee – ee – ee – ee – en awf the Isles!' or words to that effect, which Shadrach took up and warbled across his glass to Meshech, which Meshech trolled away to his brother singer, until the ditty was ended, nobody understanding a word of what it meant; not Oldboy – not the old or young Israelite minstrel his companion – not we, who were clinking our glasses – not Chisel, who was urging us and the Chairman on – not the Chairman and the guests in embroidery – not the kind, exalted, and amiable lady whose health we were making believe to drink, certainly, and in order to render whose name welcome to the Powers to whom we recommended her safety, we offered up, through the mouths of three singers, hired for the purpose, a perfectly insane and irrelevant song.

'Why,' says I to Pillkington, 'the Chairman and the grand guests might just as well get up and dance round the table, or cut off Chisel's head and pop it into a turtle-soup tureen, or go through any other mad ceremony as the last. Which of us here cares for her Majesty the Queen Dowager, any more than for a virtuous and eminent lady, whose goodness and private worth appear in all her acts? What the deuce has that absurd song about the Queen of the Isles to do with her Majesty, and how does it set us all stamping with our glasses on the mahogany?' Chisel bellowed out another toast – 'The Army'; and we were silent in admiration, while Sir George Bluff, the greatest General present, rose to return thanks.

Our end of the table was far removed form the thick of the affair, and we only heard, as it were, the indistinct cannonading of the General, whose force had just advanced into action. We saw an old gentleman with white whiskers, and a flaring scarlet coat covered with stars and gilding, rise up with a frightened and desperate look, and declare that 'this was the proudest – a-hem – moment of his – a-hem – unworthy as he was – a-hem – as a member of the British – a-hem – who had fought under the illustrious Duke of – a-hem – his joy was to come among the Bellows-Menders – a-hem – and inform the great merchants of the greatest City of the – hum – that a British – a-hem – was always ready to do his – hum. Napoleon – Salamanca – a-hem – had witnessed their – hum, haw – and should any other – hum – ho – casion which he deeply deprecated – haw – there were men now around him – a-haw – who, inspired by the Bellows-Menders' Company and the City of London – a-hum – would do their duty as – a-hum – a-haw – a-hah.' Immense cheers, yells, hurrays, roars, glass-smackings, and applause followed this harangue, at the end of which the three Israelites, encouraged by Chisel, began a military cantata – 'Oh, the sword and shield – on the battle-field – Are the joys that best we love, boys – Where the Grenadiers, with their pikes and spears, through the ranks of the foemen shove, boys – Where the bold hurray, strikes dread dismay, in the ranks of the dead and dyin' – and the baynet clanks in the Frenchmen's ranks, as they fly from the British Lion.' (I repeat, as before, that I quote from memory.)

Then the Secretary of the Tape and Sealing-Wax Office rose to return thanks for the blessings which we begged upon the Ministry. He was, he said, but a humble – the humblest member of that body. The suffrages which that body had received from the nation were gratifying, but the most gratifying testimonial of all was the approval of the Bellows-Menders' Company. (*Immense applause.*) Yes, among the most enlightened of the mighty corporations of the City, the most enlightened was the Bellows-Menders'. Yes, he might say, in consonance with their motto, and in defiance of illiberality, *Afflavit veritas et dissipati sunt.* (*Enormous applause.*) Yes, the thanks and pride that were boiling with emotion in his bosom, trembled to find utterance at his lip. Yes, the proudest moment of his life, the crown of his ambition, the meed of his early hopes and struggles and aspirations, was at that moment won in the approbation of the Bellows-Menders. Yes, his children should know that he too had attended at those great, those noble, those joyous, those ancient festivals, and that he too, the humble individual who from his heart pledged the assembled company in a bumper – that he too was a Bellows-Mender.

Shadrach, Meshech, and Oldboy, at this began singing, I don't know for what reason, a rustic madrigal, describing, 'Oh, the joys of bonny May – bonny May – a-a-ay, when the birds sing on the spray,' &c., which never, as I could see, had the least relation to that or any other Ministry, but which was, nevertheless, applauded by all present. And then the Judges returned thanks; and the Clergy returned thanks; and the Foreign Ministers had an innings (all interspersed by my friends' indefatigable melodies); and the distinguished foreigners present, especially Mr Washington Jackson, were greeted, and that distinguished American rose amidst thunders of applause.

He explained how Broadway and Cornhill were in fact the same. He showed how Washington was in fact an Englishman, and how Franklin would never have been an American but for his education as a printer in Lincoln's Inn Fields. He declared that Milton was his cousin, Locke his ancestor, Newton his dearest friend, Shakespeare his grandfather, or more or less – he vowed that he had wept tears of briny anguish on the pedestal of Charing Cross – kissed with honest fervour the clay of Runnymede – that Ben Jonson and Samuel – that Pope and Dryden, and Dr Watts and Swift were the darlings of *his* hearth and home, as of ours, and in a speech of about five-and-thirty minutes, explained to us a series of complimentary sensations very hard to repeat or to remember.

But I observed that, during his oration, the gentlemen who report for the daily papers were occupied with their wine instead of their note-books – that the three singers of Israel yawned and showed many signs of disquiet and inebriety, and that my old friend, who had swallowed the three plates of turtle, was sound asleep.

Pillkington and I quitted the banqueting-hall, and went into the tea-room, where gents were assembled still, drinking slops and eating buttered muffins, until the grease trickled down their faces. Then I resumed the query which I was just about to put, when grace was called, and the last chapter ended. 'And, gracious goodness!' I said, 'what can be the meaning of a ceremony so costly, so uncomfortable, so unsavoury, so unwholesome as this? Who is called upon to pay two or three guineas for my dinner now, in this blessed year 1847? Who is it that *can* want muffins after such a banquet? Are there no poor? Is there no reason? Is this monstrous belly-worship to exist for ever?'

'Spec,' the Doctor said, 'you had best come away. I make no doubt that you for one have had too much.' And we went to his brougham. May nobody have such a headache on this happy New Year as befell the present writer on the morning after the Dinner in the City!

THE FATAL BOOTS

January – The birth of the year

Some poet has observed, that if any man would write down what has really happened to him in this mortal life, he would be sure to make a good book, though he never had met with a single adventure from his birth to his burial. How much more, then, must I, who *have* had adventures, most singular, pathetic, and unparalleled, be able to compile an instructive and entertaining volume for the use of the public.

I don't mean to say that I have killed lions, or seen the wonders of travel in the deserts of Arabia or Persia; or that I have been a very fashionable character, living with dukes and peeresses, and writing my recollections of them, as the way now is. I never left this my native isle, nor spoke to a lord (except an Irish one, who had rooms in our house, and forgot to pay three weeks' lodging and extras); but, as our immortal bard observes, I have in the course of my existence been so eaten up by the slugs and harrows of outrageous fortune, and have been the object of such continual and extraordinary ill-luck, that I believe it would melt the heart of a milestone to read of it – that is, if a milestone had a heart of anything but stone.

Twelve of my adventures, suitable for meditation and perusal during the twelve months of the year, have been arranged by me for this work. They contain a part of the history of a great, and, confidently I may say, a *good* man. I was not a spendthrift like other men. I never wronged any man of a shilling, though I am as sharp a fellow at a bargain as any in Europe. I never injured a fellow-creature; on the contrary, on several occasions, when injured myself, have shown the most wonderful forbearance. I come of a tolerably good family; and yet, born to wealth – of an inoffensive disposition, careful of the money that I had, and eager to get more – I have been going down hill ever since my journey of life began, and have been pursued by a complication of misfortunes such as surely never happened to any man but the unhappy Bob Stubbs.

Bob Stubbs is my name; and I haven't got a shilling; I have borne the commission of lieutenant in the service of King George, and am *now* – but never mind what I am now, for the public will know in a few pages more. My father was of the Suffolk Stubbses – a well-to-do gentleman of Bungay. My grandfather had been a respected attorney in that town, and left my papa a pretty little fortune. I was thus the inheritor of competence, and ought to be at this moment a gentleman.

My misfortunes may be said to have commenced about a year before my birth, when my papa, a young fellow pretending to study the law in London, fell madly in love with Miss Smith, the daughter of a tradesman, who did not give her a sixpence, and afterwards became bankrupt. My papa married this Miss Smith, and carried her off to the country, where I was born, in an evil hour for me.

Were I to attempt to describe my early years, you would laugh at me as an impostor; but the following letter from mamma to a friend, after her marriage, will pretty well show you what a poor foolish creature she was; and what a reckless extravagant fellow was my other unfortunate parent:

To Miss Eliza Kicks, in Gracechurch Street, London

Oh, Eliza! your Susan is the happiest girl under heaven! My Thomas is an angel! not a tall grenadier-like looking fellow, such as I always vowed I would marry: on the contrary, he is what the world would call dumpy, and I hesitate not to confess, that his eyes have a cast in them. But what then? when one of his eyes is fixed on me, and one on my babe, they are lighted up with an affection which my pen cannot describe, and which, certainly, was never bestowed upon any woman so strongly as upon your happy Susan Stubbs.

When he comes home from shooting, or the farm, if you *could* see dear Thomas with me and our dear little Bob! as I sit on one knee, and baby on the other, and as he dances us both about. I often wish that we had Sir Joshua* or some great painter, to depict the group; for sure it is the prettiest picture in the whole world, to see three such loving merry people.

Dear baby is the most lovely little creature that *can possibly be* – the very *image* of papa; he is cutting his teeth, and the delight of *everybody*. Nurse says that, when he is older, he will get rid of his squint, and his hair will get a *great deal* less red. Doctor Bates is as kind, and skilful, and attentive as we could desire. Think what a blessing to have had him! Ever since poor baby's birth, it has never had a day of quiet; and he has been obliged to give it from three to four doses every week; – how thankful ought we to be that the *dear thing* is as well as it is! It got through the

January – The birth of the year

measles wonderfully; then it had a little rash; and then a nasty hooping-cough; and then a fever, and continual pains in its poor little stomach, crying, poor dear child, from morning till night.

But dear Tom is an excellent nurse; and many and many a night has he had no sleep, dear man! in consequence of the poor little baby. He walks up and down with it *for hours*, singing a kind of song (dear fellow, he has no more voice than a tea-kettle), and bobbing his head backwards and forwards, and looking, in his night-cap and dressing-gown, *so droll*. Oh, Eliza! how you would laugh to see him.

We have one of the best nursemaids *in the world* an Irishwoman, who is as fond of baby almost as his mother (but that can *never be*). She takes it to walk in the park for hours together, and I really don't know why Thomas dislikes her. He says she is tipsy, very often, and slovenly, which I cannot conceive – to be sure, the nurse is sadly dirty, and sometimes smells very strong of gin.

But what of that? – these little drawbacks only make home more pleasant. When one thinks how many mothers have *no* nursemaids: how many poor dear children have no doctors: ought we not to be thankful for Mary Malowney, and that Doctor Bates's bill is forty-seven pounds? How ill must dear baby have been, to require so much physic!

But they are a sad expense, these dear babies, after all. Fancy, Eliza, how much this Mary Malowney costs us. Ten shillings every week; a glass of brandy or gin at dinner; three pint-bottles of Mr Thrale's best porter every day, – making twenty-one in a week, and nine hundred and ninety in the eleven months she has been with us. Then, for baby, there is Doctor Bates's bill of forty-five guineas, two guineas for christening, twenty for a grand christening supper and ball (rich uncle John mortally offended because he was made godfather, and had to give baby a silver cup: he has struck Thomas out of his will: and old Mr Firkin quite as much hurt because he was *not* asked: he will not speak to me or Thomas in consequence); twenty guineas for flannels, laces, little gowns, caps, napkins, and such baby's ware: and all this out of £300 a year! But Thomas expects to make *a great deal* by his farm.

We have got the most charming country-house *you can imagine*: it is *quite shut in* by trees, and so retired that, though only thirty miles from London, the post comes to us but once a week. The roads, it must be confessed, are execrable; it is winter now, and we are up to our knees in mud and snow. But oh, Eliza! how happy we are: with Thomas (he has had a sad attack of rheumatism, dear man!) and little Bobby, and our kind friend Doctor Bates, who comes so far to see us, I leave you to fancy that we have a charming merry party, and do not care for all the gaieties of Ranelagh.

Adieu! dear baby is crying for his mamma. A thousand kisses from your affectionate

Susan Stubbs

There it is! Doctor's bills, gentleman-farming, twenty-one pints of porter a week. In this way my unnatural parents were already robbing me of my property.

February – Cutting weather

I have called this chapter 'cutting weather', partly in compliment to the month of February, and partly in respect of my own misfortunes, which you are going to read about. For I have often thought that January (which is mostly twelfth-cake* and holiday time) is like the first four or five years of a little boy's life; then comes dismal February, and the working-days with it, when chaps begin to look out for themselves, after the Christmas and the New Year's heyday and merry-making are over, which our infancy may well be said to be. Well can I recollect that bitter first of February, when I first launched out into the world and appeared at Doctor Swishtail's academy.

I began at school that life of prudence and economy which I have carried on ever since. My mother gave me eighteenpence on setting out (poor soul! I thought her heart would break as she kissed me, and bade God bless me); and, besides, I had a small capital of my own, which I had amassed for a year previous. I'll tell you what I used to do. Wherever I saw six halfpence I took one. If it was asked for, I said I had taken it, and gave it back; if it was not missed, I said nothing about it, as why should I? – those who don't miss their money, don't lose their money. So I had a little private fortune of three shillings, besides mother's eighteen-pence. At school they called me the copper-merchant, I had such lots of it.

Now, even at a preparatory school, a well-regulated boy may better himself: and I can tell you I did. I never was in any quarrels:

I never was very high in the class or very low; but there was no chap so much respected: and why? *I'd always money*. The other boys spent all theirs in the first day or two, and they gave me plenty of cakes and barley-sugar then, I can tell you. I'd no need to spend my own money, for they would insist upon treating me. Well, in a week, when theirs was gone, and they had but their threepence a week to look to for the rest of the half-year, what did I do? Why, I am proud to say that three-halfpence out of the threepence a week of almost all the young gentlemen at Doctor Swishtail's, came into my pocket. Suppose, for instance, Tom Hicks wanted a slice of gingerbread, who had the money? Little Bob Stubbs, to be sure. 'Hicks,' I used to say, '*I'll* buy you three halfp'orth of gingerbread, if you'll give me threepence next Saturday.' And he agreed; and next Saturday came, and he very often could not pay me more than three-halfpence. Then there was the threepence I was to have *the next* Saturday. I'll tell you what I did for a whole half-year: I lent a chap, by the name of Dick Bunting, three-half-pence the first Saturday for threepence the next: he could not pay me more than half when Saturday came, and I'm blest if I did not make him pay me three-halfpence *for three-and-twenty weeks running*, making two shillings and tenpence-halfpenny. But he was a sad dishonourable fellow, Dick Bunting; for, after I'd been so kind to him, and let him off for three-and-twenty weeks the money he owed me, holidays, came, and threepence he owed me still. Well, according to the common principles of practice, after six weeks' holidays, he ought to have paid me exactly sixteen shillings, which was my due. For the

First week the 3d would be	6d.	Fourth week	4s
Second week	1s	Fifth week	8s
Third week	2s	Sixth week	16s

Nothing could be more just; and yet – will it be believed? – when Bunting came back he offered me *three-halfpence*! the mean, dishonest scoundrel.

However, I was even with him, I can tell you. He spent all his money in a fortnight, and *then* I screwed him down! I made him, besides giving me a penny for a penny, pay me a quarter of his bread-and-butter at breakfast and a quarter of his cheese at supper; and before the half-year was out, I got from him a silver fruit-knife, a box of compasses, and a very pretty silver-laced waistcoat, in which I went home as proud as a king: and, what's

February – Cutting weather

more, I had no less than three golden guineas in the pocket of it, besides fifteen shillings, the knife, and a brass bottle-screw, which I got from another chap. It wasn't bad interest for twelve shillings – which was all the money I'd had in the year – was it? Heigho! I've often wished that I could get such a chance again in this wicked world; but men are more avaricious now than they used to be in those dear early days.

Well, I went home in my new waistcoat as fine as a peacock; and when I gave the bottle-screw to my father, begging him to take it as a token of my affection for him, my dear mother burst into such a fit of tears as I never saw, and kissed and hugged me fit to smother me. 'Bless him, bless him!' says she, 'to think of his old father. And where did you purchase it, Bob?' – 'Why, mother,' says I, 'I purchased it out of my savings' (which was as true as the gospel). When I said this, mother looked round to father, smiling, although she had tears in her eyes, and she took his hand, and with her other hand drew me to her. 'Is he not a noble boy?' says she to my father: 'and only nine years old!' – 'Faith,' says my father, 'he *is* a good lad, Susan. Thank thee, my boy: and here is a crown-piece in return for thy bottle-screw: it shall open us a bottle of the very best too,' says my father. And he kept his word. I always was fond of good wine (though never, from a motive of proper self-denial, having any in my cellar); and, by Jupiter! on this night I had my little skinful – for there was no stinting – so pleased were my dear parents with the bottle-screw. The best of it was, it only cost me threepence originally, which a chap could not pay me.

Seeing this game was such a good one, I became very generous towards my parents; and a capital way it is to encourage liberality in children. I gave mamma a very neat brass thimble, and she gave me a half-guinea piece. Then I gave her a very pretty needle-book, which I made myself with an ace of spades from a new pack of cards we had, and I got Sally, our maid, to cover it with a bit of pink satin her mistress had given her; and I made the leaves of the book, which I vandyked* very nicely, out of a piece of flannel I had had round my neck for a sore throat. It smelt a little of hartshorn,* but it was a beautiful needle-book; and mamma was so delighted with it, that she went into town and bought me a gold-laced hat. Then I bought papa a pretty china tobacco-stopper: but I am sorry to say of my dear father that he was not so generous as my mamma or myself, for he only burst out laughing, and did not give me so much as a half-crown piece, which was the least I expected from him. 'I shan't give you anything, Bob, this time,' says he; 'and I wish, my boy, you would not make any more such presents – for, really, they are too expensive.' Expensive indeed! I hate meanness – even in a father.

I must tell you about the silver-edged waistcoat which Bunting gave me. Mamma asked me about it, and I told her the truth, – that it was a present from one of the boys for my kindness to him. Well, what does she do but writes back to Doctor Swishtail, when I went to school, thanking him for his attention to her dear son, and sending a shilling to the good and grateful little boy who had given me the waistcoat!

'What waistcoat is it,' says the Doctor to me, 'and who gave it to you?'

'Bunting gave it me, sir,' says I.

'Call Bunting!' And up the little ungrateful chap came. Would you believe it, he burst into tears – told that the waistcoat had been given him by his mother, and that he had been forced to give it for a debt to Copper-Merchant, as the nasty little blackguard called me? He then said how, for three-halfpence, he had been compelled to pay me three shillings (the sneak! as if he had been *obliged* to borrow the three-halfpence!) – how all the other boys had been swindled (swindled!) by me in like manner, – and how, with only twelve shillings, I had managed to scrape together four guineas …

My courage almost fails me as I describe the shameful scene that followed. The boys were called in, my own little account-book was dragged out of my cupboard, to prove how much I had received from each, and every farthing of my money was paid back to them. The tyrant took the thirty shillings that my dear parents had given me, and said he should put them into the poor-box at church; and, after having made a long discourse to the boys about meanness and usury, he said, 'Take off your coat, Mr Stubbs, and restore Bunting his waistcoat.' I did, and stood without coat and waistcoat in the midst of the nasty grinning boys. I was going to put on my coat –

'Stop!' says he. '*Take down his breeches*!'

Ruthless, brutal villain! Sam Hopkins, the biggest boy, took them down – horsed me – and *I was flogged*, sir: yes, flogged! O revenge! I, Robert Stubbs, who had done nothing but what was right, was brutally flogged at ten years of age! – Though February was the shortest month, I remembered it long.

March – Showery

When my mamma heard of the treatment of her darling she was for bringing an action against the schoolmaster, or else for tearing his eyes out (when, dear soul! she would not have torn the eyes out of a flea, had it been her own injury), and, at the very least, for having me removed from the school where I had been so shamefully treated. But papa was stern for once, and vowed that I had been served quite right, declared that I should not be removed from the school, and sent old Swishtail a brace of pheasants for what he called his kindness to me. Of these the old gentleman invited me to partake, and made a very queer speech at dinner, as he was cutting them up, about the excellence of my parents, and his own determination to be *kinder still* to me, if ever I ventured on such practices again. So I was obliged to give up my old trade of lending: for the Doctor declared that any boy who borrowed should be flogged, and any one who *paid* should be flogged twice as much. There was no standing against such a prohibition as this, and my little commerce was ruined.

I was not very high in the school: not having been able to get farther than that dreadful *Propria quæ maribus* in the Latin grammar, of which, though I have it by heart even now, I never could understand a syllable: but, on account of my size, my age, and the prayers of my mother, was allowed to have the privilege of the bigger boys, and on holidays to walk about in the town. Great dandies we were, too, when we thus went out. I recollect my costume very well: a thunder-and-lightning coat, a white waistcoat embroidered neatly at the pockets, a lace frill, a pair of knee-breeches, and elegant white cotton or silk stockings. This did very well, but still I was dissatisfied: I wanted *a pair of boots*. Three boys in the school had boots – I was mad to have them too.

But my papa, when I wrote to him, would not hear of it; and three pounds, the price of a pair, was too large a sum for my mother to take from the house-keeping, or for me to pay, in the present impoverished state of my exchequer; but the desire for the boots was so strong, that have them I must at any rate.

March – Showery

There was a German bootmaker who had just set up in *our* town in those days, who afterwards made his fortune in London. I determined to have the boots from him, and did not despair, before the end of a year or two, either to leave the school, when I should not mind his dunning me, or to screw the money from mamma, and so pay him.

So I called upon this man – Stiffelkind was his name – and he took my measure for a pair.

'You are a vary yong gentleman to wear dop-boots,' said the shoemaker.

'I suppose, fellow,' says I, 'that is my business and not yours. Either make the boots or not – but when you speak to a man of my rank, speak respectfully!' And I poured out a number of oaths, in order to impress him with a notion of my respectability.

They had the desired effect. 'Stay, sir,' says he. 'I have a nice littel pair of dop-boots dat I tink will jost do for you.' And he produced, sure enough, the most elegant things I ever saw. 'Day were made,' said he, 'for de Honourable Mr Stiffney, of de Gards, but were too small'

'Ah, indeed!' said I. 'Stiffney is a relation of mine. And what, you scoundrel, will you have the impudence to ask for these things?' He replied, 'Three pounds.'

'Well,' said I, 'they are confoundedly dear; but, as you will have a long time to wait for your money, why, I shall have my revenge you see.' The man looked alarmed, and began a speech: 'Sare – I cannot let dem go vidout' – but a bright thought struck me, and I interrupted – 'Sir! don't sir me. Take off the boots, fellow, and, hark ye, when you speak to a nobleman, don't say – Sir.'

'A hundert tousand pardons, my lort,' says he: 'if I had known you were a lort, I vood never have called you – Sir. Vat name shall I put down in my books?'

'Name? – oh! why, Lord Cornwallis, to be sure,' said I, as I walked off in the boots.

'And vat shall I do vid my lort's shoes?'

'Keep them until I send for them,' said I. And, giving him a patronising bow, I walked out of the shop, as the German tied up my shoes in paper.

This story I would not have told, but that my whole life turned upon these accursed boots. I walked back to school as proud as a peacock, and easily succeeded in satisfying the boys as to the manner in which I came by my new ornaments.

Well, one fatal Monday morning – the blackest of all black Mondays that ever I knew – as we were all of us playing between school-hours, I saw a posse of boys round a stranger, who seemed to be looking out for one of us. A sudden trembling seized me – I knew it was Stiffelkind. What had brought him here? He talked loud, and seemed angry. So I rushed into the school-room, and burying my head between my hands, began reading for dear life.

'I vant Lort Cornvallis,' said the horrid bootmaker. 'His lort-ship belongs, I know, to dis honourable school, for I saw him vid de boys at chorch yesterday.'

'Lord who?'

'Vy, Lort Cornvallis to be sure – a very fat yong nobleman, vid red hair: he squints a little, and svears dreadfully.'

'There's no Lord Cornvallis here,' said one; and there was a pause.

'Stop! I have it,' says that odious Bunting. '*It must be Stubbs*!' And 'Stubbs! Stubbs!' every one cried out, while I was so busy at my book as not to hear a word.

At last, two of the biggest chaps rushed into the school-room, and seizing each an arm, run me into the playground – bolt up against the shoemaker.

'Dis is my man. I beg your lortship's pardon,' says he, 'I have brought your lortship's shoes, vich you left. See, dey have been in dis parcel ever since you vent avay in my boots.'

'Shoes, fellow!' says I. 'I never saw your face before!' For I knew there was nothing for it but brazening it out. 'Upon the honour of a gentleman!' said I, turning round to the boys. They hesitated; and if the trick had turned in my favour, fifty of them would have seized hold of Stiffelkind and drubbed him soundly.

'Stop!' says Bunting (hang him!) 'Let's see the shoes. If they fit him, why then the cobbler's right.' They did fit me; and not only that, but the name of *Stubbs* was written in them at full length.

'Vat!' said Stiffelkind. 'Is he not a lort? So help me Himmel, I never did vonce tink of looking at de shoes, which have been lying ever since in dis piece of brown paper.' And then, gathering anger as he went on, he thundered out so much of his abuse of me, in his German-English, that the boys roared with laughter. Swishtail came in in the midst of the disturbance, and asked what the noise meant.

'It's only Lord Cornwallis, sir,' said the boys, 'battling with his shoemaker about the price of a pair of top-boots.'

'Oh, sir,' said I, 'it was only in fun that I called myself Lord Cornwallis.'

'In fun! – Where are the boots? And you, sir, give me your bill.' My beautiful boots were brought; and Stiffelkind produced his bill. 'Lord Cornwallis to Samuel Stiffelkind, for a pair of boots – four guineas.'

'You have been fool enough, sir,' says the Doctor, looking very stern, 'to let this boy impose on you as a lord; and knave enough to charge him double the value of the article you sold him. Take back the boots, sir! I won't pay a penny of your bill; nor can you get a penny. As for you, sir, you miserable swindler and cheat, I shall not flog you as I did before, but I shall send you home: you are not fit to be the companion of honest boys.'

'*Suppose we duck him* before he goes?' piped out a very small voice. The Doctor grinned significantly, and left the school-room; and the boys knew by this they might have their will. They seized me and carried me to the playground pump: they pumped upon me until I was half dead; and the monster, Stiffelkind, stood looking on for the half-hour the operation lasted.

I suppose the Doctor, at last, thought I had had pumping enough, for he rang the school-bell, and the boys were obliged to leave me. As I got out of the trough, Stiffelkind was alone with me. 'Vell, my lort,' says he, 'you have paid *something* for dese boots, but not all. By Jubider, *you shall never hear de end of dem.*' And I didn't.

April – Fooling

After this, as you may fancy, I left this disgusting establishment, and lived for some time along with pa and mamma at home. My education was finished, at least mamma and I agreed that it was; and from boyhood until hobbadyhoyhood (which I take to be about the sixteenth year of the life of a young man, and may be likened to the month of April when spring begins to bloom) – from fourteen until seventeen, I say, I remained at home, doing nothing – for which I have ever since had a great taste – the idol of my mamma, who took part in all my quarrels with father, and used regularly to rob the weekly expenses in order to find me in pocket-money. Poor soul! many and many is the guinea I have had from her in that way; and so she enabled me to cut a very pretty figure.

Papa was for having me at this time articled to a merchant, or put to some profession; but mamma and I agreed that I was born to be a gentleman and not a tradesman, and the army was the only place for me. Everybody was a soldier in those times, for the French war had just begun, and the whole country was swarming with militia regiments. 'We'll get him a commission in a marching regiment,' said my father. 'As we have no money to purchase him up, he'll *fight* his way, I make no doubt.' And papa looked at me with a kind of air of contempt, as much as to say he doubted whether I should be very eager for such a dangerous way of bettering myself.

I wish you could have heard mamma's screech when he talked so coolly of my going out to fight! 'What, send him abroad, across the horrid, horrid sea – to be wrecked and perhaps drowned, and only to land for the purpose of fighting the wicked Frenchmen, – to be wounded and perhaps kick – kick – killed! Oh, Thomas, Thomas! would you murder me and your boy?' There was a regular scene. However, it ended – as it always did – in mother's getting the better, and it was settled that I should go into the militia. And why not? The uniform is just as handsome, and the danger not half so great. I don't think in the course of my whole military experience I ever fought anything, except an old woman, who had the impudence to hallo out, 'Heads up, lobster!' – Well, I joined the North Bungays, and was fairly launched into the world.

I was not a handsome man, I know; but there was *something* about me – that's very evident – for the girls always laughed when they talked to me, and the men, though they were affected to call me a poor little creature, squint-eyes, knock-knees, red-head, and so on, were evidently annoyed by my success, for they hated me so confoundedly. Even at the present time they go on, though I have given up gallivanting, as I call it. But in the April of my existence, – that is, in anno Domini 1791, or so – it was a different case; and having nothing else to do, and being bent upon bettering my condition, I did some very pretty things in that way. But I was not hot-headed and imprudent, like most young fellows. Don't fancy I looked for beauty! Pish! – I wasn't such a fool. Nor for temper; I don't care about a bad temper: I could break any woman's heart in two years. What I wanted was to get on in the world. Of course I didn't *prefer* an ugly woman, or a shrew; and when the choice offered, would certainly put up with a handsome, good-humoured girl, with plenty of money, as any honest man would.

Now there were two tolerably rich girls in our parts: Miss Magdalen Crutty, with twelve thousand pounds (and, to do her justice, as plain a girl as ever I saw), and Miss Mary Waters, a fine, tall, plump, smiling, peach-cheeked, golden-haired, white-skinned lass, with only ten. Mary Waters lived with her uncle, the Doctor, who had helped me into the world, and who was trusted with this little orphan charge very soon after. My mother, as you have heard, was so fond of Bates, and Bates so fond of little Mary, that both, at first, were almost always in our house; and I used to call her my little wife as soon as I could speak, and before she could walk almost. It was beautiful to see us, the neighbours said.

Well, when her brother, the lieutenant of an India ship, came to be captain, and actually gave Mary five thousand pounds, when she was about ten years old, and promised her five thousand more, there was a great talking, and bobbing, and smiling between the Doctor and my parents, and Mary and I were left together more than ever, and she was told to call me her little husband. And she did; and it was considered a settled thing from that day. She was really amazingly fond of me.

Can any one call me mercenary after that? Though Miss Crutty had twelve thousand, and Mary only ten (five in hand, and five

April – Fooling

in the bush), I stuck faithfully to Mary. As a matter of course, Miss Crutty hated Miss Waters. The fact was, Mary had all the country dangling after her, and not a soul would come to Magdalen, for all her £12,000. I used to be attentive to her though (as it's always useful to be); and Mary would sometimes laugh and sometimes cry at my flirting with Magdalen. This I thought proper very quickly to check. 'Mary,' said I, 'you know that my love for you is disinterested, – for I am faithful to you, though Miss Crutty is richer than you. Don't fly into a rage, then, because I pay her attentions, when you know that my heart and my promise are engaged to you.'

The fact is, to tell a little bit of a secret, there is nothing like the having two strings to your bow. 'Who knows?' thought I. 'Mary may die; and then where is my £10,000?' So I used to be very kind indeed to Miss Crutty; and well it was that I was so: for when I was twenty and Mary eighteen, I'm blest if news did not arrive that Captain Waters, who was coming home to England with all his money in rupees, had been taken – ship, rupees, self and all – by a French privateer; and Mary, instead of £10,000, had only £5,000, making a difference of no less than £350 per annum betwixt her and Miss Crutty.

I had just joined my regiment (the famous North Bungay Fencibles,* Colonel Craw commanding) when this news reached me; and you may fancy how a young man, in an expensive regiment and mess, having uniforms and what not to pay for, and a figure to cut in the world, felt at hearing such news! 'My dearest Robert,' wrote Miss Waters, 'will deplore my dear brother's loss: but not, I am sure, the money which that kind and generous soul had promised me. I have still five thousand pounds, and with this and your own little fortune (I had £1,000 in the Five per Cents!)* we shall be as happy and contented as possible.'

Happy and contented indeed! Didn't I know how my father got on with his £300 a year, and how it was all he could do out of it to add a hundred a year to my narrow income, and live himself! My mind was made up. I instantly mounted the coach and flew to our village, – to Mr Crutty's, of course. It was next door to Doctor Bates's; but I had no business *there*.

I found Magdalen in the garden. 'Heavens, Mr Stubbs!' said she, as in my new uniform I appeared before her, 'I really did never – such a handsome officer – expect to see you.' And she made as if she would blush, and began to tremble violently. I led her to a garden-seat. I seized her hand – it was not withdrawn. I pressed it; – I thought the pressure was returned. I flung myself on my knees, and then I poured into her ear a little speech which I had made on the top of the coach. 'Divine Miss Crutty,' said I; 'idol of my soul! It was but to catch one glimpse of you that I passed through this garden. I never intended to breathe the secret passion.' (oh, no; of course not) 'which was wearing my life away. You know my unfortunate pre-engagement – it is broken, and *for ever*! I am free; – free, but to be your slave, – your humblest, fondest, truest slave!' And so on ...

'Oh, Mr Stubbs,' said she, as I imprinted a kiss upon her cheek, 'I can't refuse you; but I fear you are a sad naughty man ... '

Absorbed in the delicious reverie which was caused by the dear creature's confusion, we were both silent for a while, and should have remained so for hours perhaps, so lost were we in happiness, had I not been suddenly roused by a voice exclaiming from behind us –

'*Don't cry, Mary! He is a swindling, sneaking scoundrel, and you are well rid of him!*'

I turned round. O heaven, there stood Mary, weeping on Doctor Bates's arm, while that miserable apothecary was looking at me with the utmost scorn. The gardener, who had let me in, had told them of my arrival, and now stood grinning behind them. 'Imperence!' was my Magdalen's only exclamation, as she flounced by with the utmost self-possession, while I, glancing daggers at *the spies*, followed her. We retired to the parlour, where she repeated to me the strongest assurances of her love.

I thought I was a made man. Alas! I was only an *April Fool*!

May – Restoration Day

As the month of May is considered, by poets and other philosophers, to be devoted by Nature to the great purpose of love-making, I may as well take advantage of that season and acquaint you with the result of *my* amours.

Young, gay, fascinating, and an ensign – I had completely won the heart of my Magdalen; and as for Miss Waters and her nasty uncle the Doctor, there was a complete split between us, as you may fancy; Miss pretending, forsooth, that she was glad I had broken off the match, though she would have given her eyes, the little minx, to have had it on again. But this was out of the question. My father, who had all sorts of queer notions, said I had acted like a rascal in the business; my mother took my part, of course, and declared I acted rightly, as I always did: and I got leave of absence from the regiment in order to press my beloved Magdalen to marry me out of hand – knowing, from reading and experience, the extraordinary mutability of human affairs.

Besides, as the dear girl was seventeen years older than myself, and as bad in health as she was in temper, how was I to know that the grim king of terrors might not carry her off before she became mine? With the tenderest warmth, then, and most delicate ardour, I continued to press my suit. The happy day was fixed – the ever memorable 10th of May, 1792. The wedding-clothes were ordered; and, to make things secure, I penned a little paragraph for the county paper to this effect: 'Marriage in High Life. We understand that Ensign Stubbs, of the North Bungay Fencibles, and son of Thomas Stubbs, of Sloffemsquiggle, Esquire, is about to lead to the hymeneal altar the lovely and accomplished daughter of Solomon Crutty, Esquire, of the same place. A fortune of twenty thousand pounds is, we hear, the lady's portion. "None but the brave deserve the fair."'

'Have you informed your relatives, my beloved?' said I to Magdalen one day after sending the above notice; 'will any of them attend at your marriage?'

'Uncle Sam will, I dare say,' said Miss Crutty, 'dear mamma's brother.'

'And who *was* your dear mamma?' said I: for Miss Crutty's respected parent had been long since dead, and I never heard her name mentioned in the family.

Magdalen blushed, and cast down her eyes to the ground. 'Mamma was a foreigner,' at last she said.

'And of what country?'

'A German. Papa married her when she was very young: she was not of a very good family,' said Miss Crutty, hesitating.

'And what care I for family, my love!' said I, tenderly kissing the knuckles of the hand which I held. 'She must have been an angel who gave birth to you.'

'She was a shoemaker's daughter.'

'*A German shoemaker*! Hang 'em!' thought I, 'I have had enough of them!'; and so broke up this conversation, which did not somehow please me.

Well, the day was drawing near: the clothes were ordered; the banns were read. My dear mamma had built a cake about the size of a washing-tub; and I was only waiting for a week to pass to put me in possession of twelve thousand pounds in the Five per Cents,* as they were in those days, heaven bless 'em! Little did I know the storm that was brewing, and the disappointment which was to fall upon a young man who really did his best to get a fortune.

'Oh, Robert!' said my Magdalen to me, two days before the match was to come off, 'I have *such* a kind letter from uncle Sam in London. I wrote to him as you wished. He says that he is coming down to-morrow; that he has heard of you often, and knows your character very well; and that he has got a *very handsome present* for us! What can it be, I wonder?'

'Is he rich, my soul's adored?' says I.

'He is a bachelor, with a fine trade, and nobody to leave his money to.'

'His present can't be less than a thousand pounds?' says I.

'Or, perhaps, a silver tea-set, and some corner-dishes,' says she.

But we could not agree to this: it was too little – too mean for a man of her uncle's wealth; and we both determined it must be the thousand pounds.

May – Restoration Day

'Dear good uncle! he's to be here by the coach,' says Magdalen. 'Let us ask a little party to meet him.' And so we did, and so they came: my father and mother, old Crutty in his best wig, and the parson who was to marry us the next day. The coach was to come in at six. And there was the tea-table, and there was the punch-bowl, and everybody ready and smiling to receive our dear uncle from London.

Six o'clock came, and the coach, and the man from the 'Green Dragon' with a portmanteau, and a fat old gentleman walking behind, of whom I just caught a glimpse – a venerable old gentleman: I thought I'd seen him before.

Then there was a ring at the bell; then a scuffling and bumping in the passage: then old Crutty rushed out, and a great laughing and talking, and '*How are you?*' and so on, was heard at the door; and then the parlour-door was flung open, and Crutty cried out with a loud voice –

'Good people all! my brother-in-law, Mr *Stiffelkind*!'

Mr Stiffelkind! – I trembled as I heard the name!

Miss Crutty kissed him; mamma made him a curtsey, and papa made him a bow; and Doctor Snorter, the parson, seized his hand and shook it most warmly: then came my turn!

'Vat!' says he. 'It is my dear goot yong frend from Doctor Schvis'hentail's! is dis de yong gentleman's honorable moder' (mamma smiled and made a curtsey), 'and dis his fader? Sare and madam, you should be broud of soch a sonn. And you my niece, if you have him for a husband you vill be locky, dat is all. Vat dink you, broder Croty, and Madame Stobbs, I 'ave made your sonn's boots! Ha – ha!'

My mamma laughed, and said, 'I did not know it, but I am sure, sir, he has as pretty a leg for a boot as any in the whole county.'

Old Stiffelkind roared louder. 'A very nice leg, ma'am, and a very *sheap boot too*. Vat! did you not know I make his boots? Perhaps you did not know something else too – p'raps you did not know' (and here the monster clapped his hand on the table and made the punch-ladle tremble in the bowl) – 'p'raps you did not know as dat yong man, dat Stobbs, dat sneaking, baltry, squinting fellow, is as vicked as he is ogly. He bot a pair of boots from me and never paid for dem. Dat is noting, nobody never pays; but he bought a pair of boots, and called himself Lord Cornvallis. And I was fool enough to believe him vonce. But look you, niece Magdalen, I'ave got five tousand pounds: if you marry him I vill not give you a benny. But look you what I will gif you: I bromised you a bresent, and I will give you *dese*!'

And the old monster produced *those very boots* which Swishtail had made him take back.

I *didn't* marry Miss Crutty: I am not sorry for it though. She was a nasty, ugly, ill-tempered wretch, and I've always said so ever since.

And all this arose from those infernal boots, and that unlucky paragraph in the county paper – I'll tell you how.

In the first place, it was taken up as a quiz by one of the wicked, profligate, unprincipled organs of the London press, who chose to be very facetious about the 'Marriage in High Life', and made all sorts of jokes about me and my dear Miss Crutty.

Secondly, it was read in this London paper by my mortal enemy, Bunting, who had been introduced to old Stiffelkind's acquaintance by my adventure with him, and had his shoes made regularly by the foreign upstart.

Thirdly, he happened to want a pair of shoes made at this particular period, and as he was measured by the disgusting old High-Dutch cobbler, he told him his old friend Stubbs was going to be married.

'And to whom?' said old Stiffelkind. 'To a voman wit geld, I vill take my oath.'

'Yes,' says Bunting, 'a country girl – a Miss Magdalen Carotty or Crotty, at a place called Sloffemsquiggle.'

'*Schloffemschwiegel*!' bursts out the dreadful bootmaker. 'Mein Gott, mein Gott! das geht nicht! I tell you, sare, it is no go. Miss Crotty is my niece. I vill go down myself. I vill never let her marry dat goot-for-nothing schwindler and tief.' *Such* was the language that the scoundrel ventured to use regarding me!

June – Marrowbones and cleavers

Was there ever such confounded ill-luck? My whole life has been a tissue of ill-luck: although I have laboured perhaps harder than any man to make a fortune, something always tumbled it down. In love and in war I was not like others. In my marriages, I had an eye to the main chance; and you see how some unlucky blow would come and throw them over. In the army I was just as prudent, and just as unfortunate. What with judicious betting, and horse-swapping, good-luck at billiards, and economy, I do believe I put up my pay every year, – and that is what few can say who have but an allowance of a hundred a year.

I'll tell you how it was. I used to be very kind to the young men; I chose their horses for them, and their wine: and showed them how to play billiards, or écarté, of long mornings, when there was nothing better to do. I didn't cheat: I'd rather die than cheat; – but if fellows *will* play, I wasn't the man to say no – why should I? There was one young chap in our regiment of whom I really think I cleared £300 a year.

His name was Dobble. He was a tailor's son, and wanted to be a gentleman. A poor weak young creature; easy to be made tipsy; easy to be cheated; and easy to be frightened. It was a blessing for him that I found him; for if anybody else had, they would have plucked him of every shilling.

Ensign Dobble and I were sworn friends. I rode his horses for him, and chose his champagne, and did everything, in fact, that a superior mind does for an inferior, – when the inferior has got the money. We were inseparables – hunting everywhere in couples. We even managed to fall in love with two sisters, as young soldiers will do, you know; for the dogs fall in love, with every change of quarters.

Well, once, in the year 1793 (it was just when the French had chopped poor Louis's head off), Dobble and I, gay young chaps as ever wore sword by side, had cast our eyes upon two young ladies by the name of Brisket, daughters of a butcher in the town where we were quartered. The dear girls fell in love with us, of course. And many of a pleasant walk in the country, many a treat to a tea-garden, many a smart riband and brooch used Dobble and I (for his father allowed him £600, and our purses were in common) to present to these young ladies. One day, fancy our pleasure at receiving a note couched thus:

Deer Capting Stubbs and Dobble – Miss Briskets presents their compliments, and as it is probble that our papa will be till twelve at the corprayshun dinner, we request the pleasure of their company to tea.

Didn't we go! Punctually at six we were in the little back-parlour; we quaffed more Bohea,* and made more love, than half-a-dozen ordinary men could. At nine, a little punch-bowl succeeded to the little teapot; and, bless the girls! a nice fresh steak was frizzling on the gridiron for our supper. Butchers were butchers then, and their parlour was their kitchen too; at least old Brisket's was – one door leading into the shop, and one into the yard, on the other side of which was the slaughter-house.

Fancy, then, our horror when, just at this critical time, we heard the shop-door open, a heavy staggering step on the flags, and a loud husky voice from the shop, shouting, 'Hallo, Susan; hallo, Betsy! show a light!' Dobble turned as white as a sheet; the two girls each as red as a lobster; I alone preserved my presence of mind. 'The back-door,' says I. 'The dog's in the court,' say they. 'He's not so bad as the man,' said I. 'Stop!' cries Susan, flinging open the door, and rushing to the fire. 'Take *this*, and perhaps it will quiet him.'

What do you think 'this' was? I'm blest if it was not the *steak*!

She pushed us out, patted and hushed the dog, and was in again in a minute. The moon was shining on the court, and on the slaughter-house, where there hung the white ghastly-looking carcases of a couple of sheep; a great gutter ran down the court – a gutter of *blood*! The dog was devouring his beef-steak (*our* beef-steak) in silence; and we could see through the little window the girls bustling about to pack up the supper-things, and presently the shop-door being opened, old Brisket entering, staggering, angry, and drunk. What's more, we could see, perched on a high stool, and nodding politely, as if to salute old Brisket, the *feather of Dobble's cocked hat*! When Dobble saw it, he turned white, and deadly sick; and the poor fellow, in an agony of fright, sunk shivering down upon one of the butcher's cutting-blocks, which was in the yard.

June – Marrowbones and cleavers

We saw old Brisket look steadily (as steadily as he could) at the confounded, impudent, pert, waggling feather; and then an idea began to dawn upon his mind, that there was a head to the hat; and then he slowly rose up – he was a man of six feet, and fifteen stone – he rose up, put on his apron and sleeves, and *took down his cleaver.*

'Betsy,' says he, 'open the yard door.' But the poor girls screamed, and flung on their knees, and begged, and wept, and did their very best to prevent him. '*Open the yard door*!' says he, with a thundering loud voice; and the great bull-dog, hearing it, started up and uttered a yell which sent me flying to the other end of the court. Dobble couldn't move; he was sitting on the block, blubbering like a baby.

The door opened, and out Mr Brisket came.

'*To him Fowler!*' says he. '*Keep him Fowler!*' – and the horrid dog flew at me, and I flew back into the corner, and drew my sword, determining to sell my life dearly.

'That's it,' says Brisket. 'Keep him there – good dog – good dog! And now, sir,' says he, turning round to Dobble, 'is this your hat?'

'Yes,' says Dobble, fit to choke with fright.

'Well, then,' says Brisket, 'it's my – (hic) – my painful duty to – (hic) – to tell you, that as I've got your hat, I must have your head; – it's painful, but it must be done. You'd better – (hic) – settle yourself com – comfumarably against that – (hic) – that block, and I'll chop it off before you can say Jack – (hic) – no, I mean Jack Robinson.'

Dobble went down on his knees and shrieked out, 'I'm an only son, Mr Brisket! I'll marry her, sir; I will, upon my honour, sir – Consider my mother, sir; consider my mother.'

'That's it, sir,' says Brisket – 'that's a good – (hic) – a good boy; – just put your head down quietly – and I'll have it off – yes, off – as if you were Louis the Six – the Sixtix – the Siktickleteenth – I'll chop the other *chap afterwards.*'

When I heard this, I made a sudden bound back, and gave such a cry as any man might who was in such a way. The ferocious Jowler, thinking I was going to escape, flew at my throat; screaming furious, I flung out my arms in a kind of desperation – and, to my wonder, down fell the dog, dead, and run through the body!

At this moment a posse of people rushed in upon old Brisket, one of his daughters had had the sense to summon them, and

Dobble's head was saved. And when they saw the dog lying dead at my feet, my ghastly look, my bloody sword, they gave me no small credit for my bravery. 'A terrible fellow that Stubbs,' said they; and so the mess said, the next day.

I didn't tell them that the dog had committed *suicide* – why should I? And I didn't say a word about Dobble's cowardice. I said he was a brave fellow, and fought like a tiger; and this prevented *him* from telling tales. I had the dogskin made into a pair of pistol-holsters, and looked so fierce, and got such a name for courage in our regiment, that when we had to meet the regulars, Bob Stubbs was always the man put forward to support the honour of the corps. The women, you know, adore courage; and such was my reputation at this time, that I might have had my pick out of half-a-dozen, with three, four, or five thousand pounds apiece, who were dying for love of me and my red coat. But I wasn't such a fool. I had been twice on the point of marriage, and twice disappointed; and I vowed by all the Saints to have a wife, and a rich one. Depend upon this, as an infallible maxim to guide you through life: *It's as easy to get a rich wife as a poor one*; the same bait that will hook a fly will hook a salmon.

July – Summary proceedings

Dobble's reputation for courage was not increased by the butcher's-dog adventure; but mine stood very high: little Stubbs was voted the boldest chap of all the bold North Bungays. And though I must confess, what was proved by subsequent circumstances, that nature has *not* endowed me with a large, or even, I may say, an average share of bravery, yet a man is very willing to flatter himself to the contrary; and, after a little time, I got to believe that my killing the dog was an action of undaunted courage, and that I was as gallant as any of the one hundred thousand heroes of our army. I always had a military taste – it's only the brutal part of the profession, the horrid fighting and blood, that I don't like.

I suppose the regiment was not very brave itself – being only militia; but certain it was, that Stubbs was considered a most terrible fellow, and I swore so much, and looked so fierce, that you would have fancied I had made half a hundred campaigns. I was second in several duels: the umpire in all disputes; and such a crack-shot myself, that fellows were shy of insulting me. As for Dobble, I took him under my protection; and he became so attached to me, that we ate, drank, and rode together every day; his father didn't care for money, so long as his son was in good company – and what so good as that of the celebrated Stubbs? Heigho! I *was* good company in those days, and a brave fellow too, as I should have remained, but for – what I shall tell the public immediately.

It happened, in the fatal year ninety-six, that the brave North Bungays were quartered at Portsmouth, a maritime place, which I need not describe, and which I wish I had never seen. I might have been a General now, or, at least, a rich man.

The red-coats carried everything before them in those days; and I, such a crack character as I was in my regiment, was very well received by the townspeople: many dinners I had; many tea-parties; many lovely young ladies did I lead down the pleasant country-dances.

Well, although I had had the two former rebuffs in love which I have described, my heart was still young; and the fact was, knowing that a girl with a fortune was my only chance, I made love here as furiously as ever. I shan't describe the lovely creatures on whom I fixed, whilst at Portsmouth. I tried more than – several – and it is a singular fact, which I never have been able to account for, that, successful as I was with ladies of maturer age, by the young ones I was refused regular.

But 'faint heart never won fair lady'; and so I went on, and on, until I had got a Miss Clopper, a tolerably rich navy-contractor's daughter, into such a way, that I really don't think she could have refused me. Her brother, Captain Clopper, was in a line regiment, and helped me as much as ever he could; he swore I was such a brave fellow.

July – Summary proceedings

As I had received a number of attentions from Clopper, I determined to invite him to dinner; which I could do without any sacrifice of my principle upon this point: for the fact is, Dobble lived at an inn, and as he sent all his bills to his father, I made no scruple to use his table. We dined in the coffee-room, Dobble bringing *his* friend; and so we made a party *carry*, as the French say. Some naval officers were occupied in a similar way at a table next to ours.

Well – I didn't spare the bottle, either for myself or for my friends; and we grew very talkative, and very affectionate as the drinking went on. Each man told stories of his gallantry in the field, or amongst the ladies, as officers will, after dinner. Clopper confided to the company his wish that I should marry his sister, and vowed that he thought me the best fellow in Christendom.

Ensign Dobble assented to this. 'But let Miss Clopper beware,' says he, 'for Stubbs is a sad fellow: he has had I don't know how many *liaisons* already; and he has been engaged to I don't know how many women.'

'Indeed!' says Clopper. 'Come, Stubbs, tell us your adventures.'

'Psha!' said I, modestly, 'there is nothing, indeed, to tell. I have been in love, my dear boy – who has not? – and I have been jilted – who has not?'

Clopper swore that he would blow his sister's brains out if ever *she* served me so.

'Tell him about Miss Crutty,' said Dobble. 'He! he! Stubbs served *that* woman out, anyhow; she didn't jilt *him*, I'll be sworn.'

'Really, Dobble, you are too bad, and should not mention names. The fact is, the girl was desperately in love with me, and had money – sixty thousand pounds, upon my reputation. Well, everything was arranged, when who should come down from London but a relation.'

'Well, and did he prevent the match?'

'Prevent it – yes, sir, I believe you he did; though not in the sense that *you* mean. He would have given his eyes – ay, and ten thousand pounds more – if I would have accepted the girl, but I would not.'

'Why, in the name of goodness?'

'Sir, her uncle was a *shoemaker*. I never would debase myself by marrying into such a family.'

'Of course not,' said Dobble; 'he couldn't, you know. Well, now – tell him about the other girl, Mary Waters, you know.'

'Hush, Dobble, hush! don't you see one of those naval officers has turned round and heard you? My dear Clopper, it was a mere childish bagatelle.'

'Well, but let's have it,' said Clopper – 'let's have it. I won't tell my sister, you know.' And he put his hand to his nose and looked monstrous wise.

'Nothing of that sort, Clopper – no, no – 'pon honour – little Bob Stubbs is no *libertine*; and the story is very simple. You see that my father has a small place, merely a few hundred acres, at Sloffemsquiggle. Isn't it a funny name? Hang it, there's the naval gentleman staring again' – (I looked terribly fierce as I returned this officer's stare, and continued in a loud careless voice). 'Well, at this Sloffemsquiggle there lived a girl, a Miss Waters, the niece of some blackguard apothecary in the neighbourhood; but my mother took a fancy to the girl, and had her up to the park and petted her. We were both young – and – the girl fell in love with me, that's the fact. I was obliged to repel some rather warm advances that she made me; and here, upon my honour as a gentleman, you have all the story about which that silly Dobble makes such a noise.'

Just as I finished this sentence, I found myself suddenly taken by the nose, and a voice shouting out –

'Mr Stubbs, you are *a liar and a Scoundrel*! Take this, sir, – and this, for daring to meddle with the name of an innocent lady.'

I turned round as well as I could – for the ruffian had pulled me out of my chair – and beheld a great marine monster, six feet high, who was occupied in beating and kicking me, in the most ungentlemanly manner, on my cheeks, my ribs, and between the tails of my coat. 'He is a liar, gentlemen, and a scoundrel! The bootmaker had detected him in swindling, and so his niece refused him. Miss Waters was engaged to him from childhood, and he deserted her for the bootmaker's niece, who was richer.' And then sticking a card between my stock and my coat-collar, in what is called the scruff of my neck, the disgusting brute gave me another blow behind my back, and left the coffee-room with his friends.

Dobble raised me up; and taking the card from my neck, read, 'Captain Waters'. Clopper poured me out a glass of water, and said in my ear, 'If this is true, you are an infernal scoundrel, Stubbs; and must fight me, after Captain Waters'; and he flounced out of the room.

I had but one course to pursue. I sent the Captain a short and contemptuous note, saying that he was beneath my anger. As for Clopper, I did not condescend to notice his remark; but in order to get rid of the troublesome society of these low blackguards, I determined to gratify an inclination I had long entertained, and make a little tour. I applied for leave of absence, and set off *that very night*. I can fancy the disappointment of the brutal Waters, on coming, as he did, the next morning to my quarters and finding me *gone*. Ha! ha!

After this adventure I became sick of a military life – at least the life of my own regiment, where the officers, such was their unaccountable meanness and prejudice against me, absolutely refused to see me at mess. Colonel Craw sent me a letter to this effect, which I treated as it deserved. I never once alluded to it in any way, and have since never spoken a single word to any man in the North Bungays.

August – Dogs have their days

See, now, what life is! I have had ill-luck on ill-luck from that day to this. I have sunk in the world, and, instead of riding my horse and drinking my wine, as a real gentleman should, have hardly enough now to buy a pint of ale; ay, and am very glad when anybody will treat me to one. Why, why was I born to undergo such unmerited misfortunes?

You must know that very soon after my adventure with Miss Crutty, and that cowardly ruffian, Captain Waters (he sailed the day after his insult to me, or I should most certainly have blown his brains out; *now* he is living in England, and is my relation; but, of course, I cut the fellow) – very soon after these painful events another happened, which ended, too, in a sad disappoint-

August – Dogs have their days

234 W. M. THACKERAY

ment. My dear papa died, and, instead of leaving five thousand
pounds, as I expected at the very least, left only his estate, which
was worth but two. The land and house were left to me; to
mamma and my sisters he left, to be sure, a sum of two thousand
pounds in the hands of that eminent firm Messrs. Pump, Aldgate
and Co., which failed within six months after his demise, and paid
in five years about one shilling and ninepence in the pound; which
really was all my dear mother and sisters had to live upon.

The poor creatures were quite unused to money matters; and,
would you believe it? when the news came of Pump and Aldgate's
failure, mamma only smiled, and threw her eyes up to heaven, and
said, 'Blessed be God, that we have still wherewithal to live. There
are tens of thousands in this world, dear children, who would count
our poverty riches.' And with this she kissed my two sisters, who
began to blubber, as girls always will do, and threw their arms
around her neck, and then round my neck, until I was half stifled
with their embraces, and slobbered all over with their tears.

'Dearest mamma,' said I, 'I am very glad to see the noble
manner in which you bear your loss; and more still to know that
you are so rich as to be able to put up with it.' The fact was, I
really thought the old lady had got a private hoard of her own,
as many of them have – a thousand pounds or so in a stocking.
Had she put by thirty pounds a year, as well she might, for the
thirty years of her marriage, there would have been nine hundred
pounds clear, and no mistake. But still I was angry to think that
any such paltry concealment had been practised – concealment
too of *my* money; so I turned on her pretty sharply, and continued
my speech. 'You say, ma'am, that you are rich, and that Pump
and Aldgate's failure has no effect upon you. I am very happy to
hear you say so, Ma'am – very happy that you *are* rich; and I
should like to know where your property, my father's property,
for you had none of your own – I should like to know where this
money lies – *where you have concealed it*, Ma'am; and, permit
me to say, that when I agreed to board you and my two sisters for
eighty pounds a year, I did not know that you had *other* resources
than those mentioned in my blessed father's will.'

This I said to her because I hated the meanness of concealment,
not because I lost by the bargain of boarding them: for the three
poor things did not eat much more than sparrows; and I've often
since calculated that I had a clear twenty pounds a year profit out
of them.

Mamma and the girls looked quite astonished when I made the speech. 'What does he mean?' said Lucy to Eliza.

Mamma repeated the question. 'My beloved Robert, what concealment are you talking of?'

'I am talking of concealed property, Ma'am,' says I sternly.

'And do you – what – can you – do you really suppose that I have concealed – any of that blessed sa-a-a-aint's prop-op-op-operty?' screams out mamma. 'Robert,' says she – 'Bob, my own darling boy – my fondest, best beloved, now *he* is gone' (meaning my late governor – more tears) – 'you don't, you cannot fancy that your own mother, who bore you, and nursed you, and wept for you, and would give her all to save you from a moment's harm – you don't suppose that she would che-e-e-eat you!' And here she gave a louder screech than ever, and flung back on the sofa; and one of my sisters went and tumbled into her arms, and t'other went round, and the kissing and slobbering scene went on again, only I was left out, thank goodness. I hate such sentimentality.

'*Che-e-e-eat me,*' says I, mocking her. 'What do you mean, then, by saying you're so rich? Say, have you got money, or have you not?' (And I rapped out a good number of oaths, too, which I don't put in here; but I was in a dreadful fury, that's the fact.)

'So help me heaven,' says mamma, in answer, going down on her knees and smacking her two hands, 'I have but a Queen Anne's guinea in the whole of this wicked world.'

'Then what, Madam, induces you to tell these absurd stories to me, and to talk about your riches, when you know that you and your daughters are beggars, Ma'am, – *beggars*?'

'My dearest boy, have we not got the house, and the furniture, and a hundred a year still; and have you not great talents, which will make all our fortunes?' says Mrs Stubbs, getting up off her knees, and making believe to smile as she clawed hold of my hand and kissed it.

This was *too* cool. '*You* have got a hundred a year, Ma'am,' says I – '*you* have got a house? Upon my soul and honour this is the first I ever heard of it; and I'll tell you what, Ma'am,' says I (and it cut her *pretty sharply* too): 'As you've got it, *you'd better go and live in it*. I've got quite enough to do with my own house, and every penny of my own income.'

Upon this speech the old lady said nothing, but she gave a screech loud enough to be heard from here to York, and down she fell – kicking and struggling in a regular fit.

I did not see Mrs Stubbs for some days after this, and the girls used to come down to meals, and never speak; going up again and stopping with their mother. At last, one day, both of them came in very solemn to my study, and Eliza, the eldest, said, 'Robert, mamma has paid you our board up to Michaelmas.'

'She has,' says I; for I always took precious good care to have it in advance.

'She says, Robert, that on Michaelmas day – we'll – we'll go away, Robert.'

'Oh, she's going to her own house, is she, Lizzy? Very good. She'll want the furniture, I suppose, and that she may have too, for I'm going to sell the place myself.' And so *that* matter was settled.

On Michaelmas day – and during these two months I hadn't, I do believe, seen my mother twice (once, about two o'clock in the morning, I woke and found her sobbing over my bed) – on Michaelmas-day morning, Eliza comes to me and says, '*Robert, they will come and fetch us at six this evening*.' Well, as this was the last day, I went and got the best goose I could find (I don't think I ever saw a primer, or ate more hearty myself), and had it roasted at three, with a good pudding afterwards; and a glorious bowl of punch. 'Here's a health to you, dear girls,' says I, 'and you, Ma, and good luck to all three; and as you've not eaten a morsel, I hope you won't object to a glass of punch. It's the old stuff, you know, Ma'am, that that Waters sent to my father fifteen years ago.'

Six o'clock came, and with it came a fine barouche.* As I live, Captain Waters was on the box (it was his coach); that old thief, Bates, jumped out, entered my house, and before I could say Jack Robinson, whipped off mamma to the carriage: the girls followed, just giving me a hasty shake of the hand; and as mamma was helped in, Mary Waters, who was sitting inside, flung her arms round her, and then round the girls; and the Doctor, who acted footman, jumped on the box, and off they went; taking no more notice of *me* than if I'd been a nonentity.

Here's a picture of the whole business: Mamma and Miss Waters are sitting kissing each other in the carriage, with the two girls in the back seat; Waters is driving (a precious bad driver he is too); and I'm standing at the garden door, and whistling. That old fool Mary Malowney is crying behind the garden gate; she went off next day along with the furniture; and I to get into that precious scrape which I shall mention next.

September – Plucking a goose

After my papa's death, as he left me no money, and only a little land, I put my estate into an auctioneer's hands, and determined to amuse my solitude with a trip to some of our fashionable watering-places. My house was now a desert to me. I need not say how the departure of my dear parent, and her children, left me sad and lonely.

Well, I had a little ready money, and, for the estate, expected a couple of thousand pounds. I had a good military-looking person: for though I had absolutely cut the old North Bungays (indeed, after my affair with Waters, Colonel Craw hinted to me, in the most friendly manner, that I had better resign) – though I had left the army, I still retained the rank of Captain; knowing the advantages attendant upon that title in a watering-place tour.

Captain Stubbs became a great dandy at Cheltenham, Harrogate, Bath, Leamington, and other places.* I was a good whist and billiard player; so much so, that in many of these towns, the people used to refuse, at last, to play with me, knowing how far I was their superior. Fancy my surprise, about five years after the Portsmouth affair, when strolling one day up the High Street, in Leamington, my eyes lighted upon a young man, whom I remembered in a certain butcher's yard, and elsewhere – no other, in fact, than Dobble. He, too, was dressed *en militaire*, with a frogged coat and spurs; and was walking with a showy-looking, Jewish-faced, black-haired lady, glittering with chains and rings, with a green bonnet and a bird-of-Paradise – a lilac shawl, a yellow gown, pink silk stockings, and light-blue shoes. Three children, and a handsome footman, were walking behind her, and the party, not seeing me, entered the 'Royal Hotel' together.

I was known myself at the 'Royal', and calling one of the waiters, learned the names of the lady and gentleman. He was Captain Dobble, the son of the rich army-clothier, Dobble (Dobble, Hobble and Co. of Pall Mall); – the lady was a Mrs Manasseh, widow of an American Jew, living quietly at Leamington with her children, but possessed of an immense property. There's no use to give one's self out to be an absolute pauper: so the fact is, that I myself went everywhere with the character of a man of very large means. My father had died, leaving me immense sums of money, and landed estates. Ah! I was the gentleman then, the real gentleman, and everybody was too happy to have me at table.

Well, I came the next day and left a card for Dobble, with a note. He neither returned my visit, nor answered my note. The day after, however, I met him with the widow, as before; and going up to him, very kindly seized him by the hand, and swore I was – as really was the case – charmed to see him. Dobble hung back, to my surprise, and I do believe the creature would have cut me, if he dared; but I gave him a frown, and said –

'What, Dobble my boy, don't you recollect old Stubbs, and our adventure with the butcher's daughters – ha?'

Dobble gave a sickly kind of grin, and said, 'Oh! ah! yes! It is – yes! it is, I believe, Captain Stubbs.'

'An old comrade, Madam, of Captain Dobble's, and one who has heard so much, and seen so much of your ladyship, that he must take the liberty of begging his friend to introduce him.'

Dobble was obliged to take the hint; and Captain Stubbs was duly presented to Mrs Manasseh. The lady was as gracious as possible; and when, at the end of the walk, we parted, she said 'she hoped Captain Dobble would bring me to her apartments that evening, where she expected a few friends.' Everybody, you see, knows everybody at Leamington; and I, for my part, was well known as a retired officer of the army, who, on his father's death, had come into seven thousand a year. Dobble's arrival had been subsequent to mine; but putting up as he did at the 'Royal Hotel', and dining at the ordinary there with the widow, he had made her acquaintance before I had. I saw, however, that if I allowed him to talk about me, as he could, I should be compelled to give up

September – Plucking a goose

all my hopes and pleasures at Leamington; and so I determined to be short with him. As soon as the lady had gone into the hotel, my friend Dobble was for leaving me likewise; but I stopped him, and said, 'Mr Dobble, I saw what you meant just now: you wanted to cut me, because, forsooth, I did not choose to fight a duel at Portsmouth. Now look you, Dobble, I am no hero, but I am not such a coward as you – and you know it. You are a very different man to deal with from Waters; and I *will fight* this time.'

Not perhaps that I would: but after the business of the butcher, I knew Dobble to be as great a coward as ever lived; and there never was any harm in threatening, for you know you are not obliged to stick to it afterwards. My words had their effect upon Dobble, who stuttered and looked red, and then declared he never had the slightest intention of passing me by; so we became friends, and his mouth was stopped.

He was very thick with the widow, but that lady had a very capacious heart, and there were a number of other gentlemen who seemed equally smitten with her. 'Look at that Mrs Manasseh,' said a gentleman (it was droll, *he* was a Jew, too), sitting at dinner by me. 'She is old, ugly, and yet, because she has money, all the men are flinging themselves at her.'

'She has money, has she?'

'Eighty thousand pounds, and twenty thousand for each of her children. I know it *for a fact*,' said the strange gentleman. 'I am in the law, and we of our faith, you know, know pretty well what the great families amongst us are worth.'

'Who was Mr Manasseh?' said I.

'A man of enormous wealth – a tobacco-merchant – West Indies; a fellow of no birth, however; and who, between ourselves, married a woman that is not much better than she should be. My dear sir,' whispered he, 'she is always in love. Now it is with that Captain Dobble; last week it was somebody else – and it may be you next week, if – ha! ha! ha! – you are disposed to enter the lists. I wouldn't, for *my* part, have the woman with twice her money.'

What did it matter to me whether the woman was good or not, provided she was rich? My course was quite clear. I told Dobble all that this gentleman had informed me, and being a pretty good hand at making a story, I made the widow appear *so* bad, that the poor fellow was quite frightened, and fairly quitted the field. Ha! ha! I'm dashed if I did not make him believe that Mrs Manasseh had *murdered* her last husband.

I played my game so well, thanks to the information that my friend the lawyer had given me, that in a month I had got the widow to show a most decided partiality for me. I sat by her at dinner, I drank with her at the 'Wells' – I rode with her, I danced with her, and at a picnic to Kenilworth, where we drank a good deal of champagne, I actually popped the question, and was accepted. In another month, Robert Stubbs, Esq, led to the altar, Leah, widow of the late Z. Manasseh, Esq, of St. Kitt's!

We drove up to London in her comfortable chariot: the children and servants following in a postchaise. I paid, of course, for everything; and until our house in Berkeley Square was painted, we stopped at 'Stevens's Hotel'.

My own estate had been sold, and the money was lying at a bank in the City. About three days after our arrival, as we took our breakfast in the hotel, previous to a visit to Mrs Stubbs's banker, where certain little transfers were to be made, a gentleman was introduced, who, I saw at a glance, was of my wife's persuasion.

He looked at Mrs Stubbs, and made a bow. 'Perhaps it will be convenient to you to pay this little bill, one hundred and fifty-two pounds?'

'My love,' says she, 'will you pay this – it is a trifle which I had really forgotten?'

'My soul!' said I, 'I have really not the money in the house.'

'Vel, denn, Captain Shtubbsh,' says he, 'I must do my duty – and arrest you – here is the writ! Tom, keep the door!' – My wife fainted – the children screamed, and fancy my condition as I was obliged to march off to a spunging-house along with a horrid sheriff's officer!

October – Mars and Venus in opposition

I shall not describe my feelings when I found myself in a cage in Cursitor Street,* instead of that fine house in Berkeley Square, which was to have been mine as the husband of Mrs Manasseh. What a place! – in an odious, dismal street leading from Chancery Lane. A hideous Jew boy opened the second of three doors and shut it when Mr Nabb and I (almost fainting) had entered; then he opened the third door, and then I was introduced to a filthy place called a coffee-room, which I exchanged for the solitary comfort of a little dingy back-parlour, where I was left for a while to brood over my miserable fate. Fancy the change between this and Berkeley Square! Was I, after all my pains, and cleverness, and perseverance, cheated at last? Had this Mrs Manasseh been imposing upon me, and were the words of the wretch I met at the table-d'hôte at Leamington only meant to mislead me and take me in? I determined to send for my wife, and know the whole truth. I saw at once that I had been the victim of an infernal plot, and that the carriage, the house in town, the West India fortune, were only so many lies which I had blindly believed. It was true the debt was but a hundred and fifty pounds; and I had two thousand at my bankers'. But was the loss of *her* £80,000 nothing? Was the destruction of my hopes nothing? The accursed addition to my family of a Jewish wife and three Jewish children, nothing? And all these I was to support out of my two thousand pounds. I had better have stopped at home with my mamma and sisters, whom I really did love, and who produced me eighty pounds a year.

I had a furious interview with Mrs Stubbs; and when I charged her, the base wretch! with cheating me, like a brazen serpent as she was, she flung back the cheat in my teeth, and swore I had swindled her. Why did I marry her, when she might have had twenty others? She only took me, she said, because I had twenty thousand pounds. I *had* said I possessed that sum; but in love, you know, and war all's fair.

We parted quite as angrily as we met; and I cordially vowed that when I had paid the debt into which I had been swindled by

October – Mars and Venus in opposition

her, I would take my £2,000 and depart to some desert island; or, at the very least, to America, and never see her more, or any of her Israelitish brood. There was no use in remaining in the spunging-house (for I knew that there were such things as detainers, and that where Mrs Stubbs owed a hundred pounds, she might owe a thousand): so I sent for Mr Nabb, and tendering him a cheque for £150 and his costs, requested to be let out forthwith. 'Here, fellow,' said I, 'is a cheque on Child's for your paltry sum.'

'It may be a sheck on Shild's,' says Mr Nabb; 'but I should be a baby to let you out on such a paper as dat.'

'Well,' said I, 'Child's is but a step from this: you may go and get the cash – just give me an acknowledgment.'

Nabb drew out the acknowledgment with great punctuality, and set off for the bankers', whilst I prepared myself for departure from this abominable prison.

He smiled as he came in. 'Well,' said I, 'you have touched your money; and now, I must tell you, that you are the most infernal rogue and extortioner I ever met with.'

'Oh, no, Mishter Shtubbsh,' says he, grinning still. 'Dere is som greater roag dan me – mosh greater.'

'Fellow,' said I, 'don't stand grinning before a gentleman; but give me my hat and cloak, and let me leave your filthy den.'

'Shtop, Shtubbsh,' says he, not even Mistering me this time. 'Here ish a letter, vich you had better read.'

I opened the letter; something fell to the ground: it was my cheque.

The letter ran thus: 'Messrs. Child and Co. present their compliments to Captain Stubbs, and regret that they have been obliged to refuse payment of the enclosed, having been served this day with an attachment by Messrs. Solomonson and Co., which compels them to retain Captain Stubbs' balance of £2,010 11s. 6d. until the decision of the suit of Solomonson v. Stubbs. *Fleet Street.*'

'You see,' says Mr Nabb, as I read this dreadful letter – 'you see, Shtubbsh, dere vas two debts, – a little von and a big von. So dey arrested you for de little von, and attashed your money for de big von.'

Don't laugh at me for telling this story. If you knew what tears are blotting over the paper as I write it – if you knew that for weeks after I was more like a madman than a sane man – a madman in the Fleet Prison, where I went instead of to the desert island! What had I done to deserve it? Hadn't I always kept an eye to the main chance? Hadn't I lived economically, and not like other young men? Had I ever been known to squander or give away a single penny? No! I can lay my hand on my heart, and, thank heaven, say, No! Why, why was I punished so?

Let me conclude this miserable history. Seven months – my wife saw me once or twice, and then dropped me altogether – I remained in that fatal place. I wrote to my dear mamma, begging her to sell her furniture, but got no answer. All my old friends turned their backs upon me. My action went against me – I had not a penny to defend it. Solomonson proved my wife's debt, and seized my two thousand pounds. As for the detainer against me, I was obliged to go through the court for the relief of insolvent debtors. I passed through it, and came out a beggar. But fancy the malice of that wicked Stiffelkind: he appeared in court as my creditor for £3, with sixteen years' interest at five per cent, for a *pair of top-boots*. The old thief produced them in court, and told the whole story – Lord Cornwallis, the detection, the pumping and all.

Commissioner Dubobwig was very funny about it. 'So Doctor Swishtail would not pay you for the boots, eh, Mr Stiffelkind?'

'No: he said, ven I asked him for payment, dey was ordered by a young boy, and I ought to have gone to his schoolmaster.'

'What! then you came on a *bootless* errand, ay, sir?' (A laugh.)

'Bootless! no sare, I brought de boots back vid me. How de devil else could I show dem to you?' (Another laugh.)

'You're never *soled* 'em since, Mr Tickleshins?'

'I never would sell dem; I svore I never vood, on porpus to be revenged on dat Stobbs.'

'What! your wound has never been *healed*, eh?'

'Vat de you mean vid your bootless errands, and your soling and healing? I tell you I have done vat I svore to do: I have exposed him at school; I have broak off a marriage for him, ven he vould have had tventy tousand pound; and now I have showed him up in a court of justice. Dat is vat I'ave done, and dat's enough.' And then the old wretch went down, whilst everybody was giggling and staring at poor me – as if I was not miserable enough already.

'This seems the dearest pair of boots you ever had in your life, Mr Stubbs,' said Commissioner Dubobwig very archly, and then he began to inquire about the rest of my misfortunes.

In the fulness of my heart I told him the whole of them: how Mr Solomonson the attorney had introduced me to the rich widow, Mrs Manasseh, who had fifty thousand pounds, and an estate in the West Indies. How I was married, and arrested on coming to town, and cast in an action for two thousand pounds brought against me by this very Solomonson for my wife's debts.

'Stop!' says a lawyer in the court. 'Is this woman a showy black-haired woman with one eye? very often drunk, with three children? – Solomonson, short, with red hair?'

'Exactly so,' said I, with tears in my eyes.

'That woman has married *three men* within the last two years. One in Ireland, and one at Bath. A Solomonson is, I believe, her husband, and they both are off for America ten days ago.'

'But why did you not keep your £2,000?' said the lawyer.

'Sir, they attached it.'

'Oh, well, we may pass you. You have been unlucky, Mr Stubbs, but it seems as if the biter had been bit in this affair.'

'No,' said Mr Dubobwig. 'Mr Stubbs is the victim of a *fatal attachment*.'

November – A general post delivery

I was a free man when I went out of the Court; but I was a beggar – I, Captain Stubbs, of the bold North Bungays, did not know where I could get a bed, or a dinner.

As I was marching sadly down Portugal Street, I felt a hand on my shoulder and a rough voice which I knew well.

'Vell, Mr Stobbs, have I not kept my promise? I told you dem boots would be your ruin.'

I was much too miserable to reply; and only cast my eyes towards the roofs of the houses, which I could not see for the tears.

November – A general post delivery

'Vat! you begin to gry and blobber like a shild? you vood marry, vood you? and noting vood do for you but a vife vid monny – ha, ha – but you vere de pigeon, and she was de grow. She has plocked you, too, pretty vell – eh? ha! ha!'

'Oh, Mr Stiffelkind,' said I, 'don't laugh at my misery: she has not left me a single shilling under heaven. And I shall starve: I do believe I shall starve.' And I began to cry fit to break my heart.

'Starf! stoff and nonsense! You will never die of starfing – you vill die of *hanging*, I tink – ho! ho! – and it is moch easier vay too.' I didn't say a word, but cried on; till everybody in the street turned round and stared.

'Come, come,' said Stiffelkind, 'do not gry, Gaptain Stobbs – it is not goot for a Gaptain to gry – ha! ha! Dere – come vid me, and you shall have a dinner, and a bregfast too, – vich shall gost you nothing, until you can bay vid your earnings.'

And so this curious old man, who had persecuted me all through my prosperity, grew compassionate towards me in my ill-luck; and took me home with him as he promised. 'I saw your name among de Insolvents, and I vowed, you know, to make you repent dem boots. Dere, now, it is done and forgotten, look you. Here, Betty, Bettchen, make de spare bed, and put a clean knife and fork; Lort Cornvallis is come to dine vid me.'

I lived with this strange old man for six weeks. I kept his books, and did what little I could to make myself useful: carrying about boots and shoes, as if I had never borne his Majesty's commission. He gave me no money, but he fed and lodged me comfortably. The men and boys used to laugh, and call me General, and Lord Cornwallis, and all sorts of nicknames; and old Stiffelkind made a thousand new ones for me.

One day I can recollect – one miserable day, as I was polishing on the trees a pair of boots of Mr Stiffelkind's manufacture – the old gentleman came into the shop, with a lady on his arm.

'Vere is Gaptain Stobbs?' said he. 'Vere is dat ornament to his Majesty's service?'

I came in from the back shop, where I was polishing the boots, with one of them in my hand.

'Look, my dear,' says he, 'here is an old friend of yours, his Excellency Lort Cornvallis! – Who would have thought such a nobleman vood turn shoeblack? Captain Stobbs, here is your former flame, my dear niece, Miss Grotty. How could you, Magdalen, ever leaf such a lof of a man? Shake hands vid her,

Gaptain; – dere, never mind de blacking!' But Miss drew back.

'I never shake hands with a *shoeblack*,' said she, mighty contemptuous.

'Bah! my lof, his fingers von't soil you. Don't you know he has just been *vitevashed*?'

'I wish, uncle,' says she, 'you would not leave me with such low people.'

'Low, because he cleans boots? De Gaptain prefers *pumps* to boots I tink – ha! ha!'

'Captain indeed! a nice Captain,' says Miss Crutty, snapping her fingers in my face, and walking away: 'a Captain who has had his nose pulled! ha! ha!' – And how could I help it? it wasn't by my own *choice* that that ruffian Waters took such liberties with me. Didn't I show how averse I was to all quarrels by refusing altogether his challenge? – But such is the world. And thus the people at Stiffelkind's used to tease me, until they drove me almost mad.

At last he came home one day more merry and abusive than ever.

'Gaptain,' says he, 'I have goot news for you – a goot place. Your lordship vill not be able to geep your garridge, but you vill be gomfortable, and serve his Majesty.'

'Serve his Majesty?' says I. 'Dearest Mr Stiffelkind, have you got me a place under Government?'

'Yes, and somting better still – not only a place, but a uniform: yes, Gaptain Stobbs, a *red goat*.'

'A red coat! I hope you don't think I would demean myself by entering the ranks of the army? I am a gentleman, Mr Stiffelkind – I can never – no, I never – '

'No, I know you will never – you are too great a goward – ha! ha! – though dis is a red coat, and a place where you must give some *hard knocks* too – ha! ha! – do you gomprehend? – and you shall be a general instead of a gaptain – ha! ha!'

'A general in a red coat, Mr Stiffelkind?'

'Yes, a GENERAL BOSTMAN! – ha! ha! I have been vid your old friend, Bunting, and he has an uncle in the Post Office, and he has got you de place – eighteen shillings a veek, you rogue, and your goat. You must not oben any of de letters you know.'

And so it was – I, Robert Stubbs, Esquire, became the vile thing he named – a general postman!

I was so disgusted with Stiffelkind's brutal jokes, which were now more brutal than ever, that when I got my place in the Post Office, I never went near the fellow again: for though he had done me a favour in keeping me from starvation, he certainly had done it in a very rude, disagreeable manner, and showed a low and mean spirit in *shoving* me into such a degraded place as that of postman. But what had I to do? I submitted to fate, and for three years or more, Robert Stubbs, of the North Bungay Fencibles, was —

I wonder nobody recognised me. I lived in daily fear the first year: but afterwards grew accustomed to my situation, as all great men will do, and wore my red coat as naturally as if I had been sent into the world only for the purpose of being a letter-carrier.

I was first in the Whitechapel district, where I stayed for nearly three years, when I was transferred to Jermyn Street and Duke Street – famous places for lodgings. I suppose I left a hundred letters at a house in the latter street, where lived some people who must have recognised me had they but once chanced to look at me.

You see that, when I left Sloffemsquiggle, and set out in the gay world, my mamma had written to me a dozen times at least; but I never answered her, for I knew she wanted money, and I detest writing. Well, she stopped her letters, finding she could get none from me: but when I was in the Fleet, as I told you, I wrote repeatedly to my dear mamma, and was not a little nettled at her refusing to notice me in my distress, which is the very time one most wants notice.

Stubbs is not an uncommon name; and though I saw 'Mrs Stubbs' on a little bright brass plate, in Duke Street, and delivered so many letters to the lodgers in her house, I never thought of asking who she was, or whether she was my relation, or not.

One day the young woman who took in the letters had not got change, and she called her mistress. An old lady in a poke-bonnet came out of the parlour, and put on her spectacles, and looked at the letter, and fumbled in her pocket for eightpence, and apologised to the postman for keeping him waiting. And when I said, 'Never mind, Ma'am, it's no trouble,' the old lady gave a start, and then she pulled off her spectacles, and staggered back; and then she began muttering, as if about to choke; and then she gave a great screech, and flung herself into my arms, and roared out, '*My son, my son!*'

'Law, mamma,' said I, 'is that you?' and I sat down on the hall bench with her, and let her kiss me as much as ever she liked. Hearing the whining and crying, down comes another lady from upstairs – it was my sister Eliza; and down come the lodgers. And the maid gets water and what not, and I was the regular hero of the group. I could not stay long then, having my letters to deliver. But, in the evening, after mail-time, I went back to my mamma and sister; and, over a bottle of prime old port, and a precious good leg of boiled mutton and turnips, made myself pretty comfortable, I can tell you.

December – 'The winter of our discontent'

Mamma had kept the house in Duke Street for more than two years. I recollected some of the chairs and tables from dear old Sloffemsquiggle, and the bowl in which I had made that famous rum-punch, the evening she went away, which she and my sisters left untouched, and I was obliged to drink after they were gone; but that's not to the purpose.

Think of my sister Lucy's luck! that chap, Waters, fell in love with her, and married her; and she now keeps her carriage, and lives in state near Sloffemsquiggle. I offered to make it up with Waters; but he bears malice, and never will see or speak to me. He had the impudence, too, to say, that he took in all letters for mamma at Sloffemsquiggle; and that as mine were all begging-letters, he burned them, and never said a word to her concerning them. He allowed mamma fifty pounds a year, and, if she were not such a fool, she might have had three times as much; but the old lady was high and mighty forsooth, and would not be be-holden, even to her own daughter, for more than she actually wanted. Even this fifty pound she was going to refuse; but when

I came to live with her, of course I wanted pocket-money as well as board and lodging, and so I had the fifty pounds for *my* share, and eked out with it as well as I could.

Old Bates and the Captain, between them, gave mamma a hundred pounds when she left me (she had the deuce's own luck, to be sure – much more than ever fell to *me*, I know); and as she said she *would* try and work for her living, it was thought best to take a house and let lodgings, which she did. Our first and second floor paid us four guineas a week, on an average; and the front parlour and attic made forty pounds more. Mamma and Eliza used to have the front attic; but *I* took that, and they slept in the servants' bedroom. Lizzy had a pretty genius for work, and earned a guinea a week that way; so that we had got nearly two hundred a year over the rent to keep house with – and we got on pretty well. Besides, women eat nothing: my women didn't care for meat for days together sometimes, so that it was only necessary to dress a good steak or so for me.

Mamma would not think of my continuing in the Post Office. She said her dear Robert, her husband's son, her gallant soldier, and all that, should remain at home and be a gentleman – which I was, certainly, though I didn't find fifty pounds a year very much to buy clothes and be a gentleman upon. To be sure, mother found me shirts and linen, so that *that* wasn't in the fifty pounds. She kicked a little at paying the washing too; but she gave in at last, for I was her dear Bob, you know; and I'm blest if I could not make her give me the gown off her back. Fancy! once she cut up a very nice rich black silk scarf, which my sister Waters sent her, and made me a waistcoat and two stocks of it. She was so *very* soft, the old lady!

I'd lived in this way for five years or more, making myself content with my fifty pounds a year (*perhaps* I'd saved a little out of it; but that's neither here nor there). From year's end to year's end I remained faithful to my dear mamma, never leaving her except for a month or so in the summer – when a bachelor may take a trip to Gravesend or Margate, which would be too expensive for a family. I say a bachelor, for the fact is, I don't know whether I am married or not – never having heard a word since of the scoundrelly Mrs Stubbs.

I never went to the public-house before meals: for, with my beggarly fifty pounds, I could not afford to dine away from home:

December – 'The winter of our discontent'

but there I had my regular seat, and used to come home *pretty glorious*, I can tell you. Then bed till eleven; then breakfast and the newspaper; then a stroll in Hyde Park or St. James's; then home at half-past three to dinner – when I jollied, as I call it, for the rest of the day. I was my mother's delight; and thus, with a clear conscience, I managed to live on.

How fond she was of me, to be sure! Being sociable myself and loving to have my friends about me, we often used to assemble a company of as hearty fellows as you would wish to sit down with, and keep the nights up royally. 'Never mind, my boys,' I used to say, 'Send the bottle round: mammy pays for all'. As she did, sure enough: and sure enough we punished her cellar too. The good old lady used to wait upon us, as if for all the world she had been my servant, instead of a lady and my mamma. Never used she to repine, though I often, as I must confess, gave her occasion (keeping her up till four o'clock in the morning, because she never could sleep until she saw her 'dear Bob' in bed, and leading her a sad anxious life). She was of such a sweet temper, the old lady, that I think in the course of five years I never knew her in a passion, except twice: and then with sister Lizzy, who declared I was ruining the house, and driving the lodgers away, one by one. But mamma would not hear of such envious spite on my sister's part. 'Her Bob' was always right, she said. At last Lizzy fairly retreated, and went to the Waters's. I was glad of it, for her temper was dreadful, and we used to be squabbling from morning till night!

Ah, those *were* jolly times! but Ma was obliged to give up the lodging-house at last – for, somehow, things went wrong after my sister's departure – the nasty uncharitable people said, on account of *me*; because I drove away the lodgers by smoking and drinking, and kicking up noises in the house; and because Ma gave me so much of her money – so she did, but if she *would* give it, you know, how could I help it? Heigho! I wish I'd *kept* it.

No such luck. The business I thought was to last for ever; but at the end of two years came a smash – shut up shop – sell off everything. Mamma went to the Waters's: and, will you believe it? the ungrateful wretches would not receive me! that Mary, you see, was so disappointed at not marrying me. Twenty pounds a year they allow, it is true; but what's that for a gentleman? For twenty years I have been struggling manfully to gain an honest livelihood, and, in the course of them, have seen a deal of life, to be sure. I've sold cigars and pocket-handkerchiefs at the corners of streets; I've been a billiard-marker; I've been a director (in the panic year) of the Imperial British Consolidated Mangle and Drying Ground Company. I've been on the stage (for two years as an actor, and about a month as a cad, when I was very low); I've been the means of giving to the police of this empire some very valuable information (about licensed victuallers, gentlemen's carts, and pawnbrokers' names); I've been very nearly an officer again – that is, an assistant to an officer of the Sheriff of Middlesex: it was my last place.

On the last day of the year 1837, even *that* game was up. It's a thing that very seldom happened to a gentleman, to be kicked out of a spunging-house; but such was my case. Young Nabb (who succeeded his father) drove me ignominiously from his door, because I had charged a gentleman in the coffee-rooms seven-and-sixpence for a glass of ale and bread and cheese, the charge of the house being only six shillings. He had the meanness to deduct the eighteenpence from my wages, and because I blustered a bit, he took me by the shoulders and turned me out – me, a gentleman, and, what is more, a poor orphan!

How I did rage and swear at him when I got out into the street! There stood he, the hideous Jew monster, at the double door, writhing under the effect of my language. I had my revenge! Heads were thrust out of every bar of his windows, laughing at him. A crowd gathered round me, as I stood pounding him with my satire, and they evidently enjoyed his discomfiture. I think the mob would have pelted the ruffian to death (one or two of their missiles hit *me*, I can tell you), when a policeman came up, and in reply to a gentleman, who was asking what was the disturbance, said, 'Bless you, sir, it's Lord Cornwallis'. 'Move on, *Boots*,' said the fellow to me; for the fact is, my misfortunes and early life are pretty well known – and so the crowd dispersed.

'What could have made that policeman call you Lord Cornwallis and Boots?' said the gentleman, who seemed mightily amused, and had followed me. 'Sir,' says I, 'I am an unfortunate officer of the North Bungay Fencibles, and I'll tell you willingly for a pint of beer.' He told me to follow him to his chambers in the Temple, which I did (a five-pair back), and there, sure enough, I had the beer; and told him this very story you've been reading. You see he is what is called a literary man – and sold my adventures for me to the booksellers: he's a strange chap; and says they're *moral*.

I'm blest if *I* can see anything moral in them. I'm sure I ought to have been more lucky through life, being so very wide awake. And yet here I am, without a place, or even a friend, starving upon a beggarly twenty pounds a year – not a single sixpence more, upon *my honour*.

A LITTLE DINNER AT
TIMMINS'S

Chapter 1

Mr and Mrs Fitzroy Timmins live in Lilliput Street, that neat little street which runs at right angles with the Park and Brobdingnag Gardens. It is a very genteel neighbourhood, and I need not say they are of a good family.

Especially Mrs Timmins, as her mamma is always telling Mr T. They are Suffolk people, and distantly related to the Right Honourable the Earl of Bungay.

Besides his house in Lilliput Street, Mr Timmins has chambers in Fig-tree Court, Temple, and goes the Northern Circuit.

The other day, when there was a slight difference about the payment of fees between the great Parliamentary Counsel and the Solicitors, Stoke and Pogers, of Great George Street, sent the papers of the Lough Foyle and Lough Corrib Junction Railway to Mr Fitzroy Timmins, who was so elated that he instantly purchased a couple of looking-glasses for his drawing-rooms (the front room is 16 by 12, and the back, a tight but elegant apartment, 10 ft 6 by 8 ft 4), a coral for the baby, two new dresses for Mrs Timmins, and a little rosewood desk, at the Pantechnicon* for which Rosa had long been sighing, with crumpled legs, emerald-green and gold morocco top, and drawers all over.

Mrs Timmins is a very pretty poetess (her 'Lines to a Faded Tulip' and her 'Plaint of Plinlimmon' appeared in one of last year's Keepsakes); and Fitzroy, as he impressed a kiss on the snowy forehead of his bride, pointed out to her, in one of the innumerable pockets of the desk, an elegant ruby-tipped pen, and six charming little gilt blank books, marked 'My Books', which Mrs Fitzroy might fill, he said (he is an Oxford man, and very polite), 'with the delightful productions of her Muse.' Besides these books, there was pink paper, paper with crimson edges, lace paper, all stamped with R.F.T. (Rosa Fitzroy Timmins) and the hand and battle-axe, the crest of the Timminses (and borne at Ascalon by Roaldus de

Timmins, a crusader, who is now buried in the Temple Church, next to Serjeant Snooks), and yellow, pink, light-blue and other scented sealing-waxes, at the service of Rosa when she chose to correspond with her friends.

Rosa, you may be sure, jumped with joy at the sight of this sweet present; called her Charles (his first name is Samuel, but they have sunk that) the best of men; embraced him a great number of times, to the edification of her buttony little page, who stood at the landing; and as soon as he was gone to chambers, took the new pen and a sweet sheet of paper, and began to compose a poem.

'What shall it be about?' was naturally her first thought. 'What should be a young mother's first inspiration?' Her child lay on the sofa asleep before her; and she began in her neatest hand –

LINES

ON MY SON, BUNGAY DE BRACY GASHLEIGH TYMMYNS, AGED TEN MONTHS

Tuesday

> How beautiful! how beautiful thou seemest,
>   My boy, my precious one, my rosy babe!
> Kind angels hover round thee, as thou dreamest:
> Soft lashes hide thy beauteous azure eye which gleamest.

'Gleamest? thine eye which gleamest? Is that grammar?' thought Rosa, who had puzzled her little brains for some time with this absurd question, when the baby woke. Then the cook came up to ask about dinner; then Mrs Fundy slipped over from No. 27 (they are opposite neighbours, and made an acquaintance through Mrs Fundy's macaw); and a thousand things happened. Finally, there was no rhyme to babe except Tippoo Saib (against whom Major Gashleigh, Rosa's grandfather, had distinguished himself), and so she gave up the little poem about her De Bracy.

Nevertheless, when Fitzroy returned from chambers to take a walk with his wife in the Park, as he peeped through the rich tapestry hanging which divided the two drawing-rooms, he found his dear girl still seated at the desk, and writing, writing away with her ruby pen as fast as it could scribble.

'What a genius that child has!' he said; 'why, she is a second Mrs Norton!'* and advanced smiling to peep over her shoulder and see what pretty thing Rosa was composing.

It was not poetry, though, that she was writing, and Fitz read as follows:

Lilliput Street, Tuesday, 22nd May

Mr and Mrs Fitzroy Tymmyns request the pleasure of Sir Thomas and Lady Kicklebury's company at dinner on Wednesday, at 7½ o'clock.

'My dear!' exclaimed the barrister, pulling a long face.

'Law, Fitzroy!' cried the beloved of his bosom, 'how you do startle one!'

'Give a dinner-party with our means!' said he.

'Ain't you making a fortune, you miser?' Rosa said. 'Fifteen guineas a day is four thousand five hundred a year; I've calculated it.' And, so saying, she rose and taking hold of his whiskers (which are as fine as those of any man of his circuit), she put her mouth close up against his and did something to his long face, which quite changed the expression of it; and which the little page heard outside the door.

'Our dining-room won't hold ten,' he said.

'We'll only ask twenty, my love. Ten are sure to refuse in this season, when everybody is giving parties. Look, here is the list.'

'Earl and Countess of Bungay, and Lady Barbara Saint Mary's.'

'You are dying to get a lord into the house,' Timmins said (*he* has not altered his name in Fig-tree Court yet, and therefore I am not so affected as to call him *Tymmyns*).

'Law, my dear, they are our cousins, and must be asked,' Rosa said.

'Let us put down my sister and Tom Crowder, then.'

'Blanche Crowder is really so *very* fat, Fitzroy,' his wife said, 'and our rooms are so *very* small.'

Fitz laughed. 'You little rogue,' he said, 'Lady Bungay weighs two of Blanche, even when she's not in the f — '

'Fiddlesticks!' Rose cried out. 'Doctor Crowder really cannot be admitted: he makes such a noise eating his soup, that it is really quite disagreeable.' And she imitated the gurgling noise performed by the Doctor while inhausting his soup, in such a funny way, that Fitz saw inviting him was out of the question.

'Besides, we mustn't have too many relations,' Rosa went on. 'Mamma, of course, is coming. She doesn't like to be asked in the evening; and she'll bring her silver bread-basket and her candlesticks, which are very rich and handsome.'

'And you complain of Blanche for being too stout!' groaned out Timmins.

'Well, well, don't be in a pet,' said little Rosa. 'The girls won't come to dinner; but will bring their music afterwards.' And she went on with the list.

'Sir Thomas and Lady Kicklebury, 2. No saying no: we *must* ask them, Charles. They are rich people, and any room in their house in Brobdingnag Gardens would swallow up *our* humble cot. But to people in *our* position in *society* they will be glad enough to come. The City people are glad to mix with the old families.'

'Very good,' says Fitz, with a sad face of assent – and Mrs Timmins went on reading her list.

'Mr and Mrs Topham Sawyer, Belgravine Place.'

'Mrs Sawyer hasn't asked you all the season. She gives herself the airs of an empress; and when – '

'One's Member, you know, my dear, one must have,' Rosa replied, with much dignity; as if the presence of the representative of her native place would be a protection to her dinner. And a note was written and transported by the page early next morning to the mansion of the Sawyers, in Belgravine Place.

The Topham Sawyers had just come down to breakfast; Mrs T. in her large dust-coloured morning dress and Madonna front* (she looks rather scraggy of a morning, but I promise you her ringlets and figure will stun you of an evening); and having read the note, the following dialogue passed:

Mrs Topham Sawyer. 'Well, upon my word, I don't know where things will end. Mr Sawyer, the Timminses have asked us to dinner.'

Mr Topham Sawyer. 'Ask us to dinner! What d—impudence!'

Mrs Topham Sawyer. 'The most dangerous and insolent revolutionary principles are abroad, Mr Sawyer; and I shall write and hint as much to these persons.'

Mr Topham Sawyer. 'No, d—it, Joanna: they are my constituents and we must go. Write a civil note, and say we will come to their party.' (*He resumes the perusal of 'The Times', and Mrs Topham Sawyer writes*) –

My Dear Rosa,

We shall have *great pleasure* in joining your little party. I do not reply in the third person, as *we are old friends*, you know, and *country neighbours*. I hope your mamma is well: present my *kindest remembrances* to her, and I hope we shall see much *more* of each other in the summer, when we go down to the Sawpits (for going abroad is out of the question in these *dreadful times*). With a hundred kisses to your dear little *pet*,

Believe me your attached
J.T.S.

She said *Pet*, because she did not know whether Rosa's child was a girl or boy: and Mrs Timmins was very much pleased with the kind and gracious nature of the reply to her invitation.

Chapter II

The next persons whom little Mrs Timmins was bent upon asking, were Mr and Mrs John Rowdy, of the firm of Stumpy, Rowdy and Co., of Brobdingnag Gardens, of the Prairie, Putney, and of Lombard Street, City.

Mrs Timmins and Mrs Rowdy had been brought up at the same school together, and there was always a little rivalry between them, from the day when they contended for the French prize at school to last week, when each had a stall at the Fancy Fair for the benefit of the Daughters of Decayed Muffin-men; and when Mrs Timmins danced against Mrs Rowdy in the Scythe Mazurka at the Polish Ball, headed by Mrs Hugh Slasher. Rowdy took twenty-three pounds more than Timmins in the Muffin transaction (for she had possession of a kettle-holder worked by the hands of R-y-lty, which brought crowds to her stall); but in the Mazurka Rosa conquered: she has the prettiest little foot possible (which in a red boot and silver heel looked so lovely that even the Chinese ambassador remarked it), whereas Mrs Rowdy's foot is no trifle, as Lord Cornbury acknowledged when it came down on his lordship's boot-tip as they danced together amongst the Scythes.

'These people are ruining themselves,' said Mrs John Rowdy to her husband, on receiving the pink note. It was carried round by that rogue of a buttony page in the evening; and he walked to Brobdingnag Gardens, and in the Park afterwards, with a young lady who is kitchen-maid at 27, and who is not more than fourteen years older than little Buttons.

'These people are ruining themselves,' said Mrs John to her husband. 'Rosa says she has asked the Bungays.'

'Bungays indeed! Timmins was always a tuft-hunter,'* said Rowdy, who had been at college with the barrister, and who, for his own part, has no more objection to a lord than you or I have; and adding, 'Hang him, what business has *he* to be giving parties?' allowed Mrs Rowdy, nevertheless, to accept Rosa's invitation.

'When I go to business to-morrow, I will just have a look at Mr Fitz's account,' Mr Rowdy thought; 'and if it is overdrawn, as it usually is, why ... ' The announcement of Mrs Rowdy's brougham here put an end to this agreeable train of thought; and the banker and his lady stepped into it to join a snug little family-party of two-and-twenty, given by Mr and Mrs Secondchop at their great house on the other side of the Park.

'Rowdys 2, Bungays 3, ourselves and mamma 3, 2 Sawyers,' calculated little Rosa.

'General Gulpin,' Rosa continued, 'eats a great deal, and is very stupid, but he looks well at table with his star and ribbon. Let us put *him* down!' and she noted down 'Sir Thomas and Lady Gulpin, 2. Lord Castlemouldy, I.'

'You will make your party abominably genteel and stupid,' groaned Timmins. 'Why don't you ask some of our old friends? Old Mrs Portman has asked us twenty times, I am sure, within the last two years.'

'And the last time we went there, there was pea-soup for dinner!' Mrs Timmins said, with a look of ineffable scorn.

'Nobody can have been kinder than the Hodges have always been to us; and some sort of return we might make, I think.'

'Return, indeed! A pretty sound it is on the staircase to hear 'Mr and Mrs 'Odge and Miss 'Odges' pronounced by Billiter, who always leaves his *h*'s out. No, no: see attorneys at your chambers, my dear – but what could the poor creatures do in *our* society?' And so, one by one, Timmins's old friends were tried and eliminated by Mrs Timmins, just as if she had been an Irish Attorney-General, and they so many Catholics on Mr Mitchel's jury.*

Mrs Fitzroy insisted that the party should be of her very best company. Funnyman, the great wit, was asked, because of his jokes; and Mrs Butt, on whom he practises; and Potter, who is asked because everybody else asks him; and Mr Ranville Ranville of the Foreign Office, who might give some news of the Spanish squabble; and Botherby, who has suddenly sprung up into note because he is intimate with the French Revolution, and visits Ledru-Rollin and Lamartine.* And these, with a couple more who are *amis de la maison*, made up the twenty, whom Mrs Timmins thought she might safely invite to her little dinner.

But the deuce of it was, that when the answers to the invitations came back, everybody accepted! Here was a pretty quandary. How they were to get twenty into their dining-room was a calculation which poor Timmins could not solve at all; and he paced up and down the little room in dismay.

'Pooh!' said Rosa with a laugh. 'Your sister Blanche looked very well in one of my dresses last year; and you know how stout she is. We will find some means to accommodate them all, depend upon it.'

Mrs John Rowdy's note to dear Rosa, accepting the latter's invitation, was a very gracious and kind one; and Mrs Fitz showed it to her husband when he came back from chambers. But there was another note which had arrived for him by this time from Mr Rowdy – or rather from the firm; and to the effect that Mr F. Timmins had overdrawn his account £28 18s. 6d., and was requested to pay that sum to his obedient servants, Stumpy, Rowdy and Co.

And Timmins did not like to tell his wife that the contending parties in the Lough Foyle and Lough Corrib Railroad had come to a settlement, and that the fifteen guineas a day had consequently determined. 'I have had seven days of it, though,' he thought; 'and that will be enough to pay for the desk, the dinner, and the glasses, and make all right with Stumpy and Rowdy.'

Chapter III

The cards for dinner having been issued, it became the duty of Mrs Timmins to make further arrangements respecting the invitations to the tea-party which was to follow the more substantial meal.

These arrangements are difficult, as any lady knows who is in the habit of entertaining her friends. There are –

People who are offended if you ask them to tea whilst others have been asked to dinner;

People who are offended if you ask them to tea at all; and cry out furiously, 'Good Heavens! Jane my love, why do these Timminses suppose that I am to leave my dinner-table to attend their — soirée?' (the dear reader may fill up the — to any strength, according to his liking) – or, 'Upon my word, William my dear, it is too much to ask us to pay twelve shillings for a brougham, and to spend I don't know how much in gloves, just to make our curtsies in Mrs Timmins's little drawing-room.' Mrs Moser made the latter remark about the Timmins affair, while the former was uttered by Mr Grumpley, barrister-at-law, to his lady, in Gloucester Place.

That there are people who are offended if you don't ask them at all, is a point which I suppose nobody will question. Timmins's earliest friend in life was Simmins, whose wife and family have taken a cottage at Mortlake for the season.

'We can't ask them to come out of the country,' Rosa said to her Fitzroy – (between ourselves, she was delighted that Mrs Simmins was out of the way, and was as jealous of her as every well-regulated woman should be of her husband's female friends) – 'we can't ask them to come so far for the evening.'

'Why, no, certainly,' said Fitzroy, who has himself no very great opinion of a tea-party; and so the Simminses were cut out of the list.

And what was the consequence? The consequence was, that Simmins and Timmins cut when they met at Westminster; that

Mrs Simmins sent back all the books which she had borrowed from Rosa, with a withering note of thanks; that Rosa goes about saying that Mrs Simmins squints; that Mrs S, on her side, declares that Rosa is crooked, and behaved shamefully to Captain Hicks in marrying Fitzroy over him, though she was forced to do it by her mother, and prefers the Captain to her husband to this day. If, in a word, these two men could be made to fight, I believe their wives would not be displeased; and the reason of all this misery, rage, and dissension, lies in a poor little twopenny dinner-party in Lilliput Street.

Well, the guests, both for before and after meat, having been asked, old Mrs Gashleigh, Rosa's mother – and, by consequence, Fitzroy's *dear* mother-in-law, though I promise you that 'dear' is particularly sarcastic – Mrs Gashleigh of course was sent for, and came with Miss Eliza Gashleigh, who plays on the guitar, and Emily, who limps a little, but plays sweetly on the concertina. They live close by – trust them for that. Your mother-in-law is always within hearing, thank our stars for the attention of the dear women. The Gashleighs, I say, live close by, and came early on the morning after Rosa's notes had been issued for the dinner.

When Fitzroy, who was in his little study, which opens into his little dining-room – one of those absurd little rooms which ought to be called a gentleman's pantry, and is scarcely bigger than a shower-bath, or a state cabin in a ship – when Fitzroy heard his mother-in-law's knock, and her well-known scuffling and chattering in the passage – in which she squeezed up young Buttons, the page, while she put questions to him regarding baby, and the cook's health, and whether she had taken what Mrs Gashleigh had sent overnight, and the housemaid's health, and whether Mr Timmins had gone to chambers or not – and when, after this preliminary chatter, Buttons flung open the door, announcing – 'Mrs Gashleigh and the young ladies,' Fitzroy laid down his *Times* newspaper with an expression that had best not be printed here, and took his hat and walked away.

Mrs Gashleigh has never liked him since he left off calling her mamma, and kissing her. But he said he could not stand it any longer – he was hanged if he would. So he went away to chambers, leaving the field clear to Rosa, mamma, and the two dear girls.

– Or to one of them, rather: for before leaving the house, he thought he would have a look at little Fitzroy upstairs in the nursery, and he found the child in the hands of his maternal aunt Eliza, who was holding him and pinching him as if he had been her guitar, I suppose; so that the little fellow bawled pitifully – and his father finally quitted the premises.

No sooner was he gone, although the party was still a fortnight off, than the women pounced upon his little study, and began to put it in order. Some of his papers they pushed up over the bookcase, some they put behind the Encyclopædia, some they crammed into the drawers – where Mrs Gashleigh found three cigars, which she pocketed, and some letters, over which she cast her eye; and by Fitz's return they had the room as neat as possible, and the best glass and dessert-service mustered on the study table.

It was a very neat and handsome service, as you may be sure Mrs Gashleigh thought, whose rich uncle had purchased it for the young couple, at Spode and Copeland's; but it was only for twelve persons.

It was agreed that it would be, in all respects, cheaper and better to purchase a dozen more dessert-plates; and with 'my silver basket in the centre,' Mrs G. said (she is always bragging about that confounded bread-basket), 'we need not have any extra china dishes, and the table will look very pretty.'

On making a roll-call of the glass, it was calculated that at least a dozen or so tumblers, four or five dozen wines, eight water-bottles, and a proper quantity of ice-plates, were requisite; and that, as they would always be useful, it would be best to purchase the articles immediately. Fitz tumbled over the basket containing them, which stood in the hall, as he came in from chambers, and over the boy who had brought them – and the little bill.

The women had had a long debate, and something like a quarrel, it must be owned, over the bill of fare. Mrs Gashleigh, who had lived a great part of her life in Devonshire, and kept house in great state there, was famous for making some dishes, without which, she thought, no dinner could be perfect. When she proposed her mock-turtle, and stewed pigeons, and gooseberry-cream, Rosa turned up her nose – a pretty little nose it was, by the way, and with a natural turn in that direction.

'Mock-turtle in June, mamma!' said she.

'It was good enough for your grandfather, Rosa,' the mamma replied: 'it was good enough for the Lord High Admiral, when he was at Plymouth; it was good enough for the first men in the county, and relished by Lord Fortyskewer and Lord Rolls; Sir Lawrence Porker ate twice of it after Exeter Races; and I think it might be good enough for – '

'I will *not* have it, mamma!' said Rosa, with a stamp of her foot; and Mrs Gashleigh knew what resolution there was in that. Once, when she had tried to physic the baby, there had been a similar fight between them.

So Mrs Gashleigh made out a *carte,* in which the soup was left with a dash – a melancholy vacuum; and in which the pigeons were certainly thrust in amongst the *entrées*: but Rosa determined they never should make an *entrée* at all into her dinner-party, but that she would have the dinner *her* own way.

When Fitz returned, then, and after he had paid the little bill of £6 14*s.* 6*d.* for the glass, Rosa flew to him with her sweetest smiles, and the baby in her arms. And after she had made him remark how the child grew every day more and more like him, and after she had treated him to a number of compliments and caresses, which it were positively fulsome to exhibit in public, and after she had soothed him into good humour by her artless tenderness, she began to speak to him about some little points which she had at heart.

She pointed out with a sigh how shabby the old curtains looked since the dear new glasses which her darling Fitz had given her had been put up in the drawing-room. Muslin curtains cost nothing, and she must and would have them.

The muslin curtains were accorded. She and Fitz went and bought them at Shoolbred's, when you may be sure she treated herself likewise to a neat, sweet pretty half-mourning (for the Court, you know, is in mourning) – a neat sweet barège, or calimanco, or bombazine, or tiffany, or some such thing; but Madame Camille, of Regent Street, made it up, and Rosa looked like an angel in it on the night of her little dinner.

'And, my sweet,' she continued, after the curtains had been accorded, 'mamma and I have been talking about the dinner. She wants to make it very expensive, which I cannot allow. I have been thinking of a delightful and economical plan, and you, my sweetest Fitz, must put it into execution.'

'I have cooked a mutton-chop when I was in chambers,' Fitz said with a laugh. 'Am I to put on a cap and an apron?'

'No: but you are to go to the 'Megatherium Club' (where, you wretch, you are always going without my leave), and you are to

beg Monsieur Mirobolant, your famous cook, to send you one of
his best aides-de-camp, as I know he will, and with his aid we can
can dress the dinner and the confectionery at home for *almost
nothing*, and we can show those purse-proud Topham Sawyers
and Rowdys that the *humble cottage* can furnish forth an elegant
entertainment as well as the gilded halls of wealth.'

Fitz agreed to speak to Monsieur Mirobolant. If Rosa had had
a fancy for the cook of the Prime Minister, I believe the deluded
creature of a husband would have asked Lord John for the loan
of him.

Chapter IV

Fitzroy Timmins, whose taste for wine is remarkable for so young
a man, is a member of the committee of the 'Megatherium Club',
and the great Mirobolant, good-natured as all great men are, was
only too happy to oblige him. A young friend and *protégé* of his,
of considerable merit, M. Cavalcadour, happened to be disen-
gaged through the lamented death of Lord Hauncher, with whom
young Cavalcadour had made his *début* as an artist. He had
nothing to refuse to his master, Mirobolant, and would impress
himself to be useful to a *gourmet* so distinguished as Monsieur
Timmins. Fitz went away as pleased as Punch with this encomium
of the great Mirobolant, and was one of those who voted against
the decreasing of Mirobolant's salary, when the measure was
proposed by Mr Parings, Colonel Close, and the Screw party in
the committee of the club.

Faithful to the promise of his great master, the youthful Cavalcadour called in Lilliput Street the next day. A rich crimson
velvet waistcoat, with buttons of blue glass and gold, a variegated
blue satin stock, over which a graceful mosaic chain hung in

glittering folds, a white hat worn on one side of his long curling ringlets, redolent with the most delightful hair-oil – one of those white hats which looks as if it had been just skinned – and a pair of gloves not exactly of the colour of *beurre frais,* but of *beurre* that has been up the chimney, with a natty cane with a gilt knob, completed the upper part, at any rate, of the costume of the young fellow whom the page introduced to Mrs Timmins.

Her mamma and she had been just having a dispute about the gooseberry-cream when Cavalcadour arrived. His presence silenced Mrs Gashleigh; and Rosa, in carrying on a conversation with him in the French language – which she had acquired perfectly in an elegant finishing establishment in Kensington Square – had a great advantage over her mother, who could only pursue the dialogue with very much difficulty, eyeing one or other interlocutor with an alarmed and suspicious look, and gasping out 'We' whenever she thought a proper opportunity arose for the use of that affirmative.

'I have two leetl menus weez me,' said Cavalcadour to Mrs Gashleigh.

'Minews – yes, – oh, indeed?' answered the lady.

'Two little cartes.'

'Oh, two carts! Oh, we,' she said. 'Coming, I suppose?' And she looked out of the window to see if they were there.

Cavalcadour smiled. He produced from a pocket-book a pink paper and a blue paper, on which he had written two bills of fare – the last two which he had composed for the lamented Hauncher – and he handed these over to Mrs Fitzroy.

The poor little woman was dreadfully puzzled with these documents (she has them in her possession still), and began to read from the pink one as follows: –

DÎNER POUR 16 PERSONNES

Potage (clair) à la Rigodon

Do. à la Prince de Tombuctou

Deux Poissons

Saumon de Severne   Rougets Gratinés
à la Boadicée   à la Cléopatre

Deux Relevés

Le Chapeau-à-trois-cornes farci à la Robespierre

Le Tire-botte à l'Odalisque

Six Entrées

Sauté de Hannetons à l'Epinglère

Côtelettes à la Megatherium
Bourrasque de Veau à la Palsambleu
Laitances de Carpe en goguette à la Reine Pomare
Turban de Volaille à l'Archevêque de Cantorbéry

And so on with the *entremets*, and *hors d'œuvres*, and the *rôtis*, and the *relevés*.

'Madame will see that the dinners are quite simple,' said M. Cavalcadour.

'Oh, quite!' said Rosa, dreadfully puzzled.

'Which would Madame like?'

'Which would we like, mamma?' Rosa asked; adding, as if after a little thought, 'I think, sir, we should prefer the blue one.' At which Mrs Gashleigh nodded as knowingly as she could; though pink or blue, I defy anybody to know what these cooks mean by their jargon.

'If you please, Madame, we will go down below and examine the scene of operations,' Monsieur Cavalcadour said; and so he was marshalled down the stairs to the kitchen, which he didn't like to name, and appeared before the cook in all his splendour.

He cast a rapid glance round the premises, and a smile of something like contempt lighted up his features. 'Will you bring pen and ink, if you please, and I will write down a few of the articles which will be necessary for us? We shall require, if you please, eight more stew-pans, a couple of braising-pans, eight sauté-pans, six bainmarie-pans, a freezing-pot with accessories, and a few more articles of which I will inscribe the names.' And Mr Cavalcadour did so, dashing down, with the rapidity of genius, a tremendous list of ironmongery goods, which he handed over to Mrs Timmins. She and her mamma were quite frightened by the awful catalogue.

'I will call three days hence and superintend the progress of matters; and we will make stock for the soup the day before the dinner.'

'Don't you think, sir,' here interposed Mrs Gashleigh, 'That one soup – a fine rich mock-turtle, such as I have seen in the best houses in the West of England, and such as the late Lord Fortyskewer – '

'You will get what is wanted for the soups, if you please,' Mr Cavalcadour continued, not heeding this interruption, and as bold as a captain on his own quarter-deck: 'for the stock of clear soup, you will get a leg of beef, a leg of veal, and a ham.'

'We, munseer,' said the cook, dropping a terrified curtsey: 'a leg of beef, a leg of veal, and a ham.'

'You can't serve a leg of veal at a party,' said Mrs Gashleigh; 'and a leg of beef is not a company dish.'

'Madame, they are to make the stock of the clear soup,' Mr Cavalcadour said.

'*What*!' cried Mrs Gashleigh; and the cook repeated his former expression.

'Never, whilst *I* am in this house,' cried out Mrs Gashleigh, indignantly; 'never in a Christian *English* household; never shall such sinful waste be permitted by *me*. If you wish me to dine, Rosa, you must get a dinner less *expensive*. The Right Honourable Lord Fortyskewer could dine, sir, without these wicked luxuries, and I presume my daughter's guests can.'

'Madame is perfectly at liberty to decide,' said M Cavalcadour. 'I came to oblige Madame and my good friend Mirobolant, not myself.'

'Thank you, sir, I think it *will* be too expensive,' Rosa stammered in a great flutter; 'but I am very much obliged to you.'

'Il n'y a point d'obligation, Madame,' said Monsieur Alcide Camille Cavalcadour in his most superb manner; and, making a splendid bow to the lady of the house, was respectfully conducted to the upper regions by little Buttons, leaving Rosa frightened, the cook amazed and silent, and Mrs Gashleigh boiling with indignation against the dresser.

Up to that moment, Mrs Blowser, the cook, who had come out of Devonshire with Mrs Gashleigh (of course that lady garrisoned her daughter's house with servants, and expected them to give her information of everything which took place there) – up to that moment, I say, the cook had been quite contented with that subterraneous station which she occupied in life, and had a pride in keeping her kitchen neat, bright, and clean. It was, in her opinion, the comfortablest room in the house (we all thought so when we came down of a night to smoke there), and the handsomest kitchen in Lilliput Street.

But after the visit of Cavalcadour, the cook became quite discontented and uneasy in her mind. She talked in a melancholy manner over the area-railings to the cooks at twenty-three and twenty-five. She stepped over the way, and conferred with the cook there. She made inquiries at the baker's and at other places about the kitchens in the great houses in Brobdingnag Gardens, and how many spits, bangmarry-pans, and stoo-pans they had. She thought she could not do with an occasional help, but must have a kitchen-maid. And she was often discovered by a gentleman of the police force, who was, I believe, her cousin, and occasionally visited her when Mrs Gashleigh was not in the house or spying it – she was discovered seated with *Mrs Rundell* in her lap, its leaves bespattered with her tears. 'My pease be gone, Pelisse,' she said, 'zins I zaw that ther Franchman!' And it was all the faithful fellow could do to console her.

' — the dinner!' said Timmins, in a rage at last. 'Having it cooked in the house is out of the question. The bother of it, and the row your mother makes, are enough to drive one mad. It won't happen again, I can promise you, Rosa. Order it at Fubsby's, at once. You can have everything from Fubsby's – from footmen to saltspoons. Let's go and order it at Fubsby's.'

'Darling, if you don't mind the expense, and it will be any relief to you, let us do as you wish,' Rosa said; and she put on her bonnet, and they went off to the grand cook and confectioner of the Brobdingnag quarter.

Chapter V

On the arm of her Fitzroy, Rosa went off to Fubsby's, that magnificent shop at the corner of Parliament Place and Alicompayne Square – a shop into which the rogue had often cast a glance of approbation as he passed: for there are not only the most wonderful and delicious cakes and confections in the window, but at the counter there are almost sure to be three or four of the prettiest women in the whole of this world, with little darling caps of the last French make, with beautiful wavy hair, and the neatest possible waists and aprons.

Yes, there they sit; and others, perhaps, besides Fitz have cast a sheep's-eye through those enormous plate-glass window-panes. I suppose it is the fact of perpetually living among such a quantity of good things that makes those young ladies so beautiful. They come into the place, let us say, like ordinary people, and gradually grow handsomer and handsomer, until they grow out into the perfect angels you see. It can't be otherwise: if you and I, my dear fellow, were to have a course of that place, we should become beautiful too. They live in an atmosphere of the most delicious pine-apples, blanc-manges, creams (some whipt, and some so good that of course they don't want whipping), jellies, tipsy-cakes, cherry-brandy – one hundred thousand sweet and lovely things. Look at the preserved fruits, look at the golden ginger, the outspreading ananas, the darling little rogues of China oranges, ranged in the gleaming crystal cylinders. *Mon Dieu*! Look at the strawberries in the leaves. Each of them is as large nearly as a lady's reticule, and looks as if it had been brought up in a nursery to itself. One of those strawberries is a meal for those young ladies behind the counter; they nibble off a little from the side, and if they are very hungry, which can scarcely ever happen, they are allowed to go to the crystal canisters and take out a rout-cake* or macaroon. In the evening they sit and tell each other little riddles out of the bonbons; and when they wish to amuse themselves, they read the most delightful remarks, in the French language, about Love, and Cupid, and Beauty, before they place them inside the crackers. They always are writing down good things into Mr Fubsbys's ledgers. It must be a perfect feast to read them. Talk of the Garden of Eden! I believe it was nothing to Mr Fubsby's house; and I have no doubt that after those young ladies have been there a certain time, they get to such a pitch of loveliness at last, that they become complete angels, with wings sprouting out of their lovely shoulders, when (after giving just a preparatory balance or two) they fly up to the counter and perch there for a minute, hop down again, and affectionately kiss the other young ladies, and say, 'Good-bye, dears! We shall meet again *là haut*.' And then with a whirr of their deliciously scented wings, away they fly for good, whisking over the trees of Brobdingnag Square, and up into the sky, as the policeman touches his hat.

It is up there that they invent the legends for the crackers, and the wonderful riddles and remarks on the bonbons. No mortal, I am sure, could write them.

I never saw a man in such a state as Fitzroy Timmins in the presence of those ravishing houris. Mrs Fitz having explained that they required a dinner for twenty persons, the chief young lady asked what Mr and Mrs Fitz would like, and named a thousand things, each better than the other, to all of which Fitz instantly said yes. The wretch was in such a state of infatuation that I believe if that lady had proposed to him a fricasseed elephant, or a boa-constrictor in jelly, he would have said, 'O yes, certainly; put it down.'

That Peri wrote down in her album a list of things which it would make your mouth water to listen to. But she took it all quite calmly. Heaven bless you! *they* don't care about things that are no delicacies to them! But whatever she chose to write down, Fitzroy let her.

After the dinner and dessert were ordered (at Fubsby's they furnish everything: dinner and dessert, plate and china, servants in your own livery, and, if you please, guests of title too), the married couple retreated from that shop of wonders; Rosa delighted that the trouble of the dinner was all off their hands: but she was afraid it would be rather expensive.

'Nothing can be too expensive which please *you*, dear,' Fitz said.

'By the way, one of those young women was rather good-looking,' Rosa remarked: 'the one in the cap with the blue ribbons.' (And she cast about the shape of the cap in her mind, and determined to have exactly such another.)

'Think so? I didn't observe,' said the miserable hypocrite by her side; and when he had seen Rosa home, he went back, like an infamous fiend, to order something else which he had forgotten, he said, at Fubsby's. Get out of that Paradise, you cowardly, creeping, vile serpent you!

Until the day of the dinner, the infatuated fop was *always* going to Fubsby's. *He was remarked there*. He used to go before he went to chambers in the morning, and sometimes on his return from the Temple: but the morning was the time which he preferred; and one day, when he went on one of his eternal pretexts, and was chattering and flirting at the counter, a lady who had been reading yesterday's paper and eating a halfpenny bun for an hour in the back shop (if that paradise may be called a shop) – a lady stepped forward, laid down the *Morning Herald*, and confronted him.

That lady was Mrs Gashleigh. From that day the miserable Fitzroy was in her power; and she resumed a sway over his house, to shake off which had been the object of his life, and the result of many battles. And for a mere freak – for, on going into Fubsby's a week afterwards he found the Peris drinking tea out of blue cups, and eating stale bread and butter, when his absurd passion instantly vanished – I say, for a mere freak, the most intolerable burden of his life was put on his shoulders again – his mother-in-law.

On the day before the little dinner took place – and I promise you we shall come to it in the very next chapter – a tall and elegant middle-aged gentleman, who might have passed for an earl but that there was a slight incompleteness about his hands and feet, the former being uncommonly red, and the latter large and irregular, was introduced to Mrs Timmins by the page, who announced him as Mr Truncheon.

'I'm Truncheon, Ma'am,' he said, with a low bow.

'Indeed!' said Rosa.

'About the dinner, M'm, from Fubsby's, M'm. As you have no butler, M'm, I presume you will wish me to act as sich. I shall bring two persons as haids to-morrow; both answers to the name of John. I'd best, if you please, inspect the premisis, and will think you to allow your young man to show me the pantry and kitching.'

Truncheon spoke in a low voice, and with the deepest and most respectful melancholy. There is not much expression in his eyes, but from what there is, you would fancy that he was oppressed by a secret sorrow. Rosa trembled as she surveyed this gentleman's size, his splendid appearance, and gravity. 'I am sure,' she said, 'I never shall dare to ask him to hand a glass of water.' Even Mrs Gashleigh, when she came on the morning of the actual dinner-party, to superintend matters, was cowed, and retreated from the kitchen before the calm majesty of Truncheon.

And yet that great man was, like all the truly great – affable.

He put aside his coat and waistcoat (both of evening cut, and looking prematurely splendid as he walked the streets in noon-day), and did not disdain to rub the glasses and polish the decanters, and to show young Buttons the proper mode of pre-paring these articles for a dinner. And while he operated, the maids, and Buttons, and cook, when she could – and what had she but the vegetables to boil? – crowded round him, and listened with wonder as he talked of the great families as he had lived with. That man, as they saw him there before them, had been cab-boy

to Lord Tantallan, valet to the Earl of Bareacres, and groom of
the chambers to the Duchess Dowager of Fitzbattleaxe. Oh, it was
delightful to hear Mr Truncheon!

Chapter VI

On the great, momentous, stupendous day of the dinner, my
beloved female reader may imagine that Fitzroy Timmins was sent
about his business at an early hour in the morning, while the
women began to make preparations to receive their guests. 'There
will be no need of your going to Fubsby's,' Mrs Gashleigh said to
him, with a look that drove him out of doors. 'Everything that we
require has been ordered *there*! You will please to be back here
at six o'clock, and not sooner: and I presume you will acquiesce
in my arrangements about the *wine*?'

'O yes, mamma,' said the prostrate son-in-law.

'In so large a party – a party beyond some folks' *means* –
expensive *wines* are *absurd*. The light sherry at 26s., the champagne at 42s.; and you are not to go beyond 36s. for the claret
and port after dinner. Mind, coffee will be served: and you come
upstairs after two rounds of the claret.'

'Of course, of course,' acquiesced the wretch; and hurried out
of the house to his chambers, and to discharge the commissions
with which the womankind had intrusted him.

As for Mrs Gashleigh, you might have heard her bawling over
the house the whole day long. That admirable woman was
everywhere: in the kitchen until the arrival of Truncheon, before
whom she would not retreat without a battle; on the stairs; in
Fitzroy's dressing-room; and in Fitzroy minor's nursery, to whom
she gave a dose of her own composition, while the nurse was sent
out on a pretext to make purchases of garnish for the dishes to be

served for the little dinner. Garnish for the dishes! As if the folks at Fubsby's could not garnish dishes better than Gashleigh, with her stupid old-world devices of laurel-leaves, parsley, and cut turnips! Why, there was not a dish served that day that was not covered over with skewers, on which truffles, crayfish, mush-rooms, and forced-meat were impaled. When old Gashleigh went down with her barbarian bunches of holly and greens to stick about the meats, even the cook saw their incongruity, and, at Truncheon's orders, flung the whole shrubbery into the dust-house, where, while poking about the premises, you may be sure Mrs G saw it.

Every candle which was to be burned that night (including the tallow candle, which she said was a good enough bed-light for Fitzroy) she stuck into the candlesticks with her own hands, giving her own high-shouldered plated candlesticks of the year 1798 the place of honour. She upset all poor Rosa's floral arrangements, turning the nosegays from one vase into the other without any pity, and was never tired of beating, and pushing, and patting, and *whapping* the curtain and sofa draperies into shape in the little drawing-room.

In Fitz's own apartments she revelled with peculiar pleasure. It has been described how she had sacked his study and pushed away his papers, some of which, including three cigars, and the com-mencement of an article for the *Law Magazine*, 'Lives of the Sheriffs' Officers', he has never been able to find to this day. Mamma now went into the little room in the back regions, which is Fitz's dressing-room (and was destined to be a cloak-room), and here she rummaged to her heart's delight.

In an incredibly short space of time she examined all his outlying pockets, drawers, and letters; she inspected his socks and handkerchiefs in the top drawers; and on the dressing-table, his razors, shaving-strop, and hair-oil. She carried off his silver-topped scent-bottle out of his dressing-case, and a half-dozen of his favourite pills (which Fitz possesses in common with every well-regulated man), and probably administered them to her own family. His boots, glossy pumps, and slippers, she pushed into the shower-bath, where the poor fellow stepped into them the next morning, in the midst of a pool in which they were lying. The baby was found sucking his boot-hooks the next day in the nursery; and as for the bottle of varnish for his shoes (which he generally paints upon the trees himself, having a pretty taste in that way), it could never be found to the present hour; but it was remarked that the young Master Gashleighs, when they came home for the holidays, always wore lacquered highlows* and the reader may draw his conclusions from *that* fact.

In the course of the day all the servants gave Mrs Timmins warning.

The cook said she coodn't bear it no longer, 'aving Mrs G always about her kitching, with her fingers in all the saucepans. Mrs G had got her the place, but she preferred one as Mrs G didn't get for her.

The nurse said she was come to nuss Master Fitzroy, and knew her duty; his grandmamma wasn't his nuss, and was always aggrawating her – missus must shoot herself elsewhere.

The housemaid gave utterance to the same sentiments in language more violent.

Little Buttons bounced up to his mistress, said he was butler of the family, Mrs G was always poking about his pantry, and dam if he'd stand it.

At every moment Rosa grew more and more bewildered. The baby howled a great deal during the day. His large china christening-bowl was cracked by Mrs Gashleigh altering the flowers in it, and pretending to be very cool, whilst her hands shook with rage.

'Pray go on, mamma,' Rosa said with tears in her eyes. 'Should you like to break the chandelier?'

'Ungrateful, unnatural child!' bellowed the other. 'Only that I know you couldn't do without me, I'd leave the house this minute.'

'As you wish,' said Rosa; but Mrs G *didn't* wish: and in this juncture Truncheon arrived.

That officer surveyed the dining-room, laid the cloth there with admirable precision and neatness; ranged the plate on the sideboard with graceful accuracy, but objected to that old thing in the centre, as he called Mrs Gashleigh's silver basket, as cumbrous and useless for the table, where they would want all the room they could get.

Order was not restored to the house, nor, indeed, any decent progress made, until this great man came: but where there was a revolt before, and a general disposition to strike work and to yell out defiance against Mrs Gashleigh, who was sitting bewildered and furious in the drawing-room – where there was before commotion, at the appearance of the master-spirit, all was peace and unanimity: the cook went back to her pans, the housemaid busied herself with the china and glass, cleaning some articles and breaking others, Buttons sprang up and down the stairs, obedient to the orders of his chief, and all things went well and in their season.

At six, the man with the wine came from Binney and Latham's. At a quarter-past six, Timmins himself arrived.

At half-past six, he might have been heard shouting out for his varnished boots – but we know where *those* had been hidden – and for his dressing things; but Mrs Gashleigh had put them away.

As in his vain inquiries for these articles he stood shouting, 'Nurse! Buttons! Rosa my dear!' and the most fearful execrations up and down the stairs, Mr Truncheon came out on him.

'Igscuse me, sir,' says he, 'but it's impawsable. We can't dine twenty at that table – not if you set 'em out awinder, we can't.'

'What's to be done?' asked Fitzroy, in an agony; 'they've all said they'd come.'

'Can't do it,' said the other; 'with two top and bottom – and your table is as narrow as a bench – we can't hold more than heighteen, and then each person's helbows will be into his neighbour's cheer.'

'Rosa! Mrs Gashleigh!' cried out Timmins, 'come down and speak to this gent – this – '

'Truncheon, sir,' said the man.

The women descended from the drawing-room. 'Look and see, ladies,' he said, inducting them into the dining-room: 'there's the room, there's the table laid for heighteen, and I defy you to squeege in more.'

'One person in a party always fails,' said Mrs Gashleigh, getting alarmed.

'That's nineteen,' Mr Truncheon remarked. 'We must knock another hoff, Ma'm.' And he looked her hard in the face.

Mrs Gashleigh was very red and nervous, and paced, or rather squeezed round the table (it was as much as she could do). The chairs could not be put any closer than they were. It was impossible, unless the *convive* sat as a centre-piece in the middle, to put another guest at that table.

'Look at that lady movin' round, sir. You see now the difficklty. If my men wasn't thinner, they couldn't hoperate at all,' Mr Truncheon observed, who seemed to have a spite to Mrs Gashleigh.

'What is to be done?' she said, with purple accents.

'My dearest mamma,' Rosa cried out, 'you must stop at home – how sorry I am!' And she shot one glance at Fitzroy, who shot another at the great Truncheon, who held down his eyes. 'We could manage with heighteen,' he said, mildly.

Mrs Gashleigh gave a hideous laugh.

She went away. At eight o'clock she was pacing at the corner of the street, and actually saw the company arrive. First came the Topham Sawyers, in their light-blue carriage with the white hammer-cloth and blue and white ribbons – their footmen drove the house down with the knocking.

Then followed the ponderous and snuff-coloured vehicle, with faded gilt wheels and brass earl's coronets all over it, the conveyance of the House of Bungay. The Countess of Bungay and daughter stepped out of the carriage. The fourteenth Earl of Bungay couldn't come.

Sir Thomas and Lady Gulpin's fly made its appearance, from which issued the General with his star, and Lady Gulpin in yellow satin. The Rowdys' brougham followed next; after which Mrs Butt's handsome equipage drove up.

The two friends of the house, young gentlemen from the Temple, now arrived in cab No. 9996. We tossed up, in fact, which should pay the fare.

Mr Ranville Ranville walked, and was dusting his boots as the Templars drove up. Lord Castlemouldy came out of a twopenny omnibus. Funnyman, the wag, came last, whirling up rapidly in a hansom, just as Mrs Gashleigh, with rage in her heart, was counting that two people had failed, and that there were only seventeen after all.

Mr Truncheon passed our names to Mr Billiter, who bawled them out on the stairs. Rosa was smiling in a pink dress, and looking as fresh as an angel, and received her company with that grace which has always characterised her.

The moment of the dinner arrived, old Lady Bungay scuffled off on the arm of Fitzroy, while the rear was brought up by Rosa and Lord Castlemouldy, of Ballyshanvanvoght Castle, co. Tipperary. Some fellows who had the luck, took down ladies to dinner. I was not sorry to be out of the way of Mrs Rowdy, with her dandyfied airs, or of that high and mighty county princess, Mrs Topham Sawyer.

Chapter VII

Of course it does not become the present writer, who has partaken of the best entertainment which his friends could supply, to make fun of their (somewhat ostentatious, as it must be confessed) hospitality. If they gave a dinner beyond their means, it is no business of mine. I hate a man who goes and eats a friend's meat, and then blabs the secrets of the mahogany. Such a man deserves never to be asked to dinner again; and though at the close of a London season that seems no great loss, and you sicken of a whitebait as you would of a whale – yet we must always remember that there's another season coming and hold our tongues for the present.

As for describing, then, the mere victuals on Timmins's table, that would be absurd. Everybody – (I mean of the genteel world of course, of which I make no doubt the reader is a polite ornament) – Everybody has the same everything in London. You see the same coats, the same dinners, the same boiled fowls and mutton, the same cutlets, fish, and cucumbers, the same lumps of Wenham Lake ice, &c. The waiters with white neckcloths are as like each other everywhere as the pease which they hand round with the ducks of the second course. Can't any one invent anything new?

The only difference between Timmins's dinner and his neighbour's was, that he had hired, as we have said, the greater part of the plate, and that his cowardly conscience magnified faults and disasters of which no one else probably took heed.

But Rosa thought, from the supercilious air with which Mrs Topham Sawyer was eyeing the plate and other arrangements, that she was remarking the difference of the ciphers on the forks and spoons – which had, in fact, been borrowed from every one of Fitzroy's friends – I know, for instance, that he had my six, among others, and only returned five, along with a battered old black-pronged plated abomination, which I have no doubt belongs to Mrs Gashleigh, whom I hereby request to send back mine in exchange – their guilty consciences, I say, made them fancy that every one was spying out their domestic deficiencies: whereas, it is probable that nobody present thought of their failings at all. People never do: they never see holes in their neighbours' coats – they are too indolent, simple, and charitable.

Some things, however, one could not help remarking: for instance, though Fitz is my closest friend, yet could I avoid seeing and being amused by his perplexity and his dismal efforts to be facetious? His eye wandered all round the little room with quick uneasy glances, very different from those frank and jovial looks with which he is accustomed to welcome you to a leg of mutton; and Rosa, from the other end of the table, and over the flowers, *entrée* dishes, and wine-coolers, telegraphed him with signals of corresponding alarm. Poor devils! why did they ever go beyond that leg of mutton?

Funnyman was not brilliant in conversation, scarcely opening his mouth, except for the purposes of feasting. The fact is, our friend Tom Dawson was at table, who knew all his stories, and in his presence the greatest wag is always silent and uneasy.

Fitz has a very pretty wit of his own, and a good reputation on circuit; but he is timid before great people. And indeed the presence of that awful Lady Bungay on his right hand was enough to damp him. She was in court mourning (for the late Prince of Schlippenschloppen). She had on a large black funereal turban and appurtenances, and a vast breastplate of twinkling, twiddling black bugles. No wonder a man could not be gay in talking to *her*.

Mrs Rowdy and Mrs Topham Sawyer love each other as women do who have the same receiving nights, and ask the same society; they were only separated by Ranville Ranville, who tries to be well with both: and they talked at each other across him.

Topham and Rowdy growled out a conversation about Rum, Ireland, and the Navigation Laws, quite unfit for print. Sawyer never speaks three words without mentioning the House and the Speaker.

The Irish Peer said nothing (which was a comfort); but he ate and drank of everything which came in his way; and cut his usual absurd figure in dyed whiskers and a yellow under-waistcoat.

General Gulpin sported his star, and looked fat and florid, but melancholy. His wife ordered away his dinner, just like honest Sancho's physician at Barataria.

Botherby's stories about Lamartine are as old as the hills, since the barricades of 1848; and he could not get in a word or cut the slightest figure. And as for Tom Dawson, he was carrying on an undertoned small-talk with Lady Barbara St Mary's, so that there was not much conversation worth record going on *within* the dining-room.

Outside, it was different. Those houses in Lilliput Street are so uncommonly compact, that you can hear everything which takes place all over the tenement; and so –

In the awful pauses of the banquet, and the hall-door being furthermore open, we had the benefit of hearing:

The cook, and the occasional cook, belowstairs, exchanging rapid phrases regarding the dinner;

The smash of the soup-tureen, and swift descent of the kitchen-maid and soup-ladle down the stairs to the lower regions. This accident created a laugh, and rather amused Fitzroy and the company, and caused Funnyman to say, bowing to Rosa, that she was mistress of herself, though China fall. But she did not heed him, for at that moment another noise commenced, namely, that of –

The baby in the upper rooms, who commenced a series of piercing yells, which, though stopped by the sudden clapping to of the nursery-door, were only more dreadful to the mother when suppressed. She would have given a guinea to go upstairs and have done with the whole entertainment.

A thundering knock came at the door very early after the dessert, and the poor soul took a speedy opportunity of summoning the ladies to depart, though you may be sure it was only old Mrs Gashleigh, who had come with her daughters – of course the first person to come. I saw her red gown whisking up the stairs, which were covered with plates and dishes, over which she trampled.

Instead of having any quiet after the retreat of the ladies, the house was kept in a rattle, and the glasses jingled on the table as the flymen and coachmen plied the knocker, and the *soirée* came in. From my place I could see everything: the guests as they arrived (I remarked very few carriages, mostly cabs and flies), and a little crowd of blackguard boys and children, who were formed round the door, and gave ironical cheers to the folks as they stepped out of their vehicles.

As for the evening-party, if a crowd in the dog-days is pleasant, poor Mrs Timmins certainly had a successful *soirée*. You could hardly move on the stair. Mrs Sternhold broke in the banisters, and nearly fell through. There was such a noise and chatter you could not hear the singing of the Miss Gashleighs, which was no great loss. Lady Bungay could hardly get to her carriage, being entangled with Colonel Wedgewood in the passage. An absurd attempt was made to get up a dance of some kind; but before Mrs Crowder had got round the room, the hanging-lamp in the dining-room below was stove in, and fell with a crash on the table, now prepared for refreshment.

Why, in fact, did the Timminses give that party at all? It was quite beyond their means. They have offended a score of their old friends, and pleased none of their acquaintances. So angry were many who were not asked, that poor Rosa says she must now give a couple more parties and take in those not previously invited. And I know for a fact that Fubsby's bill is not yet paid; nor Binney and Latham's the wine-merchants; that the breakage and hire of glass and china cost ever so much money; that every true friend of Timmins has cried out against his absurd extravagance, and that now, when every one is going out of town, Fitz has hardly money to pay his circuit, much more to take Rosa to a watering-place, as he wished and promised.

As for Mrs Gashleigh, the only feasible plan of economy which she can suggest, is that she should come and live with her daughter and son-in-law, and that they should keep house together. If he agrees to this, she has a little sum at the banker's, with which she would not mind easing his present difficulties; and the poor wretch is so utterly bewildered and crest-fallen that it is very likely he will become her victim.

The Topham Sawyers, when they go down into the country, will represent Fitz as a ruined man and reckless prodigal; his uncle, the attorney, from whom he has expectations, will most likely withdraw his business, and adopt some other member of his family – Blanche Crowder for instance, whose husband, the doctor, has had high words with poor Fitzroy already, of course at the women's instigation. And all these accumulated miseries fall upon the unfortunate wretch because he was good-natured, and his wife would have a Little Dinner.

HOBSON'S CHOICE

---

or, The Tribulations of a Gentleman in Search of a Man-Servant

I

Before my wife's dear mother, Mrs Captain Budge, came to live with us – which she did on occasion of the birth of our darling third child, Albert, named in compliment to a gracious Prince, and now seven-and-a-half years of age – our establishment was in rather what you call a small way, and we only had female servants in our kitchen.

I liked them, I own. I like to be waited on by a neat-handed Phillis of a parlour-maid,* in a nice fitting gown, and a pink ribbon to her cap: and I do not care to deny that I liked to have my parlour-maids good-looking. Not for any reason such as *jealousy might suggest* – such reasons I scorn; but as, for a continuance and for a harmless recreation and enjoyment, I would much rather look out on a pretty view of green fields and a shining river, from my drawing-room window, than upon a blank wall, or an old-clothesman's shop: so I am free to confess I would choose for preference a brisk, rosy, good-natured, smiling lass, to put my dinner and tea before me on the table, rather than a crooked, black-muzzled *frump*, with a dirty cap and black hands. I say I like to have nice-looking people about me; and when I used to chuck my Anna Maria under the chin, and say that was one of the reasons for which I married her, I warrant you Mrs H was not offended; and so she let me have my harmless way about the parlour-maids. Sir, the only way in which we lost our girls in our early days was by marriage. One married the baker, and gives my boy, Albert, gingerbread, whenever he passes her shop; one became the wife of Policeman X, who distinguished himself by having his nose broken in the Chartist riots;* and a third is almost a lady, keeping her one-horse carriage, and being wife to a carpenter and builder.

Well, Mrs Captain Budge, Mrs H's mother, or 'Mamma', as

she insists that I should call her, and I do so, for it pleases her warm and affectionate nature, came to stop for a few weeks, on the occasion of our darling Albert's birth, *anno Domini* 1842; and the child and its mother being delicate, Mrs Captain B stayed to nurse them both, and so has remained with us occupying the room which used to be my study and dressing-room ever since. When she came to us, we may be said to have moved *in a humble sphere*, viz. in Bernard Street, Foundling Hospital, which we left four years ago, for our present residence, Stucco Gardens, Pocklington Square. And up to the period of Mrs Captain B's arrival, we were, as I say, waited upon in the parlour by maids; the rough below-stairs work of knife and shoe-cleaning being done by Grundsell, our greengrocer's third son.

But, though Heaven forbid that I should say a word against my mother-in-law, who has a handsome sum to leave, and who is besides a woman all self-denial, with *her every thought* for our good: yet I think that, without Mamma, my wife would not have had those tantrums, may I call them, of jealousy, which she never exhibited previously, and which she certainly began to show very soon after our dear little scapegrace of an Albert was born. We had at that time, I remember, a parlour servant, called Emma Buck, who came to us from the country, from a Doctor of Divinity's family, and who pleased my wife very well at first, as indeed she did all her power to please her. But on the very day Anna Maria came downstairs to the drawing-room, being brought down in these very arms, which I swear belong to as faithful a husband as any in the City of London, and Emma bringing up her little bit of dinner on a tray, I observed Anna Maria's eyes look uncommon savage at the poor girl, Mrs Captain B looking away the whole time, on to whose neck my wife plunged herself as soon as the girl had left the room; bursting out into tears, and calling somebody a viper.

'Hullo,' says I, 'my beloved, what is the matter? Where's the viper? I didn't know there were any in Bernard Street' (for I thought she might be nervous still, and wished to turn off the thing, whatever it might be, with a pleasantry). 'Who is the serpent?'

'That – that – woman,' gurgles out Mrs H, sobbing on Mamma's shoulder, and Mrs Captain B scowling sadly at me over her daughter.

'What, Emma?' I asked, in astonishment; for the girl had been uncommonly attentive to her mistress, making her gruels and things, and sitting up with her, besides tending my eldest daughter, Emily, through the scarlet fever.

'Emma! don't say Emma in that cruel, audacious way, Marmaduke – Mr Ho – o – obson,' says my wife (for such are my two names as given me by my godfathers and my fathers). 'You call the creature by her christian name before my very face!'

'Oh, Hobson, Hobson!' says Mrs Captain B, wagging her head.

'Confound it' – ('Don't swear,' says Mamma) – 'Confound it, my love,' says I, stamping my foot, 'you wouldn't have me call the girl Buck, Buck, as if she was a rabbit? She's the best girl that ever was: she nursed Emily through the fever; she has been attentive to you; she is always up when you want her – '

'Yes; and when *you-oo-oo come home from the club*, Marmaduke,' my wife shrieks out, and falls again on Mamma's shoulder, who looks me in the face and nods her head fit to drive me mad. I come home from the club, indeed! Wasn't I forbidden to see Anna Maria? Wasn't I turned away a hundred times from my wife's door by Mamma herself, and could I sit alone in the dining-room (for my eldest two, a boy and girl, were at school) – alone in the dining-room, where that very Emma would have had to wait upon me?

Not one morsel of chicken would Anna Maria eat. (She said she dared to say that woman would poison the egg-sauce.) She had hysterical laughter and tears, and was in a highly nervous state, a state as dangerous for the mother as for the darling baby, Mrs Captain B remarked justly; and I was of course a good deal alarmed, and sent, or rather went off, for Boker, our medical man. Boker saw his interesting patient, said that her nerves were highly excited, that she must at all sacrifices be kept quiet, and corroborated Mrs Captain B's opinion in every particular. As we walked downstairs I gave him a hint of what was the matter, at the same time requesting him to step into the back-parlour, and there see me take an affidavit that I was as innocent as the blessed baby just born, and named but three days before after His Royal Highness the Prince.

'I know, I know, my good fellow,' says Boker, poking me in the side (for he has a good deal of fun), 'that you are innocent. Of course you are innocent. Everybody is, you sly dog. But what of that? The two women have taken it into their heads to be jealous of your maid – and an uncommonly pretty girl she is, too, Hobson, you sly rogue, you. And were she a Vestal Virgin, the girl must go if you want to have any peace in the house; if you want your wife and the little one to thrive – if you want to have a quiet house and family. And if you do,' says Boker, looking me in the face hard, 'though it is against my own interest, will you let me give you a bit of advice, old boy?'

We had been bred up at Merchant Taylors* together, and had licked each other often and often, so of course I let him speak.

'Well, then,' says he, 'Hob my boy, get rid of the old dragon – the old Mother-in-law. She meddles with my prescriptions for your wife; she doctors the infant in private: you'll never have a quiet house or a quiet wife as long as that old Catamaran* is here.'

'Boker,' says I, 'Mrs Captain Budge is a lady who must not, at least in *my* house, be called a Catamaran. She has seven thousand pounds in the funds, and always says Anna Maria is her favourite daughter.' And so we parted, not on the best of terms, for I did not like Mamma to be spoken of disrespectfully by any man.

What was the upshot of this? When Mamma heard from Anna Maria (who weakly told her what I had let slip laughing, and in confidence to my wife) that Boker had called her a Catamaran, of course she went up to pack her trunks, and of course we apologised, and took another medical man. And as for Emma Buck, there was nothing for it but that she, poor girl, should go to the right about; my little Emily, then a child of ten years of age, crying bitterly at parting with her. The child very nearly got me into a second scrape, for I gave her a sovereign to give to Emma, and she told her grandmamma: who would have related all to Anna Maria, but that I went down on my knees, and begged her not. But she had me in her power after that, and made me wince when she would say, 'Marmaduke, have you any sovereigns to give away?' &c.

After Emma Buck came Mary Blackmore, whose name I remember because Mrs Captain B called her Mary Blackymore (and a dark, swarthy girl she was, not at all good-looking in *my* eyes). This poor Mary Blackmore was sent about her business because she looked sweet on the twopenny postman, Mamma said. And she knew, no doubt, for (my wife being downstairs again long since), Mrs B saw everything that was passing at the door, as she regularly sat in the parlour window.

After Blackmore came another girl of Mrs B's own choosing: own rearing, I may say, for she was named Barbara, after Mamma, being a soldier's daughter, and coming from Portsea, where the late Captain Budge was quartered, in command of his company of Marines. Of this girl Mrs B would ask questions out of the 'Catechism' at breakfast, and my scapegrace of a Tom would burst out laughing at her blundering answers. But from a demure country lass, as she was when she came to us, Miss Barbara very quickly became a dressy, impudent-looking thing; coquetting with the grocer's and butcher's boys, and wearing silk gowns and flowers in her bonnet when she went to church on Sunday evenings, and actually appearing one day with her hair in bands, and the next day in ringlets. Of course she was setting her cap at me, Mamma said, as I was the only gentleman in the house, though for my part I declare I never saw the set of her cap at all, or knew if her hair was straight or curly. So, in a word, Barbara was sent back to her mother, and Mrs Budge didn't fail to ask me whether I had not a sovereign to give her?

After this girl we had two or three more maids, whose appearance or history is not necessary to particularise – the latter was uninteresting, let it suffice to say; the former grew worse and worse. I never saw such a woman as Grizzel Scrimgeour, from Berwick-upon-Tweed, who was the last that waited on us, and who was enough, I declare, to curdle the very milk in the jug as she put it down to breakfast.

At last the real aim of my two conspirators of women came out. 'Marmaduke,' Mrs Captain B said to me one morning, after this Grizzel had brought me an oniony knife to cut the bread; 'women-servants are very well in their way, but there is always something disagreeable with them, and in families of a certain rank a man-servant commonly waits at table. It is proper: it is decent that it should be so in the respectable classes: and *we* are of those classes. In Captain Budge's lifetime we were never without our groom, and our tea-boy. My dear father had his butler and coachman, as our family has had ever since the Conquest; and though you are certainly in business, as your father was before you, yet your relations are respectable: your grandfather was a dignified clergyman in the West of England; you have connections both in the army and navy, who are members of Clubs and known in the fashionable world; and (though I never shall speak to that man again) remember that your wife's sister is married to a barrister who lives in Oxford Square, and goes the Western Circuit. *He* keeps a man-servant. *They* keep men-servants, and I do not like to see my poor Anna Maria occupying an inferior

position in society to her sister Frederica, named after the Duke
of York though she was, when His Royal Highness reviewed the
Marines at Chatham; and seeing some empty bottles carried from
the table, said – '

'In mercy's name,' says I, bursting out, for when she came to
this story Mamma used to drive me frantic, 'have a man, if you
like, ma'am, and give me a little peace.'

'You needn't swear, Mr Hobson,' she replied with a toss of her
head; and when I went to business that day it was decided by the
women that our livery should be set up.

II

Peter Grundsell, the knife-boy, the youth previously mentioned
as son of my greengrocer and occasional butler, a demure little
fair-haired lad, who had received his education in a green baize
coat and yellow leather breeches at Saint Blaize's Charity School,
was our first footboy or page. Mamma thought that a full-sized
footman might occasion inconvenience in the house, and would
not be able to sleep in our back attic (which indeed was scarcely
six feet long), and she had scarcely six feet long), and she had
somehow conceived a great fondness for this youth with his pale
cheeks, blue eyes, and yellow hair, who sang the sweetest of all
the children in the organ-loft of Saint Blaize's. At five o'clock
every morning, winter and summer, that boy, before he took a
permanent engagement in my establishment, slid down our area
steps, of which and of the kitchen entrance he was entrusted with
the key. He crept up the stairs as silent as a cat, and carried off
the boots and shoes from the doors of our respective apartments
without disturbing one of us: the knives and shoes of my domestic
circle were cleaned as brilliant as possible before six o'clock: he
did odd jobs for the cook, he went upon our messages and errands;
he carried out his father's potatoes and cauliflowers; he attended
school at St. Blaize's; he turned his mother's mangle: there was no
end to the work that boy could do in the course of a day, and he
was the most active, quiet, humble little rogue you ever knew.
Mrs Captain Budge then took a just liking to the lad, and resolved
to promote him to the situation of page. His name was changed
from Peter to Philip, as being more genteel: and a hat with a gold

cord and a knob on the top like a gilt Brussels sprout, and a dark green suit, with a white galloon stripe down the trouser-seams, and a bushel of buttons on the jacket, were purchased at an establishment in Holborn, off the dummy at the door. Mamma is a great big strong woman, with a high spirit, who, I should think, could *protect herself* very well; but when Philip had his livery, she made him walk behind her regularly, and never could go to church without Philip after her to carry the books, or out to tea of an evening without that boy on the box of the cab.

Mrs Captain B is fond of good living herself; and, to do her justice, always kept our servants well. I don't meddle with the kitchen affairs myself, having my own business to attend to; but I believe my servants had as much meat as they could eat, and a great deal more than was good for them. They went to bed pretty soon, for ours was an early house, and when I came in from the City after business, I was glad enough to get to bed; and they got up rather late, for we are all good sleepers (especially Mrs B, who takes a heavy supper, which *I* never could indulge in), so that they were never called upon to leave their beds much before seven o'clock, and had their eight or nine good hours of rest every night.

And here I cannot help remarking, that if these folks knew their luck – *sua si bona nôrint*, as we used to say at Merchant Taylors; if they remembered that they are fed as well as lords, that they have warm beds and plenty of sleep in them; that, if they are ill, they have frequently their master's doctor; that they get good wages, and beer and sugar and tea in sufficiency: they need not be robbing their employers or taking fees from tradesmen, or grumbling at their lot. My friend and head-clerk Raddles has a hundred and twenty a year and eight children; the Reverend Mr Bittles, our esteemed curate at Saint Blaize's, has the same stipend and family of three; and I am sure that both of those gentlemen work harder, and fare worse, than any of the servants in my kitchen, or my neighbour's. And I, who have seen that dear, good elegant *angel** of a Mrs Bittles ironing her husband's bands and neckcloths; and that uncommonly shy supper of dry bread and milk=and-water which the Raddles family take when I have dropped in to visit them at their place (Glenalvon Cottage,

*I say this, because I think so, and will *not* be put down. My wife says she thinks there is nothing in Mrs Bittles, and Mamma says she gives herself airs, and has a cast in her eye; but a more elegant woman *I* have never seen, no, not at a Mansion House ball, or the Opera. – M. H.

Magnolia Road South, Camden Town), on my walks from Hampstead on a Sunday evening: I say, I, who have seen these people, and thought about my servants at home, on the same July evening, eating buttered toast round the kitchen fire – have marvelled how resigned and contented some people were, and how readily other people grumbled.

Well, then, this young Philip being introduced into my family, and being at that period as lean as a whipping-post, and as contented with the scraps and broken victuals which the cook gave him, as an alderman with his turtle and venison, now left his mother's mangle – on which, or on a sack in his father's potato bin, he used to sleep – and put on my buttons and stripes, waited at my own table, and took his regular place at that in the kitchen, and occupied a warm bed and three blankets in the back attic.

The effect of the three (or four or five, is it? – for the deuce knows how many they take) meals a day upon the young rascal, was speedily evident in his personal appearance. His lean cheeks began to fill out, till they grew as round and pale as a pair of suet dumplings. His dress (for the little dummy in Holborn, a bargain of Mrs Captain B's, was always a tight fit) grew tighter and tighter; as if his meals in the kitchen were not sufficient for any two Christians, the little gormandiser levied contributions upon our parlour dishes. And one day my wife spied him with his mouth smeared all over with our jam pudding; and on another occasion he came in with tears in his eyes and hardly able to speak, from the effects of a curry on which he had laid hands in the hall, and which we make (from the Nawob of Mulligatawney's own receipt) remarkably fine, and as hot, as hot – as the dog-days.

As for the crockery, both the common blue and the stone china Mamma gave us on our marriage (and which, I must confess, I didn't mind seeing an end of, because she bragged and *bothered* so about it), the smashes that boy made were incredible. The handles of all the tea-cups went; and the knobs off the covers of the vegetable dishes; and the stems of the wine-glasses; and the china punch-bowl my Anna Maria was christened in. And the days he did not break the dishes on the table, he spilt the gravy on the cloth. Lord! Lord! how I did wish for my pretty neat little parlour-maid again. But I had best not, for peace' sake, enlarge again upon *that* point.

And as for getting up, I suppose the suppers and dinners made him sleepy as well as fat; certainly the little rascal for the first week did get up at his usual hour: then he was a little later: at the end of a month he came yawning downstairs after the maids had long been at work: there was no more polishing of boots and knives: barely time to get mine clean, and knives enough ready for me and my wife's breakfast (Mrs Captain B taking hers and her poached eggs and rashers of bacon in bed) – in time enough, I say, for my breakfast, before I went into the City.

Many and many a scolding did I give that boy, until, my temper being easy and the lad getting nō earthly good from my abuse of him, I left off – from sheer weariness and a desire for a quiet life. But Mamma, to do her justice, was never tired of giving it to him, and rated him up hill and down dale. It was, 'Philip, you are a fool!' 'Philip, you dirty wretch.' 'Philip, you sloven,' and so forth, all dinner time. But still, when I talked of sending him off, Mrs Captain B always somehow pleaded for him and insisted upon keeping him. Well. My weakness is that I can't say no to a woman, and Master Philip stayed on, breaking the plates and smashing the glass, and getting more mischievous and lazy every day.

At last there came a *crash*, which, though it wasn't *in my crockery*, did Master Philip's business. Hearing a great laughter in the kitchen one evening, Mamma (who is a good housekeeper, and does not like her servants to laugh on any account) stepped down, – and what should she find but Master Philip, mimicking her to the women servants, and saying, 'Look, this is the way old Mother Budge goes!' And pulling a napkin round his head (something like the Turkish turban Mrs Captain B wears), he began to speak as if in her way, saying, 'Now Philip, you nasty, idle, good-for-nothing, lazy, dirty boy you, why do you go for to spill the gravy so?' &c.

Mrs B rushed forward and boxed his ears soundly, and the next day he was sent about his business; for flesh and blood could bear him no longer.

Why he had been kept so long, as I said before, I could not comprehend, until after Philip had left us; and then Mamma said, looking with tears in her eyes at the chap's jacket, as it lay in the pantry, that her little boy Augustus was something like him, and he wore a jacket with buttons of that sort. Then I knew she was thinking of her eldest son, Augustus Frederick York Budge, a midshipman on board the 'Hippopotamus' frigate, Captain Swang, CB (I knew the story well enough), who died of yellow fever on the West India Station in the year 1814.

III

By the time I had had two or three more boys in my family, I got to hate them as if I had been a second Herod, and the rest of my household, too, was pretty soon tired of the wretches. If any young housekeepers read this, I would say to them, Profit by my experience, and never keep a boy; be happy with a parlour-maid, put up with a charwoman, let the cook bring up your dinner from the kitchen; get a good servant who knows his business, and pay his wages as cheerfully as you may; but never have a boy into your place, if you value your peace of mind.

You may save a little in the article of wages with the little rascal but how much do you pay in discomfort! A boy eats as much as a man, a boy breaks twice as much as a man, a boy is twice as long upon an errand as a man; a boy batters your plate and sends it up to table dirty; you are never certain that a boy's fingers are not in the dish which he brings up to your dinner; a boy puts your boots on the wrong trees; and when at the end of a year or two he has broken his way through your crockery, and at last learned some of his business, the little miscreant privately advertises himself in the *Times* as a youth who has two years' character, and leaves you for higher wages and another place. Two young traitors served me so in the course of my fatal experience with boys.

Then, in a family council, it was agreed that a man should be engaged for our establishment, and we had a series of footmen. Our curate recommended to me our first man, whom the clergyman had found in the course of his charitable excursions. I took John Tomkins out of the garret, where he was starving. He had pawned every article of value belonging to him; he had no decent clothes left in which he could go out to offer himself for a situation; he had not tasted meat for weeks, except such rare bits as he could get from the poor curate's spare table. He came to my house, and all of a sudden rushed into plenty again. He had a comfortable supply of clothes, meat, fire, blankets. He had not a hard master, and as for Mamma's scolding, he took it as a matter of course. He had but few pairs of shoes to clean, and lived as well as a man of five hundred a-year. Well, John Tomkins left my service in six months after he had been drawn out of the jaws of death, and after he had considered himself lucky at being able to get a crust of bread, because the cook served him a dinner of cold meat two days running – 'He never ad been used to cold meat; it was the custom in no good fam'lies to give cold meat – he wouldn't stay where it was practised.' And away he went, then – very likely to starve again.

Him there followed a gentleman, whom I shall call Mr Abershaw, for I am positive he did it, although we never could find him out. We had a character with this amiable youth which an angel might have been proud of – had lived for seven years with General Hector – only left because the family was going abroad, the General being made Governor and Commander-in-Chief of the Tapioca Islands – the General's sister, Mrs Colonel Ajax, living in lodgings in the Edgware Road, answered for the man, and for the authenticity of the General's testimonials. When Mamma, Mrs Captain B, waited upon her, Mrs Captain B remarked that Mrs Colonel's lodgings were rather queer, being shabby in themselves, and over a shabbier shop – and she thought there was a smell of hot spirits and water in Mrs Colonel's room when Mrs B entered it at one o'clock; but, perhaps, she was not very rich, the Colonel being on half-pay, and it might have been ether and not rum which Mrs B smelt. She came home announcing that she had found a treasure of a servant, and Mr Abershaw stepped into our pantry and put on our livery.

Nothing could be better for some time than this gentleman's behaviour; and it was edifying to remark how he barred up the house of a night, and besought me to see that the plate was all right when he brought it upstairs in the basket. He constantly warned us, too, of thieves and rascals about; and, though he had a villanous hang-dog look of his own, which I could not bear, yet Mamma said this was only a prejudice of mine, and, indeed, I had no fault to find with the man. Once I thought something was wrong with the lock of my study-table; but, as I keep little or no money in the house, I did not give this circumstance much thought, and once Mrs Captain Budge saw Mr Abershaw in conversation with a lady who had very much the appearance of Mrs Colonel Ajax, as she afterwards remembered, but the resemblance did not, unluckily, strike Mamma at the time.

It happened one evening that we all went to see the Christmas pantomime; and of course took the footman on the box of the fly, and I treated him to the pit, where I could not see him; but he said afterwards that he enjoyed the play very much. When the pantomime was over, he was in waiting in the lobby to hand us back to the carriage, and a pretty good load we were – our three children, ourselves, and Mrs Captain B, who is a very roomy woman.

When we got home – the cook, with rather a guilty and terrified look, owned to her mistress that a most 'singular' misfortune had happened. She was positive she shut the door – she could take her Bible oath she did – after the boy who comes every evening with the paper; but the policeman, about eleven o'clock, had rung and knocked to say that the door was open – and open it was, sure enough; and a great coat, and two hats, and an umbrella, were gone.

'Thank 'Evins! the plate was all locked up safe in my pantry,' Mr Abershaw said, turning up his eyes; and he showed me that it was all right before going to bed that very night; he could not sleep unless I counted it, he said – and then it was that he cried out, Lord! Lord! to think that while he was so happy and unsuspicious, enjoyin' of himself at the play, some rascal should come in and rob his kind master! If he'd a know'd it, he never would have left the house – no, that he wouldn't.

He was talking on in this way, when we heard a loud shriek from Mamma's room, and her bell began to ring like mad: and presently out she ran, roaring out, 'Anna Maria! Cook! Mr Hobson! Thieves! I'm robbed, I'm robbed!'

'Where's the scoundrel?' says Abershaw, seizing the poker as valiant as any man I ever saw; and he rushed upstairs towards Mrs B's apartment, I followed behind, more leisurely; for, if the rascal of a housebreaker had pistols with him, how was I to resist him, I should like to know?

But when I got up – there was no thief. The scoundrel had been there: but he was gone: and a large box of Mrs B's stood in the centre of the room, burst open, with numbers of things strewn about the floor. Mamma was sobbing her eyes out, in her big chair; my wife and the female servants already assembled; and Abershaw, with the poker, banging under the bed to see if the villain was still there.

I was not aware at first of the extent of Mrs B's misfortune, and it was only by degrees, as it were, that that unfortunate lady was brought to tell us what she had lost. First, it was her dresses she bemoaned, two of which, her rich purple velvet and her black satin, were gone; then, it was her Cashmere shawl; then, a box full of ornaments, her jet, her pearls, and her garnets; nor was it until the next day that she confessed to my wife that the great loss of all was an old black velvet reticule, containing two hundred and twenty-three pounds, in gold and notes. I suppose she did not like to tell me of this; for a short time before, being somewhat pressed for money, I had asked her to lend me some; when, I am sorry to say, the old lady declared, upon her honour, that she had not a guinea, nor should have one until her dividends came in. Now, if she had lent it to me, she would have been paid back again, and this she owned with tears in her eyes.

Well, when she had cried and screamed sufficiently, as none of this grief would mend matters, or bring back her money, we went to bed, Abershaw clapping to all the bolts of the house door, and putting the great bar up with a clang that might be heard all through the street. And it was not until two days after the event that I got the numbers of the notes which Mrs Captain B had lost, and which were all paid into the Bank, and exchanged for gold the morning after the robbery.

When I was aware of its extent, and when the horse was stolen, of course I shut the stable-door, and called in a policeman – not one of your letter X policeman – but a gentleman in plain clothes, who inspected the premises, examined the family, and questioned the servants one by one. This gentleman's opinion was that the robbery was got up in the house. First, he suspected the cook, then he inclined towards the housemaid, and the young fellow with whom, as it appeared, that artful hussey was keeping company; and those two poor wretches expected to be carried off to jail forthwith, so great was the terror under which they lay.

All this while Mr Abershaw gave the policeman every information; insisted upon having his boxes examined and his accounts looked into, for though he was absent, waiting upon his master and mistress, on the night when the robbery was committed, he did not wish to escape search – not he; and so we looked over his trunks just out of compliment.

The officer did not seem to be satisfied – as, indeed, he had discovered nothing as yet – and after a long and fruitless visit in the evening, returned on the next morning in company with another of the detectives, the famous Scroggins indeed.

As soon as the famous Scroggins saw Abershaw, all matters seemed to change – 'Hullo, Jerry!' said he; 'what, you here? at your old tricks again? This is the man what has done it, sir,' he

said to me; 'He is a well-known rogue and prig.'* Mr Abershaw
swore more than ever that he was innocent, and called upon me
to swear that I had seen him in the pit of the theatre during the
whole of the performance; but I could neither take my affidavit
to this fact, nor was Mr Scroggins a bit satisfied, nor would he be
until he had the man up to Beak Street Police Court and examined
by the magistrate.

Here my young man was known as an old practitioner on the
treadmill, and, seeing there was no use in denying the fact, he
confessed it very candidly. He owned that he had been unfortunate in his youth: that he had not been in General Hector's service
these five years; that the character he had got was a sham one,
and Mrs Ajax merely a romantic fiction. But no more would he
acknowledge. His whole desire in life, he said, was to be an honest
man; and ever since he had entered my service he had acted as
such. Could I point out a single instance in which he had failed
to do his duty? But there was no use in a poor fellow who had
met with misfortune trying to retrieve himself: he began to cry
when he said this, and spoke so naturally that I was almost
inclined to swear that I *had* seen him under us all night in the pit
of the theatre.

There was no evidence against him; and this good man was
discharged, both from the Police Office and from our service,
where he couldn't abear to stay, he said, now that his Hhonour
was questioned. And Mrs Budge believed in his innocence, and
persisted in turning off the cook and housemaid, who she was sure
had stolen her money; nor was she quite convinced of the contrary
two years after, when Mr Abershaw and Mrs Colonel Ajax were
both transported for forgery.

THE FASHIONABLE AUTHORESS

Paying a visit the other day to my friend Timson, who, I need not tell the public, is editor of that famous evening paper, the **** (and let it be said that there is no more profitable acquaintance than a gentleman in Timson's situation, in whose office, at three o'clock daily, you are sure to find new books, lunch, magazines, and innumerable tickets for concerts and plays): going, I say, into Timson's office, I saw on the table an immense paper cone or funnel, containing a bouquet of such a size, that it might be called a bosquet, wherein all sorts of rare geraniums, luscious magnolias, stately dahlias, and other floral produce were gathered together – a regular flower-stack.

Timson was for a brief space invisible, and I was left alone in the room with the odours of this tremendous bow-pot, which filled the whole of the inky, smutty, dingy apartment with an agreeable incense. 'O *rus! quando te aspiciam?*' exclaimed I, out of the Latin grammar, for imagination had carried me away to the country, and I was about to make another excellent and useful quotation (from the 14th book of the Iliad, Madam), concerning 'ruddy lotuses, and crocuses, and hyacinths,' when all of a sudden Timson appeared. His head and shoulders had, in fact, been engulfed in the flowers, among which he might be compared to any Cupid, butterfly, or bee. His little face was screwed up into such an expression of comical delight and triumph, that a Methodist parson would have laughed at it in the midst of a funeral sermon.

'What are you giggling at?' said Mr Timson, assuming a high, aristocratic air.

'Has the goddess Flora made you a present of that bower, wrapped up in white paper; or did it come by the vulgar hands of yonder gorgeous footman, at whom all the little printer's devils are staring in the passage?'

'Stuff!' said Timson, picking to pieces some rare exotic, worth at the very least fifteenpence; 'a friend, who knows that Mrs

Timson and I are fond of these things, has sent us a nosegay, that's all.'

I saw how it was. 'Augustus Timson,' exclaimed I, sternly, 'the Pimlicoes have been with you; if that footman did not wear the Pimlico plush, ring the bell and order me out; if that three-cornered billet lying in your snuff-box has not the Pimlico seal to it, never ask me to dinner again.'

'Well, if it *does*,' says Mr Timson, who flushed as red as a peony, 'what is the harm? Lady Fanny Flummery may send flowers to her friends, I suppose? The conservatories at Pimlico House are famous all the world over, and the Countess promised me a nosegay the very last time I dined there.'

'Was that the day when she gave you a box of bonbons for your darling little Ferdinand?'

'No, another day.'

'Or the day when she promised you her carriage for Epsom Races?'

'No.'

'Or the day when she hoped that her Lucy and your Barbara-Jane might be acquainted, and sent to the latter from the former a new French doll and tea-things?'

'Fiddlestick!' roared out Augustus Timson, Esquire: 'I wish you wouldn't come bothering here. I tell you that Lady Pimlico is my friend – my friend, mark you, and I will allow no man to abuse her in my presence; I say again *no man*!' wherewith Mr Timson plunged both his hands violently into his breeches-pockets, looked me in the face sternly, and began jingling his keys and shillings about.

At this juncture (it being about half-past three o'clock in the afternoon), a one-horse chaise drove up to the **** office (Timson lives at Clapham, and comes in and out in this machine) – a one-horse chaise drove up; and amidst a scuffling and crying of small voices, good-humoured Mrs Timson bounced into the room.

'Here we are, deary,' said she: 'we'll walk to the Meryweathers; and I've told Sam to be in Charles Street at twelve with the chaise: it wouldn't do, you know, to come out of the Pimlico box and have the people cry, "Mrs Timson's carriage!" for old Sam and the chaise.'

Timson, to this loving and voluble address of his lady, gave a peevish, puzzled look towards the stranger, as much as to say, '*He's* here.'

'La, Mr Smith! and how *do* you do? – So rude – I didn't see you: but the fact is, we are all in *such* a bustle! Augustus has got Lady Pimlico's box for the *Puritani* to-night, and I vowed I'd take the children.'

Those young persons were evidently from their costume prepared for some extraordinary festival. Miss Barbara-Jane, a young lady of six years old, in a pretty pink slip and white muslin, her dear little poll bristling over with papers, to be removed previous to the play; while Master Ferdinand had a pair of nankeens* (I can recollect Timson in them in the year 1825 – a great buck), and white silk stockings, which belonged to his mamma. His frill was very large and very clean, and he was fumbling perpetually at a pair of white kid gloves, which his mamma forbade him to assume before the opera.

And 'Look here!' and 'Oh, precious!' and 'Oh, my!' were uttered by these worthy people as they severally beheld the vast bouquet, into which Mrs Timson's head flounced, just as her husband's had done before.

'I must have a green-house at the Snuggery, that's positive, Timson, for I'm passionately fond of flowers – and how kind of Lady Fanny! Do you know her ladyship, Mr Smith?'

'Indeed, Madam, I don't remember having ever spoken to a lord or a lady in my life.'

Timson smiled in a supercilious way. Mrs Timson exclaimed, 'La, how odd! Augustus knows ever so many. Let's see, there's the Countess of Pimlico and Lady Fanny Flummery; Lord Doldrum (Timson touched up his travels, you know); Lord Gasterton, Lord Guttlebury's eldest son; Lady Pawpaw (they say she ought not to be visited, though); Baron Strum – Strom – Strumpf –'

What the baron's name was I have never been able to learn; for here Timson burst out with a 'Hold your tongue, Bessy!' which stopped honest Mrs Timson's harmless prattle altogether, and obliged that worthy woman to say meekly, 'Well, Gus, I did not think there was any harm in mentioning your acquaintance.' Good soul! it was only because she took pride in her Timson that she loved to enumerate the great names of the persons who did him honour. My friend the editor was, in fact, in a cruel position, looking foolish before his old acquaintance, stricken in that unfortunate sore point in his honest, good-humoured character. The man adored the aristocracy, and had that wonderful respect for a lord which, perhaps the observant reader may have

remarked, especially characterises men of Timson's way of
thinking.

In old days at the club (we held it in a small public-house near
the Coburg Theatre, some of us having free admissions to that
place of amusement, and some of us living for convenience in the
immediate neighbourhood of one of his Majesty's prisons in that
quarter) – in old days, I say, at our spouting and toasted-cheese
club, called 'The Forum', Timson was called Brutus Timson, and
not Augustus, in consequence of the ferocious republicanism
which characterised him, and his utter scorn and hatred of a
bloated, do-nothing aristocracy. His letters in *The Weekly Senti-
nel*, signed 'Lictor', must be remembered by all our readers: he
advocated the repeal of the corn laws, the burning of machines,
the rights of labour, &c. &c., wrote some pretty defences of
Robespierre, and used seriously to avow, when at all in liquor,
that, in consequence of those 'Lictor' letters, Lord Castlereagh
had tried to have him murdered, and thrown over Blackfriars
Bridge.

By what means Augustus Timson rose to his present exalted
position it is needless here to state; suffice it, that in two years he
was completely bound over neck and heels to the bloodthirsty
aristocrats, hereditary tyrants, &c. One evening he was asked to
dine with a secretary of the Treasury (the **** is Ministerial, and
has been so these forty-nine years); at the house of that secretary
of the Treasury he met a lord's son: walking with Mrs Timson in
the Park next Sunday, that lord's son saluted him. Timson was
from that moment a slave, had his coats made at the west end,
cut his wife's relations (they are dealers in marine stores, and live
at Wapping), and had his name put down at two Clubs.

Who was the lord's son? Lord Pimlico's son, to be sure, the
Honourable Frederick Flummery, who married Lady Fanny Foxy,
daughter of Pitt Castlereagh, second Earl of Reynard, Kilbrush
Castle, county Kildare. The earl had been ambassador in '14: Mr
Flummery, his attaché: he was twenty-one at that time, with the
sweetest tuft on his chin in the world. Lady Fanny was only
four-and-twenty, just jilted by Prince Scoronconcolo, the horrid
man who had married Miss Solomonson with a plum. Fanny had
nothing – Frederick had about seven thousand pounds less. What
better could the young things do than marry? Marry they did,
and in the most delicious secrecy. Old Reynard was charmed to
have an opportunity of breaking with one of his daughters for

ever, and only longed for an occasion never to forgive the other nine.

A wit of the Prince's time, who inherited and transmitted to his children a vast fortune of genius, was cautioned on his marriage to be very economical. 'Economical!' said he; 'my wife has nothing, and I have nothing: I suppose a man can't live under *that*!' Our interesting pair, by judiciously employing the same capital, managed, year after year, to live very comfortably, until, at last, they were received into Pimlico House by the dowager (who has it for her life), where they live very magnificently. Lady Fanny gives the most magnificent entertainment in London, has the most magnificent equipage, and a very fine husband; who has his equipage as fine as her ladyship's; his seat in the omnibus, while her ladyship is in the second tier. They say he plays a good-deal – ay, and pays, too, when he loses.

And how, pr'ythee? Her ladyship is a Fashionable Authoress. She has been at this game for fifteen years; during which period she has published forty-five novels, edited twenty-seven new magazines, and I don't know how many annuals, besides publishing poems, plays, desultory thoughts, memoirs, recollections of travel, and pamphlets without number. Going one day to church, a lady, whom I knew by her Leghorn bonnet and red ribbons, *ruche* with poppies and marigolds, brass ferronière, great red hands, black silk gown, thick shoes, and black silk stockings; a lady, whom I knew, I say, to be a devotional cook, made a bob to me just as the psalm struck up, and offered me a share of her hymn-book. It was –

HEAVENLY CHORDS;

A COLLECTION OF

SACRED STRAINS,

SELECTED, COMPOSED, AND EDITED, BY THE

LADY FRANCES JULIANA FLUMMERY.

– Being simply a collection of heavenly chords robbed from the lyres of Watts, Wesley, Brady and Tate &c.; and of sacred strains from the rare collection of Sternhold and Hopkins.* Out of this, cook and I sang; and it is amazing how much our fervour was increased by thinking that our devotions were directed by a lady whose name was in the Red Book.

The thousands of pages that Lady Fanny Flummery has covered with ink exceed all belief. You must have remarked, Madam, in respect of this literary fecundity, that your amiable sex possesses vastly greater capabilities than we do; and that while a man is painfully labouring over a letter of two sides, a lady will produce a dozen pages, crossed, dashed, and so beautifully neat and close, as to be well-nigh invisible. The readiest of ready pens has Lady Fanny; her Pegasus gallops over hot-pressed satin so as to distance all gentlemen riders; like Camilla, it scours the plain – of Bath, and never seems punished or fatigued; only it runs so fast that it often leaves all sense behind it; and there it goes on, on, scribble, scribble, scribble, never flagging until it arrives at that fair winning-post on which is written 'Finis', or 'The End'; and shows that the course, whether it be of novel, annual, poem, or what not, is complete.

Now, the author of these pages doth not pretend to describe the inward, thoughts, ways, and manners of being, of my Lady Fanny, having made before that humiliating confession, that lords and ladies are personally unknown to him; so that all milliners, butchers' ladies, dashing young clerks, and apprentices, or other persons who are anxious to cultivate a knowledge of the aristocracy, had better skip over this article altogether. But he hath heard it whispered, from pretty good authority, that the manners and customs of these men and women resemble, in no inconsiderable degree, the habits and usages of other men and women, whose names are unrecorded by Debrett. Granting this, and that Lady Fanny is a woman pretty much like another, the philosophical reader will be content that we rather consider her ladyship in her public capacity, and examine her influence upon mankind in general.

Her person, then, being thus put out of the way, her works, too, need not be very carefully sifted and criticised; for what is the use of peering into a millstone, or making calculations about the figure o? The woman has not, in fact, the slightest influence upon literature for good or for evil: there are a certain number of fools whom she catches in her flimsy traps; and why not? They are made to be humbugged, or how should we live? Lady Flummery writes everything; that is, nothing. Her poetry is mere wind; her novels, stark nought; her philosophy, sheer vacancy: how should she do any better than she does? how could she succeed if she *did* do any better? If she did write well, she would not be Lady Flummery;

she would not be praised by Timson and the critics, because she would be an honest woman, and would not bribe them. Nay, she would probably be written down by Timson and Co., because, being an honest woman, she utterly despised them and their craft.

We have said what she writes for the most part. Individually, she will throw off any number of novels that Messrs. Soap and Diddle will pay for; and collectively, by the aid of self and friends, scores of 'Lyrics of Loveliness', 'Beams of Beauty', 'Pearls of Purity', &c. Who does not recollect the success which her 'Pearls of the Peerage' had? She is going to do the 'Beauties of the Baronetage'; then we shall have the 'Daughters of the Dustmen', or some such other collection of portraits. Lady Flummery has around her a score of literary gentlemen, who are bound to her, body and soul: give them a dinner, a smile from an opera-box, a wave of the hand in Rotten Row, and they are hers, neck and heels. *Vides, mi fili*, &c. See, my son, with what a very small dose of humbug men are to be bought. I know many of these individuals: there is my friend M'Lather, an immense, pudgy man: I saw him one day walking through Bond Street in company with an enormous ruby breast-pin. 'Mac!' shouted your humble servant, 'that is a Flummery ruby;' and Mac hated and cursed us ever after. Presently came little Fitch, the artist; he was rigged out in an illuminated velvet waistcoat – Flummery again – 'There's only one like it in town,' whispered Fitch to me confidentially, 'and Flummery has that.' To be sure, Fitch had given, in return, half-a-dozen of the prettiest drawings in the world. 'I wouldn't charge for them, you know,' he says: 'for, hang it, Lady Flummery is my friend.' Oh, Fitch, Fitch!

Fifty more instances could be adduced to her ladyship's ways of bribery. She bribes the critics to praise her, and the writers to write for her; and the public flocks to her as it will to any other tradesman who is properly puffed. Out comes the book; as for its merits, we may allow, cheerfully, that Lady Flummery has no lack of that natural *esprit* which every woman possesses; but here praise stops. For the style, she does not know her own language; but, in revenge, has a smattering of half-a-dozen others. She interlards her works with fearful quotations from the French, fiddle-faddle extracts from Italian operas, German phrases fiercely mutilated, and a scrap or two of bad Spanish: and upon the strength of these murders, she calls herself an authoress. To be sure there is no such word as authoress. If any young nobleman

or gentleman of Eton College, when called upon to indite a copy
of verses in praise of Sappho, or the Countess of Dash, or Lady
Charlotte What-d'ye-call-'em, or the Honourable Mrs Somebody,
should fondly imagine that he might apply to those fair creatures
the title of *auctrix* – I pity that young nobleman's or gentleman's
case. Doctor Wordsworth and assistants would swish that error
out of him in a way that need not here be mentioned. Remember
it henceforth, ye writeresses – there is no such word as authoress.
Auctor, madam, is the word. '*Optima tu proprii nominis auctor
eris*', which, of course, means that you are, by your proper name,
an author, not an authoress; the line is in Ainsworth's Dictionary,
where anybody may see it.

This point is settled then: there is no such word as authoress.
But what of that? Are authoresses to be bound by the rules of
grammar? The supposition is absurd. We don't expect them to
know their own language; we prefer rather the little graceful
pranks and liberties they take with it. When, for instance, a
celebrated authoress, who wrote a Diaress, calls somebody the
prototype of his own father, we feel an obligation to her ladyship;
the language feels an obligation; it has a charm and a privilege
with which it was never before endowed: and it is manifest, that
if we can call ourselves antetypes of our grandmothers – can
prophesy what we had for dinner yesterday, and so on, we get
into a new range of thought, and discover sweet regions of fancy
and poetry, of which the mind hath never even had a notion until
now.

It may be then considered as certain that an authoress *ought*
not to know her own tongue. Literature and politics have this
privilege in common, that any ignoramus may excel in both. No
apprenticeship is required, that is certain; and if any gentleman
doubts, let us refer him to the popular works of the present day,
where, if he find a particle of scholarship, or any acquaintance
with any books in any language, or if he be disgusted by any
absurd, stiff, old-fashioned notions of grammatical propriety, we
are ready to qualify our assertion. A friend of ours came to us the
other day in great trouble. His dear little boy, who had been for
some months attaché to the stables of Mr Tilbury's establishment,
took a fancy to the corduroy breeches of some other gentleman
employed in the same emporium – appropriated them, and afterwards disposed of them for a trifling sum to a relation – I believe
his uncle. For this harmless freak, poor Sam was absolutely seized,

tried at Clerkenwell Sessions, and condemned to six months' useless rotatory labour at the House of Correction. 'The poor fellow was bad enough before, sir,' said his father, confiding in our philanthropy; 'he picked up such a deal of slang among the stable-boys: but if you could hear him since he came from the mill! he knocks you down with it, sir. I am afraid, sir, of his becoming a regular prig:* for though he's a 'cute chap, can read and write, and is mighty smart and handy, yet no one will take him into service, on account of that business of the breeches!'

'What, sir!' exclaimed we, amazed at the man's simplicity; '*such* a son, and you don't know what to do with him! a 'cute fellow, who can write, who has been educated in a stable-yard, and has had six months' polish in a university – I mean a prison – and you don't know what to do with him? Make a *fashionable novelist* of him, and be hanged to you!' And proud am I to say that that young man, every evening, after he comes home from his work (he has taken to street-sweeping in the day, and I don't advise him to relinquish a certainty) – proud am I to say that he devotes every evening to literary composition, and is coming out with a novel, in numbers, of the most fashionable kind.

This little episode is only given for the sake of example; *par exemple*, as our authoress would say, who delights in French of the very worst kind. The public likes only the extremes of society, and votes mediocrity vulgar. From the Author they will take nothing but Fleet Ditch; from the Authoress, only the very finest of rose-water. I have read so many of her ladyship's novels, that, egad! now I don't care for anything under a marquis. Why the deuce should we listen to the intrigues, the misfortunes, the virtues, and conversations of a couple of countesses, for instance, when we can have duchesses for our money? What's a baronet? pish! pish! that great coarse red fist in his scutcheon turns me sick! What's a baron? a fellow with only one more ball than a pawn-broker; and, upon my conscience, just as common. Dear Lady Flummery, in your next novel, give us no more of these low people; nothing under strawberry leaves, for the mercy of heaven! Suppose, now, you write us

ALBERT;

OR,

WHISPERINGS AT WINDSOR.

BY THE LADY FRANCES FLUMMERY.

There is a subject – fashionable circles, curious revelations, exclusive excitement, &c. To be sure, you *must* here introduce a viscount, and that is sadly vulgar; but we will pass him for the sake of the ministerial *portefeuille*, which is genteel. Then you might do 'Leopold; or, the Bride of Neuilly', 'The victim of Würtemberg', 'Olga; or, the Autocrat's Daughter' (a capital title), '*Henri*; or, Rome in the Nineteenth Century'; we can fancy the book, and a sweet paragraph about it in Timson's paper.

Henri, by Lady Frances Flummery. – Henri! Who can he be? a little bird whispers in our ears, that the gifted and talented Sappho of our hemisphere has discovered some curious particulars in the life of *a certain young chevalier*, whose appearance at Rome has so frightened the court of the Tu-l-ries. Henri de B-rd – ux is of an age when the *young god* can shoot his darts into the bosom with fatal accuracy; and if the Marchesina degli Spinachi (whose portrait our lovely authoress has sung with a *kindred hand*) be as beauteous as she is represented (and as all who have visited in the exclusive circles of the eternal city say she is), no wonder at her effect upon the Pr-nce. *Verbum sap.* We hear that a few copies are still remaining. The enterprising publishers, Messrs. Soap and Diddle, have announced, we see, several other works by the same accomplished pen.

This paragraph makes its appearance, in small type, in the ****, by the side, perhaps, of a disinterested recommendation of bears'-grease, or some remarks on the extraordinary cheapness of plate in Cornhill. Well, two or three days after, my dear Timson, who has been asked to dinner, writes in his own hand, and causes to be printed in the largest type, an article to the following effect:

HENRI.
BY LADY F. FLUMMERY.

This is another of the graceful evergreens which the fair fingers of Lady Fanny Flummery are continually strewing upon our path. At once profound and caustic, truthful and passionate, we are at a loss whether most to admire the manly grandeur of her ladyship's mind, or the exquisite nymph-like delicacy of it. Strange power of fancy! Sweet enchantress, that rules the mind at will: stirring up the utmost depths of it into passion and storm, or wreathing and dimpling its calm surface with countless summer smiles. As a great Bard of old Time has expressed it, what do we not owe to woman?

What do we not owe to her? More love, more happiness, more calm of vexed spirit, more truthful aid, and pleasant counsel; in joy, more delicate sympathy; in sorrow, more kind companionship. We look into her cheery eyes, and, in those wells of love, care drowns; we listen to her siren voice, and, in that balmy music, banished hopes come winging to the breast again.

This goes on for about three-quarters of a column: I don't pretend to understand it; but with flowers, angels, Wordsworth's poems, and the old dramatists, one can never be wrong, I think; and though I have written the above paragraphs myself, and don't understand a word of them, I can't, upon my conscience, help thinking that they are mighty pretty writing. After, then, this has gone on for about three-quarters of a column (Timson does it in spare minutes, and fits it to any book that Lady Fanny brings out), he proceeds to particularise, thus:

The griding excitement which thrills through every fibre of the soul as we peruse these passionate pages, is almost too painful to bear. Nevertheless, one drains the draughts of poesy to the dregs, so deliciously intoxicating is its nature. We defy any man who begins these volumes to quit them ere he has perused each line. The plot may be briefly told as thus: Henri, an exiled Prince of Franconia (it is easy to understand the flimsy allegory), arrives at Rome, and is presented to the sovereign Pontiff. At a feast, given in his honour at the Vatican, a dancing girl (the loveliest creation that ever issued from poet's brain) is introduced, and exhibits some specimens of her art. The young prince is instantaneously smitten with the charms of the Saltatrice; he breathes into her ear the accents of his love, and is listened to with favour. He has, however, a rival, and a powerful one. The Pope has already cast his eye upon the Apulian maid, and burns with lawless passion. One of the grandest scenes ever writ, occurs between the rivals. The Pope offers to Castanetta every temptation; he will even resign his crown and marry her: but she refuses. The prince can make no such offers; he cannot wed her: 'The blood of Borbone,' he says, 'may not be thus misallied.' He determines to avoid her. In despair, she throws herself off the Tarpeian rock; and the Pope becomes a maniac. Such is an outline of this tragic tale.

Besides this fabulous and melancholy part of the narrative, which is unsurpassed, much is written in the gay and sparkling style for which our lovely author is unrivalled. The sketch of the Marchesina degli Spinachi and her lover, the Duca di Gammoni, is delicious; and the intrigue between the beautiful Princess Kalbsbraten and Count Bouterbrod is exquisitely painted: everybody, of course, knows who these characters are. The discovery of the manner in which Kartoffeln, the Saxon envoy, poisons the princess's dishes, is only a graceful and real repetition of a story which was agitated throughout all the diplomatic circles last year. Schinken, the Westphalian, must not be forgotten; nor Olla, the Spanish

Spy. How does Lady Fanny Flummery, poet as she is, possess a sense of the ridiculous and a keenness of perception which would do honour to a Rabelais or a Rochefoucauld? To those who ask this question, we have one reply, and that an example – not among women, 'tis true; for till the Lady Fanny came among us, woman never soared so high. Not among women, indeed! – but in comparing her to that great spirit for whom our veneration is highest and holiest, we offer no dishonour to his shrine: in saying that he who wrote of Romeo and Desdemona might have drawn Castanetta and Enrico, we utter but the truthful expressions of our hearts; in asserting that so long as Shakespeare lives, so long will Flummery endure; in declaring that he who rules in all hearts, and over all spirits and all climes, has found a congenial spirit, we do but justice to Lady Fanny – justice to him who sleeps by Avon!

With which we had better, perhaps, conclude, Our object has been, in descanting upon the Fashionable Authoress, to point out the influence which her writing possesses over society, rather than to criticise her life. The former is quite harmless: and we don't pretend to be curious about the latter. The woman herself is not so blameable; it is the silly people who cringe at her feet that do the mischief, and, gulled themselves, gull the most gullable of publics. Think you, O Timson, that her ladyship asks you for your *beaux yeux* or your wit? Fool! you do think so, or try and think so; and yet you know she loves not you, but the **** newspaper. Think, little Fitch, in your fine waistcoat, how dearly you have paid for it! Think, M'Lather, how many smirks, and lies, and columns of good three-halfpence-a-line matter that big garnet pin has cost you! the woman laughs at you, man! you, who fancy that she is smitten with you – laughs at your absurd pretensions, your way of eating fish at dinner, your great hands, your eyes, your whiskers, your coat, and your strange north-country twang. Down with this Delilah! Avaunt, O Circe! giver of poisonous feeds. To your natural haunts, ye gentlemen of the press! if bachelors, frequent your taverns, and be content. Better is Sally the waiter, and the first cut of the joint, than a dinner of four courses, and humbug therewith. Ye who are married, go to your homes; dine not with those persons who scorn your wives. Go not forth to parties, that ye may act Tom Fool for the amusement of my lord and my lady; but play your natural follies among your natural friends. Do this for a few years, and the Fashionable Authoress is extinct. O Jove, what a prospect! She, too, has retreated to her own natural calling, being as much out of place in a book as you, my dear M'Lather, in a drawing-room. Let milliners look up to her; let Howell and James swear by her; let simpering dandies caper about her car; let her write poetry if she likes, but only for the most exclusive circles; let mantua-makers puff her – but not men: let such things be, and the Fashionable Authoress is no more! Blessed, blessed thought! No more fiddle-faddle novels! no more namby-pamby poetry! no more fribble 'Blossoms of Loveliness'! When will you arrive, O happy Golden Age?

TUNBRIDGE TOYS

I wonder whether those little silver pencil-cases with a moveable almanack at the butt-end are still favourite implements with boys, and whether pedlars still hawk them about the country? Are there pedlars and hawkers still, or are rustics and children grown too sharp to deal with them? Those pencil-cases, as far as my memory serves me, were not of much use. The screw, upon which the moveable almanack turned, was constantly getting loose. The I of the table would work from its mooring, under Tuesday or Wednesday, as the case might be, and you would find, on examination, that Th. or W. was the 23½ of the month (which was absurd on the face of the thing), and in a word your cherished pencil-case an utterly unreliable time-keeper. Nor was this a matter of wonder. Consider the position of a pencil-case in a boy's pocket. You had hard-bake in it; marbles, kept in your purse when the money was all gone; your mother's purse, knitted so fondly and supplied with a little bit of gold, long since – prodigal little son! – scattered amongst the swine – I mean amongst brandy-balls, open tarts, three-cornered, puffs, and similar abominations. You had a top and string; a knife; a piece of cobbler's wax; two or three bullets; a *Little Warbler*; and I, for my part, remember, for a considerable period, a brass-barrelled pocket-pistol (which would fire beautifully, for with it I shot off a button from Butt Major's jacket); with all these things, and ever so many more, clinking and rattling in your pockets, and your hands, of course, keeping them in perpetual movement, how could you expect your moveable almanack not to be twisted out of its place now and again – your pencil-case to be bent – your liquorice water not to leak out of your bottle over the cobbler's wax, your bull's-eyes not to ram up the lock and barrel of your pistol, and so forth?

In the month of June, thirty-seven years ago, I bought one of those pencil-cases from a boy whom I shall call Hawker, and who was in my form. Is he dead? Is he a millionaire? Is he a bankrupt now? He was an immense screw *at school, and I believe to this

day that the value of the thing for which I owed and eventually
paid three-and-six pence, was in reality not one-and-nine.

I certainly enjoyed the case at first a good deal, and amused
myself with twiddling round the moveable calendar. But this
pleasure wore off. The jewel, as I said, was not paid for, and
Hawker, a large and violent boy, was exceedingly unpleasant as
a creditor. His constant remark was, 'When are you going to pay
me that three-and-sixpence? What sneaks your relations must be!
They come to see you. You go out to them on Saturdays and
Sundays, and they never give you anything! Don't tell me, you
little humbug!' and so forth. The truth is that my relations were
respectable; but my parents were making a tour in Scotland; and
my friends in London, whom I used to go and see, were most kind
to me, certainly, but somehow never tipped me. That term, of
May to August 1823, passed in agonies, then, in consequence of
my debt to Hawker. What was the pleasure of a calendar pencil-
case in comparison with the doubt and torture of mind occasioned
by the sense of the debt, and the constant reproach in that fellow's
scowling eyes and gloomy, coarse reminders? How was I to pay
off such a debt out of sixpence a week? ludicrous! Why did not
some one come to see me, and tip me? Ah! my dear sir, if you have
any little friends at school, go and see them, and do the natural
thing by them. You won't miss the sovereign. You don't know
what a blessing it will be to them. Don't fancy they are too old –
try'em. And they will remember you, and bless you in future days;
and their gratitude shall accompany your dreary after life; and
they shall meet you kindly when thanks for kindness are scant. O
mercy! shall I ever forget that sovereign you gave me, Captain
Bob? or the agonies of being in debt to Hawker? In that very term,
a relation of mine was going to India. I actually was fetched from
school in order to take leave of him. I am afraid I told Hawker of
this circumstance. I own I speculated upon my friend's giving me
a pound. A pound? Pooh! A relation going to India, and deeply
affected at parting from his darling kinsman, might give five
pounds to the dear fellow! ... There was Hawker when I came
back – of course there he was. As he looked in my scared face, his
turned livid with rage. He muttered curses, terrible from the lips
of so young a boy. My relation, about to cross the ocean to fill a
lucrative appointment, asked me with much interest about my
progress at school, heard me construe a passage of Eutropius, the
pleasing Latin work on which I was then engaged; gave me a God

bless you, and sent me back to school; upon my word of honour, without so much as a half-crown! It is all very well, my dear sir, to say that boys contract habits of expecting tips from their parents' friends, that they become avaricious, and so forth. Avaricious! fudge! Boys contract habits of tart and toffee eating, which they do not carry into after life. On the contrary, I wish I did like 'em. What raptures of pleasure one could have now for five shillings, if one could but pick it off the pastrycook's tray! No. If you have any little friends at school, out with your half-crowns, my friend, and impart to those little ones the little fleeting joys of their age.

Well, then. At the beginning of August, 1823, Bartlemy-tide holidays came, and I was to go to my parents, who were at Tunbridge Wells. My place in the coach was taken by my tutor's servants – 'Bolt-in-Tun', Fleet Street, seven o'clock in the morning, was the word. My Tutor, the Rev Edward P, to whom I hereby present my best compliments, had a parting interview with me: gave me my little account for my governor: the remaining part of the coach-hire; five shillings for my own expenses; and some five-and-twenty shillings on an old account which had been overpaid, and was to be restored to my family.

Away I ran and paid Hawker his three-and-six. Ouf! what a weight it was off my mind! (He was a Norfolk boy, and used to go home from Mrs Nelson's 'Bell Inn,' Aldgate – but that is not to the point). The next morning, of course, we were an hour before the time. I and another boy shared a hackney-coach; two-and-six: porter for putting luggage on coach, threepence. I had no more money of my own left. Rasherwell, my companion, went into the 'Bolt-in-Tun' coffee-room, and had a good breakfast. I couldn't: because, though I had five-and-twenty shillings of my parent's money, I had none of my own, you see.

I certainly intended to go without breakfast, and still remember how strongly I had that resolution in my mind. But there was that hour to wait. A beautiful August morning – I am very hungry. There is Rasherwell 'tucking' away in the coffee-room. I pace the street, as sadly almost as if I had been coming to school, not going thence. I turn into a court by mere chance – I vow it was by mere chance – and there I see a coffee-shop with a placard in the window, *Coffee, Twopence. Round of buttered toast, Twopence.* And here am I, hungry, penniless, with five-and-twenty shillings of my parents' money in my pocket.

What would you have done? You see I had had my money, and spent it in that pencil-case affair. The five-and-twenty shillings were a trust – by me to be handed over.

But then would my parents wish their only child to be actually without breakfast? Having this money, and being so hungry, so *very* hungry, mightn't I take ever so little? Mightn't I at home eat as much as I chose?

Well, I went into the coffee-shop, and spent fourpence. I remember the taste of the coffee and toast to this day – a peculiar, muddy, not-sweet-enough, most fragrant coffee – a rich, rancid, yet not-buttered-enough, delicious toast. The waiter had nothing. At any rate, four-pence, I know, was the sum I spent. And the hunger appeased, I got on the coach a guilty being.

At the last stage – what is its name? I have forgotten in seven-and-thirty years – there is an inn with a little green and trees before it; and by the trees there is an open carriage. It is our carriage. Yes, there are Prince and Blucher, the horses; and my parents in the carriage. Oh! how I had been counting the days until this one came! Oh! how happy I had been to see them yesterday! But there was that fourpence. All the journey down the toast had choked me, and the coffee poisoned me.

I was in such a state of remorse about the fourpence, that I forgot the maternal joy and caresses, the tender paternal voice. I pull out the twenty-four shillings and eightpence with a trembling hand.

'Here's your money,' I gasp out, 'which Mr P owes you, all but fourpence. I owed three-and-sixpence to Hawker out of my money for a pencil-case, and I had none left, and I took fourpence of yours, and had some coffee at a shop.'

I suppose I must have been choking whilst uttering this confession.

'My dear boy,' says the governor, 'why didn't you go and breakfast at the hotel?'

'He must be starved,' says my mother.

I had confessed; I had been a prodigal; I had been taken back to my parents' arms again. It was not a very great crime as yet, or a very long career of prodigality; but don't we know that a boy who takes a pin which is not his own, will take a thousand pounds when occasion serves, bring his parents' grey heads with sorrow to the grave, and carry his own to the gallows? Witness the career of Dick Idle, upon whom our friend Mr Sala* has been discoursing.

Dick only began by playing pitch-and-toss on a tombstone: playing fair, for what we know: and even for that sin he was promptly caned by the beadle. The bamboo was ineffectual to cane that reprobate's bad courses out of him. From pitch-and-toss he proceeded to manslaughter if necessary: to highway robbery; to Tyburn and the rope there. Ah! heaven be thanked, my parents' heads are still above the grass, and mine still out of the noose.

As I look up from my desk, I see Tunbridge Wells Common and the rocks, the strange familiar place which I remember forty years ago. Boys saunter over the green with stumps and cricket-bats. Other boys gallop by on the riding-master's hacks. I protest it is *Cramp, Riding Master*, as it used to be in the reign of George IV, and that Centaur Cramp must be at least a hundred years old. Yonder comes a footman with a bundle of novels from the library. Are they as good as *our* novels? Oh! how delightful they were! Shades of Valancour,* awful ghost of Manfrone, how I shudder at your appearance! Sweet image of Thaddeus of Warsaw, how often has this almost infantile hand tried to depict you in a Polish cap and richly embroidered tights! And as for Corinthian Tom in light blue pantaloons and hessians, *and Jerry Hawthorn from the country, can all the fashion, can all the splendour of real life which these eyes have subsequently beheld, can all the wit I have heard or read in later times, compare with your fashion, with your brilliancy, with your delightful grace, and sparkling vivacious rattle?

Who knows? They *may* have kept those very books at the library still – at the well-remembered library on the Pantiles, where they sell that delightful, useful Tunbridge ware. I will go and see. I wend my way to the Pantiles, the queer little old-world Pantiles, where, a hundred years since, so much good company came to take its pleasure. Is it possible, that in the past century, gentlefolks of the first rank (as I read lately in a lecture on George II in the *Cornhill Magazine*) assembled here and entertained each other with gaming, dancing, fiddling, and tea? There are fiddlers, harpers, and trumpeters performing at this moment in a weak little old balcony, but where is the fine company? Where are the earls, duchesses, bishops, and magnificent embroidered gamesters? A half-dozen of children and their nurses are listening to the musicians; an old lady or two in a poke bonnet passes, and for the rest, I see but an uninteresting population of native tradesmen. As for the library, its window is full of pictures of burly theologians, and their works, sermons, apologues, and so forth. Can I go in and ask the young ladies at the counter for 'Manfrone, or the One-handed Monk', and 'Life in London, or the Adventures of Corinthian Tom, Jeremiah Hawthorn, Esq., and their friend Bob Logic'? – absurd. I turn away abashed from the casement – from the Pantiles – no longer Pantiles, but Parade. I stroll over the Common and survey the beautiful purple hills around, twinkling with a thousand bright villas, which have sprung up over this charming ground since first I saw it. What an admirable scene of peace and plenty! What a delicious air breathes over the heath, blows the cloud shadows across it, and murmurs through the full-clad trees! Can the world show a land fairer, richer, more cheerful? I see a portion of it when I look up from the window at which I write. But fair scene, green woods, bright terraces gleaming in sunshine, and purple clouds swollen with summer rain – nay, the very pages over which my head bends – disappear from before my eyes. They are looking backwards, back into forty years off, into a dark room, into a little house hard by on the Common here, in the Bartlemy-tide holidays. The parents have gone to town for two days: the house is all his own, his own and a grim old maid-servant's, and a little boy is seated at night in the lonely drawing-room, poring over 'Manfrone, or the One-handed Monk', so frightened that he scarcely dares to turn round.

ON BEING FOUND OUT

At the close (let us say) of Queen Anne's reign, when I was a boy at a private and preparatory school for young gentlemen, I remember the wiseacre of a master ordering us all, one night, to march into a little garden at the back of the house, and thence to proceed one by one into a tool or hen-house, (I was but a tender little thing just put into short clothes, and can't exactly say whether the house was for tools or hens,) and in that house to put our hands into a sack which stood on a bench, a candle burning beside it. I put my hand into the sack. My hand came out quite black. I went and joined the other boys in the school-room; and all their hands were black too.

By reason of my tender age (and there are some critics who, I hope, will be satisfied by my acknowledging that I am a hundred and fifty-six next birthday) I could not understand what was the meaning of this night excursion – this candle, this tool-house, this bag of soot. I think we little boys were taken out of our sleep to be brought to the ordeal. We came, then, and showed our little hands to the master; washed them or not – most probably, I should say, not – and so went bewildered back to bed.

Something had been stolen in the school that day; and Mr Wiseacre having read in a book of an ingenious method of finding out a thief by making him put his hand into a sack (which, if guilty, the rogue would shirk from doing), all we boys were subjected to the trial. Goodness knows what the lost object was, or who stole it. We all had black hands to show to the master. And the thief, whoever he was, was not Found Out that time.

I wonder if the rascal is alive – an elderly scoundrel he must be by this time; and a hoary old hypocrite, to whom an old school-fellow presents his kindest regards – parenthetically remarking what a dreadful place that private school was; cold, chilblains, bad dinners, not enough victuals, and caning awful! – Are you alive still, I say, you nameless villain, who escaped discovery on that day of crime? I hope you have escaped often since, old sinner.

Ah, what a lucky thing it is, for you and me, my man, that we are not found out in all our peccadilloes; and that our backs can slip away from the master and the cane!

Just consider what life would be, if every rogue was found out, and flogged *coram populo*! What a butchery, what an indecency, what an endless swishing of the rod! Don't cry out about my misanthropy. My good friend Mealymouth, I will trouble you to tell me, do you go to church? When there, do you say, or do you not, that you are a miserable sinner? and saying so, do you believe or disbelieve it? If you are a M.S., don't you deserve correction, and aren't you grateful if you are to be let off? I say again, what a blessed thing it is that we are not all found out!

Just picture to yourself everybody who does wrong being found out, and punished accordingly. Fancy all the boys in all the school being whipped; and then the assistants, and then the head master (Doctor Badford let us call him). Fancy the provost-marshal being tied up, having previously superintended the correction of the whole army. After the young gentlemen have had their turn for the faulty exercises, fancy Doctor Lincolnsinn being taken up for certain faults in *his* Essay and Review. After the clergyman has cried his peccavi, suppose we hoist up a bishop, and give him a couple of dozen! (I see my Lord Bishop of Double-Gloucester sitting in a very uneasy posture on his right reverend bench). After we have cast off the bishop, what are we to say to the Minister who appointed him? My Lord Cinqwarden, it is painful to have to use personal correction to a boy of your age; but really ... *Siste tandem, carnifex*! The butchery is too horrible. The hand drops powerless, appalled at the quantity of birch which it must cut and brandish. I am glad we are not all found out, I say again; and protest, my dear brethren, against our having our deserts.

To fancy all men found out and punished is bad enough; but imagine all women found out in the distinguished social circle in which you and I have the honour to move. Is it not a mercy that so many of these fair criminals remain unpunished and un-discovered? There is Mrs Longbow, who is for ever practising, and who shoots poisoned arrows, too; when you meet her you don't call her liar, and charge her with the wickedness she has done, and is doing. There is Mrs Painter, who passes for a most respectable woman, and a model in society. There is no use in saying what you really know regarding her and her goings on. There is Diana Hunter – what a little haughty prude it is; and yet *we* know stories about her which are not altogether edifying. I say it is best, for the sake of the good, that the bad should not all be found out. You don't want your children to know the history of that lady in the next box, who is so handsome, and whom they admire so. Ah me, what would life be if we were all found out, and punished for all our faults? Jack Ketch* would be in permanence; and then who would hang Jack Ketch?

They talk of murderers being pretty certainly found out. Psha! I have heard an authority awfully competent vow and declare that scores and hundreds of murders are committed, and nobody is the wiser. That terrible man mentioned one or two ways of committing murder, which he maintained were quite common, and were scarcely ever found out. A man, for instance, comes home to his wife, and ... but I pause – I know that this Magazine has a very large circulation. Hundreds and hundreds of thousands – why not say a million of people at once? – well, say a million, read it. And amongst these countless readers, I might be teaching some monster how to make away with his wife without being found out, some fiend of a woman how to destroy her dear husband. I will *not* then tell this easy and simple way of murder, as communicated to me by a most respectable party in the confidence of private intercourse. Suppose some gentle reader were to try this most simple and easy receipt – it seems to me almost infallible – and come to grief in consequence, and be found out and hanged? Should I ever pardon myself for having been the means of doing injury to a single one of our esteemed subscribers? The prescription whereof I speak – that is to say, whereof I *don't* speak – shall be buried in this bosom. No, I am a humane man. I am not one of your Bluebeards to go and say to my wife, 'My dear! I am going away for a few days to Brighton. Here are all the keys of the house. You may open every door and closet, except the one at the end of the oak-room opposite the fire-place, with the little bronze Shakespeare on the mantelpiece (or what not).' I don't say this to a woman – unless, to be sure, I want to get rid of her – because, after such a caution, I know she'll peep into the closet. I say nothing about the closet at all. I keep the key in my pocket, and a being whom I love, but who, as I know, has many weaknesses, out of harm's way. You toss up your head, dear angel, drub on the ground with your lovely little feet, on the table with your sweet rosy fingers, and cry, 'Oh, sneerer! You don't know the depth of woman's feeling, the lofty scorn of all deceit, the entire absence of mean curiosity in the sex, or never, never would you libel us so!' Ah, Delia! dear, dear Delia! It is because I fancy I *do* know something about you (not all, mind – no, no; no man knows that) – Ah, my bride, my ringdove, my rose, my poppet – choose, in fact, whatever name you like – bulbul of my grove, fountain of my desert, sunshine of my darkling life, and joy of my dungeoned existence, it is because I *do* know a little about you that I conclude to say nothing of that private closet, and keep my key in my pocket. You take away that closet-key then, and the house-key. You lock Delia in. You keep her out of harm's way and gadding, and so she never *can* be found out.

And yet by little strange accidents and coincidences how we are being found out every day. You remember that old story of the Abbé Kakatoes, who told the company at supper one night how the first confession he ever received was – from a murderer let us say. Presently enters to supper the Marquis de Croquemitaine. 'Palsambleu, abbé!' says the brilliant marquis, taking a pinch of snuff, 'are you here? Gentlemen and ladies! I was the abbé's first penitent, and I made him a confession which I promise you astonished him.'

To be sure how queerly things are found out! Here is an instance. Only the other day I was writing in these Roundabout Papers about a certain man, whom I facetiously called Baggs, and who had abused me to my friends, who of course told me. Shortly after that paper was published another friend – Sacks let us call him – scowls fiercely at me as I am sitting in perfect good-humour at the club, and passes on without speaking. A cut. A quarrel. Sacks thinks it is about him that I was writing: whereas, upon my honour and conscience, I never had him once in my mind, and was pointing my moral from quite another man. But don't you see, by this wrath of the guilty-conscienced Sacks, that he had been abusing me too? He has owned himself guilty, never having been accused. He has winced when nobody thought of hitting him. I did but put the cap out, and madly butting and chafing, behold my friend rushes to put his head into it! Never mind, Sacks, you are found out; but I bear you no malice, my man.

And yet to be found out, I know from my own experience, must be painful and odious, and cruelly mortifying to the inward vanity. Suppose I am a poltroon, let us say. With fierce moustache, loud talk, plentiful oaths, and an immense stick, I keep up nevertheless a character for courage. I swear fearfully at cabmen and women; brandish my bludgeon, and perhaps knock down a little man or two with it: brag of the images which I break at the shooting-gallery, and pass amongst my friends for a whiskery fire-eater, afraid of neither man nor dragon. Ah me! Suppose some brisk little chap steps up and gives me a caning in St James's Street, with all the heads of my friends looking out of all the club windows. My reputation is gone. I frighten no man more. My nose is pulled by whipper-snappers, who jump up on a chair to reach it. I am found out. And in the days of my triumphs, when people were yet afraid of me, and were taken in by my swagger, I always knew that I was a lily-liver, and expected that I should be found out some day.

That certainty of being found out must haunt and depress many a bold braggadocio spirit. Let us say it is a clergyman, who can pump copious floods of tears out of his own eyes and those of his audience. He thinks to himself, 'I am but a poor swindling, chattering rogue. My bills are unpaid. I have jilted several women whom I have promised to marry. I don't know whether I believe what I preach, and I know I have stolen the very sermon over which I have been snivelling. Have they found me out?' says he, as his head drops down on the cushion.

Then your writer, poet, historian, novelist, or what not? The *Beacon* says that 'Jones's work is one of the first order.' The *Lamp* declares that 'Jones's tragedy surpasses every work since the days of Him of Avon.' The *Comet* asserts that 'J's "Life of Goody Two-shoes" is a κτῆμα ἐς ἀεὶ and enduring monument to the fame of that admirable Englishwoman,' and so forth. But then Jones knows that he has lent the critic of the *Beacon* five pounds; that his publisher has a half-share in the *Lamp*; and that the *Comet* comes repeatedly to dine with him. It is all very well. Jones is immortal until he is found out; and then down comes the extinguisher, and the immortal is dead and buried. The idea (*dies iræ!*) of discovery must haunt many a man, and make him uneasy, as the trumpets are puffing in his triumph. Brown, who has a higher place than he deserves, cowers before Smith, who has found him out. What is a chorus of critics shouting 'Bravo?' – a public clapping hands and flinging garlands? Brown knows that Smith has found him out. Puff, trumpets! Wave, banners! Huzza, boys, for the immortal Brown! 'This is all very well,' B. thinks (bowing the while, smiling, laying his hand to his heart); 'but there stands Smith at the window: *he* has measured me; and some day the others will find me out too.' It is a very curious sensation to sit by a man who has found you out, and who you know has found you out; or, *vice versa*, to sit with a man whom *you* have found out. His talent? Bah! His virtue? We know a little story or two about his virtue, and he knows we know it. We are thinking over friend Robinson's antecedents, as we grin, bow and talk; and we are both humbugs together. Robinson a good fellow, is he? You know how he behaved to Hicks? A good-natured man, is he? Pray do you remember that little story of Mrs Robinson's black eye? How men have to work, to talk, to smile, to go to bed, and try and sleep, with this dread of being found out on their consciences! Bardolph, who has robbed a church, and Nym, who has taken a purse, go to their usual haunts, and smoke their pipes with their companions. Mr Detective Bullseye appears, and says, 'Oh, Bardolph! I want you about that there pyx business!' Mr Bardolph knocks the ashes out of his pipe, puts out his hands to the little steel cuffs, and walks away quite meekly. He is found out. He must go. 'Good-bye, Doll Tearsheet! Good-bye, Mrs Quickly, ma'am!' The other gentlemen and ladies *de la société* look on and exchange mute adieux with the departing friends. And an assured time will come when the other gentlemen and ladies will be found out too.

What a wonderful and beautiful provision of nature it has been that, for the most part, our womankind are not endowed with the faculty of finding us out! *They* don't doubt, and probe, and weigh, and take your measure. Lay down this paper, my benevolent friend and reader, go into your drawing-room now, and utter a joke ever so old, and I wager sixpence the ladies there will all begin to laugh. Go to Brown's house, and tell Mrs Brown and the young ladies what you think of him, and see what a welcome you will get! In like manner, let him come to your house, and tell *your* good lady his candid opinion of you, and fancy how she will receive him! Would you have your wife and children know you exactly for what you are, and esteem you precisely at your worth? If so, my friend, you will live in a dreary house, and you will have but a chilly fireside. Do you suppose the people round it don't see your homely face as under a glamour, and, as it were, with a halo of love round it? You don't fancy you *are*, as you seem to them? No such thing, my man. Put away that monstrous conceit, and be thankful that *they* have not found you out.

OGRES

I dare say the reader has remarked that the upright and independent vowel, which stands in the vowel-list between E and O, has formed the subject of the main part of these essays. How does that vowel feel this morning? – fresh, good-humoured, and lively? The Roundabout lines, which fall from this pen, are correspondingly brisk and cheerful. Has anything, on the contrary, disagreed with the vowel. Has its rest been disturbed, or was yesterday's dinner too good, or yesterday's wine not good enough? Under such circumstances, a darkling, misanthropic tinge, no doubt, is cast upon the paper. The jokes, if attempted, are elaborate and dreary. The bitter temper breaks out. That sneering manner is adopted, which you know, and which exhibits itself so especially when the writer is speaking about women. A moody carelessness comes over him. He sees no good in anybody or thing: and treats gentlemen, ladies, history, and things in general, with a like gloomy flippancy. Agreed. When the vowel in question is in that mood, if you like airy gaiety and tender gushing benevolence – if you want to be satisfied with yourself and the rest of your fellow-beings; I recommend you, my dear creature, to go to some other shop in Cornhill, or turn to some other article. There are moods in the mind of the vowel of which we are speaking, when it is ill-conditioned and captious. Who always keeps good health, and good humour? Do not philosophers grumble? Are not sages sometimes out of temper? and do not angel-women go off in tantrums? Today my mood is dark. I scowl as I dip my pen in the inkstand.

Here is the day come round – for everything here is done with the utmost regularity: intellectual labour, sixteen hours; meals, thirty-two minutes; exercise, a hundred and forty-eight minutes; conversation with the family, chiefly literary, and about the housekeeping, one hour and four minutes; sleep, three hours and fifteen minutes (at the end of the month, when the Magazine is complete, I own I take eight minutes more); and the rest for the toilette and the world. Well, I say, the *Roundabout Paper Day* being come, and the subject long since settled in my mind, an excellent subject – a most telling, lively, and popular subject – I go to breakfast determined to finish that meal in 9 3/4 minutes, as usual, and then retire to my desk and work, when – oh, provoking! – here in the paper is the very subject treated, on which I was going to write? Yesterday another paper which I saw treated it – and of course, as I need not tell you, spoiled it. Last Saturday, another paper had an article on the subject; perhaps you may guess what it was – but I won't tell you. Only this is true, my favourite subject, which was about to make the best paper we have had for a long time: my bird, my game that I was going to shoot and serve up with such a delicate sauce, has been found by other sportsmen; and pop, pop, pop, a half-dozen of guns have banged at it, mangled it, and brought it down.

'And can't you take some other text?' say you. All this is mighty well. But if you have set your heart on a certain dish for dinner, be it cold boiled veal, or what you will, and they bring you turtle and venison, don't you feel disappointed? During your walk you have been making up your mind that that cold meat, with moderation and a pickle, will be a very sufficient dinner: you have accustomed your thoughts to it; and here, in place of it, is a turkey, surrounded by coarse sausages, or a reeking pigeon-pie or a fulsome roast-pig. I have known many a good and kind man made furiously angry by such a *contretemps*. I have known him lose his temper, call his wife and servants names, and a whole household made miserable. If, then, as is notoriously the case, it is too dangerous to baulk a man about his dinner, how much more about his article? I came to my meal with an ogre-like appetite and gusto. Fee, faw, fum! Wife, where is that tender little Princekin? Have you trussed him, and did you stuff him nicely, and have you taken care to baste him and do him, not too brown, as I told you? Quick! I am hungry! I begin to whet my knife, to roll my eyes about, and roar and clap my huge chest like a gorilla; and then my poor Ogrina has to tell me that the little princes have all run away, whilst she was in the kitchen, making the paste to bake them in? I pause in the description. I won't condescend to report the bad language, which you know must ensue, when an ogre, whose mind is ill-regulated, and whose habits of self-indulgence are notorious, finds himself disappointed of his greedy hopes. What treatment of his wife, what abuse and brutal behaviour to his children, who, though ogrillions, are children! My dears, you may fancy, and need not ask my delicate pen to describe, the language and behaviour of a vulgar, coarse, greedy, large man with an immense mouth and teeth, which are too frequently employed in the gobbling and crunching of raw man's meat.

And in this circuitous way you see I have reached my present subject, which is, Ogres. You fancy they are dead or only fictitious characters – mythical representatives of strength, cruelty, stupidity, and lust for blood? Though they had seven-leagued boots, you remember all sorts of little whipping-snapping Tom Thumbs used to elude and outrun them. They were so stupid that they gave into the most shallow ambuscades and artifices: witness that well-known ogre, who, because Jack cut open the hasty-pudding, instantly ripped open his own stupid waistcoat and interior. They were cruel, brutal, disgusting, with their sharpened teeth, immense knives, and roaring voice! but they always ended by being overcome by little Tom Thumbkins, or some other smart little champion.

Yes; they were conquered in the end there is no doubt. They plunged headlong (and uttering the most frightful bad language) into some pit where Jack came with his smart *couteau de chasse*, and whipped their brutal heads off. They would be going to devour maidens,

> But ever when it seemed
>   Their need was at the sorest,
> A knight, in armour bright,
>   Came riding through the forest.

And down, after a combat, would go the brutal persecutor, with a lance through his midriff. Yes, I say, this is very true and well. But you remember that round the ogre's cave the ground was covered, for hundreds and hundreds of years, *with the bones of the victims* whom he had lured into the castle. Many knights and maids came to him and perished under his knife and teeth. Were dragons the same as ogres? monsters dwelling in caverns, whence they rushed, attired in plate armour, wielding pikes and torches, and destroying stray passengers who passed by their lair? Monsters, brutes, rapacious tyrants, ruffians, as they were, doubtless they ended by being overcome. But, before they were destroyed, they did a deal of mischief. The bones round their caves were countless. They had sent many brave souls to Hades, before their own fled, howling out of their rascal carcasses, to the same place of gloom.

There is no greater mistake than to suppose that fairies, champions, distressed damsels, and by consequence ogres, have ceased to exist. It may not be *ogreable* to them (pardon the horrible pleasantry, but as I am writing in the solitude of my chamber, I am grinding my teeth – yelling, roaring and cursing – brandishing my scissors and paper-cutter and as it were have become an ogre). I say there is no greater mistake than to suppose that ogres have ceased to exist. We all *know* ogres. Their caverns are round us, and about us. There are the castles of several ogres within a mile of the spot where I write. I think some of them suspect I am an ogre myself. I am not, but I know they are. I visit them. I don't mean to say that they take a cold roast prince out of the cupboard, and have a cannibal feast before *me*. But I see the bones lying about the roads to their houses, and in the areas and gardens. Politeness, of course, prevents me from making any remarks: but I know them well enough. One of the ways to know 'em is to watch the scared looks of the ogres' wives and children. They lead an awful life. They are present at dreadful cruelties. In their excesses those ogres will stab about and kill not only strangers who happen to call in and ask a night's lodging, but they will outrage, murder and chop up their own kin. We all know ogres, I say, and have been in their dens often. It is not necessary that ogres who ask you to dine should offer their guests the *peculiar dish* which they like. They cannot always get a Tom Thumb family. They eat mutton and beef too; and I daresay even go out to tea, and invite you to drink it. But I tell you there are numbers of them going about in the world. And now you have my word for it, and this little hint, it is quite curious what an interest society may be made to have for you by your determining to find out the ogres you meet there.

What does the man mean? says Mrs Downright, to whom a joke is a very grave thing. I mean, madam, that in the company assembled in your genteel drawing-room, who bow here and there, and smirk in white neckcloths, you receive men who elbow through life successfully enough, but who are ogres in private: men wicked, false, rapacious, flattering; cruel hectors at home, smiling courtiers abroad; causing wives, children, servants, parents, to tremble before them, and smiling and bowing, as they bid strangers welcome into their castles. I say, there are men who have crunched the bones of victim after victim; in whose closets lie skeletons picked frightfully clean. When these ogres came out into the world, you don't suppose they show their knives, and their great teeth? A neat simple white neckcloth, a merry rather obsequious manner, a cadaverous look, perhaps, now and again, and a rather dreadful grin; but I know ogres very considerably respected: and when you hint to such and such a man, 'My dear sir, Mr Sharpus, whom you appear to like, is, I assure you, a most dreadful cannibal', the gentleman cries, 'Oh, psha, nonsense! Dare say not so black as he is painted. Dare say not worse than his neighbours.' We condone everything in this country – private treason, falsehood, flattery, cruelty at home, roguery, and double-dealing. What! Do you mean to say in your acquaintance you don't know ogres guilty of countless crimes of fraud and force, and that knowing them you don't shake hands with them; dine with them at your table; and meet them at their own? Depend upon it in the time when there were real live ogres, in real caverns or castles, gobbling up real knights and virgins, when they went into the world – the neighbouring market-town, let us say, or earl's castle – though their nature and reputation were pretty well known, their notorious foibles were never alluded to. You would say, 'What, Blunderbore, my boy! How do you do? How well and fresh you look! What's the receipt you have for keeping so young and rosy?' And your wife would softly ask after Mrs Blunderbore and the dear children. Or it would be, 'My dear Humguffin! try that pork. It is home-bred, home-fed, and I promise you, tender. Tell me if you think it is as good as yours? John, a glass of Burgundy to Colonel Humguffin!' You don't suppose there would be any unpleasant allusions to disagreeable home reports regarding Humguffin's manner of furnishing his larder? I say we all of us know ogres. We shake hands and dine with ogres. And if inconvenient moralists tell us we are cowards for our pains, we turn round with a *tu quoque*, or say that we don't meddle with other folk's affairs; that people are much less black than they are painted, and so on. What! Won't half the country go to Ogreham Castle. Won't some of the clergy say grace at dinner? Won't the mothers bring their daughters to dance with the young Rawheads? And if Lady Ogreham happens to die – I won't say to go the way of all flesh, that is too revolting – I say if Ogreham is a widower, do you aver, on your conscience and honour, that mothers will not be found to offer their young girls to supply the lamented lady's place? How stale this misanthropy is! Something must have disagreed with this cynic. Yes, my good woman. I dare say you would like to call another subject. Yes, my fine fellow; ogre at home, supple as a dancing-master abroad, and shaking in thy pumps, and wearing a horrible grin of sham gaiety to conceal thy terror, lest I should point thee out: thou art prosperous and honoured, art thou? I say thou hast been a tyrant and a robber. Thou hast plundered the poor. Thou hast bullied the weak. Thou hast laid violent hands on the goods of the innocent and confiding. Thou hast made a prey of the meek and gentle who asked for thy protection. Thou hast been hard to thy kinsfolk, and cruel to thy family. Go, monster! Ah, when shall little Jack come and drill daylight through thy wicked cannibal carcass? I see the ogre pass on, bowing right and left to the company; and he gives a dreadful sidelong glance of suspicion as he is talking to my lord bishop in the corner there.

Ogres in our days need not be giants at all. In former times, and in children's books, where it is necessary to paint your moral in such large letters that there can be no mistake about it, ogres are made with that enormous mouth and *ratelier* which you know of, and with which they can swallow down a baby, almost without using that great knife which they always carry. They are too cunning now-a-days. They go about in society, slim, small, quietly dressed, and showing no especially great appetite. In my own young days there used to be play ogres – men who would devour a young fellow in one sitting, and leave him without a bit of flesh on his bones. They were quiet gentleman-like-looking people. They got the young fellow into their cave. Champagne, pâté-de-foie-gras, and numberless good things, were handed about; and then, having eaten, the young man was devoured in his turn. I believe these card and dice ogres have died away almost as entirely as the hasty-pudding giants whom Tom Thumb overcame. Now, there are ogres in City courts who lure you into their dens. About our Cornish mines, I am told there are many most plausible ogres, who tempt you into their caverns and pick your bones there. In a certain newspaper there used to be lately a whole column of advertisements from ogres who would put on the most plausible, nay, piteous appearance, in order to inveigle their victims. You would read, 'A tradesman, established for seventy years in the City, and known, and much respected by Messrs N. M. Rothschild and Baring Brothers, has pressing need for three pounds until next Saturday. He can give security for half a million, and

forty thousand pounds will be given for the use of the loan,' and
so on; or, 'An influential body of capitalists are about to establish
a company, of which the business will be enormous and the profits
proportionately prodigious. They will require a Secretary, of good
address and appearance, at a salary of two thousand per annum.
He need not be able to write, but address and manners are
absolutely necessary. As a mark of confidence in the company, he
will have to deposit,' &c.; or, 'A young widow (of pleasing
manners and appearance) who has a pressing necessity for four
pounds ten for three weeks, offers her Erard's grand piano valued
at three hundred guineas; a diamond cross of eight hundred
pounds; and board and lodging in her elegant villa near Banbury
Cross, with the best references and society, in return for the loan.'
I suspect these people are ogres. There are ogres and ogres.
Polyphemus* was a great, tall, one-eyed, notorious ogre, fetching
his victims out of a hole, and gobbling them one after another.
There could be no mistake about him. But so were the Sirens
ogres* – pretty blue-eyed things, peeping at you coaxingly from
out of the water, and singing their melodious wheedles. And the
bones round their caves were more numerous than the ribs, skulls,
and thigh-bones round the cavern of hulking Polypheme.

To the castle-gates of some of these monsters up rides the
dapper champion of the pen; puffs boldly upon the horn which
hangs by the chain; enters the hall resolutely, and challenges the
big tyrant sulking within. We defy him to combat, the enormous
roaring ruffian! We give him a meeting on the green plain before
his castle. Green? No wonder it should be green: it is manured
with human bones. After a few graceful wheels and curvets, we
take our ground. We stoop over our saddle. 'Tis but to kiss the
locket of our lady-love's hair. And now the vizor is up: the lance
is in rest (Gillott's iron is the point for me). A touch of the spur
in the gallant sides of Pegasus, and we gallop at the great brute.

'Cut off his ugly head, Flibbertygibbet, my squire!' And who
are these who pour out of the castle? the imprisoned maidens, the
maltreated widows, the poor old hoary grandfathers, who have
been locked up in the dungeons these scores and scores of years,
writhing under the tyranny of that ruffian! Ah ye knights of the
pen! May honour be your shield, and truth tip your lances! Be
gentle to all gentle people. Be modest to women. Be tender to
children. And as for the Ogre Humbug, out sword, and have at
him.

NOTES

A SHABBY GENTEEL STORY

19 'A plum': i.e. £100,000.

22 'James Gann Esq': such a style of address, superior to the plain 'Mr', would typically be seen as a confirmation of Gann's gentlemanly pretensions. Compare the reaction of Mr Holbrook in Elizabeth Gaskell's *Cranford* (1853), who returns letters using the 'Esq' form on the grounds that his correct title is 'Thomas Holbrook, Yeoman'.

23 '*Ferronnières*': a chain worn round the head, suspending a jewel in the middle of the forehead, named after da Vinci's portrait *La Belle Ferronnière*.

24 'Mrs Coutts': Angela Burdett-Coutts (1814–1906), the granddaughter of Thomas Coutts, founder of the banking house that bears his name, and a celebrated Victorian philanthropist.

28 'I don't half like him': an example of a transitional stage in the use of the expression 'not half'. The original meaning was 'not very much at all'. However, the present usage, meaning 'more than half', i.e. considerably, was developing by the mid-nineteenth century. See K. C. Phillipps, *The Language of Thackeray*, ch. 3.

31 'Half-pay': a reduced allowance to an officer when not in actual service, or in retirement.

33 'Andrea Fitch': Fitch appears to have been modelled on the Scottish artist John Grant Brine, whom Thackeray visited in Paris in 1833 and later dismissed in a letter to his mother as 'a second-rate man, a little better than a drawing-master'. Brine later died of consumption. By the time he came to write a sequel, *Philip*, over twenty years later, Thackeray's opinion of Fitch/Brine had greatly improved. His 'genius' had 'made a little flicker of brightness': although this had now been extinguished, he possessed 'as loving, gentle, faithful, honourable a heart as ever beat in a little bosom.' See John Carey, *Thackeray: Prodigal Genius*, p.31.

34 'Pattens': wooden clogs or sandals fixed to a wooden platform or metal ring.

34 'Blucher boots': strong leather half-boots, named after the Prussian Field Marshal von Blucher.

37 'Tuft-hunter': a slang expression for a toady or sycophant, derived from Oxford and Cambridge undergraduates who wore tufts or gold tassels in their caps, signifying that they were peers or the eldest sons of peers. *Pendennis* vol. II ch. 22 recalls a minor character in his Oxbridge days 'truckling to the tufts'.

39–40 '*Manfrone; or, The One-handed Monk* ... *Thaddeus of Warsaw, Scottish Chiefs*': examples of the early nineteenth century vogue for the historical novel. Jane Porter's *Thaddeus of Warsaw* was published in 1803, and her *Scottish Chiefs* in 1810.

40 'Leslie, Maclise': Charles Leslie (1794–1859), royal painter, known, among other works, for his portrait *The Queen Receiving the Sacrament at her Coronation* (1838), and *The Christening of the Princess Royal* (1841). Daniel Maclise (1806–78), Irish painter, whose work includes the 72 lithographical portraits of contemporary celebrities and two vast frescoes for the royal gallery of the House of Lords. Thackeray appears in his sketch of the contributors to *Fraser's Magazine*.

51 'Oronooko': a type of Virginian tobacco.

58 '... an Admirable Crichton': after James Crichton (1560–82), famed for his mastery of ten languages, and a variety of other accomplishments. Sir Thomas Urquhart's account of his life, *The Discovery of a Most Exquisite Jewel* (1652) is thought to be exaggerated.

61 'Prime Hollands': Dutch gin.

62 'Brandenburg House, sir – England's injured Queen.' Brandenburg House, near Hammersmith, was the residence of Caroline of Brunswick (1768–1821), the rejected wife of George IV, during the last months of her life.

63 'Go bodkin': i.e. forced to squeeze in between two others, where there is space for two only.

69 'St. George's, Hanover Square': a fashionable venue for society weddings. The majority of Trollope's heroines, for example, are married there.

70 'As Miss Lydia Languish does in the play': the heroine of Sheridan's *The Rivals* (1775).

72 '*Mysteries of Udolpho*': the Gothic novel by Mrs Radcliffe (1764–1823), first published in 1794.

77 'Alnaschar': a beggar in the *Arabian Nights* who destroys his means of livelihood by indulging in visions of riches and grandeur.

78 'A house in Newman Street': Newman Street, which lies north of Oxford Street, was by the mid-nineteenth century a popular residential area for successful artists, although see Thackeray's disparaging remarks in 'The Artists' q.v.

78 'In the song of Mr Thomas Moore': Thomas Moore (1779–1852), national lyricist of Ireland and author of *Irish Melodies* (1807–34).

79 'Landon or Mrs Hemans': Laetitia Landon (1802–38), whose works included the poem 'Rome' (1820) and the semi-autobiographical novel *Ethel Churchill* (1837). Felicia Hemans (1793–1835), poet and friend of Scott and Wordsworth, was known, among other works, for her *Translations from Camoens and Other Poets* and *Lays of Many Lands*.

87 'Form a pretty good idea of my age': Thackeray was twenty-nine at the time of writing.

95 'Milled': Sporting slang for 'beat' or 'thrashed'.

103 'Astley's Amphitheatre': Philip Astley (1742–1814), the celebrated equestrian performer, opened Astley's Royal Amphitheatre in London in 1798. Destroyed by fire in 1803, it was rebuilt in the following year.

108 '*Galignani's Messenger*': *Galignani's English Messenger*, an English-language newspaper, founded in 1815 and circulated throughout Europe, largely for the benefit of English travellers on the continent.

GOING TO SEE A MAN HANGED

110 'To see Courvoisier killed': François Benjamin Courvoisier, a Swiss valet, had been convicted of the murder of his master, Lord William Russell, at the latter's house in Norfolk Street on 5 May 1840. He was executed at Snow Hill on 6 July. For an account of the trial, which excited tremendous public interest, see the appendix to the *Annual Register 1840*, pp.229–45.

113 'Jack Ketch': Public executioner from *c*. 1663 to 1686. As a result of his barbarity at the executions of William Lord Russell, the Duke of Monmouth and others, and also from the association with the verb 'ketch' (catch), the name became synonymous with 'hangman'.

114 'When Lord Stanley withdrew his Irish bill the other night': throughout 1840 Melbourne's Liberal administration came under continuous attack from Sir Robert Peel's Conservative opposition. The Irish Municipal Corporation Bill was withdrawn by Lord Stanley on 6 July, having failed in nine of the ten divisions forced upon it, in consequence of the lateness of the session.

120 'After Thistlewood and his companions were hanged': Arthur Thistlewood (b. 1774), ringleader of the Cato Street conspiracy (1820), whose object was the assassination of the Cabinet as they sat at dinner.

THE ARTISTS

126 'The quarter of Soho': Soho, whose boundaries at this stage extended north of Oxford Street, remains a favourite haunt of Thackeray's artistic characters. Becky Sharp's father has a house there (*Vanity Fair* I ch. 2), while Clive Newcome occupies a studio in Charlotte Street, not far from Mr Gandish's art school.

126 'Pattens': see note to *A Shabby Genteel Story*, p.34.

127 'Lord Lyndhurst ... the Duke': all much-copied subjects for early Victorian painters: Lord Lyndhurst (1782–1863) was a Lord Chancellor; Lady Peel the wife of Sir Robert Peel. 'Miss Croker' is presumably a reference to Marianne Croker (d. 1854), the wife of Thomas Crofton Croker (1798–1854), the Irish antiquary; the Duke is Wellington.

133 'The naughty sirens lured the passing seaman'. See note to *Ogres*, p.330.

MEMORIALS OF GOURMANDISING

143 'Olla podrida': a Spanish dish whose literal translation is 'rotten pot', that is, food on the point of turning bad, cooked into a stew to disguise its unappetising flavour.

144 'Barmecide': one who offers imaginary food or illusory benefits. In the *Arabian Nights* the Barmecides were Baghdad princes, one of whom placed a succession of empty dishes before a beggar, pretending that they contained a sumptuous repast. The deceit was humorously accepted by the beggar.

149 'Spermaceti': a fatty substance found in the head and other parts of the sperm whale, in the nineteenth century used in the manufacture of candles.

151 'Heliogabalus': or Elagabalus, b. AD 204, Roman Emperor, AD 218–222 and famous for his eccentric behaviour. His homosexual orgies outraged Roman opinion.

155 'Negus': named after Colonel Francis Negus (d. 1732). Wine, especially port or sherry, and hot water, sweetened and flavoured with lemon and spice.

156 'Banyan days': another name for the Indian fig-tree, famous for its

extensive and shady branches. A 'banyan day', consequently, is synonymous with leisure.

160 *'Lunel'*: a sweet Muscat wine, originally from the town of Lunel in France.

160 *'Noctes'*: the *Noctes Ambrosianae*, imaginary conversations on literary and other topics, appeared in *Blackwood's magazine* from 1822 to 1835.

161 'Gil Blas': hero of *The Adventures of Gil Blas of Santillane*, a picaresque romance by Alain le Sage (1668–1747), published from 1715 to 1735.

166 'Upas plant': a highly poisonous Javanese tree.

166 'Themis': the ancient Greek goddess of law and justice.

CAPTAIN ROOK AND MR PIGEON

170 'Don Carlos ... Queen Christina': the chief protagonists of the first Carlist War (1833–9). Don Carlos (1788–1855), the second surviving son of Charles IV of Spain and brother of Ferdinand VII, was excluded from the throne by Maria Christina I (1806–78), the latter's queen consort, who persuaded her husband to alter the law of succession in favour of their daughter Isabella. The ensuing conflict involved the employment of numerous foreign mercenaries.

170 '(see the romances of Adam Smith, Malthus and Ricardo, and the philosophical works of Miss Martineau)': Adam Smith (1723–90), social philosopher and political economist, best known for *An Enquiry into the nature and cause of the Wealth of Nations* (1776). David Ricardo (1772–1823), economist, whose chief work was *Principles of Political Economy and Taxation* (1817). Thomas Malthus (1766–1834), economist and demographer, whose works included *An Essay on the Principles of Population* (1798) and *Principles of Political Economy Compared with a View to their Practical Application* (1820). Harriet Martineau (1802–76), who enjoyed an influential career as a writer on social, economic and political subjects, first attracted public attention with her popularisations of classical economics, especially the ideas of Ricardo and Malthus. Her publications in this field included *Illustrations of Political Economy* (23 vols, 1832–4), *Poor Laws and Paupers Illustrated* (10 vols, 1833–4), and *Illustrations of Taxation* (5 vols, 1834).

175 'I need not tell Freddy's name': the use of the name Pigeon, meaning an impressionable and easily duped young man, recurs in Thackeray. In *Vanity Fair* II ch. 28 Mr Frederick Pigeon claims that, under the watchful

gaze of Becky Sharp, 'he was hocussed at supper and lost eight hundred pounds to Major Loder and the Honourable Mr Duceace', that is, stupefied with drugs and then tricked at cards. These scenes are closely linked to Thackeray's own experiences as a young man. At Cambridge his freehandedness with money attracted the attention of a group of professional gamblers, who took rooms opposite his college, invited him to dinner and *ecarté*, and by the end of the evening had relieved their guest of £1,500.

178   'The gentlest hint in the world that he had better sell out': until the army reforms of 1871 military commissions could be bought and sold.

A DINNER IN THE CITY

187   'Calipash and calipee': i.e. the edible parts of the turtle.

187   'Vitellius': AD 15–69, the last of Nero's three short-lived successors in the year of the four Emperors. His popular reputation as a fabulous glutton is based largely on propaganda.

188   'Gog and Magog': in Scripture Gog is the hostile power ruled by Satan that will manifest itself immediately before the end of the world (Revelation 20). Here and in other passages in Judaeo–Christian apocalyptic literature, Gog is joined by a second hostile force named Magog, but elsewhere in the Bible Magog is apparently a geographical locality and the place of Gog's origin. Thackeray probably has in mind the two colossal wooden effigies in the Guildhall, thought to represent the survivors of a race of giants destroyed by the Trojan Brutus and brought to London to act as porters at the gate of the royal palace. Several times destroyed by fire, these have been replaced as recently as 1953.

188   'Smoking a dhoodeen': or dudeen, the Irish name for a short clay tobacco-pipe.

189   '*George Barnwell*': *The History of George Barnwell, or The London Merchant*, a domestic tragedy in prose by George Lillo (1693–1739), first produced in 1731.

195   'His Boanerges of a Clerk': 'Sons of Thunder', the name given by Christ to the two sons of Zebedee (Mark 3:17), hence a loud, vociferous preacher or orator.

THE FATAL BOOTS

200   'Sir Joshua': Sir Joshua Reynolds (1723–92), portrait painter and aesthetician, a dominant figure in English artistic life in the mid- to late eighteenth century.

203 'Twelfth-cake': short for twelfth-night or twelfth-tide cake, a large cake eaten at the festival of Twelfth Night, usually frosted or otherwise ornamented and containing a bean or coin which would determine the 'king' or 'queen' of the feast.

206 'Which I vandyked very nicely': points made in material, in the manner of the collars with deeply cut edges worn by subjects in Van Dyke's portraits.

206 'Hartshorn': the powdered horn or antler of the hart, at that time a chief source of ammonia.

216 'The famous North Bungay Fencibles': a militia regiment, composed of persons who undertook voluntary military service in time of domestic emergency, in this case the threat of French invasion.

216 'In the Five per Cents': stock or shares paying 5 per cent annual interest on their nominal value, and the principal support of private incomes.

219 'Five per Cents, as they were in those days': by the mid-nineteenth century investment values had fallen and such stock typically produced a 4 per cent return.

224 'We quaffed more Bohea': black China tea, then regarded as choice.

236 'And with it came a fine barouche': a four-wheeled horse-drawn carriage with a retractable hood over the rear half. Possession of such a vehicle was a conspicuous sign of wealth, in particular an indication that the owner was not concerned with the reduction in tax granted to two-wheeled vehicles, known consequently as 'tax carts'. In *Vanity Fair* I ch. 34 James Crawley is embarrassed when out driving in his aunt's barouche to encounter 'on the cliff in a tax cart drawn by a bang-up pony ... his friends the Tutbury Pet and the Rottingdean Fibber'.

237 'Cheltenham, Harrogate, Bath, Leamington and other places': all fashionable early nineteenth-century spa towns.

242 'Cursitor Street': compare Rawdon Crawley's imprisonment in *Vanity Fair* II ch. 16.

A LITTLE DINNER AT TIMMINS'S

257 'At the Pantechnicon': originally a bazaar for the sale of all kinds of artistic work, the Pantechnicon subsequently became a warehouse for storing furniture. In *Vanity Fair* II ch. 26 the Osborne family property is conveyed there after old Mr Osborne's death to await his grandson's majority. The implication, consequently, is that Mrs Timmins has purchased her desk second-hand.

258 'A second Mrs Norton': Caroline Norton (1808–77), author of *The Dream and other Poems* (1840) and other works. Her matrimonial difficulties and efforts to secure legal protection for married women made her a celebrated figure in mid-Victorian society. In particular, she was instrumental in the passing of the 1839 Infant Custody Act and the 1857 Divorce Act.

260 'Madonna front': artificial hair, in this instance braided on either side of the face in the manner of Italian representations of the Madonna.

262 'Tuft-hunter': see note to *A Shabby Genteel Story*, p.37.

263 'Mr Mitchel's jury': John Mitchel (1815–75), Irish nationalist and editor of the 'United Irishman', whose letters to Lord Clarendon were an open incitement to rebellion. He was arrested and tried for sedition in 1848, but the case could not proceed owing to the unreliability of Irish juries. As a result, Mitchel was rearrested under the recently passed Treason Felony Act, tried at a Dublin commission court and sentenced to 14 years' transportation. However, he escaped to America, subsequently returning to Ireland in 1875 where, shortly before his death, he was elected MP for Tipperary.

263 'Ledru-Rollin and Lamartine': two of the architects of the French Second Republic of 1848. Alexandre Auguste Ledru-Rollin (1807–74), a radical lawyer, was Minister of the Interior in the provisional government of 1848 and, for a few hours, head of the provisional administration which attempted to overthrow Louis-Napoleon in 1849. He subsequently fled to England, but was allowed to return to France under the general amnesty of 1870. Alphonse de Lamartine (1790–1869), poet and statesman, was the author of *Meditations poetiques* (1820), which established him as an important figure in the French Romantic movement. After the 1848 revolution he too was briefly head of a provisional government.

273 'Rout-cake': a small rich cake suitable for a 'rout' or reception. Mrs Elton supplies them in *Emma* ch. 34; Joseph Sedley eats twenty-four at a sitting in *Vanity Fair* I ch.3.

278 'Lacquered highlows': a type of covering for the foot and ankle, so called because they were too high to be called a shoe and too low to be called a boot, and something of an obsession for Thackeray, who invested them with enormous social significance. In the *Book of Snobs* ch.15, for example, 'highlows and no straps' are an infallible sign of the lower orders. At university Arthur Pendennis is beaten in mathematics by 'very vulgar young men, who did not even use straps to their trousers so as to cover the abominably thick and coarse shoes and stockings which they wore' (*Pendennis* II ch.18). Later in the same novel Fanny Bolton cannot help but compare Pendennis's footwear with that worn by her vulgar

admirer, Huxter. The former's shining boot is 'so, so unlike Sam's highlow' (*Pendennis* II ch.20).

HOBSON'S CHOICE

285 'A neat-handed Phillis of a parlour-maid': a generic name in pastoral poetry for a rustic maiden. Also, after Milton, a 'neat-handed' table-maid or waitress.

285 'The Chartist riots': the last great outburst of Chartism, the working-class movement for parliamentary reform named after its proclamation of a 'People's Charter', took place in 1848 and involved widespread social disruption.

288 'Bred up at Merchant Taylors together': the London public school (founded 1560–1) endowed by the Merchant Taylors' Company of London, an incorporated group of craftsmen tailors. Other schools with the same name, founded by different livery companies, exist elsewhere in England.

288 'Catamaran': a cross-grained person, especially a woman, presumably derived from 'cat'.

298 'A well-known rogue and a prig': by the mid-nineteenth century 'prig' had a number of meanings, among them a fop or conceited young man, a precisian in religion (especially a Non-Conformist minister), or, more generally, a hypocrite. Thackeray uses the word in the older sense of 'petty thief'.

THE FASHIONABLE AUTHORESS

301 'Nankeens': trousers made of nankeen, a kind of cotton originally manufactured in Nanking, China, from a yellow variety of cotton, subsequently from ordinary cotton dyed yellow.

303 'Being simply a collection … Sternhold and Hopkins': Thackeray here refers to a number of celebrated hymn-writers: Isaac Watts (1674–1748), Charles Wesley (1707–78), Nahum Tate (1652–1715) and Nicholas Brady (1659–1726). Tate and Brady collaborated on a metrical version of the Psalms, first published in 1696. Thomas Sternhold (d. 1549) and John Hopkins (d. 1570) were joint versifiers of the Psalms; a collection of forty-four appeared in the year of Sternhold's death.

307 'Prig': see note to *Hobson's Choice* p.298.

TUNBRIDGE TOYS

313 'He was an immense screw at school': i.e. a miser. Becky Sharp's letter to Amelia from Queen's Crawley (*Vanity Fair*) gives a contemporary definition: 'This gentleman and the guard seemed to know Sir Pitt very well, and laughed at him a great deal. They both agreed in calling him an old screw, which means a very stingy, avaricious person.'

315 'Mr Sala': G. A. Sala (1828–95), prolific journalist and author of, among much else, *The Strange Adventures of Captain Dangerous* (1861). Thackeray printed many of his contributions in the *Cornhill*.

316 'Shades of Valancour ... vivacious rattle': see note to *A Shabby Genteel Story* p.39–40.

316 'Hessians': high boots with tassels in front at the top, named after the Hessian troops who originally wore them. Like highlows (see note to *A Little Dinner at Timmins's* p.278), a subject of some interest to Thackeray. Hessians are the cause of Bob Stubbs's downfall in *The Fatal Boots*. Jos Sedley in *Vanity Fair* wore them at school, and the youthful George Osborne is severely punished on one occasion for cutting off the tassels.

ON BEING FOUND OUT

320 'Jack Ketch': see note to *Going to see a Man Hanged*, p.113.

OGRES

330 'Polyphemus': the one-eyed giant in Homer's *Odyssey* ix.

330 'But so were the Sirens ogres': a recurrent image in Thackeray. Sirens with sinister white arms, surrounded by bleached human bones, are a feature of his imagination. They first appear in *The Artists* (see pp.133), where they masquerade as models and devour young artists, and can also be glimpsed in *The Newcomes*, in connection with la Duchesse d'Ivry – 'I fancy a fish's tail is flapping under her fine flounces, and a forked fin at the end of it.' See Carey, *Thackeray: Prodigal Genius*, p.89.

THACKERAY AND HIS CRITICS

There is scarcely any extended critical comment on Thackeray's early writings. George Saintsbury's prefaces to the 1908 collected edition, reprinted as *A Consideration of Thackeray* (1931), are mostly concerned with the full-length work. George Orwell's essay 'Oysters and Brown Stout', which appeared in *Tribune* in 1943, played an important part in the rediscovery of Thackeray's early work. Later critics such as John Carey have acknowledged their debt to Orwell. Carey's comments on 'Going to see A Man Hanged', taken from *Thackeray: Prodigal Genius* (1977), form part of a wider discussion of Thackeray's early style.

1. George Orwell: 'Oysters and Brown Stout'

G.K. Chesterton said once that every novelist writes one book whose title seems to be a summing-up of his attitude to life. He instanced, for Dickens, *Great Expectations*, and for Scott, *Tales of a Grandfather*.

What title would one choose as especially representative of Thackeray? The obvious one is *Vanity Fair*, but I believe that if one looked more closely one would choose either *Christmas Books, Burlesques*, or *A Book of Snobs* – at any rate, one would choose the title of one of the collections of scraps which Thackeray had previously contributed to *Punch* and other magazines. Not only was he by nature a burlesque writer, but he was primarily a journalist, a writer of fragments, and his most characteristic work is not fully separable from the illustrations. Some of the best of these are by Cruikshank, but Thackeray was also a brilliant comic draughtsman himself, and in some of his very short sketches the picture and the letter-press belong organically together. All that is best in his full-length novels seems to have grown out of his contributions to *Punch*, and even *Vanity Fair* has a fragmentary quality that makes it possible to begin reading in it at almost any place, without looking back to see what has happened earlier.

At this date some of his major works – for instance, *Esmond* or *The Virginians* – are barely readable, and only once, in a rather short book, *A Shabby Genteel Story*, did he write what we should now regard as a serious novel. Thackeray's two main themes are snobbishness and extravagance, but he is at his best when he handles them in the comic vein, because – unlike Dickens, for instance – he has very little social insight and not even a very clear moral code. *Vanity Fair*, it is true, is a valuable social document as well as being an extremely readable and amusing book. It records, with remarkable fidelity so far as physical detail goes, the ghastly social competition of the early nineteenth century, when an aristocracy which could no longer pay its way was still the arbiter of fashion and of behaviour. In *Vanity Fair*, and indeed throughout Thackeray's writings, it is almost exceptional to find anyone living inside his income.

To live in a house which is too big for you, to engage servants whom you cannot pay, to ruin yourself by giving pretentious dinner parties with hired footmen, to bilk your tradesmen, to overdraw your banking account, to live permanently in the clutches of money-lenders – this is almost the norm of human behaviour. It is taken for granted that anyone who is not half-way to being a saint will ape the aristocracy if possible. The desire for expensive clothes, gilded carriages and hordes of liveried servants is assumed to be a natural instinct, like the desire for food and drink. And the people Thackeray is best able to describe are those who are living the fashionable life upon no income whatever – people like Becky Sharp and Rawdon Crawley in *Vanity Fair*, or the innumerable seedy adventurers, Major Loder, Captain Rook, Captain Costigan, Mr Deuceace, whose life is an endless to-and-fro between the card-table and the sponging-house.

So far as it goes, Thackeray's picture of society is probably true. The types he depicts, the mortgage-ridden aristocrats, the brandy-drinking army officers, the elderly bucks with their stays and their dyed whiskers, the match-making mothers, the vulgar City magnates, did exist. But he is observing chiefly externals. In spite of endless musings on the French Revolution, a subject that fascinated him, he does not see that the structure of society is altering: he sees the nation-wide phenomenon of snobbery and extravagance, without seeing its deeper causes. Moreover, unlike Dickens, he does not see that the social struggle is three-sided: his sympathies hardly extend to the working class, whom he is conscious of chiefly as servants. Nor is he ever certain where he himself stands. He cannot make up his mind whether the raffish upper class or the money-grubbing middle class is more objectionable. Not having any definite social, political or, probably, religious convictions, he can hardly imagine any virtues except simplicity, courage and, in the case of women, 'purity'. (Thackeray's 'good' women, incidentally, are completely intolerable.) The implied moral of both *Vanity Fair* and *Pendennis* is the rather empty one: 'Don't be selfish, don't be worldly, don't live outside your income.' And *A Shabby Genteel Story* says the same thing in a more delicate way.

But Thackeray's narrow intellectual range is actually an advantage to him when he abandons the attempt to portray real human beings. A thing that is very striking is the vitality of his *minor* writings, even of things that he himself must have thought of as purely ephemeral. If you dip almost anywhere in his collected works – even in his book reviews, for instance – you come upon the characteristic flavour. Partly it is the atmosphere of surfeit which belongs to the early nineteenth century, an atmosphere compounded of oysters, brown stout, brandy and water, turtle soup, roast sirloin, haunch of venison, Madeira and cigar smoke, which Thackeray is well able to convey because he has a good grip on physical detail and is extremely interested in food.

He writes about food perhaps more often even than Dickens, and more accurately. His account of his dinners in Paris – not expensive dinners, either – in 'Memorials of Gourmandising' is fascinating reading. 'The Ballad of the Bouillabaisse' is one of the best poems of that kind in English. But the characteristic flavour of Thackeray is the flavour of burlesque, of a world where no one is good and nothing is serious. It pervades all the best passages in his novels, and it reaches its perfection in short sketches and stories like 'Dr Birch and his Young Friends', *The Rose and the Ring*, 'The Fatal Boots' and 'A Little Dinner at Timmins's'.

The Rose and the Ring is a sort of charade, similar in spirit to *The Ingoldsby Legends*, 'A Little Dinner at Timmins's' is a relatively naturalistic story, and 'The Fatal Boots' is about midway between the two. But in all these and similar pieces Thackeray has got away from the difficulty that besets most novelists and has never been solved by any characteristically English novelist – the difficulty of combining characters who are meant to be real and exist 'in the round' with mere figures of fun.

English writers from Chaucer onwards have found it very difficult to resist burlesque, but as soon as burlesque enters the reality of the story suffers. Fielding, Dickens, Trollope, Wells, even Joyce, have all stumbled over this problem. Thackeray, in the best of his short pieces, solves it by making *all* his characters into caricatures. There is no question of the hero of 'The Fatal Boots' existing 'in the round'. He is as flat as an ikon. In 'A Little Dinner at Timmins's' – one of the best comic short stories ever written, though it is seldom reprinted – Thackeray is really doing the same thing as he did in *Vanity Fair*, but without the complicating factor of having to simulate real life and introduce disinterested motives. It is a simple little story, exquisitely told and rising gradually to a sort of crescendo which stops at exactly the right moment. A lawyer who has received an unusually large fee decides to celebrate it by giving a dinner party. He is at once led into much greater expense than he can afford, and there follows a series of disasters which leave him heavily in debt, with his friends alienated and his mother-in-law permanently installed in his home. From start to finish no one has had anything from the dinner party except misery. And when, at the end, Thackeray remarks, 'Why, in fact, did the Timminses give that party at all?' one feels the folly of social ambition has been more conclusively demonstrated than it is by *Vanity Fair*. This is the kind of thing that Thackeray could do perfectly, and it is the recurrence of farcical incidents like this, rather than their central story, that makes the longer novels worth reading.

Tribune, 22 December 1944

2. John Carey: extract from *Thackeray: Prodigal Genius*

A masterpiece of impressionistic reporting, this work ['Going to See a Man Hanged'] draws together a mesh of light-effects (growing more garish as the sun rises), and of intensely relished physical images, so that the vividness of life stands out clamorously against the darkness into which Courvoisier is to be plunged. That he is to be, as it were, blacked-out – hooded and dropped into a dark hole from which the executioner's hands reach up to pull his legs and strangle him – is the aspect of his fate that seems most horrific to Thackeray. At the start of his account he reconstructs Courvoisier's last night from the published reports: how he ground his teeth in his sleep, was woken by the jailer at four, wrote to his mother, refused breakfast. Keenly contrasted with this is the elegant *petit déjeuner* Thackeray and his friends enjoy – coffee, fowl, sherry and soda – and the lovely scraps of the morning scene which their eyes take in as they drive to the scaffold: the drab-silk coach linings, the cigar smoke, white and pure in the clear air, the dew on the grass in Gray's Inn and the windows in a flame, and the crowd hurrying along the broad, bright street, with blue shadows marching after them. Mixing with the crowd round the gallows, Thackeray records types and faces in a seemingly disconnected way, so that the sense of waiting around for something to happen is preserved. But actually his observations distinguish rigorously (and understandably) between the spectators on the ground, like himself, and those who occupy the better vantage points who are more glaringly exposed to the early sunlight. With the groundlings he feels democratic sympathy that extends to the condemned man. The others disgust him. The group which most excites his contempt comprises several tipsy, dissolute-looking young people, with one man 'lolling over the sunshiny tiles, with a fierce sodden face', while the women of the party:

> were giggling, drinking and romping, as is the wont of these delicate creatures; sprawling here and there, and falling upon the knees of one or other of the males. Their scarves were off their shoulders, and you saw the sun shining down upon the bare white flesh, and the shoulder-points glittering like burning glasses.

Thackeray's objection is not precisely moral. A young thief's mistress in the crowd, who swaps ribaldry with the standers-by, behaves quite as disreputably as the roof-top group, yet he feels attracted to her and her 'devil-may-care candour'. The harshly-lit women perched on the roof repel him because they create a cruel, raucous light-effect with their bare shoulders, besides being immodest. His sensitivity to light and his morals are intertwined.

When Courvoisier appears on the scaffold it is Thackeray's genius for rapidly caught facial expressions that makes the scene unforgettable:

> His arms were tied in front of him. He opened his hands in a helpless kind of way, and clasped them once or twice together. He turned his head here and there, and looked about him for an instant with a wild

imploring look. His mouth was contracted into a sort of pitiful smile. He went and placed himself at once under the beam.

The smile is the astonishing thing. It suggests a sort of half-embarrassed resignation, like that of a child agreeing to take part in a game it has really grown too old for. Courvoisier smiles almost apologetically, it seems, at the self-destructive role he has to play, as he goes to stand under the beam.

1977

SUGGESTIONS FOR FURTHER READING

The standard biography of Thackeray by Gordon N. Ray (2 vols, *Thackeray: The Uses of Adversity*, 1955, *Thackeray: The Age of Wisdom*, 1958) is long out of print. A good recent introduction is Catherine Peters's *Thackeray's Universe: Shifting Worlds of Imagination and Reality* (1987), which makes excellent use of Thackeray's illustrations to his text. John Carey's *Thackeray: Prodigal Genius* (1977) is an essential starting-point for any critical consideration of Thackeray. A more specialist work, which affords many insights into Thackeray's style, is K. C. Phillipps, *The Language of Thackeray* (1977).

ACKNOWLEDGEMENTS

The editor and publishers are grateful to Secker & Warburg Ltd and Penguin Books for permission to reproduce 'Oysters and Brown Stout' from George Orwell, *Collected Essays, Letters and Journalism*, vol. 3, 1968 (Penguin edition 1970), and to Faber and Faber Ltd for permission to reproduce an extract from John Carey, *Thackeray: Prodigal Genius*, 1977.

SHORT STORY COLLECTIONS
IN EVERYMAN

A SELECTION

**The Secret Self
Short Stories by Women**
'A superb collection' *Guardian* **£4.99**

**Selected Short Stories
and Poems**
THOMAS HARDY
The best of Hardy's Wessex in a
unique selection **£4.99**

**The Best of
Sherlock Holmes**
ARTHUR CONAN DOYLE
All the favourite adventures in one
volume **£4.99**

**Great Tales of Detection
Nineteen Stories**
Chosen by Dorothy L. Sayers **£3.99**

Short Stories
KATHERINE MANSFIELD
A selection displaying the
remarkable range of Mansfield's
writing **£3.99**

Selected Stories
RUDYARD KIPLING
Includes stories chosen to reveal the
'other' Kipling **£4.50**

**The Strange Case of
Dr Jekyll and Mr Hyde
and Other Stories**
R. L. STEVENSON
An exciting selection of gripping
tales from a master of suspense **£3.99**

**Modern Short Stories 2:
1940-1980**
Thirty-one stories from the greatest
modern writers **£3.50**

**The Day of Silence and
Other Stories**
GEORGE GISSING
Gissing's finest stories, available for
the first time in one volume **£4.99**

Selected Tales
HENRY JAMES
Stories portraying the tensions
between private life and the outside
world **£5.99**

£4.99

£6.99

AVAILABILITY

All books are available from your local bookshop or direct from
**Littlehampton Book Services Cash Sales, 14 Eldon Way, LinesideEstate,
Littlehampton, West Sussex BN17 7HE.** PRICES ARE SUBJECT TO CHANGE.

To order any of the books, please enclose a cheque (in £ sterling) made payable to
Littlehampton Book Services, or phone your order through with credit card details (Access,
Visa or Mastercard) on 0903 721596 (24 hour answering service) stating card number and
expiry date. Please add £1.25 for package and postage to the total value of your order.